DARCY

The Collection

Dear Reader,

I must confess I write stories to entertain myself and because I am easily bored, I aim to make every one of them something new and excitingly different. The following three stories are a fine sample of the variety I offer you and I hope they will bring you as much pleasure as they've given me.

I have always loved mysteries—the suspense, the tension of not knowing and the shock when the truth finally emerges. At the beginning of *Always Love*, I pushed my heroine, Genevra, into taking a leap of faith about the hero, Christian Nemo. Is her belief in him right or wrong? As she gets in deeper and deeper with him, the uncertainties build until... But I'm not going to tell you the end which is wonderfully explosive and passionate.

Apart from the mystery angle of the romance, I'm very fond of this book since it vividly recalls my first trip to England. My husband and I stayed at The Dorchester while in London, spent one sumptuous night in The Hollyhock Suite at Le Manoir aux Quat'Saisons, and a wonderful weekend in Tregenna Castle Hotel at St Ives. I loved it so much, I had to share it with everyone, so I hope these backdrops to the story give you the same sense of delicious luxury and pampering.

The second story, *To Tame a Wild Heart*, is set in the Australian outback. I have written three outback stories, each of them enormously demanding. It is so dominant to the lives of the people who inhabit it, one cannot simply concentrate on the relationship between the heroine and the hero. Their relationship to the land has to be an integral part of everything that happens. I think of each outback story as a big unforgettable, almost spiritual experience, and the people in them have to be extra special.

Rebecca Wilder is one of the strongest heroines I've ever written, and the man who finally softens her heart is certainly of heroic mettle. There is a greatness about both of them, a greatness we don't see much of in today's world. But this is another world.

I offer here a journey you will get nowhere else—past, present, future, bound into a pioneering spirit that endures in the oldest land on this planet. I hope this story imparts some of this feeling. I want you to know it, at least as much as I can get it across to you.

The third story, *The Seduction of Keira* is fun. People often ask me where I get my ideas. Well, have you ever seen a woman so stunning you just can't stop looking at her? I saw one in an airport and people were bumping into each other and tripping over things because no one wanted to tear their eyes off her. So she became my heroine, Keira, who blithely floats through life without any real comprehension of her effect on people. I hope you are as amused by this as I was.

So my heroine leapt to life for me, but what of the story? Haven't we all had the fantasy of coming face to face with a man who is 'The One'? What if it really happened? And what if he instantly wanted to sweep you away with him and you let him, not even knowing who he was? And for one night he was everything you ever wanted in a lover...

I had a delicious time with this story, creating a beautiful dream. But, as in real life, we often get a rude awakening. What's a story without surprises?

Trust me, though, it ends well. In fact, I couldn't resist using my sister-in-law's admonition to her children—'I only want to hear the good news!'

To me, that is very much what romance is all about—*the good news.* I hope, by the time you've finished reading these three stories, you're feeling really good...satisfied...pleased...glad you spent this time with me. It's a wonderful thing to be able to smile and truly say...that was good!

With love —
Emma Darcy

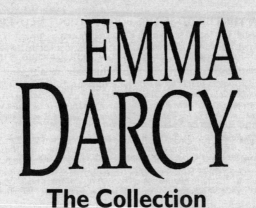

EMMA DARCY

The Collection

ALWAYS LOVE

TO TAME A WILD HEART

THE SEDUCTION OF KEIRA

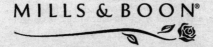

MILLS & BOON®

*All the characters in this book have no existence outside the imagination
of the author, and have no relation whatsoever to anyone bearing the same
name or names. They are not even distantly inspired by any individual
known or unknown to the author, and all the incidents are pure invention.*

*MILLS & BOON and MILLS & BOON with the Rose Device
are registered trademarks of the publisher.
Harlequin Mills & Boon Limited,
Eton House, 18-24 Paradise Road,
Richmond, Surrey, TW9 1SR*

EMMA DARCY THE COLLECTION
© by Harlequin Books SA

Always Love, To Tame a Wild Heart and *The Seduction of Keira* were
first published in separate, single volumes by Mills & Boon Limited.
Always Love in 1988 and *To Tame a Wild Heart*
and *The Seduction of Keira* in 1993.

Always Love © Emma Darcy 1988
To Tame a Wild Heart © Emma Darcy 1993
The Seduction of Keira © Emma Darcy 1993

ISBN 0 263 81252 9
62-9808

*Printed and bound in Great Britain
by Caledonian Book Manufacturing Ltd, Glasgow*

Emma Darcy nearly became an actress until her fiancé declared he preferred to attend the theatre with her. She became a full-time wife and mother of three sons. Later, when her sons had grown up, she took up oil painting and pottery—unsuccessfully, she remarks. Then her husband suggested she try architecture, and she ended up designing the family home, which stands on twenty-five acres in a lovely valley on the Central Coast of New South Wales.

Next came romance writing— 'the hardest and most challenging of all the activities', she confesses. To her it was like acting—she played the roles of all her characters, feeling all their emotions as the story unfolded. Mills & Boon® published her first novel in 1983, and since then Emma has written over sixty books, which have been distributed worldwide.

ALWAYS LOVE

CHAPTER ONE

GENEVRA could not eat the lunch she had ordered. The tension inside her grew with every passing minute that brought her closer and closer to the meeting with Matthew. Finally she left the hotel dining-room and returned to her room, where she paced the floor, trying to calm her inner agitation.

She had made the right decision, no question about it. Her mind was made up, and she was not going to be diverted from her purpose, regardless of what Matthew said. She had to find out about Luke, and Matthew was the only one who could help her. He wouldn't approve of the course she had set her mind on, but that didn't matter. Only learning the truth about Luke mattered. She could no longer bear not knowing.

Luke had loved her. The bond between them had been too strong for Genevra to ever doubt that. They had spent six weeks together... six weeks of long, magical days that she would never forget... a romantic dream that had come true.

He had come into her bookshop at St Ives one bright spring morning; a tall, darkly tanned, and very handsome stranger... an Australian, she quickly discovered, in England on business. But he was taking a holiday break and he found the fishing village of St Ives fascinating. More fascinating by the minute!

Their eyes had sparkled at each other, and Luke had stayed in the shop, chatting to her in between customers. The holiday break had been extended, and extended again, until the call came from home, pleading for his immediate return. His sister was very ill, asking for him. Luke had left within twenty-four hours, and Genevra had never seen him again. The letter had come a month later.

The shock and the pain of it still lingered in her heart, and she had read the words so many times, they were indelibly printed in her memory.

> 'My darling Genevra,
>   I don't know how to write what I must. I know too well the pain it will give you, and wish with all my heart that I did not have to make this choice, but I cannot turn my back on the love and obligations I owe my family. I could not be happy within myself, nor could I make you happy, knowing I had refused to answer their needs when they have given me so much.
>   I cannot marry you as we planned, Genevra, and I will not ask you to wait for me. I must honour the commitment I am about to make for as long as it lasts. By the time you receive this letter, I will be married.

It will be best for both of us to try and forget
what could have been. Goodbye, my love.'

'Goodbye...', 'forget what could have been...'
But Genevra had not been able to forget the love
they had shared, nor bring herself to really believe
in his goodbye. The hurt had been unbearable. To
lose the man she loved to another woman, when
she had only just learnt she was carrying his
child... Genevra had been unable to accept it. She
had read and re-read behind the lines of that letter.

Luke had been forced into a marriage he didn't
want, to a woman he didn't love, and whatever the
pressures that had driven him into such a course
they would lessen in time. If she waited long
enough, he would come back to her. He would free
himself of that woman as soon as he could do so
without hurting his family, and then...

But he hadn't come back, nor had there been one
word from him in all that time, and Genevra
couldn't bear to go on waiting any longer. Time
had eroded her certainty in his love for her. If Luke
was still married, then it was because he wanted to
be, and she had been deluding herself with a dream
that would never come true. It was better to know
than to go on dreaming... wasn't it?

She suddenly caught her reflection in the mirror
and paused in mid-step. If Luke walked back into
her life today, would he still think her beautiful?
The years had changed her. The experience of being

a single parent had slimmed her girlish face into the firmer lines of a woman, and the curves of her figure had become more pronounced. Motherhood had dropped her waistline and brought a larger fullness to her breasts, as well as sharpening her mind to the harsher realities of life.

She had kept her black hair long because Luke had liked it that way, its thick waves rippling from a centre parting to cloud around her pale, oval face and long, slender neck. But the warm innocence had long since disappeared from her eyes, and the mental and emotional torment of the last few days had taken its toll. The thickly fringed blue eyes were startlingly dark—glittering bruises in a face that seemed too delicate to support them. Her straight, little nose had a pinched look about the nostrils, and her normally soft, generous mouth was a tight red line.

The navy-blue suit and the white silk shirt emphasised her pallor, a mistake that was too late to correct. But that didn't matter, either. She wasn't going to see Luke. She hadn't seen him for four years, and today... today was the day of decision. All she had to do was confront Matthew and tell him what she wanted, and then, with her mind free of this turmoil, she could meet the American publisher, Christian Nemo, with more equanimity than she could manage now.

It was the American's letter that had started this present torment over Luke, sharpening the ache in her heart. If Christian Nemo hadn't asked her to meet him at the Dorchester Hotel for afternoon tea, reminding her of that last afternoon with Luke... but it was time she did something positive, instead of blindly waiting for a man who might never return to her.

She almost jumped when the telephone rang, and her hand was trembling as she picked up the receiver.

'Miss Kingsley?'

'Yes.'

'Reception desk. Mr Hastings' car is here for you, Miss Kingsley.'

'Thank you.'

She glanced anxiously at her watch as she snatched up her handbag. It was only one-twenty; Matthew was ten minutes early. She had meant to be in the foyer, waiting for him. As it was, he had done her the favour of fitting her into his busy schedule at late notice.

Her heart fluttered with nervous apprehension as she hurried downstairs and out to the white Rolls-Royce which stood at the kerb. The chauffeur had the passenger door open for her, and she quickly slid in next to Matthew.

She flicked him an apologetic look. 'I didn't expect you this soon.'

As usual, he looked very much the eminent solicitor. The shock of white hair gave him the distinguished air of a patriarch. His face had the weathered strength of character that shouted of an ingrained discipline of mind. He wore respectability like a well-fitted glove, his dark suit the epitome of conventional quality, his manner impeccably that of a gentleman, born and bred. He projected the image one expected of a top solicitor from Gray's Inn.

He shook his head at her in fond indulgence. 'Genevra, why do you persist in staying at a hotel in Bloomsbury when you come up to London? There is no need . . .'

'It suits me,' Genevra cut in quickly, tired of Matthew's attempts to get her to spend the trust money that he administered for her.

He sighed. 'You can afford better, Genevra. It's absolutely ridiculous that . . .'

She turned on him, too wrought up to be patient. 'I've told you, Matthew. I'm saving that money for Johnny. It's his birthright. I'll spend it if I need to, but I'm doing quite well without it. I can make a reasonable living out of the bookshop, and I'm even seeing a publisher later today about a book he wants to commission.'

'That's splendid!' he said, obviously pleased for her. 'But even so, those two tourist books you wrote have only brought in a few hundred pounds, and the bookshop provides little more than subsistence living. The point is, my dear, that *you* are the beneficiary of the Anna Christie Trust, not your son.'

But she wasn't really. Genevra had never felt right about that money, even though Matthew had assured her from the very beginning that it was legally hers, to do with as she wished. She had needed it then. Needed it desperately. Luke had gone, she was carrying their child, and her father had left a mountain of debts on the bookshop which was her only means of support. It wasn't until after all the debts had been paid and she had given birth to Johnny that Genevra began to wonder...and it had preyed on her mind all these years, just as Luke had. So why not find out about that, too?

'Matthew, that's one of the things I would like you to do for me.'

The words burst off her tongue with more force than she had intended, and Matthew raised his eyebrows in surprised enquiry.

'I want you to find out about Anna Christie,' she said, in a more subdued voice, but with no less conviction.

He gave one of his dismissive shrugs. 'There's nothing to find out. I've told you all I know. She was a Canadian.'

'Haven't you ever thought it strange?' Genevra persisted, wanting his understanding. 'You know what my circumstances were at the time—three months pregnant with Johnny, threatened with bankruptcy, no one to turn to for help. Maybe I would have survived anyway, but it was the lowest point of my life. And suddenly...there was the Anna Christie Trust!'

'God looks after his angels!' His hands gesticulated the dismissal of any fanciful nonsense as he addressed himself to her more seriously. 'What do you want to believe? That a woman on the other side of the Atlantic Ocean died for your convenience? You weren't even named in the trust deed, Genevra. It was your father who was the beneficiary, and then his next of kin. If you had not survived your father, the money would have gone to the International Red Cross.'

'Why should some woman I've never heard of leave all that money to my father? It doesn't make sense!' Genevra retorted in bewilderment.

Matthew sighed and linked his hands across his pin-striped waistcoat. It was a mannerism that indicated he was about to give her the wisdom of his sixty years. At another time, Genevra would have smiled and accepted that he knew better than she did, but not today.

'Maybe she once loved your father. Maybe he saved her life. Who knows? Obviously there was some connection between them, probably before you were ever born. It doesn't matter.'

'It matters to me,' she said stubbornly. 'I want to know, Matthew. I've lived too long with the torment of wondering about things. From this day onwards, I'm going to learn what I want to know.'

He stared at her, frowning over the glittering determination in her eyes. His hands slowly lifted in a gesture of submission. 'So be it, then. I'll contact the Canadian firm of solicitors who set up the trust for Anna Christie. If they can't come up with the information you want, then we can proceed with an investigation.'

'Thank you.' She knew Matthew was indulging her, and she felt a rush of affection for the kindly old solicitor for conceding to her point of view without too much argument. She hoped he would not feel it necessary to caution her against her next request, because it was the really important one.

The Rolls-Royce pulled up outside Matthew's chambers at Gray's Inn. Genevra tried to get her thoughts in some coherent order as Matthew led her inside. She had to say what she had come to say, but the pain inside her was like the growth of a terminal illness that was about to be openly confronted.

Matthew closed the door of his office behind them, escorted Genevra to a chair, then rounded the huge mahogany desk and dropped into the leather chair behind it.

The Anna Christie file was already on the desk in front of him. It was the only business that ever brought Genevra to these chambers, and undoubtedly Matthew's secretary had placed it there. Matthew opened it, made a note, then closed it again, looking up at her with an encouraging smile.

'Sit down, Genevra. You can tell me now what the real problem is.'

But she couldn't sit down. Her nerves were jumping too much. For a moment, she panicked. Did she really want to know? Yes, came the agonised cry from her heart. But, despite her resolution, despite the need churning through her, Genevra could not hold Matthew's enquiring gaze. She fumbled open her handbag, withdrew the card on which she had written Luke's name and the only address he had given her, and placed it on Matthew's desk.

A self-conscious flush burnt a swift path up her throat and into her cheeks, and she turned away, pacing distractedly around the room as she forced the words out, all too painfully aware of the strained stiffness of her voice.

'There's a man I want to find out about. His name is Stanford... Luke Stanford. He's an Australian, an engineer... thirty-three years old. The last I heard of him, he was living in New South Wales. Near Sydney. But the address I've written on that card is four years old. He may not be there any more. He . . . he married at about that time.'

Tears pricked her eyes and she fought them back. She had made up her mind. She couldn't go on waiting, not knowing what had happened, not knowing if he ever really meant to come back to her. She blinked hard and fought down the lump in her throat. Then, with unflinching determination, she swung around and defiantly met the eyes of the man whose help was absolutely critical to her cause.

'I want to find out if he's still married. Can you arrange that for me, Matthew?'

His whole face seemed to sag with a sad weariness as he looked down at his hands. For long, tense moments his fingers dragged at the age-spots on the skin just above the knuckles. 'I take it that Luke Stanford is Johnny's father.'

It was not a question. It was a flat statement of fact, carefully drained of any emotion. He lifted his eyes and the knowledge in them was tempered by a sympathy that recognised and understood human failings all too well.

'Yes.' She almost choked on the word. She had never told anyone outside her family before, but it was the obvious answer, and there was no point in denying it. Yet it was not for Johnny's sake that she had to find out about Luke. Her three-year-old son wasn't eating his heart out for a father he had never known. It was for herself. Even after four years of silence, she could not stop loving Luke Stanford.

Matthew nodded. His gaze slowly swept back to her, and his mouth took on a sad, ironic twist as he spoke. 'I know you don't want to hear the advice I'm about to give, Genevra, but I would not be serving you well if I don't give it.'

He paused to lend emphasis to his words. 'Let the past go. You're only twenty-five, young enough and beautiful enough to attract any number of men. Don't look back, Genevra. Look forward. And open your heart to what can be...for your sake, and Johnny's sake.'

She shook her head. He didn't understand. Even if she showed him Luke's letter, he wouldn't understand. He hadn't known Luke as she had known him. 'I can't do that, Matthew. Maybe...after I know...I can do what you say. But not until then.'

Matthew's face hardened. 'Genevra, he left you to marry another woman. He left you carrying his child...'

'Luke didn't know that!' she cried, her eyes painfully protesting against the accusation. 'And I don't intend to tell him. I have no intention of interfering with...with his life, Matthew. I don't want him to know anything about this inquiry. I just want to know if he's still married. I need to know. That's all,' she pleaded.

'It will only bring you grief.'

'No more than I've lived with for the past four years. Grief is nothing new to me, Matthew.'

The passionate conviction of her retort won a reprieve from argument. Matthew's mouth tightened over whatever he had been about to say. His gaze dropped to the card she had placed on his desk. He picked it up, fingering it with an air of distaste. Disapproval emanated from him but, when he finally spoke, it was with curt decisiveness.

'I don't personally know of any private investigation firms in Australia, but I have contacts who can advise me. I'll let you know as soon as I get the information you want; and I'll insist that all inquiries be carried out with maximum discretion.'

Genevra almost sagged with relief. Her legs started to shake. She put out a hand and gripped the back of a chair to steady herself. 'Thank you,' she whispered, her voice deserting her now that the battle had been won.

Matthew's gaze shot up to pin hers. 'I hope this will be the finish of it, Genevra.'

No, it would never be finished, Genevra thought with a dull sense of resignation, but she didn't say that. 'At least then I'll know,' she replied on a wistful sigh.

And that was all she could achieve, hopeless as that might prove to be. But the wheels had been set in motion. The waiting and wondering would soon be over. And then...then she would know if her life was ever again to have any meaning.

CHAPTER TWO

MATTHEW insisted that Genevra take his car to her appointment with Christian Nemo. He had always been kind to her and, despite their sharp difference of opinion, he seemed even more solicitous than usual as he escorted her out of his chambers; asking after Johnny and Auntie May and their life in St Ives, handing her into the Rolls-Royce himself, and wishing her all the best with the publisher.

Genevra thanked him once again, but she was relieved when he finally shut the car door, releasing her from the strain of his presence. The memory of their altercation over Luke was still pulsing painfully.

She asked the chauffeur to drop her off at one of the entrances to Hyde Park. Although her talk with Matthew had seemed to go on for an eternity, she still had more than half an hour to fill in before she had to be at the Dorchester.

She relaxed back into the plush leather seat of the Rolls and closed her eyes, half regretting what she had just done.

She felt curiously drained, almost as if she had betrayed a trust she should have kept. But the

silence had been too long. Even the most desperate
hope needed something to feed on.

'Hyde Park, madam.'

Genevra jolted upright. The car was stationary,
and the chauffeur had opened the door for her. She
stepped out on to the pavement, thanked the man,
and walked briskly into the park.

It was a fine, sunny day, the trees a vibrant
summer green, roses coming into bloom, the rolling
expanse of grass invitingly lush. Just as it had been
that last day with Luke.

The sweet memories crept into her mind:
lounging on the grass under the trees, idly watching
others play makeshift games of soccer and baseball
while she and Luke talked...and touched; strolling
around the Serpentine, feeding the swans, laughing
at the amateur canoeists...loving one another.

As she walked along, Genevra felt a strong sense
of all that had happened before; past and present
in parallel time-streams...shifting, crossing,
merging into one. Luke's presence was so strong
that she could almost imagine he was walking beside
her, as he had done on that last afternoon, four
years ago, taking her to afternoon tea at the
Dorchester Hotel.

Genevra had never indulged in such luxury before
or since, but Luke had wanted to take her somewhere special. It was something of a tradition in

London, afternoon tea at the Dorchester, but not for ordinary people like her, of course.

The snobbery of England meant nothing to Luke. She had wanted a cup of tea, and he had insisted on taking her to the most prestigious place in London. He had blithely swept aside all her protests that they were not dressed correctly and they couldn't really go *there*!

She remembered how awed she had felt as they waited at the entrance to the Promenade Room until a waiter in black tails and white bow-tie had come to show them to a table. The room glowed so richly, with its long colonnade of marble columns veined in a soft russet and topped with bands of beautifully worked gilt. The ceiling was indented with gilt friezes, and huge cages made of glass and brass hung from it, glittering with the candles that lit the room. Other candle-fittings were centred on wall mirrors, and between the mirrors were quiet paintings, lending further elegance to the unique ambience of the room.

Between the columns were beautiful potted palms, surrounded by trailing vines, and Indian statues from the British Raj. A grand piano of polished red mahogany sat in the centre of the room, and an accomplished pianist played a selection of songs from popular musicals.

Genevra had clung nervously to Luke's arm as the waiter led them down the room, past the groupings of sofas and chairs that were so richly upholstered in red and gold striped velvet. Softly patterned carpets in tonings of red and green and peach were set into the grey and white marble slabs on the floor. Genevra had watched her footing, terrified that she might trip and make a fool of herself.

Not only was the room the last word in elegant luxury, the tea service was exquisite: starched white linen serviettes, silver teapots, sugar bowls, tea strainers, milk and cream jugs; delicate china crockery; dainty little pots of jam, rosettes of butter, scones, cakes, a selection of finger sandwiches served from a silver tray with silver tongs.

And the patrons had been equally fascinating: groups of stylish Americans, the British upper class with their careless arrogance, the beautifully mannered Orientals...Genevra had stared unashamedly at an Arab sheik who had walked by.

Luke, in his egalitarian Australian way, had laughed her out of her sense of awe, taking all the fabulous service for granted since he was paying for it, and making up wicked stories about the people around them. He had made it a magical experience, one she would remember vividly all her life...even if he never came back to her.

Genevra paused on the footpath just across from the Dorchester, waiting for a break in the traffic. She watched the hotel doorman, in his top hat and tails, opening the passenger door of a Silver Cloud

Rolls-Royce. An ironic smile curled her mouth. After four years of friendly association with Matthew Hastings, she was no longer in awe of luxury cars or places.

All the same, the Dorchester Hotel seemed an odd choice of venue for a meeting with a publisher. But Mr Christian Nemo was an American. While in London, he probably enjoyed tasting the best of English traditional fare.

The traffic break came, and she quickly crossed the road. It was just three o'clock as she walked into the hotel foyer.

Her eye was immediately caught by the magnificent hydrangeas in the two huge urns which stood like sentinels on either side of the entrance to the Promenade Room. She paused there, admiring the huge blooms, until a girl in a smart black suit enquired if she could be of service.

'Yes. I'm to meet a Mr Christian Nemo,' Genevra explained, flicking a look down the length of the room to see if she could spot a lone gentleman. 'I believe he has...'

Shock cut off her speech. The man walking past the piano to the far end of the room...she could not believe her eyes! Even from the back view, she couldn't be mistaken. His height, the shape of his head, the close-set ears, the bulk of his shoulders, the way his thick, dark hair curled around the nape of his neck. It had to be him!

For a moment she was totally mesmerised, unable to move or even breathe. Then her heart started to pound, sending painful vibrations through her chest. A great welling of love poured through her body. No matter that her mind told her it was impossible. She could not doubt the truth of what she saw.

Genevra didn't stop to think, to reconsider. Her heart was pounding faster than a jackhammer now. She brushed past the girl and barely restrained herself from breaking into a run. 'Luke!' she called, the name half choked as it left her lips. He didn't turn around.

She hastened her step. He had reached the table where they had sat four years before. He paused at the same chair he had occupied. She was certain now. Excitement pumped her heart even faster. She did run the last couple of yards and grabbed his arm before he could sit down.

'Luke!' she breathed ecstatically, but all her wild elation burst into a thousand stabbing icicles as the man turned slowly towards her.

The face was one she had never seen before, cruelly hurt in some accident a long time ago. A black patch covered one eye, and the skin of his face was marked with a faint criss-crossing of pale lines, the result of an immense amount of corrective surgery. A more prominent scar sliced through the eyebrow above the patch. The jawline was subtly different to Luke's, not so square; and the shape of the nose...it wasn't right, either.

But Genevra did not care. Shock gave way to a surge of fierce love. If it was Luke, she would throw herself into his arms and kiss away the pain of all those terrible injuries. She waited for him to nod, to say yes, to acknowledge his identity...waited in growing desperation for a sign that never came.

'I'm afraid you are mistaken, young lady.'

His voice was soft, kindly, but the accent was unmistakably American...not Australian! His gaze held hers steadily, without flinching.

'My name is Nemo,' he continued slowly. 'Christian Nemo.'

CHAPTER THREE

'No!'

The word exploded from Genevra before she could control herself. Shock had shattered into violent disbelief. She half raised her hand in negation of what he had said, and barely stopped herself from accusing him of playing some cruel trick on her.

She had been so sure, so certain that the man was Luke, that he had come back for her. Until she saw his face, heard his accent, she would have sworn on a stack of Bibles that this man standing in front of her had to be Luke.

Yet how could she deny the evidence of her eyes and ears? The face...the voice...both of them contradicted her conviction so strongly. In sheer desperation, she searched for something that would confirm the identity of the man beyond question.

Luke's eyes had been gray.

Christian Nemo's were a tawny brown.

The blood drained from Genevra's head. A trembling weakness seeped into her legs. She swayed on her feet as the realisation of how wrong she had been hit home.

The man clutched her arm hard, steadying her. 'I'm sorry. I know my face comes as a bit of a shock to most people.' His mouth curled into a twist of self-mockery. 'That's why I chose the most unobtrusive table in this room. I don't wish to put people off their afternoon tea.'

'It's not that bad,' Genevra blurted out, instinctively protesting his misreading of her reaction, even as she struggled to accept that he wasn't Luke. This was the man she had come to meet, the American publisher whom she had wanted to impress!

The blood came rushing back to her face in a heated burst of embarrassment. 'What I mean is...' She floundered, searching for some tactful way to explain her mistake. 'I thought you were someone else, you see. It was so stupid of me. You must think I'm quite mad.'

'No. Our minds play all sorts of tricks on us at times. I'm sorry I've upset you, however unwittingly it was. Would you like to sit down for a few moments?'

His kindness made Genevra feel worse. Any chance of carrying off this introduction with dignity was long gone. All she could do now was give him the courtesy of looking him straight in the eye while she owned up to her own identity.

'The fact is, Mr Nemo, I'm Genevra Kingsley, and I hope you can overlook my...'

'Miss Kingsley!' Warm pleasure lighted his expression and softened the harsh lines of his face, making him look more open and approachable. He released his grasp on her arm and took her hand in his. 'I am delighted to meet you. I must confess I was expecting someone not . . . quite so beautiful.'

The smile, the way his fingers had curled around hers, the tingling reaction to the light pressure of his hand . . . God! She was going mad! If he wasn't Luke . . . But he had denied that he was, and she had to make some reply.

'That's very kind of you.'

She was so frozen and confused inside, she wondered how she got the words out.

'Do please sit down,' he invited.

Genevra sat, concentrating hard on pulling herself together. Luke had been so heavily on her mind that she had obviously projected her need for him on to this man. That he had looked exactly like Luke from a back view was simply an uncanny coincidence. She was lucky that Christian Nemo was generous enough to forgive her blunder.

She watched him lower himself into a chair, noticing for the first time that he used a walking cane—black oak, with a silver tip and a chased silver knob. His left leg obviously gave him some trouble, although he had not walked with any stiffness. She couldn't quite fit that elegant walking-cane with her image of Luke, nor the conservative cut of the dark grey suit. The quality tailoring, the silk stripe in his white shirt, the rich statement of the red and silver tie—they added up to a man who put considerable stock in his appearance...or a man who wanted to create that impression.

The clothes did not disguise the toughness of his physique: the broad chest and muscular shoulders, the strength in his hands. In some strange way, his facial disfigurement actually enhanced the aura of masculinity, suggesting that he would always rise above any adversity, unbeaten.

His lips curved into a dry smile under her intense scrutiny. 'Beauty and the Beast?' he drawled, making light of her rudeness in staring.

'No!' Genevra retorted sharply, distressed by a reference which was so demeaning to himself. She imagined the mountain of hurts that had forced the building of such a flippant façade, and her stomach churned with hatred for all the people who had made him feel so conscious of his scars. If he had been Luke... Without giving it another second's thought, Genevra burst into speech, defending him from himself as well as other people.

'If you want me to stay, I don't want to hear you talk like that! Never again! I can't tolerate your thinking of yourself in...in such terms. I won't stand for it!'

Her chest was heaving with the expulsion of her pent-up emotion and, as the last word of her ul-

timatum faded into a dreadful silence, Genevra
wished the floor would open up and swallow her.
Christian Nemo wouldn't want to do business with
her after that outburst. Yet she had only spoken
the truth. She couldn't have borne to have him talk
about himself in such a way.

His face had stiffened in mute shock. They stared
at each other like grim antagonists. Genevra felt
drained, but the tension emanating from him kept
her nerves on edge. It was a relief when he finally
broke the silence.

'You speak just as you write, Miss Kingsley. Directly, and without pretension.'

His stiff manner of speech contrasted sharply to
the pleasant flow of his previous statements, and
Genevra's heart sank. She hadn't meant to offend
him. She just couldn't seem to keep her emotions
under control. The strain of the last few days in
coming to a decision, her preoccupation with
Luke...she was in no fit state to carry on a business
discussion.

'I'm sorry,' she sighed. 'I really am sorry, Mr
Nemo. I don't expect you to understand...' She
started to rise.

He stretched out a hand in protest, restraining
any further movement. 'Please... please don't go.
It seems to me that I'm the one who should be
apologising. I beg you to forgive me for making
you feel uncomfortable. It is...sometimes dif-

ficult . . . to meet a stranger. I was trying to put you at ease . . .' his grimace was full of savage irony ' . . . not drive you away. Could we start again?'

Genevra slowly nodded her agreement. She didn't know if she really wanted to stay. Christian Nemo was too disturbing a reminder of Luke. He had opened up the wounds of loving a man who was beyond her reach. She no longer cared about the commission he had in mind for her, but she couldn't turn her back on his appeal. It would be brutally insensitive after what she had said.

Christian Nemo resettled himself with an air of relief. 'May I call you Genevra?'

'Yes, of course,' she murmured.

'When I read your books on Devon and Cornwall, I knew you were the writer I wanted on this project. You did a splendid job of blending the right mixture of human interest with factual material.'

'Thank you.' It was incredibly difficult to focus her mind on to business. She felt as if she was split in two, one part of her accepting that Christian Nemo was a complete stranger, the other part in total conflict with such an acceptance. When she forced herself to speak, her voice sounded both defensive and aggressive.

'How did you happen to get hold of my books, Mr Nemo? They're only of local interest, and their distribution is very limited.'

'I was in Hampshire a couple of weeks ago, and I picked them up at a little village bookshop. I can't remember the name.'

The deep timbre of his voice struck a chord of recognition. The American accent was distracting, but it did not disguise the tonal quality that echoed out of Genevra's memory. Still, four years was a long time. Christian Nemo was built like Luke. It wasn't beyond the realms of possibility that his voice carried the same deep vibrancy.

Genevra made another effort to carry her end of the conversation. 'I must confess I've never heard of your publishing house, but then I'm barely acquainted with those in England. Do you publish a lot of tourist books?'

He smiled. 'They make up a good, constant market.'

That smile was so typical, so reminiscent— Genevra's heart leapt, then fell into an erratic pounding. Christian Nemo was driving her crazy, evoking memories of the man she loved. She studied his mouth as he talked—the shape of it, the way his lips moved, the occasional flash of white teeth— and she could see Luke talking just like that. She found herself wondering how she would react if those lips were to touch her own. Would they excite the same response? The thought jolted her so much that she barely heard Christian Nemo's series of statements, outlining the project he had in mind.

'What I envisage is a number of articles which will detail all that is of interest about the great historic country mansions and castles that have been converted to hotels. We'll do the best of them, the most unique and the most expensive.'

His voice gathered enthusiasm. 'Even if the readers can never afford to stay in such places, I want to give them the vicarious experience of doing so. Of course, your expenses will be paid, and we'll set an outright fee on each completed article. Besides that, you'll receive royalties on the book.'

Genevra was quite stunned by the offer. 'You mean, you actually want me to stay at these places so that I can write everything about them?'

'Of course.'

'And it won't cost me a thing?'

'Not in money. It will cost you time and effort.'

She was still digesting the proposition when a waiter arrived to ask their preference in tea, earnestly detailing the various types that were on offer. 'Darjeeling,' Genevra replied, automatically making the same choice that had sprung to her lips four years ago. The waiter departed, having received a nod of agreement from Christian Nemo.

'Can we do business together?' he asked.

It was a dream job, no doubt about it. An extraordinary offer to someone who was little more than an amateur author. Could she do credit to such a fantastic assignment? Christian Nemo apparently thought so, and why should she question his judgement? There was no reason for not trying her hand at it, and it certainly would be exciting to stay in such wonderful places, providing she could manage the trips away from home without compromising on what was really important to her.

She was not about to neglect her son. Auntie May adored Johnny and took wonderful care of him, but Genevra did not want to be a part-time mother. Nor could she expect her shop assistant, Beryl Parker, to manage the bookshop on her own for long periods of time. If Christian Nemo was in a hurry for a finished product, she couldn't possibly accept the job.

'Would I have to work to deadlines?' she asked, quickly adding, 'I do have other commitments that I can't ignore.'

'You can work at your own pace,' he assured her.

'How many places do you have in mind?'

'It's open-ended. Thirty...perhaps more... Really, it's up to you.'

'That will take a very long time,' Genevra warned.

'Yes. To do it properly would certainly take a long time.' The thought seemed to give him satisfaction. 'As I said before, I'm not concerned about time.' He hesitated a moment, then slowly added, 'There is one other thing...'

'Yes?'

His gaze held hers with steady deliberation. 'I want to see these places myself. I've already been to a couple in Hampshire. One of them—Chewton Glen—inspired the idea for this project. I'd like to follow through on the idea, and since I'm on convalescent leave for a few months, I intend to come with you. Call it self-indulgence. I hope you don't mind.'

Genevra struggled hard to conceal her dismay. To be closely associated with this man for months and months, sharing dinners and breakfasts across the same table, hours and hours of his company...haunting her with his smile...reminding her continually of the man she didn't have...could she cope with it? Would familiarity gradually diminish the disturbing impact he had on her?

Her long hesitation prompted a sharp look of concern from Christian Nemo. 'I assure you, I'm not suggesting anything improper in this arrangement. I'm well aware that I'm not...' He clamped his mouth shut, and frowned in frustration.

Genevra was painfully reminded of the ultimatum she had delivered earlier. It seemed horribly ironic that he should think himself unattractive. The problem was that his likeness to Luke made him far too attractive for her peace of mind.

'I didn't think that,' she said quietly, and was grateful that the arrival of afternoon tea saved her from being pressed for an immediate decision. She needed more time to consider the position.

The tea service was all set out on the low table in front of them. Genevra accepted a couple of finger sandwiches, hoping they might help to settle her stomach. The tea was poured into their cups and, all too soon, Genevra was once more alone with Christian Nemo.

He looked at her expectantly and her heart quivered with indecision. As much as she wanted to take the job, being close to Christian Nemo, with his uncanny similarities to Luke, would surely constitute a form of self-torture that she would be stupid to invite upon herself. Yet she instinctively recoiled from saying anything that might hurt him, and she certainly didn't want him to take her rejection of his offer as a rejection of himself.

She sought for some tactful way out of the dilemma. 'How can you make such a project pay?' she asked. 'You'll never cover the costs.'

'I don't assess all my projects in purely dollar terms,' he replied drily. 'You have no need to worry about money.'

He was making it very difficult for her to refuse him. Genevra didn't know what to do. Then she thought of Johnny. No doubt Christian Nemo was expecting to move from one hotel to another, and she couldn't possibly do that.

'There is one difficulty, one that I might not be able to get over...'

He had been adding sugar to his tea. Very slowly and deliberately, he set the teaspoon down on the saucer. When he lifted his face to her, it was stripped of all expression. 'There's usually a way around most problems. If you'll tell me what's troubling you...'

'I'm not entirely free to do what you want, Mr Nemo,' she replied, her own careful expression softening as she thought of her son. 'I have a child. A little boy. And I can't...'

His teacup clattered across the table, dropped to the marble floor and smashed into a thousand fragments. Tea was splashed everywhere: over the scones, the butter, the jam-pots. Christian Nemo stood up as waiters descended on them.

His face was white and pained, the criss-crossing of scars showing up more sharply on the strained pallor of his skin. Not once did he look at Genevra while order was being restored, but his distress was so palpable that she felt her own nerves tighten. She didn't understand why such a simple, commonplace accident should upset him so much.

The waiters departed and Christian Nemo sat down again. Still he did not look at her. He stared down at his hands, the fingers of one stroking savagely over the other. 'Please excuse my clumsiness.

Occasionally I get a nerve spasm. Nothing I can do about it,' he said grimly.

'It doesn't matter,' Genevra sympathised.

But his distress did not ease. And it went deeper than distress. He was concealing it as best he could, but Genevra could feel his despair as if it was a tangible thing, crawling around her, tapping at her heart, and somehow it was a more frightening thing than anything she had ever experienced.

When he finally lifted his gaze to her, it was only for the most fleeting glance of acknowledgement. 'I didn't realise you were married. I should have asked before. Of course, the whole thing is impossible. I'm sorry for wasting your time.'

'I'm not married!'

His curt, clipped speech had somehow drawn the blunt retort from her. His head jerked up again, and Genevra coloured under the sharp reassessment.

'Unmarried mothers are not uncommon these days,' she said defensively.

'How old is the boy?' he rapped out, almost before she finished speaking.

'Johnny is three. Three and a half, to be exact.'

He looked as though she had slapped a brick in his face. To hell with him and his damned project, Genevra thought on a fierce surge of anger. If he thought any the less of her because she had Johnny, then she didn't want to do business with him, anyway.

'I'm sure you understand that a child needs his mother, and I consider his needs before anything else,' she said in belligerent defiance of any moral censure. 'I couldn't leave him for the length of time you're envisaging. So you're quite right, Mr Nemo. The whole thing is impossible!'

He gave a little shake of his head, and again he looked pained. 'You love him, Genevra?'

The soft, wistful question plunged her into confusion. The anger melted into a helpless vulnerability that wanted, needed his approval. 'Johnny is the best part of my life,' she blurted out, unconsciously revealing some of the loneliness of being a single parent.

The silence that followed her declaration held a strange stillness, like being in the eye of a storm. Genevra wondered why she didn't get up and go. Finish it. Yet she couldn't find the strength to make the break. Somehow, Christian Nemo held her tied to him with an emotional power that she didn't understand. If he had been Luke . . .

He suddenly smiled at her, and Genevra's heart turned over. 'Of course you must consider your son's welfare first,' he agreed warmly. 'But that's something we can get over, Genevra. We can arrange our schedule so that you needn't be away longer than one or two nights at a time. Do one place a week, or every fortnight. Even do only one a month, for that matter. And, if it's what you want, we could take Johnny with us to the places that would allow us to...'

He plunged on, answering every possible objection to her acceptance of his plans. Time didn't matter to him; he was happy to wait on her convenience; he was sure he could spend the intervals very pleasantly in St Ives; he liked children.

He was casting a net around her, leaving no loophole for escape, and Genevra stared helplessly at him, mesmerised by the mouth that was so like Luke's. The turmoil pounded through her again, urgently demanding answers that needed to be settled. How would she cope with being put through an emotional wringer every time she was in Christian Nemo's company? Would it be different the next time she saw him? Was it only the strain of today that had her so hopelessly off balance?

She wanted to do the job. It was a marvellous assignment, staying in all those exciting places and writing about them. But if she committed herself... what would she be committing herself to in accepting such a close association with Christian Nemo? If only there was some way of knowing...

'Are you happy with that arrangement?' he asked.

Genevra's nerves prickled, sensing his need for her acquiescence. Why was she so aware of him, so sensitive to his feelings? She couldn't even bring herself to refuse him outright, despite her deep misgivings. The sense of something terribly important hanging in the balance was clouding her judgement, pressing her towards a course she knew could not be in her best interests... could it? She searched desperately for a compromise, and finally found one.

'Mr Nemo, you'll be spending a lot of money on this project, and I'm not sure I can deliver what you want. Before we start signing contracts or whatever, could we have a test run, so to speak? Go to one of these places—I'll pay my own way— and just see if I can satisfy your requirements. If not...'

'Certainly we can do that,' he declared, almost with an air of triumph, and again he took control, making arrangements so fast that Genevra had no time to reconsider.

He would pick her up from her hotel tomorrow afternoon, and they would stay overnight at the best hotel he could find at such short notice. Then he would see her safely home to St Ives the following day. As she agreed to this timetable, he visibly relaxed, but Genevra found her inner tension rising.

The decision had been made, for better or worse. She took her leave of Christian Nemo, feeling the oddest sensation that their lives were now inexorably intertwined, and there would be no escape. Ever.

If he had been Luke, coming back into her life, Genevra would not have questioned what she was feeling . . . but why was she reacting so strongly to a total stranger?

CHAPTER FOUR

NONE of the famous London landmarks made any impression whatsoever on Genevra as the taxi wove through the afternoon traffic. The trip to her hotel was blurred by wave after wave of chaotic emotion, and all of them swirled around the enigma of Christian Nemo.

She had been so certain he was Luke. It seemed impossible that two men could be so alike. Not the face—she couldn't refute the cruel evidence of those altered features—but all the rest: his physique, the smile, the deep timbre of his voice, even the touch of his hand had felt like Luke's.

It was madness to keep going over it all, yet Genevra could no more control her thoughts than she had been able to control her reactions to Christian Nemo. Not once in all these years of waiting for Luke had any man caused so much as a flutter in Genevra's heart, let alone played havoc with it. Even now, her pulse was racing at the thought of being with him tomorrow. And tomorrow night. And the next day.

Only Luke had ever...only Luke!

It *was* him!

It *had* to be!

The taxi pulled up at her hotel, and Genevra stepped out, sternly telling herself to get her feet back on the ground. She had to be wrong. Christian Nemo had flatly denied being Luke when they had first met. He talked like an American. His eye colour was different.

She recited those facts over to herself as she went up to her room, but she could not dispel the power of that wild idea. It kept growing, gathering force, taking over her mind. They had to be one and the same person! Surely it was the only answer that made sense of what she was feeling.

Madness, her mind screamed, but her heart beat a jubilant tattoo, and every instinct in her body played clarions of approval, drowning out the shrill voice of reason. And with all the force of her being Genevra commanded herself to forget Christian Nemo's face and the wrong eye colour, forget the American accent and everything else that couldn't be explained away. Somewhere there was an explanation. Had to be!

The meeting at the Dorchester, it was no coincidence at all. Luke would have chosen that venue to meet her again...at the same table they had shared before!

And her recognition of him had been instant and certain! She had felt no hesitation or confusion until he had turned around, and even then her instincts had still insisted it was Luke. There could be no doubt at all about the way he had made her feel.

But why would he pretend to be someone else? What motivation could he possibly have to play such a heartless game with her? Did he think she might not love him after all this time...or might not love the man he had become? Genevra found that a sobering thought.

She kicked off her shoes, hung up her suit-coat, then flopped down on the bed, intent on focusing her whole concentration on the problem.

Maybe he didn't feel he could present himself as the man who had swept her off her feet four years ago. He had been very, very conscious of the injuries to his face. And what other injuries had he sustained? Genevra wondered, remembering the walking-cane, the stiffness of his left leg when he sat down, and the nerve spasm in his hand. Another, even more pertinent thought sped into Genevra's mind...how long had all that corrective surgery taken?

What if Luke had lied to her in that letter, four years ago? What if he had been in some terrible accident soon after returning to Australia, had been disfigured, perhaps even partially paralysed, with little prospect of ever leading the kind of life he had wanted with her? Might he not have backed off from the marriage they had planned, deliberately cutting her free from any sense of obligation to him?

'I could not be happy within myself, nor could I make you happy... It will be best for both of us to try and forget what could have been...'

The words he had written leapt out of Genevra's memory, taking on a new meaning.

How many operations had he suffered through in order to emerge as the man who had introduced himself as Christian Nemo? And the project... surely that was simply a plan to spend time with her, to see if it was possible to recapture the love they had once shared. If such was the case, the money wouldn't mean anything to him, nor the time. And he would make every accommodation in the world to fit in with the son he hadn't known he had.

Johnny! The teacup knocked flying... she had just begun to tell him that she had a child. The shock, his pain and agitation, and then the despair she had sensed when he had thought she was married...now she understood! And her heart wept tears of blood for him.

His life—the life he had so painfully reconstructed—had been hanging on her answer, and she had been so close, so terribly close to turning her back on the future she had been waiting for all these years. She could well imagine the uncertainties that had racked him, forcing him to adopt the measures he had. He wasn't to know she still loved him, and *would* love him, no matter how he looked or what had happened to him.

She had to show him, reassure him, convince him, wipe any uncertainty out of his mind! A fierce exultation swept through Genevra's body. Tomorrow couldn't come fast enough. Her mind filled with all sorts of exciting plans.

She had time to go shopping in the morning. She would go to Harrods and be wildly extravagant. Matthew had urged her to spend some of the trust money on herself, and what better purpose could it be used for than pursuing her one chance for happiness? She wanted to look beautiful for Luke. She had to make him see that she found him as desirable as ever, that she wanted to attract his desire, that nothing could change her love for him.

A tiny bell of caution rang across her fevered thoughts. What if she was wrong? What if Christian Nemo was exactly what he said he was...an American publisher?

No! Everything within her heaved an instant rebellion against any doubt. She was not going to let herself be confused again. Not even the colour of his eyes could change her mind.

And yet...how could she explain that away? The colour of people's eyes didn't change. Not from grey to brown. It was inexplicable.

But that didn't matter. There had to be some explanation, because Genevra was now certain that she was right. Whatever the consequences to herself, she was going to act on that unalterable certainty, and somehow she would prove that Christian Nemo and Luke Stanford were one and the same person.

Positive action, that was what she had vowed to herself before approaching Matthew this afternoon. Genevra wished she had gone to him weeks before. Then she wouldn't have had to rely on her intuition. She would have had confirmation of Luke's accident. But she couldn't wait for that now. There had to be a quicker way to prove Luke's identity and force him to reveal the truth.

The mole! No two men could have exactly the same mole, and she remembered precisely where it was...remembered lying in bed with him, her fingers lightly brushing over it just below the pit of his back. All she had to do was get him to undress!

Well, she could always seduce him, Genevra thought on a mad wave of positive thinking; then softly laughed at herself. She was no *femme fatale*, practised in the art of seduction. There had only ever been Luke for her, and what had happened between them had simply happened because they both wanted it so much.

A ripple of remembered pleasure coursed through her body, and Genevra hugged it tightly to herself, wanting it to last, wanting to capture it again. It had been so long...so long since she had lain in Luke's arms, sharing all the wonderful intimacies of loving.

Surely he craved it, too? If she touched him, he would have to respond, just as he had always done. And if she dressed up for him, showed him in her manner and speech that nothing had changed for her, how could he resist the temptation she would offer him?

The need for his loving, her own need to love him was an ache that urgently demanded some appeasement. And what better way of proving to him that he was the man she wanted? She would make it up to him for all he had suffered to come back to her, show him that nothing else mattered but having him with her again. A blissful contentment spread through her, bringing relaxation for the first time in many days.

A small worm of sanity insisted that if Christian Nemo was truly Christian Nemo, and not Luke Stanford, she was about to make the most disastrous mistake of her life, but she swept the thought aside. She was not going to be a passive victim of her emotions any longer. She had made her decision and nothing...*nothing* was going to shift her from it.

Yves Saint Laurent—never in her life had Genevra worn a designer-label outfit, but as she slipped the top on over the brilliantly striped skirt, and admired the total effect, she thought it would be very easy to become addicted to buying such wonderful clothes.

She felt more vibrantly alive than she had done in years, and vibrant was certainly the key-word, she thought with a delighted grin. The skirt and matching top featured brilliant bands of fuchsia-pink, red, orange, violet, green and turquoise, as well as black and white; and the beautifully set white collar on the low V-neckline of the sleeveless top was the crowning touch of class.

Not to mention the Christian Dior sandals! The soft leather cross-over straps were the same marvellous shade of fuchsia-pink as in the dress, and the black button at the side of the ankle-strap and the black high heels lent a very sexy elegance to the design.

A warm tingle of excitement brought a glowing colour to Genevra's cheeks. She didn't look pale and pinched today. Her blue eyes were sparkling with happy anticipation, and her whole face seemed to have acquired a youthful bloom overnight. She felt like dancing on top of the world and shouting out to everyone that the man she loved had come back to her.

And she was ready for him now! Genevra's gaze fell exultantly on all the shopping bags strewn over the bed in her hotel room. She had spent an absolute fortune, over a thousand pounds, but the outlay was well worth every penny if she could make Luke drop his pose of being a stranger. And if the dress she had bought for tonight didn't spark off a desire to make love to her, then he would have to be made of iron!

Genevra checked her watch. It was still twenty minutes short of two o'clock, twenty minutes before Luke . . . She had to remember to call him Christian Nemo until he admitted his true identity.

Genevra packed the new clothes into her suitcase and dispensed with the shopping-bags, then, feeling a little guilty about her uncharacteristic extravagance, she rang Matthew to warn him that a large account would be coming in to be paid from the trust fund. She had never done such a thing before but, when she confessed her spending spree to Matthew, his oft-repeated comment of 'Splendid!' expressed a ringing approval that satisfactorily cleared her conscience.

Anticipation lightened her step as she went down to the reception desk to pay her hotel bill. The clerk behind the desk cast a frankly appreciative eye over her, and Genevra's heart gave a skip of elated triumph. She really did look good! She was still smiling over his very courteous attention when the Silver Cloud Rolls-Royce pulled up outside the hotel entrance.

Genevra stared in surprise as Luke stepped out of it. Christian Nemo, she swiftly corrected herself. She hadn't expected him to travel in that degree of luxury, although the kind of hotels he had described for the project would certainly be catering to people of the highest wealth-bracket. Did a construction business generate that kind of money? Then she remembered that Luke had flown first-class from England to Australia. She simply hadn't realised how well off he was.

She turned towards him as he entered the hotel foyer and her heart did more than skip a beat when he stopped dead in his tracks and stared at her. Several pulse-galloping moments passed before he took a deep breath and moved forwards, holding out his hand to her.

'I thought you beautiful yesterday, Genevra,' he said in a deep, husky voice. 'But today...'

The intensity of his gaze choked the breath in Genevra's throat. She existed only for him as he slowly took in the sparkling blue of her eyes, the becoming flush of colour in her cheeks, the shiny ripple of black waves falling to her shoulders, the soft fullness of her mouth.

'... but today you look ravishing,' he finished softly.

His hand curled around hers, subtly pressing an ownership that she gladly gave up to him. 'Thank you,' she all but whispered, then laughed out of sheer happiness. 'I thought I'd better dress up to the assignment.'

He laughed too, and it was the strongest possible echo of the past when he replied, 'Dress doesn't matter.' His smile curled around Genevra's heart as he added, 'But I feel very privileged to have your company, and I hope you'll enjoy your stay at Le Manoir aux Quat'Saisons.'

He tucked her hand around his arm, directed the clerk to get the suitcase carried to the car, then led Genevra outside and handed her into the Rolls-Royce. It looked like the same car that she had seen arriving at the Dorchester Hotel yesterday afternoon, and Genevra decided that it probably was, since Luke had only been a minute or two ahead of her.

She watched him covertly as he settled back into the seat beside her.

He was less formally dressed today, but the light grey trousers, white shirt and navy blazer were still conservative, as was the tasteful grey tie with its thin red, white and navy stripes. She remembered Luke's love of sporty, casual clothes, and wondered if his taste had really changed. Not that it mattered to her.

'Do you always motor around in a Rolls-Royce?' she asked curiously.

'No, only in England. I need a chauffeured car here.' He turned his head slightly away from her so that the black eye-patch was hidden from her sight before adding, 'I have a problem judging distances with only one eye, and I can't get an international driver's licence.'

'I don't mind, you know,' Genevra said softly.

A dry smile curved his mouth. 'Not many people do mind riding in such cars.'

'I didn't mean that. I meant the scars and whatever else you feel you have to hide,' she said in a rush, sensing an emotional retreat from her and anxious to stop it.

'Why do you think I've got something to hide?'

His sharp frown warned her that she was going too fast, and Genevra instantly back-pedalled. 'You spoke yesterday of choosing that table at the Dorchester so as to be out of view of the people there. I just want you to know that I don't find the view of your face at all offensive. Quite the contrary, in fact. So please don't turn away from me.'

He probed the sincerity in her eyes for a long moment before giving a bemused little shake of his head. 'Are you always this direct?'

'I would like you to be direct with me,' she retorted fearlessly.

He sliced her a slightly guarded look. 'What do you want to know?'

'You must have been in a frightful accident,' she prompted. 'Do you mind telling me what happened?'

He did not reply immediately, and she could feel him closing up, even before he spoke. 'Morbid curiosity?'

She flushed at the implied reprimand. 'I'm sorry. If you prefer not to talk about it . . .'

'I much prefer,' he answered curtly.

Genevra bit her tongue and stared at the back of the chauffeur's head as he started the car and steered it smoothly into a stream of traffic. She had blundered again, too eager to fill in the lost years. The craving to know all that had happened to him was hard to repress.

On the other hand, she could understand that Luke had no desire to recall a time that must have been terribly painful, both physically and mentally. She was an insensitive fool to have mentioned it. Wasn't it enough that he was here with her now?

But she would like to know if she was right about his letter, that it was the accident which had forced him into denying her, and not marriage to another woman.

'Is there anything else?' he asked in a matter-of-fact tone that effectively cut through the tense silence which had fallen between them.

Genevra's relief at the opening he had given her was almost instantly checked by the realisation that he might be offended again if he thought she was questioning his sense of morality. She tried a more indirect approach.

'If I'm to be with you, staying at hotels, there are some things I need to know...'

'Go on,' he urged as she hesitated.

Genevra took a deep breath and plunged on. 'Well, you made the point with me yesterday, so I think it's fair to ask you...' She turned to meet his gaze, and found the same guarded expression she had seen before. 'Are you married?' she asked point-blank.

A fleeting look of sadness accompanied his brief answer. 'Not any more.'

Somehow, Genevra covered up her shock, nodding an acknowledgement of the reply before turning her gaze back to the chauffeur's head. As hurt welled over the shock, she looked out the side window, pretending an interest in their route.

Not any more...so what was he? Divorced? Widowed? And why the look of sadness? The fact of the marriage hurt badly enough, although he had spelled it out to her in the letter. But the sadness! Why should he feel sad about the end of a marriage he hadn't wanted? Or did he feel sad because he had been forced to hurt her with his marriage to another woman?

The squeeze on Genevra's heart eased a little. 'I know too well the pain it will give you——' that was what he had written '—and wish with all my heart that I did not have to make this choice...'

Maybe it was the accident—his injuries—that had brought about the end of the marriage. Whatever had happened, he was free now. That was the important thing. And he had come back to her. Nothing else really mattered.

'Genevra...'

It was a soft appeal for her attention and, feeling once more in command of herself, Genevra had no hesitation in turning back to him. 'Yes?'

'I would not compromise you in any way. Please don't doubt that,' he said seriously. 'If you ever feel I'm imposing on your time, and you'd prefer to be by yourself...'

She reached over to touch his arm in a quick, reassuring gesture. 'But I'm very happy for us to be together,' she said; then, seeing his surprise, she quickly added, 'I need all the help you can give me. How else will I know exactly what you want?'

His smile was slow in coming, but it spilled an exultant joy into Genevra's heart. 'I'm glad you see it that way.'

Her own smile held all the love that had always been his. 'Tell me about this place we're going to. I don't even know where it is.'

The air of tense reserve completely disappeared. He relaxed and spoke in a tone of happy anticipation. 'It's in Oxfordshire. We should be there in under an hour. The Manoir is actually situated in the village of Great Milton, just five miles from

Oxford. The building is mainly an eighteenth-century manor house, but its origins go back to the fourteenth century. The Egon Ronay Guide gives the hotel a de-luxe rating and the restaurant three stars—one of the finest in Britain. The wine list is outstanding . . .'

Genevra watched him talk. She listened, too, nodding and smiling in all the right places, asking questions about the hotel that had impressed him so much in Hampshire, Chewton Glen.

He recalled all the details that he thought were pertinent to his concept of the project. Genevra actually began to wonder if Luke had left construction work and gone into publishing since his accident. But it was the way he was responding to her that held most of her attention.

He forgot about his face and, as Genevra got used to the altered features, she decided that the surgeon had done a masterly job. The altered nose was the right shape to balance the jawline. The barely visible scars were obviously the result of skin-grafts, and would probably fade altogether in time.

Luke was just as handsome as he had always been, although in a different way. The tawny-brown eye colour was quite startlingly attractive with his dark eyelashes and hair. She wondered if he was wearing a contact lens. Was it possible to get tinted ones? There had to be some answer to the puzzle.

She loved his smile. Loved all of him with a passion that could hardly wait for tonight. He was trying to hold back, to keep up his role of being a stranger, but Genevra knew she was wearing the barriers down. She could feel the rapport creeping back, that same magic rapport that had leapt between them four years ago.

Twice his gaze clung to hers while he forgot what he had been saying, and she sensed his need and his incredulity at the need that she was projecting. Each time, he gave a slight shake of his head before distractedly resuming the line of conversation that had been left hanging.

The third time, he actually jerked his head away and she saw his hand clench. Genevra was certain that he had wanted to reach out and touch her. 'We're coming into Great Milton now,' he announced, and the strained note in his voice was like a chord of beautiful music to Genevra's ears. She didn't doubt for one moment that he wanted her as much as ever, and the restraint he was forcing upon himself could not last long, particularly if she applied some real pressure.

Great Milton was a pretty village, more picturesque than most, with the well-kept neatness of its thatched cottages spread around the village green. Luke half leaned across her to point out the almost perfect symmetry of one cottage: chimneys at each end of the thatched roof, attic windows positioned directly above the windows on either side of the central door, window-boxes with identical flowers, and matching pot-plants hanging just under the eaves.

Genevra nodded her appreciation, but she was far more conscious of the nearness of Luke's body. His blazer had fallen open, and she could almost feel the warmth of his broad chest. All she had to do was turn towards him and she would virtually be within the circle of his arms. But before she could act on the temptation, he drew back and the moment was gone. She found herself clenching her own hands as she fought to calm her disordered pulse.

A leafy lane took them to a very old village church with a clock tower. Its high stone walls extended to the impressive gateway of the Manoir.

'Here we are.' His fingers lightly brushed her forearm, as if he could no longer resist the impulse to touch her.

However, his gaze was rather pointedly fixed on the grounds they were entering, and Genevra could not make anything positive out of the light contact. Reluctantly, she turned her attention to the subject she was supposed to write about.

The driveway was lined with trees and garden beds that were ablaze with yellow violas. On the beautifully kept lawn to their right were tables and chairs of white aluminium lace, shaded by bright pink umbrellas. The chauffeur turned the Rolls-Royce into the spacious, gravelled courtyard that fronted the stately manor house, and parked it near the entrance doorway which was framed with climbing roses.

Genevra could not disguise her own air of heightened excitement as Christian Nemo helped her to alight from the car. He took her by the arm, drawing her close to him, and she had no doubt that his need to feel her body next to his was as uncontrollable as her own. It was no longer a matter of her seducing him, but of how long they would have to wait before they were alone together.

They walked into a rather small reception room, but Genevra noted it was strikingly furnished with antiques, and the floral arrangements were nothing short of magnificent. Conscious that their sexual tension might be all too evident to the receptionist, Genevra deliberately feasted her eyes on everything else while Christian spoke to the woman.

'I've given Miss Kingsley the Hollyhock Room. You're in Hydrangea, Mr Nemo,' the receptionist announced, then added with a touch of pride, 'All our rooms are named after flowers and decorated accordingly. I hope you'll both enjoy your stay here.'

A porter took Genevra's suitcase and led the way upstairs. At the top landing, he indicated that the Hydrangea Room was up a few more stairs at the end of the hallway, then turned in the opposite direction to show them to the Hollyhock Room.

Genevra felt a stab of disappointment at the distance between the two rooms, but she quickly dismissed the idea that any distance could keep them apart now.

When the porter opened her door and invited Genevra to step inside, she hastened forwards, impatient for the formalities to be over. However, her first glance at the room left her absolutely stunned.

Its luxurious size, the superb elegance of its furnishings, the sheer marvellous richness of everything drew her forwards in gaping wonder.

She heard the porter say something about bringing up the other suitcases, but Genevra was so entranced by what was in front of her that she didn't notice his departure. She had seen pictures of fantastic bedroom suites, but the reality was almost too much to take in.

The double bed looked fabulous with its ornamental canopy hanging from the wall above it. The use of the hollyhock fabric, with its sprays of flowers scalloped by a print of blue ribbon, was the touch of a brilliant decorator. The side-drapes from the canopy were complemented by a tightly gathered central drape of hollyhock-pink silk. The bedhead and quilt were padded in the floral fabric, while the valance around the base of the bed repeated the pink silk. At least half a dozen white lace pillows were piled up in front of the bedhead.

And the bed was only the start!

A four-seater Louis the fourteenth sofa, upholstered in blue silk, graced the window position in front of the wide stretch of hollyhock curtains. There were two wing-backed armchairs in pink silk, a coffee-table, a writing-table with a matching Chippendale chair, another table draped with a white lace cloth on which stood a complimentary bowl of fruit, two elegant dining-chairs, a beautifully polished antique chest of drawers, a cheval-glass, paintings on the walls, graceful lamps...

'Like it?'

She turned sparkling eyes back to Christian Nemo. 'I love it!'

He was smiling indulgently at her. 'This must be the bathroom,' he said, moving towards a door on the left of the entrance.

In a burst of pleasurable anticipation, Genevra whirled back and hugged his arm as he opened the door.

The bathroom was perfectly matched to the bedroom décor. Even the thick beige carpet extended inside, and the mirror above the vanity bench was surrounded by a padded frame of the hollyhock fabric. The tiles were a pearly-pink, and the bath, basin and shower all had gold fittings. A potted palm sat on a ledge above the bath, and beautiful dishes held Lancôme toilette products.

'This is positively decadent,' Genevra breathed.

Christian Nemo gave a soft laugh which abruptly stopped as she looked up at him. She saw the sharp conflict between desire and caution, felt the muscle in his arm tighten under her touch. As of one accord, they turned to each other. Genevra's hand feathered up the lapel of his blazer, ready to curl around his neck. He gripped her waist, fingers sliding around to draw her closer.

There was a knock on the door!

'Mr Nemo?'

His fingers suddenly dug into her flesh, forcibly halting their encircling progress. His head jerked up. 'Yes?' he replied on a swiftly indrawn breath.

'I've brought your bags up, sir. Would you like to be shown to your room now?'

'Yes. Thank you,' he clipped out, and in a stiff, defensive move, he held Genevra still as he stepped back from her, and only when he had put some distance between them did he meet the urgent plea in her eyes.

But he didn't answer it! To her hurt bewilderment, he even pretended not to see it. Somehow, he had managed to pull a mask of formality over his own feelings and, when he spoke, his voice projected a flat denial of anything explosive between them.

'I'll leave you to settle in, Genevra. Give you time to really look around and enjoy what's here. Perhaps in an hour or so you'd like to walk around the grounds. Take everything in.'

'Yes. Yes, I would like that,' she murmured, feeling completely deflated by his withdrawal.

'Fine. I'll call by your door then.'

'Fine,' she echoed.

And he left her without a backward glance, his gait stiff, his shoulders decisively squared.

Genevra felt so frustrated that she almost slammed the door after him. He needn't have gone, she thought angrily. He could have told the porter to put the bags in his room and leave the key in the door. Why, why, why had he turned away from her like that?

She paced the floor, trying to fathom his reasons, totally uncaring of the luxury around her. Was he still unsure of how she felt about him? Was he afraid of a rebuff if he went too fast? He had sworn not to compromise her in any way; did he feel honour-bound not to take advantage of the situation?

Genevra shook her head, not knowing what to think. But one way or another, she would crack open that façade of control before tonight was over.

As far as she was concerned, the waiting was a thing of the past. This man wanted her and she wanted him. Genevra was certain who he was, and she was not going to let anything stand in the way of their coming together.

CHAPTER FIVE

THE man who called himself Christian Nemo came to her room an hour later. He wore an air of reserve.

Genevra gave him the full brilliance of her smile, closed her door, and slid her hand around his. There was a momentary passivity, then almost convulsively his fingers closed around hers.

She chattered gaily to him on their way downstairs; not giving him a chance to be at all sober or serious; and once outside she effervesced with happy enthusiasm over everything in sight. He relaxed. He smiled. He laughed. He looked at her as if he wanted to devour all that she offered him.

And dancing through Genevra's mind was an exultant refrain... "He's mine, mine, mine! And no one else can ever have him from now on."

The surrounds of the Manoir were fascinating: paths cutting through manicured lawns and bordered by wonderful rose-gardens; magnificent trees; shrubs shaped by the art of topiary; flowering vines dressing the old stone walls; a splendid, if somewhat crumbling dovecote; picturesque outbuildings that had once housed carriages, but which now contained service rooms for the hotel; an enclosed swimming pool surrounded by the now-familiar white furniture and pink umbrellas; and beyond the immediate environs were twenty-seven acres of country fields and the chef's extensive kitchen garden.

It was an exhilarating walk, every step forging a more intense awareness of each other. They saw other guests enjoying the peaceful beauty of the grounds. They even talked to a couple of gardeners, pretending an interest in the contents of the igloo hot-houses. But all the words they spoke and all the walking they did was just a game, a marvellous game of driving anticipation to its most exquisite limits.

When it was time to dress for dinner, Genevra parted from Luke at the top of the staircase, almost skipping away from him in teasing provocation— wanting to dress up for him, wanting to drive him out of his mind with desire so that there could never, never be any turning away, wanting it to be the most magical night of their lives. And she was pulsatingly aware of the yearning that emanated from him as he watched her go.

She sang in the shower. She made lavish use of the Lancôme products. She deliberately dispensed with wearing a bra. She felt deliciously, wickedly wanton as she twirled around in the new dress, assessing its sexiness in the cheval-glass.

It was a beautiful dress, predominantly pink, but patterned with streaks of white and two shades of blue. The full, graceful three-quarter-length sleeves were in a matching fabric, with deeper shades of the same colours, as were the inset gores of the lovely swinging skirt. A wide, elasticised waistband accentuated the curves of her figure. A scalloped satin-stitch of the two shades of blue featured the low V-neckline, and from the neck-edge of the shoulder seam fell string ties ending in silk tassles, which, when tied loosely at the base of her throat, added the classy touch that dispensed with any need for jewellery.

Genevra's blue eyes sparkled with delight at her reflection. The dress was not overtly sexy, but it certainly showed off the fact that she was a woman, and the silky sensuousness of the softly flowing fabric made her feel very physically aware of herself. She lifted a hand and ran it experimentally over the thrusting fullness of her breasts, and felt her nipples leaping into hard prominence.

Rampant thoughts on how Luke would touch her tonight sent ripples of excitement through her body. She couldn't think of him as Christian Nemo. Besides, after tonight there would be no need to. After they had made love and she had found the mole which would prove his identity, the truth had to come out. And then they would make love again in the full knowledge of each other and . . .

When his knock came, Genevra's breathing had already become ragged from her feverish imaginings. She opened the door and almost melted on the spot as he stared at her, speechless, the quick rise and fall of his chest revealing his own sexual tension.

'Genevra...' It was a whisper of hungry, compelling desire. His gaze lifted to hers, glazed with need. 'Tell me this is not a game with you. Tell me I'm not imagining this...'

'It's no game. And it's as real as it ever was...' She barely stopped herself from calling him Luke. Not yet. Not until he admitted it, she cautioned herself.

He shook his head, trying to break the spell of desire that bound them together. 'You hardly know me.'

'I know you as well as you know me,' she reminded him.

Painful doubt looked back at her. 'I didn't think...didn't expect...'

'Because it's been so long?' she asked softly, then stepped forwards, reaching up to caress the faintly lined cheek. 'Or because of this?'

'Don't!' It was a hoarse, explosive whisper. He plucked her hand away, as if he couldn't bear her touch. His fingers worked over hers in extreme agitation. 'It's too soon! I can't risk losing control and spoiling our relationship at this early stage. Don't tempt me, Genevra. We need...to know each other better. To talk...about things.'

A happy triumph burst through her. He was going to confess his real identity! 'Then let's go down to dinner and talk.'

Her amenability to his need for more time brought a short laugh of sheer relief. 'God knows how I'm going to do the meal justice with you sitting across from me! You're the most terrible temptation any man could have, Genevra.'

'But there's only one man I want,' she said, and her eyes quite blatantly declared her desire for him.

He made no reply to her assertion until they were seated in the dining-room and served with champagne and a platter of appetisers. He looked at her over his glass of wine, his gaze drifting down the rippling cascade of shiny black hair, skating over the jutting fullness of her breasts, then finally met the unflinching directness of her eyes.

'You were right upstairs. It has been a long time since I've been with...or even wanted to be with a woman. And the truth is, you affect me in a way no other woman has ever affected me. I would do anything for you.'

Beautiful, marvellous, glorious words that Genevra revelled in. 'It seems I've been waiting for ever for you,' she murmured fervently. 'Don't make me wait any longer.'

'Genevra...' A look of anguish crossed his face. 'I didn't come prepared for...for this contingency.

I don't want you...conceiving a child that's not planned.'

'I'm older and wiser now,' she replied softly, understanding the guilt he obviously felt over Johnny, and loving him all the more for his caring. 'It can't happen tonight,' she assured him, and silently vowed to see her doctor as soon as she got back to St Ives. There would be time for another baby in the future, but not too soon. Johnny deserved to have his father's sole attention for a while.

She smiled as she sensed his relief. With it came the slow release of the restraint he had been tightly holding on to, but he did not smile back at her. The accelerated pulse of his emotion was too strong for smiling.

'Tell me about your life...your son. I want to know everything about you,' he commanded, need throbbing behind every word.

He meant the lost years, Genevra thought, and for a moment the pain of separation that he had inflicted on both of them held her tongue. She wanted him to tell her the full truth about his marriage, the accident, all that had happened to him; but then she realised that such topics could only bring them both pain, whereas telling him about his son would give them pleasure.

She told him everything she could think of about Johnny's childhood, and not for one moment did he look the slightest bit bored with the subject. He listened with rapt attention, encouraged her into more and more detail, seemingly enthralled by her relationship with her son. The son he should have shared with her, Genevra thought sadly. But he was sharing now! What point was there in regretting time that had gone when she had now?

The meal was superb: a terrine of *bouillabaisse* with fennel, baby leeks and virgin olive oil; tender fillet of lamb, fanned into a central rosette and served with perfect baby turnips, snow peas, peeled broad beans and small circles of crisped potato; then a lemon soufflé, so light and delicate that it vanished in the mouth.

The setting was elegant, the service impeccable, the French wine as smooth as silk; all contributing an extra edge of magic to this night of nights. But best of all for Genevra was the feeling of being where she belonged, with Luke, sharing all that could be shared.

With each minute that passed, the need to touch grew stronger. It wasn't enough to talk or to look or to even hold hands, which only fed the desire for greater intimacy. Coffee and *petits fours* were served and ignored by both of them. They couldn't tear their eyes off each other. Silence fell between them, a silence that grew tense with unfulfilled passion.

'Do you want this coffee?' he asked, a rough edge furring his voice.

'No,' she breathed through a sudden constriction in her throat.

He stood up, stepping quickly to hold her chair for her. Genevra's thighs quivered in anticipation as she rose to take his arm. Neither of them spoke a word as they walked up to her room. The door shut the rest of the world out.

He tore off his jacket as she reached for him. He gathered her hard to him, her breasts crushed to the thundering beat of his chest, her lower body thrust into a more urgently pulsing hardness. Their mouths sought a swifter means of mutual possession, their fierce kiss initiating an erotic prelude for what was to come: tasting, teasing, tangling with an avid need for the passionate mingling of flesh, wildly hungry for every exciting nuance of intimacy.

Her hands were raking up his back, thrusting into his hair, then dragging down to close convulsively over his tight buttocks as she arched into him. He wrenched his mouth from hers, groaning his need. His voice held a hoarse, driven sound as he gasped, 'I can't wait, Genevra.'

'I don't want you to,' she breathed, exulting in her power to arouse him beyond his control, wanting to give him the pleasure that would ease his pain and bring them both the ultimate peace of total union.

His hands slid down her thighs and gathered up her skirt as his mouth claimed hers again. His fingers grazed up to the bare skin of her stomach, pushed under the band of her wispy lace panties and peeled them down, making her flesh leap with excitement at his every touch. He reached for the fever-heated apex between her thighs, caressing her with a delicate pressure that sent quivers of pleasure-shock through her whole body. Her knees buckled. An iron-tight arm held her pinned to him as he moved her to the bed and quickly disposed of her shoes and panties.

She reached for him, but her fingers were weak, boneless, merely brushing down the swollen hardness of his erection. His stomach contracted with tension. His gaze glittered over her as he threw off his tie and attacked the buttons of his shirt. Somehow, she found the strength to push herself up and lift her dress over her head. He straightened from removing his trousers and she flung her arms around his waist, pressing her cheek to the moist nakedness of his heaving chest.

'God almighty!' It was a tremulous gasp.

'You're mine now. Mine!' she said fiercely, and her lips pressed her claim in a sensuous trail of kisses.

'Genevra!' The cry echoed with years of aching need. He arched back, the powerful thrust of his manhood sliding through the soft valley of her breasts. His hands gripped her under her arms and lifted, hauling her up for his mouth to ravage hers as he carried her with him down on to the pillows.

He smothered her face with kisses, punctuating them with hoarse words of wild adoration. He shaped her breasts to his mouth and sucked on them as if he would draw the very essence from her soul. The most exquisite pleasure spurted through her, making her writhe and arch in uninhibited abandonment to all he would do to her.

He caressed her legs apart, his fingers delving into the intimate crevices and manipulating a sensitivity that drove her beyond madness. She felt her inner muscles convulsing out of control, and almost wept with relief as he pushed into her, a hot, heavy fullness that made her tremble with ecstatic satisfaction. Her hands shot down to drag at his powerful thighs, pulling him deeper. Her legs instinctively curled around his, lifting herself up to him, urging that final devastating plunge that took him all the way into her womb.

And that sensation eclipsed all others, the feel of him at the centre of her being, possessing and possessed. His hands curved around her buttocks, supporting her there with him, of him, together. She opened her eyes and it was Luke's body hovering above hers: beautiful, strong, a streamlined symphony of taut flesh and muscle, sheened with the heat of their desire for each other.

She lifted a limp hand and stroked a sensual line from belly to groin. He shuddered and unleashed a fiery rhythm of stroking thrusts that drove electric tingles into every cell of her body, fusing them into a sweet, aching sea of pleasure-pain that swelled to a climactic crest and crashed into pure bliss.

And still there was the exquisite movement inside her, faster, faster, spilling her into wave after wave of glorious sensation, and the ultimate spasms of his climax brought the final intense fulfilment of all the dreams she had ever had. He toppled forwards and she caught him to her, hugging him with all the love in her heart, pressing soft little kisses to his throat and cheek, until he lifted his head to sweep her mouth with his own in a tender salute of love.

'You know what I'm thinking?' he smiled down at her.

'Tell me,' she murmured, her eyes shining with a languorous happiness.

'I'm the luckiest man alive. And even now, I don't know why or how, only that I am.'

'Because you're you,' she replied, loving his smile, loving everything about him.

He stroked her hair, fanning the long tresses out on the pillow. 'Are you a sorceress, Genevra?'

She laughed up at him. 'I only have magic for you.'

'I want it to go on and on,' he said with serious fervour. 'Do you want that, too?'

'For ever,' she breathed, her need for him glittering in her eyes as she wound her arms around his neck and pulled his head down to hers.

Their kiss held no urgent passion, but it awakened a purely sensual desire to touch and taste each other in less frantic haste. They found a beautifully erotic delight in pleasuring with caresses and kisses, savouring every intimate knowledge gained and greedy for more.

Like seasoned partners in a primitive pagan ritual, they moved around each other; exciting, soothing, teasing, building slowly to the final mating ceremony, which they performed with a restrained, sensual deliberation, heightening every fragmented awareness of sliding together, becoming one, again and again and again until they could not bear the control any longer, their need exploding into a barbaric wildness that left them both exhausted and totally sated.

Then they lay in each other's arms, too drained to speak or move, knowing there were no words or actions left that could express the sense of belonging that bound them together. Nothing could have been more total, more complete.

Genevra listened contentedly to the soft sigh of her lover's breathing, and knew he was at peace. The long separation was over, and they would never be parted again. Her hand glided down his back in a wholly possessive caress, and it was only then that she remembered about the mole.

She smiled to herself. As if she needed proof now! It wasn't possible that two different men could draw such a basic response from her.

There was no question in her mind as her hand continued its downward slide. She knew him so intimately that the mole merely represented another small dimension of familiarity. Her fingers lightly swept the area of skin near the pit of his back, seeking the different texture she knew was there.

She couldn't find it. She concentrated more carefully on the task, willing her fingertips to detect what had to be detected. But there was no different texture, no change at all in the pattern of his smooth flesh, not even when she searched further afield, in case she had forgotten the exact position.

The man lying in her arms, intimately entwined with her... the man to whom she had just given herself body and soul... did not have a mole on his back!

CHAPTER SIX

GENEVRA fought back the sick, panicky feeling that clawed at the edges of her new-found happiness. Lots of people had moles removed, it meant nothing. The shape of his body, the way he made her feel...there could be no doubt that he was Luke, no matter what he called himself.

But she had been so sure the mole would be there. Its absence eroded her confidence, opening her mind to other disturbing thoughts. He had not confessed his deception, despite the most positive proof of her feelings towards him. He lay asleep in her arms as if he hadn't a care in the world. What if he really was Christian Nemo, a stranger whom she had only met yesterday?

No, that was impossible! Every instinct clamoured an instant rejection. He was no stranger!

And yet, when she had first met Luke, he hadn't felt like a stranger, either. Was it possible for two men to be so alike that she could love them both with the same intensity?

The idea tortured Genevra for several moments before it was forcefully dismissed. It was madness to even contemplate it after what had happened between them tonight. She knew him...knew him to

the very depths of her being, and there had to be
some way of proving that Luke and Christian were
one and the same person.

She fretted over the problem until an answer
slowly dawned. All she had to do was see his
passport. Surely it would hold the truth. To adopt
a false name in a foreign country where nobody
knew you was a relatively simple matter, but she
couldn't imagine it would be very simple to obtain
a false passport.

The temptation to look for it became too great
to resist. Very gently, she eased herself out of his
embrace and slid silently off the bed. His trousers
lay in a crumpled heap on the floor, and she picked
them up and folded them neatly across the seat of
a chair. She retrieved the coat which had been
dropped near the doorway and, feeling uncomfortably like a sneak-thief, she checked the pockets.

The only contents was a slim leather wallet, and
although it probably contained identifying credit
cards Genevra could not bring herself to open it.
She argued to herself that they wouldn't prove anything, anyway. A man who had gone to so much
trouble in setting up this hotel project would almost
certainly have covered his name-change on any
cards he used. She had to find his passport.

It wasn't in his clothes, so it had to be in his
room. She couldn't go there tonight, but at the first
opportunity... the run of darting thoughts came to

a dazed halt. Genevra stood in the middle of the room, appalled by what was happening to her. The man she loved had come back to her. Couldn't she show a little faith in him?

The physical barrier between them had been broken tonight, but there were other adjustments to be made... like with Johnny! Maybe he thought it was better to earn his son's love before presenting himself as his father. What other reason could he have for not declaring who he was? Maybe he would tell her first thing in the morning. All she really had to do was wait.

Her gaze shifted to the bed, and her eyes gloated lovingly over the powerfully muscled body that lay there. Her man, she thought with intense pride. There was something touchingly vulnerable about his nakedness that brought a lump of emotion to her throat. She suddenly remembered his uncertainty tonight when he had come to take her to dinner. He *was* vulnerable where she was concerned. She had to remember that, and not judge his words and actions too hastily.

He stirred in his sleep, his arm moving restlessly over the empty space where she had lain. Genevra ran back to the bed and snuggled up to him, lifting his arm around her waist. It instantly hugged her closer, and his mouth brushed against her temple.

'Genevra...' The dreamy sigh held so much longing and love that tears pricked her eyes.

'I'm here,' she whispered, her heart swelling with her love for him. 'I'll always be here.'

She awoke the next morning to find him looking down at her, a soft, wondering expression on his face. A satisfied little smile curved her lips. 'It wasn't a dream,' she assured him.

He laughed, and it was the sound of bubbling happiness. He said nothing about being an impostor, but somehow the omission didn't dim Genevra's pleasure at all as they made love, slowly and exquisitely. Then, wrapped in the thick, cosy bathrobes the hotel provided, they stole along the empty hallway to the Hydrangea Suite and made exhilarating use of the jacuzzi in his luxurious bathroom.

The bedroom was longer and narrower than Genevra's, but just as beautifully furnished. It had a balcony that overlooked the rose garden, and here they had breakfast brought to them. The sun was shining, the air was freshly scented and life was marvellous, far too marvellous to be entertaining any doubts whatsoever.

Even when she had the opportunity, Genevra didn't look for his passport. If Luke wanted to be Christian Nemo for a while, she didn't mind at all. As long as he was with her, loving her, a different name didn't mean a thing, and she even talked herself into calling him Christian.

They did not travel to St Ives in the Rolls-Royce. The car had been dismissed the previous afternoon. Christian had arranged for a helicopter to pick them up at the Manoir and fly them down. The countryside looked so pretty from the air that the whole trip was an absolute delight, but best of all was the aerial view of St Ives just before they landed.

The sea was sparkling, the beaches blazed white, colourfully dotted by the changing tents and deckchairs and sunbathers and towels; the boats moored inside the harbour lent their picturesque flavour to the scene, and the neat nestling of the village around the waterfront tugged at Genevra's heart.

She had lived all her life here. She wondered how she would feel about leaving it when the time came.

She glanced at the man beside her. He smiled and squeezed her hand. The noise of the helicopter made conversation a shouting affair, but words were unnecessary between them at the moment. Genevra knew she would go anywhere with him...to Australia or America, or wherever his life was based now.

The helicopter landed on the front lawn of Tregenna Castle Hotel, which took up a dominant place on the hill above the village. The impressive façade, with its battlement-style walls and flags flying from the turrets that flanked the entrance, was largely accentuated by the extensive grounds which contained a private golf course, tennis courts, swimming pool, all edged with lovely trees and gardens. The hotel was a popular tourist place, and Genevra was not surprised when Christian had named it as their destination. It was where Luke had stayed during that long-ago summer.

He ordered a taxi as soon as they reached the reception desk, and declared his intention of seeing her safely home. Genevra smiled, sensing his eagerness to meet Johnny, and only too happy to comply with his wishes. He removed a large parcel from his luggage and grinned a little sheepishly at her as he laid it on top of her suitcase.

'A present for a little boy. I hope you don't mind. I thought . . . well, I like kids, and I . . .'

'I don't mind at all,' she said quickly, wanting him to have every possible joy in their son. Her own joy in his anticipation broke into a wide grin. 'What did you buy?'

He gave a dismissive shrug, trying to downplay any intensity of feeling. 'Oh, just a small race-track and a couple of remote-controlled cars. I'll help him set it up. If that's all right with you,' he added, unable to keep the hopeful appeal out of his voice.

'I'd be very grateful if you would,' she assured him. 'I'm not much good at mechanical things.'

The taxi arrived, and Christian wore a happy, satisfied smile all the way down to the waterfront where Genevra's shop was situated. He gave the taxi driver an enormous tip. Genevra was riding on a wild high as she led him into the bookshop.

Fortunately Beryl was attending to a customer, so Genevra did not have to stop and introduce him. She gave her assistant a 'hello' wave which was acknowledged with an interested lift of the eyebrows. Genevra grinned at her, mouthed 'later', then ushered Christian to the staircase at the back of the shop.

'I hope that race-track is small, because we haven't got much room up here,' she warned, ruefully recalling that the Hollyhock suite at the Manoir had been bigger than the floor above them. It was divided into four rooms: kitchen, living-room, bathroom, and Auntie May's bedroom, then the two attic bedrooms up another flight of stairs.

'It only needs about four feet of floor. I'll teach Johnny how to dismantle it,' Christian assured her.

And of course he knew where it would fit in the living-room, Genevra assured herself. Luke had been in her home dozens of times.

'I'm home!' she called, excitement spilling the words out as soon as she opened the door into the living-room.

'Mummy!' Johnny shrieked from the kitchen, and came pelting out to greet her.

Genevra swept him up into her arms, hugging him with a fierce mother-love as she turned to show him off to his father. And as Christian drank in the small, boyish features that stamped him as their son, Johnny stared back at him, his gray eyes widening with fascination.

'Are you a pirate?' he asked.

Christian laughed. 'I'm afraid not. But I did bring you some booty.'

He held out the parcel encouragingly, and Johnny wriggled down from Genevra's embrace to take possession of it. 'For me?' he asked, a little over-whelmed by the size of the gift.

'All for you,' Christian affirmed, his smile so en-gaging that Johnny instantly responded with a happy grin before excitement got the better of him and he bent his head over the intriguing parcel, giving it his full attention. Christian's hand reached out, instinctively wanting to touch, and in a loving, fatherly way it gently ruffled the dark, curly head that was so like his own.

Auntie May appeared in the kitchen doorway, obviously drawn by the strange voice. She looked Christian up and down as Genevra introduced them, her blue eyes alight with curiosity and her interest very definitely aroused when she realised that he was the publisher that Genevra had gone to meet in London.

She patted back the wisps of grey hair that had escaped the bun at the back of her head, straightened the cover-all apron she invariably wore in the kitchen, and almost twittered with pleasure at the honour of meeting him.

When Christian proceeded to explain his presence in St Ives, she fairly beamed with approval, her expression telling Genevra with every glance that this was a man who should be encouraged. In no time at all, she was pushing cups of tea and her home-made cookies at him, and she was so intent on making him feel welcome, she even insisted that he call her May, instead of Miss Kingsley.

Christian charmed her even further by getting down on the living-room floor to help Johnny set up the race-track and show him how to work the remote control for the cars. Johnny, of course, was beside himself with excitement at having such a marvellous toy to play with, and positively basked in the attention Christian gave him as they played races with the cars.

Genevra felt more intensely happy than she had ever done in her life. When she accompanied her aunt into the kitchen to cut some sandwiches for lunch, she couldn't help smiling broadly at Auntie May's sly observation that Christian would make a very good father.

'Doesn't he remind you of someone, Auntie May?' she asked impulsively.

A puzzled frown came and went. 'No, I can't say he does. Except...' The frown returned, accompanied by a firm shake of the head. 'It's time you forgot him, Genevra. Turn over a new leaf. Don't spoil anything by looking back.'

'But you felt it too, didn't you?' Genevra insisted, elated by the tacit admission.

'He has the same kind of confidence and charm. That's all.' She heaved a sigh. 'And you take care this time. Don't think I can't see what's in front of my eyes. You're as smitten with him as you were before.'

Genevra laughed and hugged her aunt in a rush of grateful affection. 'I promise I'll take care.'

Auntie May had come to live with Genevra and her father when George Kingsley had been struck down by his first heart attack eight years ago. She was his older sister, a spinster who had made a career of private nursing, and she had been kind and loving and supportive to Genevra from the very first day.

Genevra's mother had died young, and for a decade there had only been her father and herself, but Auntie May quickly took the place of a mother in Genevra's heart. Her aunt had seen her through the grief of her father's death and the grief of Luke's desertion, stood by her throughout her pregnancy, and helped to look after Johnny ever since he was born. How Genevra would have managed without her these last few years was too bleak a thought to even contemplate.

It was on the tip of her tongue to tell her aunt that Christian Nemo was, in fact, the same person she had met four years ago, but she bit down on the words, keeping them for a better time. He couldn't hold out on her much longer. Then he could tell Auntie May himself.

Despite the family atmosphere that prevailed, Christian said nothing that gave any hint of his true identity in front of Johnny or Auntie May. Genevra didn't really expect him to. But he certainly made an effective start of establishing himself in Johnny's affections before he took his leave of them after lunch.

'Would you be able to have dinner with me at the Castle tonight, Genevra?' he asked as she accompanied him downstairs.

'If you can wait until after I've put Johnny to bed. Eight o'clock?'

'Fine!'

And they smiled at each other, anticipation dancing in their eyes.

Tonight, Genevra thought with utter certainty. He would tell her tonight!

He came for her in a taxi, right on the dot of eight o'clock. Genevra was ready and waiting, and the moment he took her hand the excitement of last night started pumping through her. As they rode back up to the Castle, Christian spoke of Johnny, saying what a fine boy he was, and what a wonderful job she had done in turning him into such a bright, happy child. His comments gave her deep pleasure, but she could hardly think beyond the fact that they were together again.

'Every time I see you, you're even more beautiful,' Christian murmured as they walked into the hotel dining-room, and she knew he was feeling the same urgent desire.

As soon as they were seated at a table, the waiter handed them menus. Genevra's eyes ran through the courses listed, but the words didn't register on her fevered brain.

'What do you fancy?' Christian asked.

She looked at him. Her stomach curled at the way he looked at her.

'I'm not very hungry,' she said on a ragged breath.

'Neither am I,' he replied huskily. 'One course?'

She nodded.

They ordered roast beef.

The meal seemed to take for ever to come. They made small efforts to talk from time to time, but the words quickly trailed into silence again, swamped by the intensity of their desire for each other. They ate with single-minded purpose—to get the meal over. Then, with almost indecent haste, they left the dining-room.

'The elevator's slow,' Christian said.

They took the stairs.

Genevra suddenly laughed; a wild, slightly hysterical laugh. 'We're being quite mad,' she said.

'Yes,' Christian agreed. 'I'm not sure that I want to be sane ever again.'

A fierce wave of possessiveness made her ask, 'Have you ever felt like this with any other woman, Christian?'

'No.' He unlocked his door and swept her inside his room, hugging her tightly to him as he pushed the door shut. His mouth brushed across her temples with the same fervour that throbbed in his voice as he added, 'Only you, Genevra. Only you.'

And somehow that declaration lent an extra-special dimension to their lovemaking, giving Genevra the emotional security she had secretly craved. He was not only hers now, he had always been hers, despite his marriage and the years of separation. No other woman had ever stirred him so deeply.

Genevra thought she had known the ultimate contentment last night, but she had only brushed the surface of it. As she lay quietly in Christian's arms, after every passionate demand had been made and met, she felt that love had no limits. It could just go soaring on to infinity.

'Genevra?' His voice held a slightly tentative note that barely registered through the haze of her happiness.

'Yes?' she murmured, pressing her lips over his heart.

His fingers threaded through her hair to hold her head still, gently pressing for her full attention. She sensed the slight rise of tension in him even before he spoke again.

'There's something I want to tell you. And ask you. I hope...' His chest lifted as he drew in a quick breath. 'I hope you'll understand.'

She smiled, both relieved and elated that the moment of truth had come at last. 'I'm listening,' she said in soft encouragement.

'I have a daughter, Genevra...'

A daughter! All her happy anticipation withered into numb shock. He was the father of some other child besides Johnny...another woman's child! For him to have married another woman was painful enough, but to have fathered...and it was a daughter!

'She's a few months younger than Johnny,' he continued.

He said more. Genevra vaguely heard words floating over her head, but her mind was swamped with wave after wave of black jealousy. All this time he had been giving another child the love and attention that should have been Johnny's! A daughter... by the woman he had married... while his son... *their* son...

'Genevra?'

His tone implied he was waiting for an answer, but she hadn't heard the question. Her heart was still pounding in her ears. He moved, sliding down beside her so that he could make a more direct appeal. He tenderly pushed her tumbled hair away from her face, and even in the darkening shadows of twilight she could see his taut concern.

'To be like this with you . . . it's what I want most of all. But I can't ignore Felicity, Genevra, any more than you can ignore Johnny. They're parts of our lives. I want you to meet her. I want her to meet you and Johnny. I want . . .' He hesitated, then heaved a deep sigh. 'Is it too much to ask, or too soon to ask it?'

He was right, of course. Her rational mind told her so. She would never give up her son for anyone, and she couldn't expect him to put aside a daughter. Genevra fought back the jealousy, knowing that she had to accept the child if she wanted to have this man's love.

'Where is she?' Her voice sounded wary, reserved, and she made a more concentrated effort to meet his needs. 'I mean . . . I don't understand. Does she live with you?'

'Yes. And always has done. At present, Felicity is staying with her grandfather in London. She is happy with him, but it's only a temporary arrangement. I had intended flying back and forth to visit her but, now that I've met Johnny, I've been thinking...hoping...that our children might get on well together. But if I'm going too fast for you, Genevra, just tell me so.'

'No,' she answered quickly. The last thing she wanted was for him to back off from her. She would cope with his daughter somehow. 'When do you want me to meet her?'

He hesitated, but his eagerness was all too evident as he asked, 'Would tomorrow afternoon be too soon?'

Genevra swallowed hard and stuck to her resolution. 'I have to work in the shop tomorrow, Christian. But if you and your daughter would like to come for dinner at six o'clock tomorrow night, I'm sure that'll be fine.'

His relief and gratitude were poured into a long, tender kiss. 'Thank you,' he whispered huskily.

And for the first time Genevra felt she understood the conflict of interests that had driven him to adopt a different identity. Certainly there was the change in his physical appearance, but there were other changes in his life that had further-reaching consequences...like his daughter! And, despite her love for him, Genevra knew that accepting the child of his marriage was not going to be easy.

CHAPTER SEVEN

GENEVRA was miserable. Auntie May thought it lovely that Christian Nemo had a little girl of Johnny's age, and Johnny was all excited about the 'family' dinner-party.

The two of them had been happily planning the menu for tonight when Genevra left to open the bookshop. Ashamed of her own lack of enthusiasm, she had been glad of the excuse to remove herself from any more talk of Felicity.

She tried to reason herself out of the reserve she felt. Whatever the sins of the parents, a child could not be held accountable for them. Felicity was even younger than Johnny, a total innocent, deserving of being accepted for herself. Genevra recited all this over and over again, yet still the jealousy nibbled at her, and it wasn't entirely on Johnny's account, either.

If Felicity favoured her mother in looks instead of her father, Genevra didn't know how she was going to bear it. To have a living reminder of the woman he had married, right under her eyes all the time... just the thought of such an eventuality made her feel sick.

It took hours of intense resolution to fight the black feeling into a neutral grey. That marriage was finished. Nothing could be gained by brooding over the past, and a happy future depended on her accepting Felicity, whatever she was like.

The day sped by all too fast, and Christian arrived ten minutes early. He walked into the shop while Genevra was still serving a customer, and her heart sank at first sight of the little girl at his side. She was beautiful—too beautiful for Genevra's peace of mind—and her features bore no relationship to Johnny whatsoever.

Father and daughter stood by one of the bookstands, waiting for her to be free for them, and Genevra was extremely conscious of two big brown eyes peering up at her from under a wheat-gold fringe. The shiny fair hair fell to just below her shoulders, straight and thickly textured enough to look good at that length. She wore a dainty but not overly fussy dress in a blue and white Laura Ashley print. Long white socks showed off sweetly curved legs, and her feet were encased in pretty blue shoes. She leaned shyly against her father's leg and chewed on her lower lip, obviously apprehensive about meeting strangers.

Genevra ushered the customer out of the shop, quickly locked the door after him, then fixed a determined smile on her face before turning to greet her two visitors. Christian smiled back at her, but the little girl's face remained grave.

The brown eyes seemed to grow more enormous as Genevra crouched down in front of her, and the hopeful appeal in them was so touching that Genevra could not resist it. Her smile warmed into real welcome. 'Hello,' she said softly.

'Hello.' It was a shy little echo. Felicity drew a quick breath and thrust out the small, gift-wrapped packet she had been holding. 'Daddy and me bought this for you.'

'How kind! Thank you both very much. May I open it now?'

Felicity gravely nodded. Genevra wondered if she ever smiled, and wished she'd had the foresight to buy her a gift. Too late now, she thought regretfully, and quickly unwrapped what turned out to be a velvet jeweller's box. Her pulse leapt erratically as she opened the lid. On a bed of white satin lay an exquisite Victorian necklace, a delicate pattern of gold suspending a beautiful, heart-shaped amethyst.

'Daddy said your eyes were that colour,' Felicity said in a breathy little rush.

'Do you think so?' Genevra asked.

Another grave nod.

'It's the loveliest gift I've ever been given. Would you hold the box for me while I put the necklace on?'

Felicity took the box and stared fixedly at Genevra as she fastened the catch and centered the pendant at the base of her throat. 'Have I got it right?'

Again came the nod. Then she looked up at her father for his approval. Christian smiled down at her, prompting her into offering a shy little smile to Genevra.

'I have a little boy who's been looking forward to meeting you all day,' Genevra said encouragingly. 'In fact, he got Auntie May to cook a chocolate cake, just because you were coming. Do you like chocolate cake?'

Another nod.

'Then let's go upstairs.' Genevra held out her hand as she straightened up, and a little hand crept into it. Genevra had the feeling that she had just won a marathon, and the grateful look that Christian gave her made every step of it worth while.

Johnny virtually pounced on Felicity the moment they appeared in the living-room, and the little girl tamely followed in his ebullient wake as he showed her everything that he considered of interest to a kindred spirit. Johnny simply didn't recognise shyness, and he soon coaxed his very obliging new playmate on to the living-room floor, where he quickly demonstrated how to operate one of the remote-controlled cars. Felicity concentrated hard on pleasing Johnny, and he absolutely adored being looked to as the authority on everything.

Auntie May quickly winkled Felicity out of her shyness when they sat down to dinner. The little girl chattered away to her as if she had known her all her life, but, where Genevra was concerned, she remained tongue-tied. The big brown eyes kept stealing glances at her but, whenever Genevra tried to engage the child in conversation, Felicity instantly reverted to nods, almost as if she was afraid to speak to her in case she said something wrong.

It was highly disconcerting, particularly since Genevra now wanted to win the little girl's affection. She was intensely grateful when dinner was over, and Auntie May tactfully shepherded the children into the living-room to play, leaving Genevra and Christian alone to do the dishes.

'Why is Felicity so shy with me?' she asked him anxiously. 'Am I doing something wrong?'

'No, not a thing,' he assured her.

'But...'

He pulled her into his arms and pressed her close to him, rubbing his cheek over her hair. 'I told Felicity that you're a very special person, and that you're important to me. Perhaps she's a little afraid of what that might mean to her.'

He drew back a little, and his expression held a plea for understanding. 'Felicity has had a lot of upsets in her short life, Genevra. They were unavoidable, but they've left her with certain fears that are difficult to counteract. She's not old enough to reason very well. She needs time to come to terms with what's taking place. That's all.'

Any last trace of jealousy was wiped out by Christian's explanation of his daughter's behaviour. Genevra felt a strong wave of compassion for the little girl. Johnny had never had a moment's doubt of his place in Genevra's and Auntie May's life. He had been wrapped in a secure cocoon of love from the moment he was born. The years that followed had an unbroken pattern which imbued him with a natural confidence that had never even been shaken.

'I'm afraid Johnny doesn't know the meaning of fear,' Genevra remarked with a dry smile.

'Neither do you,' Christian murmured huskily. 'I've never seen anyone give their trust so readily. You've done so much for me, I'll be for ever in your debt, Genevra.'

'It's enough that you're here with me,' she whispered, and kissed him with all the fierce conviction of the love that had been waiting years for such whole-hearted expression.

In the days that followed, Christian had many opportunities to confess the truth of the past to Genevra, but he turned aside all her attempts to lead him into it. He embraced the present as if there was no past . . . or none that he had any inclination to recall. And gradually Genevra thought less and less about it, too happy with their relationship to drag it into question.

Christian took the children out every day. They built sandcastles on the beach, flew kites at Land's End, went out on a fishing-boat, visited the ruins of King Arthur's castle at Tintagel . . . always some exciting or interesting activity that brought them home with glowing faces and shining eyes.

Auntie May frequently accompanied them, and Genevra too, whenever Beryl was available to take over the shop. From the very first day, Johnny adopted a big-brother attitude to Felicity, encouraging her to follow wherever he led, and quickly dismissing any nervous reluctance on her part by showing what fun everything was. The little girl blossomed into a happy, carefree child under Johnny's tutelage, and slowly but surely her shyness with Genevra was overcome.

One week slipped into another. No mention was made of visiting another hotel for the book project. In fact, Genevra hadn't written a word on Le Manoir Aux Quat'Saisons, and Christian hadn't asked for it. Their involvement with each other was so deep and immediate that nothing else mattered. Whenever Genevra thought of the book proposition she smiled to herself, sure in her own mind that it had only ever been a means to the end which had already been achieved.

The inquiry that she had asked Matthew Hastings to carry out on Luke Stanford had also lost any relevance to her. It had actually slipped so far out of her mind that she did not initially connect it with Matthew's startling appearance in her bookshop on the Saturday afternoon, just over two weeks after her visit to him.

'Matthew! What brings you all the way to St Ives?' she exclaimed, surprised to see him away from his London habitat.

He cast a troubled frown at a browsing customer. 'When will you be free, Genevra? I'd like to see you alone. Somewhere private, if that's possible.'

The request brought a nervous flutter to Genevra's heart. The gravity of Matthew's manner suggested that it was important, yet she couldn't imagine why he had felt it necessary to make a personal visit on her behalf. That this wealthy old London bachelor would spend a whole day of his free time on coming to see her seemed incredible.

Then she remembered the inquiry. If Matthew had found out that Luke Stanford was in England, he might feel distressed for her. Matthew had always treated her in a fatherly way, taking a kindly and sincere interest in her personal welfare. It would genuinely upset him to see her hurt and, if he could do anything to prevent it, he would.

Feeling reassured about Matthew's purpose for this visit, Genevra quickly eased the customer out of the shop and locked up. She invited Matthew to follow her upstairs, thinking that it would be curiously ironic if Christian came back with Auntie May and the children while the solicitor was still presenting his evidence.

She saw Matthew settled in the most comfortable armchair in the living-room, propped herself on the armrest of another, and smiled her appreciation of his kind consideration. 'You shouldn't have done it, Matthew, but it's terribly good of you to come all this way for me.'

'I had nothing else to do,' he said in casual dismissal, as his shrewd blue eyes observed her keenly. 'You look more relaxed and happy than when I saw you last, Genevra.'

She laughed. 'I have reason to be. Life couldn't be better at the moment.'

'I'm relieved to hear it.' He nodded a couple of times, then remarked rather heavily, 'Much better to live in the present than dwell on the past. I was concerned that the news I have for you . . . I wasn't sure how you'd react.'

'Not badly now, Matthew,' she assured him, confident that she knew what was on his mind. 'It's about Luke Stanford, isn't it?'

'Yes. You wanted to know if he was still married...'

'And he's not,' Genevra rushed on.

'That's true,' Matthew nodded gravely. 'The marriage ended three years ago. When his wife died.'

'She...died?' Genevra echoed, more in shock than disbelief. She hadn't actually asked Christian what had happened with his wife, more or less taking it for granted that they had been through a rather nasty divorce, since Felicity was in his custody.

'From some kind of kidney failure related to acute nephritis,' Matthew said in confirmation.

Genevra felt discomfited by this knowledge. She had certainly wanted the marriage dissolved, but not through death. Death didn't give anyone a choice.

Matthew rose from his chair and came over to her, taking her hand and putting his other arm around her shoulders in a comforting hug. 'It's never pleasant to hear about another's death,' he said in soft sympathy.

She flashed him an ironic look. 'I didn't know her. Not even her name. But I wasn't expecting that.'

'No. One never does with young people.' He sighed and looked even more troubled. 'I'm sorry, Genevra...' He paused, biting his lower lip, then

dragging in another breath before he continued,
'Luke Stanford only survived his wife by a few
weeks...'

The quiet statement sent a queer little chill
through Genevra's heart. She looked sharply at
Matthew, unable to accept his choice of words.
'That can't be right! Luke is alive. I know it!' she
rapped out impatiently.

'He's dead, Genevra. He's been dead for the last
three years.'

'No!' She could feel the blood draining from her
face even as she pushed herself up from the chair
to vehemently deny what Matthew was saying. 'I
don't believe it! It can't be so!'

But there was no evasion in Matthew's eyes. They
were soft with compassion, but steadily intent on
making her face irrefutable facts. 'He was a passenger in a light plane which crashed just after takeoff, killing everyone on board. There's no question
about it, Genevra. The inquiry agent sent a photo-
copy of a newspaper report on the crash. The plane
exploded into flames soon after impact with the
ground. There were no survivors.'

Her hand lifted to her forehead, but she couldn't
still the sickening whirl in her mind...

Dead...

Luke was dead...

Dead ...

She felt herself falling, but the blackness was rushing in on her, and she couldn't push it back. For the first time in her life, Genevra fainted.

CHAPTER EIGHT

'GENEVRA! Genevra!'

Someone was calling her name, patting her hand, stroking her face, drawing her out of the black, dizzying well that had swallowed her. She struggled to meet the urgency in the voice, wanting to answer it. She forced her eyes open, and Matthew Hastings' face swam in front of her. Memory came flooding back, and a moan of sheer anguish tore from her throat.

'I'm most terribly sorry, my dear. I thought it would be a shock, but . . . stupid of me not to lead into it more gradually. All my fault . . .'

The agitated bursts of speech served as a goad for Genevra to gather some control over herself. She was in an armchair. Matthew was fussing over her. Luke was dead. He had not come back to her. He never would. And Christian Nemo was . . . Christian Nemo.

Somehow, she managed a wan smile to appease Matthew's concern. 'I've never fainted before. Thanks for looking after me, Matthew. I'll be fine now.'

He was not completely convinced, eyeing her pale listlessness with a worried frown. 'I'll make you a cup of tea. Best thing. You just sit there, Genevra. I'll manage.'

She didn't protest, although she vaguely wondered if Matthew had ever made a pot of tea in his life before. A man of his position and wealth would have always had it served to him, but she heard him clattering around in the kitchen and supposed he knew what he was doing. It didn't really matter, anyway. She needed the time to straighten things out in her mind.

She found it almost impossible to accept that Christian wasn't Luke. Her emotions were so entwined with that identification that she was frightened to even try to separate them. How much of her love belonged to Luke, how much to Christian? She had established her present love on the past. Take that foundation away, and what did she have left?

How could her instincts have been so wrong?

And why hadn't she felt something... a sense of loss... something... when Luke's life had ended?

Three years... three years of waiting and hoping and still loving him, and all that time he had been dead! It didn't feel right. Yet how could she deny it? Matthew certainly wouldn't lie to her, and the inquiry agent had no reason to report anything but the truth.

But Christian was the living proof that... Genevra shook her head, forcing herself to acknowledge that there was no proof. Christian had denied being Luke. There had been no mole on his back. He had never given her any real evidence that he was Luke. She had simply interpreted his actions and responses in ways that supported her own secret belief, and turned a wilfully blind eye to anything that didn't.

All along she had been emotionally committed to a man who didn't exist any more. Dead... killed... his life wasted for no purpose or reason. Just another victim of a plane crash.

Tears welled into Genevra's eyes and trickled down her cheeks as that long-ago summer of happiness rolled through her mind, bringing back the memory of Luke's intense vitality, the warmth and strength of him. Was such a futile death a fitting climax of all that passion for life?

Grief swelled from Genevra's heart. Luke had loved her. She had never doubted that, not even when the letter came. And they'd had so little time together. She wished she had written to him, telling him about Johnny. He should have known he had a son. It might have been some consolation to him in those last few moments when he must have known death was inevitable. Had he thought of her? Why hadn't she felt something? How could he be alive to her all these years when he was dead?

Matthew returned with a tea-tray, which he set down on the small table near her chair. He pulled his own chair closer and kept a sympathetic silence until Genevra had mopped up her tears. He poured out the tea, adding the appropriate amounts of milk and sugar. Practically every time she had visited his office, Matthew had fixed her appointment around morning or afternoon tea. She suddenly realised he had never really treated her in a businesslike fashion.

'You've always been so kind to me,' she blurted out. 'Why is that, Matthew?'

A soft, whimsical smile curled his mouth. 'In my line of business, you mostly see the worst side of human nature—greed, envy, hatred, malice. But you, Genevra, have shown me over and over again that there is another side. You needed so much and asked for so little. I've always found it a rare pleasure to be with you, and talk with you.'

He heaved a sigh and gave a sad shake of his head. 'If I could give you happiness, I would, but not even wealth can manufacture happiness.' His eyes met hers with a sudden gleam of sharp determination. 'But what I can do is save you some grief over Luke Stanford.'

Tears pricked her eyes again, and she had to swallow hard to get rid of the lump in her throat. She was deeply touched by what Matthew had said of his feeling for her, but he didn't understand about Luke. 'I know it looks bad . . . that he left me as he did, but Luke did love me, Matthew.'

'No!' His mouth thinned with barely repressed anger. 'He never did! I'm sorry, Genevra, he sold you out. He married money, a great deal of it, and gave you away. And that's what I want you to face. Luke Stanford wasn't worthy of your love, and the sooner you realise that, the sooner you can dismiss him from your heart.'

She stared at him disbelievingly, her eyes still sheened with tears. 'You don't know what you're saying, Matthew. You didn't know him.'

'Did *you* really know him, Genevra?' he asked in a gentler tone. 'Just listen to the facts and judge for yourself. To begin with, the woman he married was virtually his sister...'

Protest burst from her lips. 'That's not possible! It can't be so!' It was illegal, unnatural, and the man she had known was good and fine and...

'Victoria Preston was no blood-relation, but she was his sister in every other sense,' Matthew cut back with prosecuting force. 'Luke Stanford was the foster son of John Preston. He'd lived in the Preston household since childhood. When he married Preston's daughter, and only child, Victoria, he married into a full half-share of Preston's construction company. And that partnership was worth at least twelve million dollars, probably more.'

Genevra's mind was reeling with the implications that Matthew was forcing on her, but still she clutched to her faith in Luke's basic honesty. 'There were family problems. He had to help them. That's why...'

'Open your eyes, Genevra!' Matthew retorted, then continued with implacable logic. 'The partnership was tied to the marriage. The Preston construction company was a success story. Luke Stanford chose the security of wealth and position. The price he had to pay was letting you go. And he did! You see, my dear, when it comes to that much money, love invariably comes second. And you were a long way away.'

Matthew's face was drawn into lines of weary cynicism as he added, 'It happens often enough, Genevra. I've seen it many times. A chance at the jackpot comes along, and love flies out the window. When you have wealth, you can have your choice of any number of women. Whatever he said to you in excuse for his betrayal was only window-dressing. The cold, hard truth is . . . you were dispensable.'

He hitched himself forwards in his chair in earnest appeal. 'Don't waste any more time or emotion on Luke Stanford, Genevra. He's dead. Bury him, and get on with your own life.'

Every word of Matthew's relentless exposition had left her feeling a little more hollow and uncertain. Had she been fooling herself all these years, living on a fantasy of her making? Like the fantasy she had built around Christian? She didn't know what was true any more, couldn't trust her own judgements.

She sat in a numb daze, so shaken and confused that there didn't seem to be anything she could hold fast to. Luke was a shattered image. Christian had been coloured with figments of her imagination. Her eyes lifted helplessly to Matthew's, recognising him as the one dependable solid in a sea of shifting uncertainties.

'What will I do?' she whispered.

'Stop looking back,' Matthew answered promptly. 'Think about expanding your horizons. Do some travelling. Use the trust money, Genevra. Invest in your own life. You're in a static rut here.' He raised his eyebrows in quizzical fashion. 'Did anything come of that meeting you had with the publisher in London?'

Colour flooded back into Genevra's face. Far too much had eventuated from that first meeting with Christian, and yet . . . could she honestly say she regretted any of it? 'Yes. Yes it did,' she said slowly.

'So what are you writing about now?'

Her smile twisted with irony. 'Nothing really. It's more a personal thing. Christian brought me back to St Ives. He's staying up at Tregenna Castle.'

'Ah!' said Matthew, with such a satisfied air that Genevra's cheeks burnt even more fiercely. 'He's . . . uh . . . not married, is he, Genevra?'

'He was. But not any more,' she muttered, thinking how stupid she was not to have questioned Christian with more persistence. In actual fact, she knew very little about him, just as she had known very little about Luke. Matthew was so right. It was well past time she opened her eyes, instead of acting on blind instinct.

'Well, if he's in the publishing business, no doubt you have much in common,' Matthew declared cheerfully.

It suddenly struck Genevra that she and Christian had barely spoken of books since that afternoon at Le Manoir Aux Quat'Saisons. She really knew nothing about his business, beyond what he had told her at the Dorchester. She hadn't even believed in it then.

'We do have children in common,' she said, seizing on the one definite parallel in their lives. 'Christian has a little girl a few months younger than Johnny. He and Auntie May have taken them both down to the beach this afternoon.'

'Splendid!' said Matthew with ringing approval. 'Does Johnny like him?'

'Yes.'

Even though Christian wasn't Johnny's real father, and Felicity wasn't Johnny's half-sister, the sense of a family unit had developed over the last two weeks. That was real enough, and Genevra grasped on to it as if it was a lifeline into the future.

Christian Nemo was a good man, a caring parent, and a wonderful lover. Even though he wasn't Luke, he wasn't any less than the man she thought he had been. Possibly, he was more!

Matthew suddenly grinned. 'So that was why you had a shopping spree at Harrods! And why you looked happy when I arrived. I hope this Christian—what's his full name, Genevra?'

'Nemo. Christian Nemo.'

'Nemo,' Matthew echoed musingly. 'What a curious name!'

'He's an American,' Genevra supplied helpfully, recalling now that he had never once sounded the least bit Australian.

Matthew shook his head. 'Nemo is Latin, Genevra. In English, it means no one. Still, with Americans, anything is possible.' He smiled benevolently at her. 'And how do you find his daughter? A likeable child?'

'Yes. She's very sweet.' And all her heartburn over Felicity had been based on a totally false premise, Genevra thought ruefully. She had no more reason to be jealous of Felicity's existence than Christian had to be jealous of Johnny's.

'Well then, I'm glad I came down and got this Luke Stanford business cleared away.' Matthew stood up with an air of beaming optimism. 'As I said, nothing to be gained by dwelling on the past. I'll be going now, Genevra.'

She rose from the chair and Matthew took her hands in his, giving them a light squeeze. 'You have my best wishes, my dear.'

'Thank you.' She leaned forwards and pressed a grateful kiss on his cheek.

Matthew's eyes twinkled with pleasure. 'And don't be worrying about the Anna Christie Trust, either. I'll let you know all about it when the report comes in.'

'It's not urgent, Matthew. Just curiosity, really. But I do appreciate, very deeply, all you've done on my behalf.'

His mouth quirked. 'I must admit that this little trip wasn't exactly for your sake, Genevra. It has lifted a burden from my mind. Now I can look forward to seeing you next time.'

Genevra escorted him downstairs and saw him on his way. She did not reopen the shop for business. There was little enough time left before she would have to face Christian again, and she was afraid that she would no longer react naturally to him.

The cold, hard facts stated that Luke Stanford had been dead for three years. Barely two hours ago, Genevra had thought she was waving him off to the beach with Auntie May and the children. But the man who would return... who was he? What did he really mean to her?

She thought she had known Luke through and through, yet he had proved to be faithless and mercenary. Matthew had to be right. Luke hadn't really loved her, or he wouldn't have sacrificed the future they could have shared, no matter how much money he had been offered. An engineer with his years of experience could have earned a good living anywhere. They wouldn't have been penniless. Life might not have been so easy, but at least they would have had each other.

How could he have put her aside so soon after...had his loving her all been a lie? Had she only ever been a holiday affair to him, a bit of magical fantasy that had worn off as soon as he had returned to the reality of his life in Australia?

Genevra shook her head in hurt bewilderment as the words of his letter drifted once more through her mind. All a lie, she thought with a deep sense of desolation, a romantic lie to end a romantic interlude that had had no lasting meaning for him. The only genuine sentiment he had written was the last line: 'It will be best for both of us to try and forget what could have been.' And no doubt so many millions of dollars were a great aid to forgetting!

Bitterness welled over the hurt, and Genevra curled herself into an armchair and opened the door on her memories of Luke Stanford, reviewing them all with a new-born cynicism.

She had been a naïve, trusting fool, handing him her heart on a platter, believing all his empty promises. Luke Stanford had used her, used her and dropped her when she no longer meant anything to him.

Bury him, Matthew had advised, and the weight of Genevra's disillusionment buried him deep.

So intense was her brooding over the past, she didn't at first hear the noises that heralded the return of the children with Auntie May and Christian Nemo. It was the sound of footsteps on the stairs that first impinged upon her consciousness and, as Genevra realised what that sound meant, a rush of curdling panic shot her out of the chair.

She wanted to run away and hide, do anything that would keep Christian at a distance until she could adjust herself to this new situation. But there was no escape from what she had done and, even as she teetered on the point of flight, the living-room door was pushed open.

CHAPTER NINE

THE children gave Genevra a few moments to gather a semblance of normal composure before facing the man to whom she had so recklessly and wantonly given her love.

Johnny burst into the living-room with Felicity at his heels, their faces aglow with excitement, and Genevra focused her attention on them, desperate for any distraction that postponed the inevitable confrontation.

'Felicity's staying here with me tonight,' Johnny crowed. 'Auntie May's going to fix a bed for her in my room so we can talk and talk and talk.'

'Yes!' Felicity breathed, her big brown eyes sparkling with delight.

Brown eyes, and Christian's a tawny-brown ... God, what a fool she had been! Genevra forced a smile. 'Aren't you going to sleep at all?'

'If Felicity gets tired, I'll let her go to sleep,' Johnny granted handsomely, then grabbed Felicity's hand. 'Come on. There's cookies in the kitchen.'

'You children wash your hands first,' Auntie May called as they skipped off.

'Yes, Auntie May,' they chorused.

She slanted a knowing look at Genevra in passing. 'And don't be worrying about them tonight. They'll be just fine with me.' She looked back before following the children into the kitchen, a sly twinkle enlivening her eyes. 'And I'm sure Christian will look after you.'

Genevra's heart lurched at the meaningful emphasis her aunt gave the words. It implied a further development to the relationship which was already far too intimate for Genevra's peace of mind. Every nerve in her body quivered with apprehension when Christian's arm curled around her shoulders, turning her into a loose embrace. She hoped that none of her fears showed as she reluctantly met his smiling gaze.

'I'm taking you somewhere special tonight,' he said in a voice that throbbed with suppressed excitement. 'Will you wear that beautiful pink dress for me, Genevra? And pack an overnight bag.'

'An overnight...' Genevra bit her lips as panic surged again.

He chuckled, misreading the burning rush of colour to her cheeks. 'We're not going to offend your aunt's sensibilities. May approves of my intentions.' He dropped a teasing kiss on her forehead. 'I'll be back for you in an hour.'

Genevra stood rooted to the spot for several moments after Christian had left. Her blood ran hot and cold as she contemplated the kind of night

Christian had in mind. He was going to propose marriage to her! How else would he get Auntie May's approval of his intentions? And he had every right to expect Genevra to welcome his proposal and be madly happy about spending a night of love with him. And she would have been...up until a few hours ago!

What had she done? And what could she do now? Impossible to explain to him that she had thought he was someone else. It would be so insulting. She couldn't hurt Christian like that. He loved her. And she had wilfully and wantonly encouraged his love, even to the point of seducing him when he would have held back to give their relationship time to grow. She had made her bed with a vengeance, and now...did she have any other choice but to lie in it?

In a daze of frightening indecision, Genevra forced herself to get moving. Christian expected her to be ready for him at six-thirty. Auntie May expected it. The children expected it. She was trapped in a web of her own making, and there was no backing out of the situation. She had to face up to Christian and...and what? Accept him, or make some hopelessly contrived excuse for putting him off?

With a sickening dread in her heart, she bathed and dressed and packed an overnight bag. Her nakedness in the bath reminded her too sharply of

Christian's intimate knowledge of her body. She put on a bra under her pink dress, ashamed of the way she had flaunted herself on that first night. And, as she packed the bag, she was all too aware that Christian would not have arranged a separate room for her tonight.

She heard him arrive. The children shrilled happy greetings. Auntie May called out for her. Genevra took a deep breath, picked up her bag, and slowly descended the stairs from her attic bedroom. Her legs felt wobbly and unreliable. Her heart was a painful hammer. Her mouth was an arid desert.

Christian had both children juggled in his arms, and all three faces turned towards Genevra, their eyes shining happily at her. She paused on the stairs, her pulse beating even faster as she felt the emotional tug of the man and the boy and the girl, linked together in a powerful claim on her heart.

'You look so pretty, Mummy!' Johnny said proudly.

'Beautiful!' Felicity declared in round-eyed admiration.

Christian smiled.

Genevra's gaze fastened on the smile, and she tried her utmost to separate it from her memory of Luke.

Christian put the children down and moved forwards to take the bag from her hand. He was dressed in the dark grey suit he had worn at the

Dorchester, and he was an impressive figure of a man, so very masculine. The black patch over his eye gave him a rakish air that was both intriguing and sexy.

His smile tilted in amusement. 'You look as if you were seeing me for the first time.'

The awful irony of these words was not lost on Genevra. 'I was just thinking how handsome you are,' she said, hoping that she didn't sound as strained as she felt.

He laughed and took her hand to draw her down the last two stairs. 'I've got a taxi waiting for us.'

Genevra felt dreadfully self-conscious as she kissed the children goodbye and took her leave of Auntie May. Christian took her arm in a proprietorial way, making her tremblingly aware of how many times he had possessed her. Physically! There was no doubting that she still found him immensely attractive, but her mind and emotions were in terrible chaos.

He sat close to her in the taxi, his fingers threaded through hers, stroking across the back of her hand. Genevra felt choked by the sheer magnetism of his presence. She wished that Matthew had never come, that she had never been told that the man beside her could not be Luke. But that emotional security had been ripped away from her, and she couldn't pretend otherwise.

'Where are you taking me?' she asked as the taxi headed out of town.

Again he smiled, making her heart lurch with the happy look of anticipation that lit his face. 'To Boscundle Manor. It's near St Austell, and I've booked us in for the night.'

Another exclusive country hotel, Genevra thought with a guilty pang. 'Christian, I didn't write an article about Le Manoir Aux Quat'Saisons,' she confessed.

'Genevra, this has nothing to do with the project we discussed. It's only to do with you and me, and planning for the future.'

The future together, he meant, and Genevra still had no answer to the proposal which intuition told her was hovering on his lips. The need for evasion, postponement, made her grasp for some other line of conversation, and she chattered on about the children, asking Christian what they had done this afternoon.

He obliged her with an amusing description of the children's activities, and out of the turmoil in Genevra's mind came one absolute certainty— Johnny would benefit from having Christian as his stepfather. Christian really did like children. And she herself was very drawn to his shy little daughter. If she accepted Christian as a husband...

And why not? a savage little voice urged. Luke Stanford had married for the security of wealth.

She wouldn't ever have to worry about money again if she married Christian. Why shouldn't she be just as mercenary as the man who had betrayed her? What was love worth, anyway? A lot of heartache and bitter disillusionment!

It wasn't as if she didn't like Christian. And she could hardly say she shrank from sharing his bed! On any common-sense level she would be a fool to reject the future he could offer her. Luke was dead. He had never even been the man she had clung on to in her dreams, anyway. It was Christian who had unwittingly fulfilled her fantasy, being the kind of man she had thought Luke was. Maybe she *did* love Christian. At least he was real, she thought fiercely.

Boscundle Manor was a lovely old building, partially Georgian in style, but with many rambling additions that gave it a charming informality. Its beautiful hillside garden and the adjoining woodland gave the whole setting a peaceful, rural atmosphere. Genevra's inner tension eased a little as she stepped out of the taxi. There was a sense of solid permanence about the place that was vaguely comforting.

Genevra felt bone-weary of uncertainties. She looked up at Christian, who wanted to offer her something solid and permanent, and she made her decision. She wanted what he could give her, and in return she would be a good wife to him, and a good mother to Felicity.

They were greeted by a very welcoming couple and shown to their room, which was furnished with an elegant simplicity that was also comforting. Genevra did not want to be distracted from the decision which needed all her concentration if she wasn't to waver again. As soon as she and Christian were left alone, he drew her into his arms and she pressed closer, needing the physical reassurance of his warmth and strength.

'Hold me tight, Christian,' she whispered urgently. 'Never let me go.'

'Never!' he vowed with a deep conviction that was emphasised by the aggressive power of his body as he wrapped her in a crushing embrace. 'Say you'll marry me, Genevra. I can't wait any longer. It has to be. It has to be,' he repeated with such a yearning ache in his voice that Genevra's heart instinctively surrendered to it without any urging from her mind.

'I'll marry you, Christian,' she answered, and felt a tidal wave of relief, as if all responsibility for her actions had been lifted from her shoulders.

And she felt relief wash through him, too—the ragged expulsion of breath, the light shudder that ran through his body. He pressed a fervent trail of kisses over her hair, interspersing them with murmurs of love that floated into her mind and kept all doubts at bay.

He loosened his embrace to smile down at her; a funny little smile, mixed with apology and self-mockery. 'I've done this all wrong. I meant to make it a big moment with champagne and...' He sighed and dragged a small velvet pouch from his pocket. His fingers shook a little as he fumbled it open and withdrew a ring—a fabulous, deep blue sapphire, surrounded by diamonds.

'I hope it fits,' he breathed as he took her left hand and slid the ring on to her third finger.

'It's beautiful, Christian,' Genevra whispered, awed by the glittering size of the stones.

The ring faltered on her second knuckle, with Christian loath to give it the necessary push, but Genevra quickly thrust it into place.

'It fits,' she smiled up at him.

He laughed out of sheer exuberant feeling. 'I'll be even happier to see a wedding ring with it. I can't tell you how much this means to me, Genevra. I feel as if...' He shook his head, and once more took her in his arms and held her close, his cheek rubbing softly over her hair. 'It's as if I've waited all my life for this moment.'

Genevra was intensely moved by the wistful note of longing in that soft murmur. She didn't even think of herself. She just wanted to fulfil his dreams and make him happy.

He took her down to a dining-room, which gleamed with polished mahogany and shining silverware, but the glow of happiness on Christian's face outshone everything else. They drank champagne. They feasted on sole Véronique, and duckling with cherry and brandy sauce. They talked of the future.

'Where will we live?' Genevra asked.

'Wherever you wish,' Christian replied with grand unconcern.

'But what about your business?' she queried.

'I employ people who are paid a great deal, more than they are worth, to make sure that all my business interests keep running smoothly and successfully. I don't need to work, Genevra, and neither do you. You will never have to worry about money again,' he said with almost grim satisfaction.

'But . . . I have to consider Auntie May,' she protested worriedly.

'May is only too happy to come and live with us, wherever we go. She fancies the role of nanny to our children.'

'You've already spoken to her?'

'This afternoon.'

Genevra shook her head in bemusement. 'You've really thought of everything, haven't you?'

'Everything I can that will make you happy to be my wife,' he said with an intensity of feeling that humbled Genevra.

'I hope I can be everything you want in a wife, Christian,' she said with deep sincerity.

He looked at her with so much love and desire that her toes curled. 'You *are* everything, Genevra. Everything I've ever dreamed of and wanted and needed. If I couldn't have you, I wouldn't want to live.'

'Don't say that,' she implored, a little frightened that his happiness depended so much on her.

'It's true.' A faintly self-mocking smile curved his lips as he saw her reluctance to believe him. 'When we met at the Dorchester...I felt it then. I knew I had to do all I could to keep you in my life.'

And suddenly Genevra remembered her own strong reaction to him, the sensation that somehow their lives were inexorably intertwined...and that had been *before* she reasoned out that Christian and Luke were one and the same person. She had actually felt that she shouldn't walk away from Christian Nemo, which was why she had agreed to a test run of the project he had outlined.

She stared at him, her heart pounding with wild excitement over the revelation. It was Christian himself who had drawn that response from her, not a superimposed image of Luke Stanford! Christian, the man she was going to marry, joining her life with his for the rest of her days. Her instincts had not been wrong at all. This was a man she could love, *did* love!

'Yes,' she murmured, awed by the certainty that thrilled through her.

His hand reached across the table and gripped hers. 'You felt it, too?' he asked, emotion furring his voice.

She nodded. 'I hated it when you made that comment about Beauty and the Beast. I wanted to take away all the hurts you had suffered and make you...' She hesitated, groping for the right words to express her feelings.

'...and make me whole,' Christian supplied softly. 'You did that, Genevra. And I'll spend the rest of my life loving you in every way I can, because you make life worth while.'

He meant it. He really did need her. She was necessary to him. Genevra was swept by the most extraordinary feeling, as if the whole purpose of her existence had lain dormant until this moment. She had thought her life had no meaning, but it did. Christian gave it meaning. And purpose.

'Thank you,' she breathed, her whole body pulsing with a glorious exultation.

He shook his head. 'You have nothing to thank me for, Genevra.' He lifted her hand and pressed it to his cheek, covering it there with his own. Pain flickered over his expression before determination banished it. 'I'll give you all the world can offer. You'll never want for anything again.'

She smiled, her eyes adoring him for his boundless generosity. 'I only want you, Christian.'

He drew in a sharp breath and slid her hand to his mouth, pressing fervent little kisses across her palm. Genevra's stomach contracted. She wanted him now, wanted to smother him with kisses and make him feel as precious to her as she was to him, wanted to hold him in her arms and love him with all that she was.

'Christian . . .'

It was a husky plea which he instantly answered, rising to his feet, holding her chair, taking her arm, linking her to him with a caring possessiveness that warmed her very soul.

The urgency of her desire melted into a wonderful sense of well-being. There was no need for haste. Christian would never leave her. From now on, he would always be at her side. She hugged closer to him as they walked up to their room, revelling in the security of their togetherness.

Christian either sensed her change of mood or felt the same need to savour this moment of total commitment to each other. He kissed her with a tenderness that twisted her heart, and Genevra knew that tonight there would be no rush to passion. Tonight they would know each other in every possible way.

'I love you,' she whispered, and kissed him with a soft reverence that expressed her total awareness of the man he was.

Their undressing was slow and deliberate, a conscious revelation of their bodies to each other. They touched, kissed, caressed, savouring every sensual nuance of being together. Only when their control moved from exquisite pleasure to painful need did they surrender to the ultimate mating of their bodies; melting into each other, fusing into one entity, exulting in the union that was so uniquely theirs.

Not the slightest shadow of doubt clouded Genevra's happiness as she lay in Christian's arms, his body curved around hers like a cradle of warm security. This love was real. Christian would never desert her or betray her as Luke had done. No amount of money in the whole world could buy him away from her. He would always be hers.

CHAPTER TEN

THE next morning, Genevra felt she had been reborn to a new life. A little smile of irony curved her mouth as she noticed Christian's passport on the bedside table, lying next to his wallet and key-case. An American passport. If only she had looked for it a fortnight ago...but it didn't matter now. Better that she hadn't, or she might not have learned to love Christian as she did.

He was still shaving. More out of idle curiosity than a need for information, Genevra picked up the passport and opened it. The photograph was a grim-looking one, and she wrinkled her nose at it. Christian was much more handsome when he smiled. Place of birth—Rochester.

'Where's Rochester?' she asked as he emerged from the bathroom.

'On the U.S. side of Lake Ontario.'

'Is it nice?'

He shrugged. 'Haven't been there since I was a little kid. And talking about kids...' His face lit up with a grin of pure pleasure. '...I'm looking forward to telling ours the good news.'

Genevra laughed from sheer happiness. 'I know Johnny will be ecstatic. What about Felicity?'

'She'll think all her Christmases have come at once.'

And, indeed, when they returned to St Ives later that morning and broke the news to the children, both Johnny and Felicity could hardly contain their excitement. Apparently they had talked the matter over between themselves, both envying each other's parent and secretly wanting to belong to the one family. Auntie May, of course, clucked over all of them like a smug mother hen, saying again and again that she had known everything would work out right.

Christian took them all to lunch at Tregenna Castle. The children were too excited to have an afternoon nap, and they played around the grounds while the adults relaxed in deck-chairs on the front lawn. Eventually they all strolled down to the waterfront to have fish and chips for tea, and Felicity insisted that she stay overnight again with Johnny. Christian and Genevra tucked both their children into bed and gave them goodnight kisses, much to their wriggling delight.

'Will it always be like this now, Daddy?' Felicity asked hopefully, her eyes shining at Genevra with shyly possessive love.

'Always, sweetheart,' Christian promised her.

'I've wished and wished for a mummy,' she whispered to Genevra.

'And I've wished for a daughter, just like you,' Genevra whispered back, and Felicity breathed a sigh of huge contentment as she snuggled into her pillow.

A question about Christian's ex-wife flitted across Genevra's mind, but Johnny's more boisterous goodnight distracted her from it. The rest of the evening was spent with Auntie May, discussing plans for the future.

Christian was all for getting married as soon as possible, even though it would take some time to settle up Genevra's business. They talked about where they might live, without coming to any definite conclusion. Christian had leased a house in Eaton Square in London, and they would take up residence there initially.

Auntie May retired early, tactfully leaving the two lovers alone, but Christian didn't stay long. They were both tired, and Genevra insisted she had to work in the morning. She was yawning as she climbed the attic stairs to her bedroom, yet once she was between the sheets her mind was still too full of the day's events for sleep to come easily.

When she heard the soft, whimpering noises, Genevra did not at first connect them to a child, but as they began to be punctuated with sobs she suddenly realised they were coming from Johnny's bedroom. In an instant she was out of bed and flying across the landing. She found Felicity crouched into a huddle, her little body shaking with sobs.

Alarmed by the inexplicable distress, Genevra scooped her up in her arms and cradled her like a baby, making soft, soothing sounds as she carried her out of Johnny's room and into her own.

'G'evra...'

'Yes, darling. Were you having a bad dream?' Genevra asked, climbing into bed and cuddling her close for comfort.

'G'evra, I don't want you to die and go to heaven,' the little girl pleaded brokenly.

'I'm not going to die, Felicity,' Genevra assured her, wondering what fear had conjured up such a thought.

'But mummies want to have babies and...' she sucked in a long, quivering breath '...you'll die. And I want to keep you.'

'That won't happen, Felicity, I promise you.'

But not even the promise consoled the child. She looked up at Genevra, her huge eyes brimming with tears. 'My mummy had to die to get me born.'

Somehow, Genevra managed to swallow the shock of that bald statement, and spoke as calmly as she could. 'Who told you that, Felicity?'

'Daddy.' Another deep breath and the whole story came pouring out in jerky little bursts. 'He said Mummy wasn't strong enough to have a baby, but she wanted me so much that she had me anyway. He said I was more important than anything else to Mummy, and that's why she called me Felicity. 'Cause that means happiness. And I gave Mummy a lot of happiness when I was born. But I want a Mummy who's here, G'evra, not in heaven.'

The tearful plea was so heart-wrenching that Genevra felt tears prick her own eyes, but she firmly blinked them away and set about explaining that not all mothers died when they had babies, citing herself and Johnny as an obvious example. However, it took a lot of talking to banish Felicity's fear and, even when the little girl finally fell into a contented sleep, Genevra kept her in her own bed for extra reassurance.

She herself lay awake for a long time, pondering Christian's first marriage. She wondered what had been wrong with Felicity's mother. The child had been too distressed for Genevra to ask, but it was a tantalising question in Genevra's mind. Few women died from childbirth these days, and even fewer women knowingly put their lives at risk to have a child.

More important than anything else, Felicity had said. More important than her husband and the love they had supposedly shared? Genevra knew which choice she would have made. She would have lived for Christian and remained childless.

The choice Felicity's mother had made, and her subsequent death, would almost certainly have left deep emotional scars on Christian. Little wonder that he had never wanted to talk about his marriage. And Genevra recalled his concern over her getting pregnant that first night at the Manoir... perhaps he harboured the same irrational fear as his daughter, and wouldn't want to have any more children. That was something they hadn't discussed, and Genevra decided it needed talking about. But not in front of Felicity. It would have to wait until tomorrow night.

The next morning, Genevra started taking an inventory of the shop contents. She wondered if she should have a closing-down sale, or if a buyer would want to take over the stock with the business. Since she didn't know the legalities of selling leases, she telephoned Matthew Hastings for his advice.

'Matthew, Christian and I are going to get married,' she announced, imagining his delighted smile.

'Splendid! I am very happy for you, Genevra. Any chance of my meeting the chap?'

'Of course. I'd like you take the place of my father at the wedding,' she said impulsively.

She heard him clear his throat, and knew he was deeply touched by the request. 'I'd be honoured,' he said with deep sincerity.

Genevra felt an extra glow of happiness. Matthew had always been like a father to her. 'I'll let you know the date as soon as we've fixed it. Meanwhile...'

She explained what she needed to know about the bookshop, and Matthew outlined the various options open to her. When they had covered everything to their satisfaction, Genevra started to thank him, but Matthew interrupted her.

'Genevra...' He hesitated a moment, and there was a faint note of disquiet in his tone as he continued. 'That information you wanted on Anna Christie came in this morning. It's...umm...rather curious.'

'Oh?' Genevra prompted.

'Anna Christie was the maiden name of Luke Stanford's mother. The trust wasn't actually set up by her at all. She died twenty-four years ago. The Canadian solicitor received his instructions from an Australian solicitor, and those documents were signed by Luke Stanford himself.'

'But why?' It all seemed so convoluted; Genevra was at a loss to understand Luke's motives.

'Well, he obviously used his mother's name to keep himself distanced from you, but it appears that he wasn't quite the rotter I thought him. Even if it was only a feeling of guilt that prompted him into it, he went to a great deal of trouble to see that you would never be in any financial want. Of course, he could afford it easily enough, but it was decent of him. Most people wouldn't have bothered.'

Blood money, Genevra thought with angry bitterness. Luke had sold her out for millions and set up a trust fund of fifty thousand pounds to appease his conscience. She was glad now that she had used so little of it on herself. She didn't want anything from Luke Stanford.

But Johnny had a right to that money. As Luke's son, he had every right to it, and she would see that every penny of it was kept for him from now on.

'Genevra? You're not worrying about this, are you?' Matthew asked anxiously.

'No. I was just thinking that it really is Johnny's inheritance. I always had a funny feeling that it was, somehow. Thanks for finding out for me, Matthew.'

'Since Luke Stanford never knew of his son's existence, I could argue that point with you, Genevra,' he said drily. 'However, he certainly owes Johnny something, and if you're happier to accept it on that basis...'

'I'd hand it over to the Red Cross rather than touch another penny of it myself,' she declared decisively. 'If you don't mind, Matthew, just keep re-investing the interest for Johnny.'

'Well, I'm glad that's settled,' he said with satisfaction. 'And you'll let me know about the wedding...'

Genevra was only too happy to switch her mind back on to Christian. She did not want to think of Luke Stanford ever again. All her memories of him had been completely soured. The deception he had played on her was unforgivable, and she was doubly grateful that Christian had proved so worthy of her trust.

She did not get the chance to talk with him alone until after the children had been put to bed that night. He suggested a stroll around the harbour in the lingering twilight, and Genevra eagerly agreed. She needed to know what his attitude was towards having a family. As it turned out, no sooner had she broached the subject than he set her mind at rest.

'We'll have as many children as you want, Genevra,' he said, without even a glimmer of reserve.

'It won't worry you?' she queried.

'Of course not. Why should it?'

She hesitated, reluctant to remind him of his first wife, yet feeling she should mention what Felicity had told her. However, as she related the previous night's incident with his daughter, Christian's sudden tension was disquieting, and not until she had finished speaking did that tension ease.

'I'll talk to her. I didn't realise...' He stopped, his face taking on a look of grim determination.

'That's in the past, Genevra. I won't have anything marring our future. I'll make Felicity understand.'

'Christian, do be careful,' Genevra warned, troubled by his rather extreme attitude. 'It's only natural that Felicity is affected by what happened to her mother.'

'We all were,' he muttered darkly, then in an abrupt change of mood he smiled at her. 'Don't worry about it, Genevra. She'll get over it fast enough. All Felicity needs, and all *I* need, is to be with you. You're a miracle for both of us.'

She relaxed and laughed. 'I think you're the miracle-worker. Do you realise we've only known each other for about three weeks?'

He shook his head. 'We knew each other in another life. We just re-met, that's all.'

Her eyes danced teasingly at him. 'Do you really believe that?'

'Yes,' he replied gravely, then smiled. 'My heart knew you instantly.'

'That's a lovely thing to say,' she sighed, and snuggled her head on to his shoulder as they walked along the harbour wall.

'There's someone I want you to meet, Genevra,' Christian said, throwing her a slightly anxious glance. 'I hope you'll like him.'

'If you do, then I'm sure I shall,' she assured him with happy confidence.

'It's Felicity's grandfather. My... father-in-law.'

Genevra frowned over the relationship. 'Will he want to meet me, Christian?'

'Very much so. Jack knows all about you, Genevra. I should explain that he and I are very close. As I told you, my own parents are dead. And Jack's alone now too, except for me and Felicity. He took care of her when...when I couldn't. Given me every possible support over the last three years.'

Christian stopped walking and turned to her, his expression pleading for her understanding. 'He's been like a father to me, Genevra.'

Like Matthew to me, she thought, and smiled. 'I'm glad he stood by you, Christian, and I'll be very happy to meet him.'

His answering smile was full of relief. 'He could come down from London tomorrow. Would dinner tomorrow night be all right?'

'Fine!' she agreed. 'And there's someone I want you to meet, too...' And she told him about Matthew, and how kind he had been to her over the years.

Genevra had no ill-feeling of premonition over the forthcoming meeting with Christian's father-in-law. Quite clearly, he was anxious not to lose access to his granddaughter, and she could well understand that. If the man held no prejudice against her taking his dead daughter's place, then Genevra would accept him unconditionally, too.

Nevertheless, as she rode up to the Castle with Christian the next evening, she did feel slightly nervous, and hoped she would make a good impression on him. And she was aware that Christian also was a little apprehensive that the meeting should go off well. His hand was squeezing hers tightly as they entered the drawing-room where his father-in-law was waiting for them.

A big man instantly rose to his feet from an arm-chair near the window. He was well over six feet, broad-shouldered and barrel-chested. His hair was starkly white, above a face that was darkly tanned and weathered with lines that suggested many sorrows in his life. His smile was slightly wistful as his gaze travelled quickly over Genevra, but the brown cycs gave her an unreserved welcome.

'Genevra, this is my father-in-law...Jack Preston.'

Preston! Jack...John Preston? For a moment, Genevra's mind reeled. Common sense instantly argued there were probably thousands of Prestons in the world. She forced her hand out to take the one offered to her. 'How do you do, Mr Preston,' she said a little too stiffly, still rocked by the coincidence.

Her hand was engulfed warmly by his. 'Let's make that Jack. I'm delighted to meet you, Genevra, and even more delighted to have this opportunity to wish you every happiness for the future.'

It was a generous speech, but Genevra barely registered a word of it. He had spoken with an Australian accent. Not American...Australian! An Australian John Preston whose daughter had died three years ago!

All Genevra's bright, shining dreams of ever-lasting love splintered into the most devastating nightmare as the implications pounded her brain. In sheer, piercing horror she screamed, and the scream echoed into a moan of the most terrible anguish.

CHAPTER ELEVEN

BOTH men stared at Genevra in blank shock, but she didn't care. She didn't care if the whole hotel staff came running to check on what was happening. She wouldn't have cared if there'd been a hundred people in the room starting up in alarm at the way she had screamed.

She snatched her hand out of Jack Preston's warm clasp and hugged it under her arm, out of reach. She was alone. Alone in a far more desperate way than she had ever been before. And these men had done it to her with their deceit and treachery.

'Genevra...' The man who had called himself Christian Nemo reached out to her. 'What's wrong?'

She recoiled from his touch. 'How could you?' she whimpered, lost for a moment in the pain he had given her. 'You should have told me! You should have...'

Then a bitter rage billowed over the pain, feeding off the cruel deception he had played on her. She was sure now, but she would put the matter beyond all doubt. She wheeled on Jack Preston, her eyes blazing with contempt as she flew into venomous attack. 'Tell me your daughter's name, Mr Preston.'

He frowned and shot a worried look at his son-in-law.

'Tell me, Mr Preston...' Genevra's voice sharpened with cutting savagery. 'Was it Victoria?'

'Genevra!' Christian's voice... Luke's voice... pleading for forbearance, but she ruthlessly shut him out as he had done to her four years ago.

'Answer me!' she commanded. 'It was Victoria, wasn't it?'

The old man's face sagged with pain. 'Yes, that's so, my dear. But we always called her Vickie.'

'Genevra...' A hand clutched her arm. 'Please, you must listen to me...'

She swung on the man to whom she had so foolishly given her love, and beat his arm away from her. She felt no love for him now. 'Lies... all lies!' she panted, shaken by a fury so deep that all she wanted was to wound as she had been wounded. 'They said you were dead! Killed in a plane crash! But it's all been one huge deception, hasn't it...' Her mouth twisted with vicious mockery as she hurled his real name at him. '...Luke Stanford!'

She could say it now without the slightest shadow of doubt. Luke Stanford... the man she had loved and lost, the man who had betrayed and deceived her and put her through a hell of uncertainty.

Matthew had been right about the name, Nemo. It did mean no one. Christian Nemo did not exist. He was Luke Stanford!

The face that had fooled her into believing him contorted with agonised denial. 'I'm not that man any more, Genevra. Isn't that plain enough? I did what was necessary, only what was necessary to free you from any tie you might feel to the past. How could I come to you after what happened?'

Genevra's rage weakened for a moment, allowing that he had suffered during their separation, but then she remembered her own suffering, which had all been so unnecessary if he had ever really thought of her instead of himself.

Her teeth gnashed as she scorned his explanation. 'How you belittle me! And the love I once bore you! Did you even stop to think what I felt when you denied who you were at the Dorchester Hotel?'

'I wanted your love. Not your pity. Do you think it was easy for me to hold back after all these years of craving for you?' He stepped forwards, grasping her roughly by the shoulders. 'Genevra, I love you. I...'

'No!' she screamed at him, twisting out of his hold and sweeping out an arm that vehemently dismissed his claim. 'You never loved me! You never did...' her shrill voice choked into an anguished sob '...or you wouldn't have left me and married

Vickie. You wouldn't have done all the things you did...'

'Genevra, I couldn't have lived with myself if I hadn't tried to give Vickie the love she wanted. We'd lived together for so many years...'

'Then how could you promise me what you did? How could you lead me on, make love to me...'

'Because I loved you,' came the fierce answer, and he cupped her face to forcibly hold her attention. 'And Vickie left me no other choice. I had to do my best to make her happy...'

'Make *her* happy!' Genevra repeated bitterly, and the rage consumed her again. She threw her head back in proud disdain and stepped away from him, her eyes accusing him of base betrayal. 'I know better than that, Luke! You did it for the money. All the millions that her father offered you...'

'That's not true!' Jack Preston shouldered his way vehemently into the argument, clutching her arm to press his defence. 'Luke was always...'

'Get your hand off me!' Genevra seethed at him. 'You got your daughter what she wanted, and you didn't care what it cost. Johnny and I were expendable.'

He shook his head in pained protest. 'No, it wasn't that way!'

'Oh, yes it was!' She backed away from him so that both men were in her sights, and she attacked with all the concentrated power of the pain they had dealt her over the years, her voice lashing out at them like a scourging whip.

'The truth is that I was discarded to bear my child alone, while Luke was bedding his new wife and getting her pregnant. The truth is that she had all the security of marriage and wealth, all the care and attention, all the love...' She choked as tears of desolation brimmed her eyes.

'Genevra...please, please listen to me.'

She turned tortured eyes to the man she could never trust again. 'I waited for you, Luke. Waited to hear from you every day of four long, lonely years. I believed in our love. I made excuses for the silence. I wove fantasies to explain why you didn't come back to me.'

'I couldn't! Not until now,' he pleaded. 'I came as soon as I could offer you a reasonable kind of life.'

Her voice broke with anguish. 'You could have called me three years ago, Luke. I would have come. I would have accepted anything, forgiven you anything, just to be reunited with you. But my love wasn't enough for you. It came last on your list of priorities.'

'You were better off anywhere than with me!' he cried in violent denial.

'Yes. Better off without you,' Genevra agreed, a deathly numbness spreading through her. She looked at him with bleak, wintry eyes. 'That's what

Matthew told me when the report from the inquiry agent came back. You see, Luke, the waiting and the silence from you had gone on too long. I couldn't bear not knowing what had happened to you, so I asked my solicitor to find out. And then I knew... I knew how deeply you had betrayed me.'

His hands reached out to her in despairing appeal. 'Genevra, I didn't know about Johnny. I didn't want to make the choice I did...'

'You didn't think of me, Luke. You *never* thought of me!'

'It was only the thought of you that kept me alive. I swear to you...'

She flapped her hands in despairing rejection as he started towards her. 'No more lies, Luke. No more deception. I don't know how you did it—the colour of your eyes, the American passport, and all the other things. I don't even know *why* you did it. And I don't care any more. I never want to see you again.'

'You don't mean that, Genevra,' he begged in a hoarse, driven voice.

'Yes, I do. I can't take any more. And I'm not going to. You cheated me. And you cheated Johnny.'

She closed her eyes to the haunted look on his face and turned her back on him, moving her trembling legs towards the doorway.

'No!' Rough hands caught her and spun her around. His arms imprisoned her in a vicelike embrace, as his face worked to bring turbulent emotion under control. 'I won't let you do this. I love you, Genevra. And you love me. We've got to talk this out and put it behind us. You can't walk away from me now.'

'You did, Luke,' she reminded him, too soul-sickened to answer any of his needs or desires. 'You walked away from me four years ago. And you never came back. Did you know what Nemo means, Luke? It means no one.'

'Stop it, Genevra!' He shook her in sheer desperation. 'We've got the rest of our lives together. You know you want that as much as I do.'

'Not any more. Let me go, Luke.'

He stared down at her, fighting the finality stamped on her cold, closed face. And slowly the fight drained out of him and his arms dropped away from her. 'I love you,' he said defeatedly. 'I tried...' He turned away from her, his shoulders slumped, his head turning helplessly from side to side. 'There just wasn't ... a right choice.'

'Well, you certainly didn't make any of the right choices where I was concerned,' she said flatly, and on that note of fatal judgement she forced herself to walk away—out of his life, out of Tregenna Castle, along the hotel driveway to the path which led down to the village where she had lived all her life . . . before Luke, and after Luke.

At least that was constant.

The numbness wore off as she walked. Misery welled out of her soul, giving birth to inconsolable despair. How could she love a man who had practised so much deceit on her? And yet she knew that there would never be anyone else for her. Twice he had come into her life and stolen her heart. Just like a thief, uncaring of what damage he did, as long as he got what he wanted. A thief in disguise.

Tears blinded her, and when her foot caught a mossy patch on the path she almost slipped over. Shaken, and too upset to keep going, Genevra took temporary refuge on the slatted bench-seat that marked a resting-point for the steep pathway. Situated as it was under the trees, and surrounded by hydrangea bushes and other shrubs, it provided her with sorely needed privacy. It was too early to go home. She couldn't bear to face Auntie May tonight. Tomorrow would be soon enough to tell her the truth.

And what *was* the truth? Genevra wasn't sure of anything any more. The lies Luke had told her, the lies he had lived since he came back . . . nothing that he had said or done could be trusted. How could a happy, secure future be built on such a rotten foundation? How long had he meant to keep up the deception? If she hadn't known about John Preston, if she had married him . . .

A fresh gush of tears flowed down her cheeks, and she doubled over in anguished shame as she remembered all the times they had made love. Only it wasn't love. He didn't love her. She had given herself to a man who had never appreciated what she had given. He had put it aside until he felt a need for it. He had never cared about her needs.

The soft crunch of approaching footsteps drove her into a huddle at the furthest end of the bench-seat away from the path. Her heart beat a sickening protest as the person paused. She mentally begged whoever it was to go on, to leave her alone with her misery. The continuing silence was an added torture to her jagged nerves.

'Genevra, I have to speak to you.'

The Australian voice of Jack Preston was soft, but it fired a bitter turmoil of resentment through Genevra's aching heart. She turned a tear-streaked face to him. 'Go away. Just go away,' she sobbed, hating him for seeing her distress.

'I'm sorry, but I can't do that.' He slowly lowered himself on to the other end of the seat, his face set in grave lines of determination.

It was abundantly clear that he didn't intend to let her escape him. There was a formidable strength in his bearing that stifled any further protest from Genevra. She bit her lips and turned her head away, pointedly ignoring his presence, although it oppressed her further.

'Why can't you leave me alone? Haven't you done enough?' she demanded wearily.

His sigh was heavy. 'Luke is like a son to me, Genevra.'

'And I am nothing,' she said in painful derision.

'You're the key to the life I want him to have.'

'The key's been too abused for it to work any more, Mr Preston.'

'You've been badly hurt, Genevra, but believe me, Luke has walked a harder road than you to reach this point.'

She looked at him in scathing disbelief, but his gaze held hers steadily and with steely purpose. 'I've watched the woman I loved die. I've watched the daughter I loved die. I've watched Luke go through agonies that I wouldn't wish on my worst enemy. And I will not stand by now and let his one chance at happiness be destroyed by misunderstandings and misconceptions.'

He shook his head, as if burdened too heavily with what had to be revealed. 'I'll tell you the truth, Genevra, and when you've listened to all I have to say, then you can judge the man you've just rejected. I won't stop you if you still want to walk away. You have the right to decide your own destiny. But Luke deserves a fair hearing, and since you won't give it to him, I'm prepared to force it down your throat. If I have to.'

'And how will I know if it's the truth?' Genevra shot at him, although he had stirred a treacherous fever of curiosity with his claims.

He gave her a grim smile. 'Because nothing else will serve now.'

CHAPTER TWELVE

GENEVRA slumped back in the seat and stared unseeingly at the greenery that enclosed herself and Jack Preston in a private little world. The trees formed a canopy above them. The shrubbery was so thick that one couldn't see the adjoining golf course, nor the village below. The sounds of civilisation were shut out, and an almost unnatural hush seemed to hang around them.

The tension slowly drained out of Genevra. She felt like a limp sponge waiting for the words that might or might not inject new life into her. She did not even feel hostile towards Jack Preston any more. He was simply there, an unknown entity that didn't really impinge on her life. Only his words could do that.

'Go ahead,' she invited listlessly. 'Talk all you want. I'm not going anywhere.'

'I hope you don't choose to live your life as I've had to live mine,' he said with a wealth of sadness. 'I'm considered a great success. Looked up to. Envied. But none of it—the success, the wealth or the power—nothing can compensate for the loss of the woman I loved.'

158

'Your wife?' Genevra asked, a little impatient with his philosophising. What possible bearing could his love-life have on her relationship with Luke Stanford?

'No. Anna Christie...Anna Christie Stanford,' he replied, his eyes suddenly swimming with tears.

Genevra quickly turned her head away, discomfited by the naked emotion.

'When I met Anna, she had already been married to Luke's father for ten years. My own marriage was over in any real sense. Only a few months after Vickie was born, my wife took a fall from her horse while show-jumping, and suffered such extensive brain damage that...' The clearing of his throat was harsh before he dragged out the brutal reality. 'She was in an eternal coma. They kept her alive on machines, but there was no hope of her ever recovering.'

'How terrible for you!' Genevra whispered sympathetically.

'You could not imagine...but at least I had Vickie to love. And then I met Anna.'

He paused, and Genevra sensed he could remember that moment as vividly as if it was happening now. There was a softness, a wonder, even awe in those last few words. He recollected himself and spoke on.

'I'd gone to the United States on business. Anna worked for a secretarial service. The moment I saw her... it was like instant recognition. A soul-mate. I cannot explain to you the power, the magic of meeting her eyes and...' His breath hissed out in a whisper of longing. 'But perhaps you do know how it feels... when it happens. I would have done anything for that woman. But she would not have me.'

His hands clenched, even now wanting to fight that decision. 'She loved me, I know she did. Although she would never admit it. She had said she could never leave her husband and son. I promised her I'd accept her son as my own, but there was a deep fear in her that she wouldn't explain... until it was too late.

'Vickie contracted scarlet fever and I had to fly home. Anna wrote and begged me not to come back. She said I would only cause her pain if I did.' He slumped forwards, propping his head in his hands. His voice came brokenly, half-muffled. 'I should have gone. Should have taken her and Luke way out of reach of the maniac she had married. Three months later, she wrote another letter, begging me to come.'

His shoulders hunched over further and Genevra sensed that he was weeping behind his covering hands. She sat there in helpless silence, knowing she could do nothing to appease his grief.

'She was in hospital with broken ribs, a punctured lung, and other internal injuries. He'd beaten her up. And her son, who had tried to protect her. I took the first flight that was possible, but by the time I got there Anna was barely hanging on to life. She asked me if I'd take Luke, bring him up as my boy. I promised I would. I had only a few hours with her and she just...just slipped away from me.'

He groped in a pocket for a handkerchief, and took his time blowing his nose. Genevra managed to stem her own tears by blinking hard. She felt so sorry for him...first his wife and then Anna. He expelled a shuddering breath and sagged back on to the bench-seat.

'Anna's husband couldn't be found. I took Luke home with me. He was nine years old, and very much his mother's son. Vickie was only two then, and in very delicate health. She was one of the un-lucky ones. The scarlet fever had left her with com-plications, in this instance, acute nephritis, a kidney disease that circumscribed her life, making it im-possible for her to lead a normal existence. I suppose both Luke and I always indulged her in our different ways.

'Luke was very protective of her, right from the beginning, and Vickie adored him. He looked after her, did all he could to keep her happy. We both did. Her life expectancy was not good. There were always health problems. I don't know when the love for her big brother changed to a womanly love.'

He rubbed his eyelids in a gesture of intense despair. Genevra said nothing, caught up in the story he was unfolding for her. She had seen how Luke was with Felicity and Johnny, and could well imagine how caring he would be to a frail little sister.

Jack Preston heaved a tired sigh and continued, 'Sometimes she showed a jealous possessiveness when Luke had casual attachments to other women, but he always laughed it off, saying she was the only important woman in his life. Apparently, Vickie was satisfied with that. Certainly, there were no serious love affairs to make her feel that her own secret desires were threatened. Until he came to England and met you, Genevra. It was obvious from his phone calls and letters that he was very serious about you.

'Vickie went into a depression that I couldn't shake her out of. She didn't take care of herself. She became so ill that she had to be rushed to hospital, and the doctors said she was refusing to co-operate with their treatment.

'I called Luke home. He was on his way when Vickie told me that she had nothing to live for any more. And she told me why.'

His hand lifted in a helpless little gesture. 'Luke was lost to her and she wanted to die. By that time, she'd done so much irreversible damage to herself that even with the greatest possible care, she would only live a few more years.'

His eyes sought Genevra's, pleading for her understanding. 'You spoke truly a little while ago when you said you were nothing to me. You were only a name, and I didn't care about you. Vickie had such little time left. I wanted her to have her heart's desire before she died. I begged Luke to give himself to her for that time, to give her the fulfilment of her dreams. He could go back to you afterwards.'

His mouth turned down in a grimace of self-abasement. 'I demanded things of him that should not be demanded of anyone. I used every piece of emotional blackmail I could think of to force his hand. But in the end, it was his own love for Vickie that forced the choice. He didn't love her as he loved you, Genevra, but he made Vickie believe he did for the fifteen months that she lived.'

Tears filled Genevra's eyes as she remembered the words Luke had written to her so long ago. 'I cannot turn my back on the love and obligations I owe my family. I could not be happy within myself, nor could I make you happy, knowing I had refused to answer their needs when they have given me so much.'

She wished he had written the whole truth, but she understood it now. She even understood why he had felt he didn't have the right to ask her to wait for him while he spent the intervening period making another woman feel loved.

'Money never entered into it, Genevra. The partnership papers had been drawn up while Luke was in England. It had always been planned that he would eventually take over the business from me. He is my son in everything but name. It was pure coincidence that the legalities were finalised at the time of his marriage to Vickie. Money would never have persuaded Luke, anyway. He's not the kind of person that can be bought.'

Genevra believed him, but it was a blessed relief to have it spelled out so convincingly. Her instincts had told her Matthew was wrong. She should have been guided by them, instead of accepting Matthew's pragmatic interpretation of the facts.

'I think you know that Vickie died in giving birth to Felicity?'

'Yes,' Genevra whispered, too choked up to answer more firmly.

'She was determined to have a baby. It was a nine-month suicide. She refused to have an abortion to prolong her life. She lived just long enough to hold Felicity in her arms. She died happy, as if there could be no greater fulfilment for having lived.'

He paused and took a deep breath. 'I was shocked when Luke told me he'd booked a flight to England a few weeks later. It was so soon after...but one look in his eyes and I knew there was no stopping him. I hadn't realised until then what you meant to him. He was desperate for you, Genevra.'

'The plane he boarded was to take him from Muswellbrook, where we had a power station under construction, to Mascot Airport in time to link with his international flight to London. I saw Luke on to the plane and watched it take off. It suddenly faltered in the air. Flames burst out of one engine. The plane nosedived to the ground and exploded.'

He shook his head, his face etched in appalled memory of the scene. 'I don't know how Luke survived the crash. No one else did.'

'The newspaper report sent by my inquiry agent stated that no one survived,' Genevra told him, half asking for an explanation of the inaccuracy.

His mouth made an ironic grimace. 'Luke was pronounced dead on arrival at the hospital. If a reporter had a deadline to meet, he wouldn't have bothered rechecking later. And it was a small plane crash. Yesterday's news. I didn't even look at newspapers while Luke was in such a critical state, so I didn't see the report. Even if I had, I doubt I would have asked for a correction. At the time, Luke could have taken his last breath at any minute. I'm sorry, Genevra.'

'It's not your fault,' she sighed, thinking that the inquiry agent could have done a bit more checking. 'But I don't understand how Luke could be pronounced dead if he wasn't.'

'He had terrible injuries. He looked... unrecoverable. I rode with him in the ambulance to the hospital. The paramedics kept working on him all the way. His heart stopped as they wheeled him into the casualty ward, but I wouldn't let the doctors give up on him, despite what they told me. Despite what I could see for myself. I needed Luke to live.

'They hammered his chest and got his pulse working again. Then the rest had to be attended to. His face was cut open and burnt. One eye completely gone, the other's sight affected by the fire. His body was broken in so many places that he was in hospital for months before he could even be moved. They said he'd never walk again.'

'My God!' Genevra breathed, horrified by the toll of injuries. 'If only he'd sent for me. I could have...'

'No, Genevra! He was in enough trauma as it was. Your presence would have been an additional torment. He couldn't have borne it.'

'Why?' she cried in protest. 'At least I could have given him emotional support.'

'Or emotional torture?' came the pointed reply.

Genevra frowned at him in non-comprehension.

'Luke was crippled,' came the harsh reminder. 'He couldn't make love to you. He was helpless, disfigured, his life hopelessly changed from what it had been when you fell in love with him. And he had given up all claim to your love by marrying Vickie. How could he possibly ask you to come to him under those circumstances? Would you have asked it of him if the situation was reversed?'

Genevra paused to think through what she might have felt. Despair... utter despair. And no... she would never have called him, no matter how desperately she might have wanted to. Luke had not been selfish, after all. Had never been selfish in all the time she had known him. He had given everything in his love for her and for Vickie.

Genevra looked up at Jack Preston and shook her head. Understanding was slowly penetrating, and not for a moment did she doubt that he was telling her anything but the unvarnished truth. 'I would have done what Luke did. Fought it out alone.'

'As you did, my dear,' the old man said quietly. 'Don't think I don't appreciate what you've been through. When Anna chose to stay with her husband... I know the burning ache of loss all too well.'

The compassion in his eyes reached into Genevra, and in that instant they knew each other and a close bond of understanding was forged. 'How did Luke recover from his paralysis?' she asked softly.

'I took him to a neuro-surgery clinic in America. I couldn't even begin to enumerate the operations he suffered through so that he could walk again.

One leg ended up shorter than the other. So he followed through a hell of a program to stretch it back to size. There's still a weakness that forces him to use a walking-stick occasionally.'

'He hasn't used it at all since that afternoon at the Dorchester,' Genevra observed thoughtfully. 'Maybe his leg is stronger now.'

A musing little smile was thrown at her. 'The power of love.'

Genevra flushed and quickly redirected the conversation. 'How long did all the healing take?'

'Until very recently. You see, the cosmetic surgery to his face took years...taking bone from his hips...skin grafts...and the corneal graft on his eye...it seemed never-ending. He still has to wear a tinted lens to reduce glare.'

'Oh!' she breathed. 'So that's why...'

'His eye colour looks different? Yes. And, as for the American passport, Luke was born an American citizen and still is. He changed his name by deed-poll. All perfectly legal.' His mouth took on an ironic twist. 'I'm afraid I haven't got used to it yet. He's been Luke to me for far too long.'

'Why Christian?' Genevra asked.

'He's never said. I think perhaps it's a twist of his mother's name. Anna Christie—Christian. He loved her very much.'

She nodded, thinking of the Anna Christie Trust. Luke had done what he could to solve her financial difficulties over the bookshop and ensure that she would never be in any real want until he could come back to her. He had not really deserted her. Or deceived her. Except over his actual identity.

'Why did he come back as Christian Nemo, instead of as Luke?'

'He said he didn't want any emotional pressures hanging over from the past. And he's not the same man he was, Genevra. Too much has happened. And too much time had passed for him to be at all confident of your love. After all, he had broken his promises to you and married someone else. He felt he had no right to expect anything from you.'

He gave a dry little smile. 'If you want my opinion, he was afraid that you would reject him out of hand. As you did tonight. But if you fell in love with Christian Nemo... to have you, Genevra, he would have been Christian Nemo for the rest of his life.'

The smile drooped into a sad grimace. 'He told you the truth, you know. It was only the thought of you that kept him alive, that drove him to suffer through all he suffered so he could come back to you as a man who could give you the kind of life he wanted to give you. And that is love, Genevra. The deepest kind of love a man can feel. And give.'

She heaved a long sigh, expelling the last lingering doubt from her heart. 'I've been a terrible fool, haven't I?'

'No. I thought Luke was foolish to take the course he did. The truth is best. If Anna had told me the truth about her husband's violent nature...'

He sighed too, then reached over and took Genevra's hand, pressing it in a comforting way. 'You do love him, don't you?'

'Yes.'

'Then I think you should go back to him now, Genevra. He's been through too much. If you let him keep thinking he's lost you...'

Her heart leapt with fear. Christian—Luke—had said he would not want to live without her. 'I've got to run,' she gasped, jumping to her feet and pulling her hand free. 'Thank you...thank you for everything!' she called back as she flew up the path.

He answered something, but her heart was pounding too loudly for her to decipher the words, and she could not stop. She had to get to Luke as fast as her legs would carry her.

CHAPTER THIRTEEN

GENEVRA'S mind whirled through the possibilities as she ran. Luke would not have stayed in the drawing-room where she had left him. Her gaze darted around the grounds, but there was no un-accompanied man in sight, and she was almost certain he would seek the privacy of his room. Or Felicity's.

A child was a reason for living. Johnny had been her only consolation throughout the four lonely years she had waited for Luke. Her son had given her life some meaning. Even though Felicity was down in the village with Johnny, Luke might have gone into her adjoining hotel room in an instinctive need to feel he had some purpose left to fulfil.

Genevra ran down the wide reception hallway, ignoring the startled exclamations of the staff on duty at the desk. She pounded up the stairs and virtually threw herself at the door to Luke's room, thumping it with both hands as she called his name in high-pitched agitation.

The door was not opened. There was no audible reply. Genevra propelled herself to the next door and banged on it with all her might, pleading with

171

Luke to let her in, but again there was no answer
to her frantic attempts to reach him.

Genevra could not believe that Luke would completely ignore her. He wasn't here. She felt no sense
of his presence behind these walls. She leaned
against the door to Felicity's room, her forehead
pressed to the panelling as she tried to think where
else to look for him.

Her mind was too jammed with fear to come up
with any answers. In a frantic need to do something, Genevra rushed back down to the reception
desk. 'Have you seen Mr Nemo in the last hour or
so?' she demanded sharply.

The two men raised their eyebrows at each other
and shook their heads in unison. 'We only came
on duty ten minutes ago, madame,' the older man
replied. 'Would you like me to call his room?'

'No...no...' Genevra answered distractedly and
turned away, feeling totally bereft.

Where? Where would he go? She was afraid to
ask herself what he would do, but the question
edged through the fear as she walked blindly out
of the hotel. Reverse the position, she told
herself...what would she do? And instantly the
answer flashed into her mind. Felicity!

Of course, he would not leave his daughter in
Genevra's home after that bitterly total condemnation of him and his kin. She had said she never
wanted to see him again, and by association that

meant Felicity, too. Guilt and shame wrung
Genevra's heart as she thought of the little girl's
bewilderment and distress at being abruptly removed from a home where she had finally felt
emotionally secure. If it was not already too late,
she had to stop Luke from doing it.

She hesitated a moment, undecided whether to
take the pathway which was a quicker route to the
village, or take the road in case Luke was already
in a taxi on his way back to the hotel with Felicity.
She did not want to miss him, yet she didn't want
to waste any precious minutes, either. Genevra was
still dithering when Jack Preston rounded the
corner of the hotel, and the sight of him inspired
a better idea.

'Mr Preston, did you drive a car to St Ives?' she
asked, pouncing on him in anxious haste.

'Yes. It's parked around here.' He waved in the
direction from whence he had just come.

'Please, will you drive me down to the village?
I've got to get home as fast as I can. I suspect Luke's
gone there to pick up Felicity.'

To Genevra's mind it was almost a certainty, not
a suspicion. Her intuition had never played her false
where Luke was concerned. Hadn't she known from
his letter that he wanted her to wait for him? Hadn't
she known Christian Nemo was Luke, despite all
the evidence to the contrary? She could not be
wrong about his intentions now! It was only the

timing that could go wrong. She desperately hoped that she wouldn't be too late. Not now, when everything her life meant depended on it.

Jack Preston did not pause to question. He moved swiftly, leading her straight to a Daimler and settling them both into it with an economy of action for which Genevra was intensely grateful. 'You will have to direct me,' was all he said as he headed the car towards the exit from the hotel grounds.

They met no taxi on the way. Genevra anxiously scanned the footpaths and narrow lanes for a man with a little girl, but there was no such couple in sight. Jack Preston parked the Daimler just outside the bookshop. 'I'll wait for you,' he said.

'Luke has to be here!' Genevra said on a tight, frantic note, and dashed out of the car, the shop-key ready in her hand. Once inside the shop, with the door relocked behind her, Genevra paused to take a deep, steadying breath, and in that momentary silence she heard the thud of the upstairs door being firmly closed, then footsteps coming down the staircase to the shop. She froze, tension screaming along every nerve.

He walked slowly, heavily, his head bent broodingly over the sleeping child in his arms. It was not until he stepped on to the shop-floor that he glanced up and saw Genevra. His whole body stiffened to a halt, and the dark pain on his face wrung Genevra's heart.

'I was just...getting Felicity,' he said with a strained catch in his voice. 'I'll be going now,' he added in a bare whisper.

'I'm sorry,' Genevra rushed out. 'You mustn't go! What I said up there...'

He was shaking his head. 'I can see now what I did to you. I'm not going to hurt you any further, Genevra.'

His mouth twisted into a bleak grimace. 'There are some broken pieces of life that can never be put back together, no matter how desperate the need is. I should have left you alone. I'm sorry.'

'No! I wanted you to come back, Luke. I never wanted anything so desperately. I've never loved any other man. I never will,' Genevra pleaded, frightened by his retreat from her.

He winced, as though her claim turned a knife in an agonising wound. 'Genevra, I can't take back what's been done, and if I had the choice again, I couldn't do any differently. Vickie...'

His gaze fell to the small bundle of humanity he held in his arms. 'She was even younger than Felicity when Jack took me into his home. She was...very dear to me. I couldn't let her down...not when she was going to die...not when she needed me so badly.' His arms tightened convulsively around the child, and he lifted a face which was engraved with years of agony. 'I did what I had to.'

'I know,' she said softly. 'It was the right choice, Luke. The only choice.'

'Genevra...' Need and despair roughened his voice. 'I wish...I wish we hadn't met until now.'

'Then we wouldn't have Johnny, would we? Or Felicity,' she reminded him, walking down the shop to where he stood, then lovingly caressing the little girl's baby-soft cheek. 'Would you really wish that, Luke?'

He seemed stunned, unable to accept what her words and actions implied. Felicity stirred in his arms and opened her eyes.

'G'evra...' she murmured sleepily.

'Yes, darling?'

'Can I come into bed with you?'

Genevra smiled down at her. 'Not right now, Felicity. But your Daddy and I will tuck you into your bed and kiss you goodnight. And in the morning you can come into my bed. Will that do?'

'Mmm,' she sighed contentedly.

Genevra looked up at the man she loved, her eyes imploring his forgiveness for her hasty judgements. 'My need for you is as great as Vickie's ever was. You're not going to let me down now, are you, Luke?'

'You still...want me, Genevra?' he asked incredulously.

'Till the day I die, and beyond,' she answered with vehement conviction. 'I'm sorry for all the cruel things I said to you. I was terribly wrong about everything. Can you forgive me?'

'Forgive you?' he choked. 'It's I who should be asking...'

'No.' She placed a hushing finger to his lips. 'I'm glad you gave Vickie that time, Luke. We have so many years ahead of us, I'll never begrudge her that brief happiness, I promise you. As for the rest, I'm just thankful that you did come back to me, under any name.'

'You really mean this, Genevra?' he breathed, hardly daring to believe her.

'With all my heart. I love you too much to ever let you go again,' she said simply.

Naked yearning throbbed from him as relief and desire furred his speech. 'I never stopped loving you...thinking of you...wanting you with me...'

She touched the child he was still clutching tightly. 'Let's put Felicity to bed. Then we can discuss...whatever is necessary,' she said, but her eyes promised a far more expressive way of communicating their need for each other.

Genevra led the way upstairs. She surprised Auntie May, pacing the living-room floor and wearing a harried expression. 'Genevra!' she cried. 'Christian came and...' Her gaze lifted to the man who had followed her niece. 'Oh! You've come back!'

Genevra gave her aunt a comforting hug. 'Not to worry. Nothing's wrong. We had a . . . a tiny misunderstanding, that's all,' she explained quickly.

'Oh!' Auntie May sagged with relief. 'I thought... well, never mind. Is there anything I can do for you?'

Genevra suddenly remembered Jack Preston, waiting outside in the Daimler.

She described him to Auntie May, and asked her to let him know that there were no more problems. Christian and Felicity were here.

Auntie May's normal air of good cheer returned as she said she'd be only too happy to have a little chat with Felicity's grandfather; and off she went, obviously pleased to have such a message to deliver.

Christian carried Felicity up the stairs to Johnny's attic bedroom, and Genevra tucked her into bed. As she bent to kiss the little girl goodnight, Felicity's arms reached out and curled possessively around her neck.

'Are you my mummy now, G'evra?'

The whispered plea held a plaintive need that tugged at Genevra's heart. She lifted Felicity up, hugging her with reassuring fervour. 'Yes, I am. And Johnny's your brother. And we're always going to be a family.' Her eyes met Luke's over Felicity's head. 'She needs so much love.'

'We both do,' he answered huskily.

'Let's take her into my bed for a while. We'll always have each other, Luke.'

'Yes.' He smiled, and the warm glow of that smile filled Genevra with the richest happiness of all.

'Mummy? Is Felicity sick?'

They turned quickly to Johnny who had hitched himself up in his bed.

'No. She just wanted a cuddle,' Luke told him and swung him out of bed, lifting him high in squealing delight before planting him on his broad shoulder.

They grinned at each other, father and son sharing an indulgent awareness of a girl's need for cuddles. 'Do you think you and I could fit into Mummy's bed, too?' Luke asked laughingly.

'Yes!' Johnny crowed.

So they all bundled into Genevra's bed, the children in the middle and their parents stretched out on either side of them. Luke told them stories and, underneath the pillows, his hand found Genevra's and gripped tight.

This is what life is all about, Genevra thought with blissful contentment: to be with the man she loved, sharing a happy time with their children, forging a bond that would never be shaken again. Her fingers squeezed his, and their eyes met without any of the doubt and pain that had shadowed the past. Their togetherness was complete and secure.

CHAPTER FOURTEEN

EVERYTHING had worked out perfectly, Genevra thought with a happy glow of satisfaction. All she had to do was sign the contract Matthew had ready, and her last personal responsibility for her single life would be discharged. The bookshop and residence at St Ives would pass to the new owner.

She and Johnny and Auntie May had already moved to the house Luke had leased in Eaton Square. Of course, it was a big jump from their old life in the village, but there were no regrets.

Johnny was enchanted with London, and this morning Luke had taken him and Felicity for a Thames boat-ride to Greenwich to see the Cutty Sark, which Luke had informed them was one of the fastest sailing ships ever made.

And the most extraordinary thing of all—Auntie May and Jack Preston were obviously finding a new lease of life in each other's company. 'A fine gentleman,' Auntie May had pronounced the morning after she had met him. But now it was, 'That Jack Preston is a lovely man, Genevra. He needs someone to look after him.' And Jack was looking ten years younger with the 'looking after' Auntie May was giving him.

Genevra couldn't help grinning to herself as she mounted the stairs to Matthew's chambers, but there was one sobering thought at the back of her mind. She still had to tell Matthew about Christian Nemo's real identity.

After Genevra's business was settled, Luke was meeting them both for lunch at the Dorchester Hotel, and Genevra didn't want Matthew under any delusions about the man she loved.

She recalled Auntie May's initial confusion over the situation, but Auntie May had been so enamoured of Christian Nemo that, if he was Luke Stanford, they were both fine men and couldn't do any wrong. It had all been 'an unfortunate tragedy' and 'all's well that ends well'.

Genevra doubted that Matthew would take quite the same simplistic view as Auntie May, but he wouldn't be able to argue with the facts she gave him. And he had said he wanted her to be happy. If he could not see she was brimming over with happiness then he would have to be blind.

And Matthew was certainly not blind when his secretary ushered Genevra into his office. He rose instantly to greet her, his shrewd blue eyes twinkling with appreciation. 'I've never seen you look so lovely, Genevra! Positively blooming!' he said with a beaming smile.

Genevra laughed and gave him an affectionate kiss.

He took her hands, pressing them in delighted approval. 'I am very much looking forward to meeting this man who's put such a beautiful sparkle in your eyes.'

'Yes . . . well, I think *you'd* better sit down this time, Matthew, because I have something to tell you and I don't want you fainting on me,' Genevra said teasingly.

The eyebrows arched in a good-humoured, quizzical fashion. It was obvious from Genevra's mood and manner that any shock she might deliver could not be an unpleasant one. 'Just as well I asked Beverley to bring in a tea-tray,' he observed drily.

He saw Genevra settled in a comfortable chair before resuming his own, then gestured an invitation for her to enlighten him.

'You remember that day I asked you to find out about Luke Stanford?'

Matthew nodded.

'I went from here to the Dorchester to meet Christian. I saw a man walking down the Promenade Room, and from the back view I was certain he was Luke.'

'Good heavens!' Matthew exclaimed, his eyebrows lowering into a frown of sympathetic concern.

Genevra smiled. 'I raced after him, but when he turned around his face was different. It bore the scars of a terrible accident, and the nose and jawline were the wrong shape. He introduced himself as Christian Nemo, which completely rattled me.'

Her mouth curved in whimsical remembrance. 'But the touch of his hand, his voice, and his smile were so like Luke's that, by the time I left him that afternoon, I was certain that Christian Nemo was really Luke Stanford, and that he had stayed away from me all those years because something dreadful had happened to him.'

'Oh, my dear! No wonder you were shocked when I told you Luke Stanford was dead,' Matthew said in quick sympathy.

'Yes. But he wasn't dead, Matthew. Christian is Luke.'

His jaw dropped open and his secretary timed her entrance with the tea-tray to perfection. Genevra got up and served Matthew while he recovered himself. Then she told him all about Luke's marriage to Vickie and the plane crash which had delayed his return for so many years.

'Then it wasn't the money?' Matthew observed, shaking his head in bemusement over the whole affair.

Genevra grinned at him. 'The trouble with you, Matthew, is that you've seen too much greed, envy, hatred, and malice.'

He laughed. 'Well, I'm very happy they didn't apply in this case.'

Genevra's grin dropped into a grimace. 'Except for me. I almost messed everything up. When Christian introduced me to Jack Preston, I knew the inquiry agent had been wrong about Luke's death, and I turned on him, accusing him of the basest treachery. I was so jealous of Vickie and all that he'd given her while I...' She gave a wry shrug. 'You know what I mean.'

He nodded gravely. 'I'm sorry, Genevra. I certainly didn't do you a good turn in getting that information to you, or interpreting it as I did.'

'Yes, you did,' Genevra corrected him quickly. 'It forced the truth into the open. And Matthew...I really learnt something important. You're a much better and happier person if you think of others instead of yourself. Luke is such a wonderful human being. I'm so lucky to have him back.'

Matthew's mouth curved into a whimsical smile. 'I'm of the opinion that he's lucky to have you back, Genevra. If I were thirty years younger, I might have contested his claim on you.'

Genevra's eyes danced appreciation of the compliment. 'I'm afraid I would have disappointed you, Matthew. There's only ever been one man for me. Christian or Luke—the name didn't matter—I loved him from the very first meeting.'

And her love was such a live, vibrant thing that it held Matthew in awed silence for several moments. 'He is a very lucky man,' he finally sighed.

'You'll soon see what a wonderful person he is,' Genevra assured him. 'And you will be free for our wedding day next week?' she added anxiously.

'I've cleared the day of all appointments. Even ordered a new morning-coat.'

She happily related all the wedding and honeymoon plans. Matthew kept nodding benevolently, finding enormous pleasure in the play of joyful anticipation on Genevra's face. He eventually drew her attention to the documents which needed her signature. She didn't bother reading them, and for once he did not insist. After all, he had prepared them himself and, as always, had been meticulous in looking after Genevra's interests.

And it did his heart good to see her with the man she loved when they lunched together at the Dorchester. By the time he left them, he no longer harboured any reservations about her husband-to-be. Genevra would be safe with him. 'To love and to cherish...' the words from the marriage service ran through his mind and he smiled to himself.

A week later, he listened to Luke Stanford repeating them to Genevra in a sacred vow, and the depth of emotion that throbbed through the words brought a blur of tears to Matthew's eyes. This is how it should always be, he thought, and when the clergyman turned to him and said, 'Who gives this woman...' Matthew handed Genevra into the keeping of the man she loved, knowing that God's will was surely being done this day.

Bright sunshine flooded through the glass doors which led out on to the balcony, brighter sunshine than Genevra had ever seen in England this early in the morning. But she and Luke had flown out of England after the wedding, and they were spending one glorious month alone in this beautiful villa on the French Riviera.

She stretched with lazy pleasure, then turned on her side to gaze possessively at her new husband. As much as she loved Johnny and Felicity, Genevra felt an almost overwhelming greed to have Luke to herself for a while. And it wouldn't hurt the children. Not when they had Auntie May and Grandpa indulging their every whim.

Luke was still asleep, but she couldn't resist touching him. The sensuality of last night's lovemaking was still a vivid memory, and she ran featherlight fingertips over his back, savouring the texture of firm flesh and muscle. He stirred and she pressed her mouth to his shoulder to prevent his turning over.

'Are you awake?' she whispered.

'No. This has to be a dream,' he answered, but she heard the smile in his voice.

'If you dare doubt that it's real, I'll scratch you all over,' she threatened, pressing her nails into the pit of his back.

He gave a lovely, deep chuckle, and started to roll towards her.

'No. Don't move,' she commanded, pushing him back and snuggling her body around his. 'I've got you covered and I want the truth.'

'I love you,' he said with very satisfactory fervour.

'I know that,' she said, feeling blissfully smug about it. 'What I don't know is what happened to your mole.'

He heaved himself up, dropping her back on to the pillows as he loomed over her. 'What mole?' he asked laughingly.

'The mole near the pit of your back, and don't tell me you don't know what mole,' she insisted with mock truculence. 'That mole has given me a bad time. That mole has a lot to answer for. If that mole had been where it should have been, you wouldn't have lasted as Christian Nemo past that first night at the Manoir.'

'Good God! Are you saying that you deliberately seduced me to look for a mole?'

'That was the plan. But things got carried away a bit. You always did have this terribly distracting influence on me, Luke.'

He shook his head at her, a bemused grin on his face. 'You really were certain it was me?'

'Well, then I was. Things got a little trickier later on. But I do think it's time you cleared up the mystery of the mole.'

She pouted in mock sulkiness and he kissed her, kissed her so thoroughly and erotically that Genevra forgot all about the mole. And the kissing didn't stop at her mouth.

'What are you doing?' she gasped, squirming with sensuous delight.

'Seducing you as deliberately as you seduced me.'

And he showed her no mercy at all, ravishing her senses with such a wicked knowledge of how to give pleasure that Genevra was still tingling with it long after the climax of their passion for each other was reached and passed.

'It was cut out,' he murmured, nibbling her ear teasingly.

'What was cut out?' Genevra mumbled, sighing with sweet contentment.

'During one of the operations. The surgeon mentioned it in passing. Thought he might as well take it off while he was wielding the knife.'

Laughter suddenly bubbled up in her, and she rolled on to her back to give full vent to it, her eyes twinkling exultantly at Luke until she caught her breath enough to speak. 'You mean, you didn't have that mole deliberately removed?'

His face was stamped with surprised innocence. 'Never thought of it.'

'Oh, Luke! Don't ever try to deceive me again. You're hopeless at it.'

He sighed and drew her back into his embrace, stroking her with almost reverent tenderness. 'You are everything to me, Genevra. You always will be. Don't ever doubt that, whatever I might do. But I promise you now, there will never be anything but truth between us.'

'And love,' she whispered.

'There was always love,' he said, hugging her tightly to him. 'Always.'

TO TAME A WILD HEART

CHAPTER ONE

SLADE CORDELL SHIFTED restlessly in the high-backed leather chair that had belonged to his father before him. It *was* uncomfortable, damned uncomfortable. Like a lot of things in this boardroom, he decided.

The thought was part of a chain of discontented thoughts that had passed through his mind since the beginning of this particular meeting. Just lately—no, it was more than just lately—for longer than he cared to remember, all his responsibilities concerning Cordell Enterprises had begun to pall on him.

His eyes flicked around the men seated on either side of the long mahogany table. They were all top executives. Otherwise they wouldn't be holding the positions they did. Slade wondered if he was really necessary or nothing more than a figurehead. Could he let the reins slide, or would everything start to fall apart if he wasn't there to hold it together in a cohesive working pattern? It was an interesting thought.

Cordell Enterprises was a vast octopus organisation. The oil fields in Texas had started it, together with a small minority holding in a company that made bits for mining drills. That had been the foundation of the Howard Hughes fortune. Cordell Enterprises had shared in it, albeit to a much smaller degree. Now the octopus had tentacles that stretched halfway around the world, embracing such diverse interests as electronics and pharmaceuticals and beef cattle. The American corporate offices took up six floors of the modern office block on Park Avenue, right in the heart of New York, but this was only the nerve centre. There were other offices: Dallas, London, Paris...

For more than ten years Slade had kept tabs on the rapidly shifting inner worlds of international business, sometimes stealing a step on them, never falling behind. He didn't like losing—never had—yet the spice of winning simply wasn't there any more. He was tired—tired of thinking, tired of travelling, tired of listening to reports on which he was always expected to pass judgement, tired and bored!

Maybe he just needed a long vacation to get rid of this burnt-out feeling. Yet a man could hardly be burnt out at thirty-six. He had too many years ahead of him to allow that as a reality. He simply needed something to liven up this dog-day existence. An adventure. A new sense of purpose. But what?

He dragged his concentration together and listened to the end of the report being given on future oil contracts and prices. Nothing to worry about there. Hinkman was one of the best directors on the board, comprehensive in his diligence, even when the incomprehensible happened, which it did from time to time.

The door to the boardroom burst open.

Slade's attention was galvanised. Board meetings were secret, privileged and inviolable!

A woman in red whirled into the room, hurling a defiant message over her shoulder. "If this is a full board meeting, I couldn't have chosen a better time!"

She swung on her heel and strode purposefully to the foot of the table where she came to a halt. Her eyes blazed straight down the length of it to where Slade sat in the high-backed leather chair, which designated his status. Her chin tilted in resolute pride and self-determination.

"Mr. Slade Cordell..." Her fist made a belligerent ball and pressed down on the table in an emphatic gesture of intent. "I've come to add one more item to the agenda of this meeting. As a matter of urgency, sir!"

The "sir" held a trace of contempt that piqued his curiosity. The accent was unmistakably Australian, which piqued his curiosity even more. Skin bronzed, athletic build, loose-limbed. She looked as if she could go anywhere, do anything... and get her own way. Slade felt a very real stirring of interest. She was also quite strikingly attractive.

There had been a surfeit of beautiful women in Slade's life, and beauty alone was no longer a drawing card to him. They had to have more than that—an individuality, a charm. But even those words seemed lukewarm for this woman. There was an aura of boldness about her, a fiery steel that nothing had ever tempered.

A couple of the board members started to rise, preparing to eject her. Slade made a motion with his hand to stop them. Ron Colson, the secretary who was supposed to ensure there were no interruptions, made an agitated appearance in the doorway.

"I beg your pardon, sir. She went straight past me without a—"

Slade flicked a look at the flustered secretary, silencing the man without a word. In the usual course of events he would not tolerate such a breach of privacy. Later on the secretary would certainly get the broadside he deserved. Apart from anything else, it kept the staff on its toes. More importantly, it ensured that in future he anticipated what had never happened before! That, surely, was his job!

However, Slade was not displeased with this particular diversion. In a perverse kind of way he welcomed something wild happening, especially when it wasn't supposed to. He rose to his feet to get a better look at the situation.

The young woman's chin tilted higher as she took in his full height. His six-foot-four-inch frame was amply filled. Slade had played football in college, and the physique developed then was in no way diminished. He was well aware that most people found him formidable, and not only because he headed Cordell Enterprises. But this woman wasn't intimidated. Not in any shape or form. She glared at him as though he was nothing but a big ape who needed to be put in his place.

"How do you do, ma'am?" he said in his most exaggerated Texas drawl, then gave her a smile designed to wipe out all hostility within its radius. "You got it right. I surely am Slade Cordell."

The look of surprise on her face was worth this bit of acting. She hadn't expected that. She had erupted into the room, all steamed up for a fight and determined to win. Well, she wasn't going to get a fight.

He glanced around the table. Everyone was tensely waiting for his true reaction, not believing for one moment that this good humour was genuine. One or two tried a smile just in case it was what he wanted.

Yes-men! Maybe that was the source of his problem. He needed someone who could stand up to him, someone with balls, someone without fear who had the courage of his convictions, someone like this woman who was emanating the kind of boldness that refused to recognise backward steps.

Not even Hinkman did that. They were all good executives, but only managers. Slade saw that more clearly now. They had reached the top rung of their abilities. He *was* necessary, the linchpin that set them all in motion.

Well, he would make certain he was right about that.

He turned an affable face towards the secretary, who was too frightened to believe in it. "Mr. Colson, would you be kind enough to bring this young lady a chair so that she can sit in and help this board with its deliberations?''

That should create a volcanic explosion, Slade thought. One or more of these board members should erupt the way Krakatoa did, back in 1883. The world should move!

Dead silence.

No eruption.

No one moved.

Not a word of protest was uttered.

All yes-men!

No, not quite all. Ross Harper's eyes met his, a quizzical challenge in them. Harper was the most junior board member. New blood brought in from outside the organisation and still feeling his way. Someone to be watched and encouraged, Slade noted approvingly.

After a few frozen seconds, Colson nervously propelled himself into action. A chair was brought. The lady was seated. Slade waved Colson out. The door closed very quietly behind him. The board members sat around the table, looking down at the papers in front of them. They knew they should have demurred, knew they should have opposed this unbelievably ridiculous idea that an absolute stranger could help them make top-level business decisions. They hadn't. Only Ross Harper had even thought of doing so.

It cleared Slade's mind of a lot of misconceptions. He was most assuredly needed here. Without him, Cordell Enterprises would be an octopus without a head, its tentacles turning in on themselves, all momentum coming to a halt. All these executive positions needed a real shake-up. Fancy letting a young woman get the better of them! It both amused Slade and disgusted him.

He sat back in his chair. It felt more comfortable than it had in a long time. He suddenly felt more alive than he had done in a long time. Sparking on all cylinders! His eyes drifted to the woman in red. In his mind, Slade raised an imaginary hat. *Thank you, ma'am,* he said to himself. *You don't know how much you've already helped me.*

She stared at him, a curious look of reassessment in her eyes. Shrewd and intelligent, he thought. Certainly she hadn't missed some of the nuances of what was going on in this room and she was concentrating solely on him, dismissing all the others as unimportant ciphers. Which was how they had acted. Slade took his time returning her appraisal. It was a deliberate tactic—testing her nerve, reinforcing his authority and noting all the details that revealed information about her.

The linen suit she wore was not precisely red. It was a more subtle shade, coral, perhaps, but all the more distinctive for being slightly unusual. Silk blouse. Nice pieces of jewelry, rather Victorian in style but undoubtedly genuine. A woman of considerable class, he decided, from a family of some wealth. Possibly a lot of wealth.

Slade turned his attention to reading what character he could from her face.

Her glossy black hair was pulled back from a striking widow's peak and wound into a neat coif around her head. The severe hairstyle suggested that vanity came second place to practicality. Nevertheless, it did serve to accentuate the wide brow and prominent cheekbones and draw attention to the fine elegance of a squarish jawline. There was no hint of weakness in those features. Her nose seemed rather thin for such a strong-boned face, but the flare of her nostrils was wide enough to complement the full-lipped mouth.

Passion, he thought. She certainly had passion. It was a thought that stirred another kind of interest. He wondered how passionate she would be ... but this was the boardroom, not a bedroom. Slade dragged his mind back to business.

She had borne his study of her without the minutest reaction, not even a slight flinch or quiver. Slade knew there were few men who could have withstood such an examination with complete sang-froid. It took a strength of character, or purpose, that would not be shaken under any duress.

Admiration kindled his interest further as he levelled his gaze on hers—green eyes, thickly lashed and blazing with pride and anger. He had no doubt, however, that the anger was under control. She was merely letting him know that his long silent scrutiny had induced only a measure of scorn from her. There was not the slightest waver in eye contact. A blistering challenge. Rock-steady.

Slade found her response intriguing, all the more so since she looked so young. He placed her age in the early twenties, but he could be mistaken about that. She had the kind of face that would hold age indefinitely. Whatever her experience of life, she had learned an inner strength that was rare among the women he knew. His curiosity deepened.

"I have not had the pleasure of your acquaintance, ma'am," he said, his mouth curling into a smile that was meant to disarm her. "If you would be so kind as to introduce yourself..."

She did not smile back. She did not relax one muscle. There was a bitter flash in her eyes as she answered him. "Rebecca Wilder, Mr. Cordell. I am the granddaughter of Janet Wilder."

She spoke those names as though they should have meant something to him, as though she had taken the biggest piece of artillery out of the U.S. arsenal, aimed it between his eyes and pressed the trigger. Yet they meant nothing to him. He mentally processed all the names he knew. None fitted.

"I'm pleased to meet you, ma'am," he said.

The glitter of savage mockery in her eyes told him that she didn't believe him, that she no longer believed her mission could be accomplished, whatever it was. But she had to feel passionately about that mission or she would not have broken into this boardroom to confront him.

"What can we do for you?" he asked softly, every instinct telling him that there was something wrong about this situation. Something badly wrong. And he felt a strong need to make it right, because Rebecca Wilder... Darn it! Was it Miss or Mrs.? He would have to watch her hands for rings.

"I do not like to see cattle suffer, Mr. Cordell. Not even your cattle," she bit out angrily. "My grandmother has done all she can to prevent that from happening up until now. But no more, Mr. Cordell. You either sell off the cattle your land won't support or Devil's Elbow will become their graveyard."

"Devil's Elbow?" A stirring of memory that he couldn't place accurately yet.

Scorn glared back at him. "It was called that long before you bought it, Mr. Cordell. For good reason, if you had ever bothered to find out. However, your new name for it—may God have mercy on your avaricious soul—is Logan's Run."

Facts slotted into place. He had renamed that property in Australia after Grandfather Logan. At the time it had seemed a good idea even though he had never seen the cattle ranch in question. It had just been another acquisition among many.

What had gone wrong? What gross mismanagement was going on behind his back? What was being hidden from him? Maybe it was time he looked beyond executive levels and did some spot checks on the lower echelons of his organisation.

"You're telling me that the cattle on Logan's Run are in danger of dying?" His voice held a cutting edge that had no shade of affability left in it. None at all. His mind was very sharply back on business.

"That's precisely what I'm telling you," she confirmed. "Unless we see some positive action from you within a week—action that will redress the situation you've created—we will take whatever steps are necessary to protect ourselves and others from your blind intransigence. In case you are in any doubt as to the outcome, Mr. Cordell, that means your cattle will start to die. And that's all I have to say to you."

She stood up, her bearing one of haughty contempt as she looked down the table at him. "I've travelled halfway around the world to tell you that, Mr. Cordell. I've spent the last five days trying to reach you to tell you that." Her eyes glittered their scorn for him and his organisation. "I tried the telephone, the telex, the fax and any other machine I could get hold of. I tried . . ."

Her left hand performed an expressive dismissal. No rings, Slade noted.

"Well, I tried just about everything. And I tried everybody I could find. Without success. But now you've been told, Mr. Cordell. And I know you've been told," she said with grim satisfaction.

Her chin lifted in determined pride. "I've done what I came to do. We've had no co-operation from your people at Devil's Elbow, no co-operation from your people in Brisbane, no co-operation from anyone here at your headquarters in New York. And I expect none from you. But at least now we can make our decisions with a completely clear conscience. You have a week, Mr. Cordell. No more."

Her smile was one of utter disdain. "Have a nice day, Mr. Cordell," she said in mocking mimic of the words that had been tossed so carelessly and meaninglessly at her all week. Then she turned to go.

"Miss Wilder..." He had to stop her. He had to make things right. He wasn't about to let her go on this unsatisfactory note. He didn't want to let her go at all!

She paused. Slade saw the fullness of her lips tighten into a thin line then relax to their natural shape. Very slowly her head turned towards him. One eyebrow was raised in disdainful challenge.

"I'm very grateful to you," Slade said with absolute precision, his words measured like a metronome as he whipped his mind off the personal angle and took the business implications in. "I'd be even more grateful if you would sit down again and clarify this matter, ah, further. It may come as a surprise to you—it comes as a considerably unpleasant surprise to me—" he shot a baleful look around the table "—that I had no knowledge of this situation whatsoever. I aim to remedy that right now. So, please ... would you be so kind as to bear with me, and the board, just a little while longer?"

Slade could see she didn't want to. She had no reason to want to. If what she said was true, he was unreasonable to ask it of her. Yet with all the power at his command he willed her to stay, to sit down again, to help him sort out the truth and put everything right between them.

For what seemed a very long time, but was probably only seconds, her eyes bored into his, questioning the integrity of his appeal. Slade savagely regretted his earlier flippancy. It had served one purpose better than he had ever anticipated, but it told against him now. He could feel her weighing everything he had said and done. He didn't know what tipped the balance in her mind, but she sat down again.

The tension eased out of his body.

He had won.

The pleasure, the triumph that rippled through his mind—the tingle of excitement in his belly—stirred Slade to another realisation. He couldn't remember anyone ever challenging him as this woman was; those eyes, glittering green daggers scouring his soul. The urge—the desire—to tame her was the strongest feeling he'd had in a long, long time.

He hadn't won much from her yet, only the most minimal stay of judgement, but he would win a lot more before he was finished with her. Oh, yes, he would!

CHAPTER TWO

FOOL! Rebecca berated herself. She should have walked out. She should have shown Slade Cordell and his men her utter contempt for them and their kind by turning her back on them and walking out without another word. She had finally done what she had set out to achieve, what she had promised Gran she would achieve. The warning had been delivered, right to the top. There was no point in staying.

Yet there had been something compelling in those dark blue eyes, a need, a demand that challenged her to stay, despite all she had been through. A strong man, Slade Cordell. His eyes hadn't once shifted from hers. Not the slightest waver. He had absorbed what she had hurled at him and was demanding more from her.

It was weak and stupid to give in to his wishes now, but no one could ever say of her that she hadn't been absolutely fair. She was bending over backwards to be fair!

"Thank you," he said. As if he really meant it.

Two-faced, she thought furiously. Multi-faced! A face for every situation, switched on and off at will. He wanted to use her. That was why he had asked her to stay. He had been using her from the moment she had stepped into this room, playing some private hand of his own for the purpose of testing his power. Why she had come had been completely irrelevant. Did he think she was so lacking in perception that she couldn't see that?

He leaned forward, resting his forearms on the table. "Now, Miss Wilder," he began.

And that was another thing! How did he know she wasn't married if he truly knew nothing about her? She hadn't told him. He hadn't asked. She looked down at her hands and understood. There should have been rings, if only...

"Would you be kind enough to tell me and the board precisely why my cattle are going to die?"

Rebecca lifted her gaze reluctantly. The dark blue eyes looked keenly interested. Was Slade Cordell a consummate actor? What on earth was being played out here behind the scenes?

Rebecca shrugged off the thought. It wasn't her problem. At least by staying she could get a few shots of her own in. Futile, most likely, but it would ease the heartburn she had suffered over the last few days. However, someone pre-empted her reply.

"Mr. Cordell."

It was one of the members of the board on the left side of the table. He had leaned forward, his heavy-jowled face turned towards the high-backed leather chair, to the man who occupied that chair with almost chilling dominance.

It was not that Slade Cordell was simply a big man, although he had left no doubt in Rebecca's mind that he used his imposing height and physique to forceful effect. His face was also an asset. It was the kind of face that belonged to a leader, a hard masculine face, uncompromising, authoritative in every line. The wide sweep of his brow was framed by dark hair, almost as dark as her own, thick and straight and cut short with no concession towards the fashion of the day. His nose was sharply ridged but it flared to his cheeks in strong planes. A firm mouth. An even firmer chin. But the power of the man resided in his eyes, those deeply set blue eyes that were now turned coldly to the man who had spoken.

"You have something to say, Mr. Petrie?" The words were drawled from a mouth that curled as it delivered them. The tone was just as soft as before but it now carried a dangerous undercurrent that would make any person think twice before interrupting again.

The man's jowls shook a little as he swallowed.

The blue eyes swung to Rebecca. "Mr. Petrie has the responsibility of reporting to me on our Australian holdings, Miss Wilder. In the normal channelling process of this organisation, you would be passed through him to get to me."

There was a tangible rise of tension around the table. Slade Cordell was certainly a lot younger than Rebecca had expected. He looked to be the youngest man in this room. Nevertheless, there was no doubting who held the whip hand, even in this high-powered company.

"Sir." Mr. Petrie forced a sharp authority into his voice. "If you will simply ask Miss Wilder to wait outside, I'll clear this matter up after the board meeting."

"I have a mind to clear it up myself, Mr. Petrie. I take it you were aware that Miss Wilder was in New York this week . . . having come all the way from Australia to see me?"

"Yes. But—"

"That she has been shuttled around these offices for days on end?"

"Yes. But—"

"That she was blocked in her purpose no matter what she tried?"

"I was preparing my report for this meeting, sir," Mr. Petrie excused himself.

"Did it occur to you that Miss Wilder might have something to add to your report?" came the softly spoken retort, the dangerous undercurrent even more in evidence. "May I suggest to you that you look up your report on Logan's Run so that you might have something constructive to add to this discussion?"

Mr. Petrie's face tightened. "I have, sir. I assumed that Miss Wilder's visit here was a negotiating tactic. It seemed the better tactic for us to ignore her request to see you, sir. There is a requisition to our Brisbane branch for the funds to buy the property owned by—"

"We will never sell!" Rebecca hurled at him, infuriated to discover that she had been the victim of tactics on an issue over which there could be no further meaningful discussion. Ever since Pa had died, Cordell Enterprises had been at Gran to sell, as if she ever would! They had been plying their offers for two years now, obdurately intent on changing Gran's mind, never listening to reason, pushing, pushing, pushing. Scorn coated Rebecca's voice as she added, "Your people have been told and told and..."

Mr. Petrie sneered at her. "Miss Wilder, we have the leverage, not you. You're wasting—"

"Leverage, Mr. Petrie?" Slade Cordell sliced in, interposing his formidable authority.

The man rushed to justify his actions. "The report on the property, Wildjanna, indicates that it is mortgaged to the hilt. The owner will not be able to withstand—"

Rebecca's eyes flashed their angry frustration at Slade Cordell. "My grandmother has told your people over and over again. We are not selling! Neither she nor I will sell Wildjanna!"

Mr. Petrie snorted contempt at her assertion. "It can only be a matter of time. You're playing a fool's game. One old woman and a girl trying to run a place like that. You'll crack. Everyone does. And everyone has their price!"

Rebecca was on her feet before she knew it. Her hands were spread on the table, her body bent forward, words spitting off her tongue. "One old woman! That old woman, Mr. Petrie, could run rings around you. She and my grandfather pioneered that land. She'll die on that land where her husband and children have lived and died. Nothing you can do or say will ever shift her. Or me. It's our home, Mr. Petrie. And any time you want to step foot on it, that old woman and I will comprehensively show you how much of a fool's game we play."

She swept a scathing look around the rich room. "You sit up here in your little eyrie high above the real world and move your figures around like pieces in an elaborate chess game. All you do is flex the power that your money gives you. But money is only paper! Little bits of paper, or figures on a computer. And you can't touch us with money, Mr. Petrie. We're the backbone of this world. We're the earth, the producers on the land, the substance from which everything else takes its existence."

Petrie gave her a mocking clap. "That sounds fine, Miss Wilder. That's all it is. A fine sound. It won't help you when the bank forecloses on your property. Then you'll see how much paper money is worth," he jeered.

Rebecca's chin lifted in utter disdain for his claim. "There is not one bank in Australia that would foreclose on Wildjanna, Mr. Petrie. We are totally, irrevocably out of your reach!"

"We have ways and means to—"

"Mr. Petrie!" Slade Cordell's voice speared at his executive, steel-edged with the kind of command that would not brook defiance. "We will listen to what Miss Wilder has to say, Mr. Petrie. It appears to me that someone should have listened to Miss Wilder a long time ago. I would not care for another interruption, Mr. Petrie, so please don't speak again unless you're spoken to."

A rush of blood suffused Mr. Petrie's neck and cheeks with angry colour, but his lips tightened over the words he was bursting to say. The cold blue gaze of Slade Cordell dismissed him and returned to Rebecca.

"Now, Miss Wilder..." His voice resumed a polite and gently encouraging tone. "Would you kindly explain to me about no bank foreclosing?"

Rebecca was wary. She didn't know what to believe about Slade Cordell. Although he had just put his own man down in favour of hearing what she had to say, it was impossible to tell if he was playing a game or was deadly serious. Was he on her side? She wanted him to be. Suddenly she wanted that very much. A strong man, with the ultimate authority to crush anyone beneath him. She shivered at that thought then quickly concentrated her mind on the issue that had brought her to him.

This was the final showdown. She would leave no loopholes for any excuses not to do what should be done at Devil's Elbow. She met those compelling blue eyes with steely resolution.

"In our country, Mr. Cordell, it takes three generations to put a property where it is safe from all disasters. I'm the third generation at Wildjanna. It is true that we are mortgaged to the hilt at the moment. This is not at all unusual when times are as bad as these. We may lose most of our stock. We may go to the wall in every financial sense you like to think of. But if we go under, so would every other property owner in the north. So no bank will ever foreclose on us. The government wouldn't allow it to happen."

"Why are you so sure of that, Miss Wilder?" It was an inquisitive question, not implying doubt, simply a request for elaboration.

Rebecca smiled, totally confident in her reply. "There's no one better equipped to recover the losses than we are, Mr. Cordell. You see, the land always does recover. And in good times, the Channel Country can compete with the finest grazing lands in the world. If worse comes to worst, the government will always step in to help us. In our country, they don't have any other option."

He nodded. While he was still weighing her words Rebecca spiked any misconception he might still be nursing. "We will never sell, Mr. Cordell. When my grandmother dies, I inherit. If I die without children, the land is willed to the Aboriginal people who live on the station. They will never sell. They know too well what it's like to be a disinherited people. So even if my grandmother and I meet with some...unforeseen accident, Cordell Enterprises will not get its hands on Wildjanna. No matter what happens."

His smile softened the ruthless cut of his face and lent it considerable charm. His eyes actually twinkled with amusement. Rebecca felt a strong pull of attraction. It was highly disconcerting. The last thing she had ever expected was to find Slade Cordell attractive in any way whatsoever.

"I would never wish an 'unforeseen accident' on you, Miss Wilder, but I have one hypothetical question. What if you marry?"

Rebecca knew in her heart she would never marry. Not unless Paul changed his mind, and then she would marry him. In the three years since he had broken their engagement, he had not shown the slightest wavering from his conviction that she must marry someone else, a man who could give her the kind of marriage she needed, the kind that he could no longer offer. Yet how could she ever do that? She owed him her love and loyalty...

"Miss Wilder?" Slade Cordell asked softly.

She snapped out of her deep introspection. Slade Cordell was waiting for an answer. "Should I ever marry, there'll be another man at Wildjanna," she stated unequivocally. "And a fourth generation."

That closed all the loopholes. The situation was now spelled out in capital letters. No mistakes could be made about it.

"Thank you for being so patient with me, Miss Wilder. I accept that as conclusive."

The gleam of intense satisfaction in his eyes suggested that Rebecca had given him the answer he wanted to hear. Although why that should be so, she couldn't imagine. He must be playing some deep game, she thought dismissively.

"Having now settled the question of tenure beyond any doubt," he continued smoothly, "I would like very much to get back to my original question. Please sit down and be comfortable, Miss Wilder. You were going to tell us why my cattle are going to die. It is a matter of considerable concern to me, a matter that both you and I want resolved. If you'd be so good as to oblige..."

Rebecca sat down again.

But didn't feel comfortable.

It seemed absurdly incongruous to even talk about cattle in this richly panelled room with its plush carpeting and the expensively suited men who were so sleekly tailored for international business. Everything about this place, these people, seemed far more than half a world away from home. It was a totally alien environment to her with no common reference point at all.

What could these men care about cattle? Beef prices yes, but hooves in the dust, the bellowing stampede to water, the plaintive bleat of calves left behind...what reality did that have in a room such as this? But if Slade Cordell wanted reality, she would give it to him.

"Water," she stated glumly. "We've had four years of drought, Mr. Cordell. My grandmother and I have done our best to keep the peace, but with the stock levels on your property so high—" she shot a glare at Mr. Petrie "—and kept deliberately high to pressure us, the situation is getting critical. If we keep watering your herd, Emilio Dalvarez will go short.''

''You mean Logan's Run doesn't control the water?'' Slade Cordell looked·appalled.

''No, it doesn't, Mr. Cordell.'' It gave her a rich sense of satisfaction to drive this point home. ''That's why it's called Devil's Elbow. Was called Devil's Elbow before your organisation bought it four years ago. We control the water in times of drought.''

''You and your grandmother.''

''Wildjanna. Our property, Mr. Cordell. The creek dries up on your land first. Then on Emilio Dalvarez's land. Wildjanna has been the only cattle station in our area to hold water even through the worst droughts. And one of them lasted as long as seven years,'' she added, just to make sure he realised what might be in front of him. ''That could be another three years . . . or more.''

''Is Logan's . . . Devil's Elbow out of water now?'' he asked.

''Yes.''

Concern furrowed the wide brow and narrowed the blue eyes. ''Are we buying water from you?''

She gave him a scornful look. ''We don't sell water! That's not the way we do things in our part of the world, Mr. Cordell. Access to our water is freely given, but your people aren't playing by the rules. If you don't cut down on your stock, then we may all have to go short. For the first time in over sixty years we have to think about limiting your access.''

''You came six thousand miles to tell me this?'' Slade Cordell inquired softly, his concern focused entirely on her now.

Rebecca's heart did a funny flip. He seemed to care . . . really care . . . yet how could he? But at least he was listening to her. She decided to ignore his expressions and simply lay out the facts.

"My grandmother and I decided you had to be told. Because the situation could turn very ugly if you don't act soon. Not only for us, Emilio—"

"Who is Emilio Dalvarez?"

"Our neighbour. He's an émigré Argentinian, and for all that he's been in Australia for thirty years, he's lost none of his Latin hot-bloodedness, nor his ingrained sense of honour. He can see as well as anyone what is happening and his sense of injustice is burning on a very short fuse."

"Where's his ranch?"

"To the west of Wildjanna. Your station, or ranch as you call it, is to the south. You and he share one common boundary. The altercations have already started. Emilio will resort to cutting down your herd with bullets if we don't come up with a satisfactory solution soon. As I said, we are doing our best to keep the peace, but your people have been less than co-operative, Mr. Cordell."

She finished on a note of intense bitterness. She had spent thousands of dollars in this last-ditch effort to get someone at Cordell Enterprises to see sense. And she hadn't liked leaving Gran to handle everything at home alone. Indomitable she might be, but she was old, and this last month had shortened Emilio Dalvarez's temper. Not that Gran would back off from using a shotgun if she had to. If only Pa hadn't died...Rebecca shook her head at the futile thought.

"I'm sorry you've been put to so much trouble on our account, Miss Wilder."

She looked up, startled not by the apology so much as the way he had seemed to read her thoughts. It gave her an odd, vulnerable feeling. "I've told you the truth, Mr. Cordell," she said sharply. "Take it or leave it. You have a week in which to act. If you don't, we will."

"Something will be done, Miss Wilder. Most assuredly so. I will see to it personally."

He sounded sincere but Rebecca had heard verbal assurances all week in these offices. They were meaningless. When the management at Devil's Elbow started moving stock to sale yards she would believe she had accomplished something, not before.

"I hope you do," she said wearily. It had been a long, hard week. She rose from the chair, tall, dignified and dismissive of all that Cordell Enterprises stood for. "I've had enough of this place, Mr. Cordell. I'm going home."

He was on his feet before she had even turned towards the door. And he was smiling at her again. Her heart fluttered. It must be because he's so big, Rebecca thought, although she wasn't the least bit nervous of him. She had no reason to be. She had truth, right and justice on her side.

"I think I might just come with you."

His voice wasn't a soft drawl this time. It resounded with a rich depth and was surprisingly pleasant. What he meant by his words was more obscure. Probably he was going to escort her out of the boardroom, out to the lift. The look in his eyes suggested he admired her, or at least appreciated the presentation she had made of her case. He damned well should appreciate it, too, Rebecca reminded herself. It hadn't cost him a cent but it had cost her plenty.

"We are deeply in your debt," he continued, disconcerting her anew with his seeming ability to read her thoughts.

"Yes, you are," Rebecca said tartly. "I hope you remember it. Now, if you'll excuse me . . ."

"Of course. You've been more than generous with your time."

He strode down the room towards her, clearly intent on seeing her out. He certainly looked imposing in his three-piece suit. The fancy red and navy silk tie was a class touch on the pristine white shirt. He could well afford class, Rebecca thought cynically. He reached her side, and all she had done was turn towards him. She was tired. Worn out. Prey to all sorts of silly fancies. How could she even think that Slade Cordell was attractive? He was so different from Paul...

"Before you go home—"

"My return flight was booked before I came, Mr. Cordell," she said tersely, discomfited by the comparison she had just made. "I leave this afternoon from Kennedy Airport. I'm going now to pick up my luggage from my hotel and—"

"What time is your flight?" he cut in, his brows drawing together as if in displeasure.

"Four-fifteen."

He glanced at his watch. "I'll have someone take you to my office. Please wait there, Miss Wilder. I'll arrange a car for you. It's the least I can do."

Why not? Rebecca thought. It would save her some hefty taxi fares. "Very well. Thank you."

He smiled, satisfaction glinting in his eyes. Then he took her arm and led her out of the boardroom.

Rebecca was quite relieved to be handed over to someone else. Whether it was his size or the forcefulness of his character, she wasn't quite sure, but Slade Cordell certainly made his presence felt close up. Even his hand on her arm had a penetrating touch. She wanted to rub the feeling away when he released her but she controlled the urge. After all, she was never going to see him or be subjected to his presence again.

He had certainly treated her with courtesy. She had to say that for him. She hoped he was a man of integrity. If he kept his word that he would personally see to correcting the problem, then all the trouble would be over. Rebecca had no doubt about that. Slade Cordell was not the kind of man who tolerated anyone flouting his authority.

She wondered what it would be like to have a man like him at her side, a man who would not let anything beat him. A need stirred deep inside her. The need that Paul might have filled if the accident hadn't happened. Yet Paul hadn't had the invincible quality that emanated from Slade Cordell. The big American wouldn't have backed out of the life she offered just because he was tied to a wheelchair. He would have found a way to conquer whatever needed to be conquered.

Rebecca shook her head at such foolish whimsy. Slade Cordell was a city man. Not for him, her kind of life. And his kind of life was not for her. She was going home, away from his world. A long way away.

CHAPTER THREE

REBECCA CHECKED HER WATCH as she was ushered into Slade Cordell's office. Strange as it seemed—was it only an hour since she had decided she would barge in on Slade Cordell wherever he was?—it was only a few minutes past eleven. She had plenty of time to make it to the airport.

She refused the refreshments offered by her escort and was left alone. If she required anything, she was told, she only needed to press a button on the telephone and she would be given instant service. This was on a massive desk top of black marble, the focal dramatic feature of a vast room mostly furnished in blues and greys.

The décor was starkly modern—leather sofas, small tables made of slabs of marble balanced on polished chrome bases, glass shelves set on chrome structures and filled with books or graced with modern sculptures, which invited the eye to imagine what it liked. Rebecca wondered whether Slade Cordell had bought them himself or if they were simply the selection made by an expensive interior decorator.

The only thing she had no doubt about was the placement of the massive desk. Slade Cordell would certainly have ordered that. It was opposite the wall of plate glass, which presented a panoramic view of the city skyline. Since the office was situated on the thirty-fifth floor, this was something to behold, and Rebecca was sure it gave the head of Cordell Enterprises a feeling of enormous power.

She looked out on the thrusting concrete and glass skyscrapers of this mighty city and shuddered. How could people spend their lives in structures such as these, year after year? To her it was soulless. The huge monoliths of Manhattan were like monuments to some god that she couldn't worship. It was totally incomprehensible. Yet it existed, this life in the sky. Let them have it, she thought. I'll take the land.

She didn't know how long she stood there. She only knew that she belonged somewhere else, with red earth and grey-green trees and brilliant blue skies that could dazzle the eyes. A place where the sun both blistered and caressed with warmth, where water was a life-giving thing and unpolluted by chemicals, where people and animals knew their life cycle was bound to the land.

Her mind slowly drifted onto what would happen at home if Slade Cordell was as good as his word. Gran would be able to force Emilio to back off and keep to the course that she stipulated for getting through the drought. It would take some time for the ill will that had been generated to die down but they could weather that. All it took was resolution, and neither Gran nor she was about to cave in on anything.

The sound of the door opening startled her out of her intense reverie. She swung around and was even more startled to see Slade Cordell enter the room. "Is your board meeting over?" she asked, confused by his unexpected appearance.

"I've adjourned the meeting until further notice," he said, his eyes glinting with some secret triumph. "You've been enjoying the view?"

"I don't like it. It's not my world at all," she blurted out. "But I wish to thank you for hearing me out."

"The least I could do," he assured her.

Something fluttered between them—an empathy, a brief locking of souls. It was weird, unreal, and Rebecca forcefully rejected it. A city man like him . . . impossible! There wasn't one shred of compatibility to form the remotest link!

"I've made all the necessary arrangements for us," he said, coupling them together as if he hadn't rejected it at all. "If you'll give me the name of your hotel, your luggage will be picked up while we have lunch."

He stepped over to the desk and picked up the telephone receiver. "Your hotel?" he prompted softly.

Rebecca gave it somewhat stiffly, not at all sure that she wanted to have lunch with him. Slade Cordell's strong personality was a little too forceful for her liking, assuming an acceptance of an invitation that wasn't even offered.

On the other hand, if he wanted to pump her for more background information on the problems at home before she left New York, it would be stupid of her to begrudge him the opportunity. Besides, he was saving her considerable trouble, and undoubtedly he would insist on paying for lunch, as well. Another small recompense for the treatment she had suffered this week.

She watched him give instructions over the telephone, her mind preoccupied with eliminating any feeling of attraction towards him. He was certainly well-proportioned for his height. But that didn't make him any more of a man than Paul. It simply emphasised his maleness and gave an impression of powerful virility. Which could easily be false. As for his face . . .

Rebecca forgot about assessing Slade Cordell's face. His eyes were wandering over her, and not in the same kind of cool, testing appraisal he had made before. Every female instinct she had started prickling with sensitivity as his gaze lingered on the firm thrust of her breasts, then roved slowly down the curve of her hips to the long line

of her legs, and even more slowly to the slim fineness of
her ankles before skating back up to her face. The blue
eyes reflected an intense inner satisfaction and Rebecca
burnt with the knowledge that he had just measured her
sexual appeal to himself and the answer he had come up
with was extremely positive.

Rebecca was suddenly assailed by a mental image of
what he might look like stripped of his ultra-civilised
tailoring. What it might be like if... Another wave of heat
raced through her veins as she clamped down on her
crazy imaginings. She couldn't really want that! Not since
the time of her engagement to Paul had she felt even a
glimmer of sexual desire for a man. On the other hand,
she hadn't met anyone quite like Slade Cordell.

Not that she would ever go to bed with him. He would
only use her for his own private pleasure. However,
Rebecca could not help wondering how good he was at
giving that kind of pleasure. Except for Paul she might
have been tempted. Even now... She put the thought
behind her. Utter madness.

She was going home this afternoon, away from New
York, away from Slade Cordell and his high-powered
business world. Nevertheless, it gave her a deep satisfaction to know that the attraction she was feeling was not
one-sided. Although it couldn't lead anywhere, the fact
that Slade Cordell found her desirable was a flattering
compliment to her femininity. A much nicer compliment than Emilio's reason for wanting the same thing.

Despite the fact that the Argentinian was twice
Rebecca's age, Emilio Dalvarez had enough arrogance in
his manliness to consider himself a suitable partner for
her. He hadn't spoken yet, hadn't made a single move,
but Rebecca was aware that he was considering it. There
had been the odd testing comment about Paul, the occasional remark about Wildjanna needing a man in
charge. Emilio would like very much to be in control of

Wildjanna. That would be far more important to him than having Rebecca share his bed. Whereas Slade Cordell...

He put down the telephone and started walking towards her.

Rebecca stiffened, appalled at the thought that he might have read her mind again. The way he had picked up on her thoughts before was positively uncanny. Embarrassment flooded through her, sharpened by a sense of disloyalty to the love that still bonded her to Paul.

There was a perceptive hesitation in his step, then he smoothly changed course, an affable smile breaking the intentness that had alarmed her. "Would you like me to close the curtains?" he asked with all the politeness of a considerate host. "Since you don't like the view," he added as Rebecca stared blankly at him.

"It doesn't matter. I'm going," she reminded him. And herself. This was his world and she wanted no part of it. Or him. This sexual speculation was a momentary aberration on both their parts. Quite clearly he had just dismissed it from his mind and she must dismiss it from hers.

"I'd like you to be comfortable while you're here. I've ordered lunch to be brought up," he informed her casually. "It saves us the bother of going to a restaurant and gives us more time to get to know each other better before we have to leave for the airport."

Rebecca's mind whirled into confusion again. "What do you mean, *we?* Are you taking me to the airport?" she asked, latching onto that point because the "getting to know each other" part was raising flutters in her stomach.

"As I said, I'm coming back to Australia with you. I'll make certain that the difficulties you have with Cordell Enterprises will be sorted out on the spot. I also wish to convey my gratitude personally to your grandmother, and pay my respects to her. She sounds just like someone else I used to know. I also want to apologise to her for all the worry my people have caused her.''

He was closing the curtains as he spoke, tossing the words out in a matter-of-fact tone. It was not often that Rebecca was struck speechless. She simply stared at him, unable to believe he actually meant what he said.

He turned to her with an ironic little smile that she couldn't read at all. ''You see, Miss Wilder,'' he said in his soft Texas drawl, ''there are people in this country who are just like yours. And we don't like to see cattle suffer, either.''

The shock of Slade Cordell's calmly spoken announcement was compounded by the realisation that he was completely serious. The slight smile on his lips was not echoed in his eyes. Those dark blue eyes held an intensity of purpose, a firmness of resolution that would allow nothing and no one to get in his way.

''That's very handsome of you, Mr. Cordell,'' Rebecca said dazedly. And even that was an understatement. For him to drop everything else to take a personal hand in sorting out a problem on the outermost perimeter of his business empire...

''Let's make it Slade,'' he said, and there was nothing unreadable about his smile this time. It was one hundred per cent charm—open, warm, friendly, appealing—demolishing at one stroke the barriers of culture, background, status and any other differences between them. Except the one elementary difference that he was a man and she was a woman. The smile did a fine job of emphasising that basic point.

''Are you called Rebecca, or do you prefer some shortened version of your name?'' he asked, pressing for the familiarity in a way that made rejection of it seem totally churlish.

"Rebecca," she replied, feeling hopelessly confused by what he was projecting. He wouldn't go so far, do something so extreme, just because he felt attracted to her, would he? "Surely it's inconveniencing you a great deal to break off your business to accompany me," she said in an attempt to probe his motives.

"This *is* my business," he returned softly. "And it inconvenienced you and your grandmother a great deal more to bring the matter to my attention, Rebecca."

"But . . ." She floundered under the disturbing intentness in his eyes. She couldn't really believe this concentrated interest in her. He couldn't really care about her. "My grandmother will welcome you," she finished limply, certain of nothing except that this was a result she had never envisaged in her list of possibilities.

"I'm counting on that," he said, and his eyes gleamed with a private satisfaction that suggested he had more on his mind than making peace. "Come. Sit down and relax," he invited, waving towards a conversational grouping of leather sofas. "I want to know a lot more about what I'm likely to meet at Devil's Elbow."

Rebecca accepted the invitation to sit down but she did not relax. He settled on the sofa facing her, but even with a table between them, Slade Cordell's strong presence aroused a tension in her that she couldn't dispel. She wasn't used to men like him, men who did as they liked and didn't count the cost. Perhaps that was an exaggeration. A person in his position had to calculate costs, but in this instance he had decided to disregard them. Or whatever it was he wanted was worth any cost at all.

"Have you had some personal involvement with cattle, Mr. Cordell?" she asked, forcing her mind onto business. It was difficult to suppress the treacherous feeling of excitement building from the thought that she would be seeing a lot more of this man.

He gave her a teasing little smile. "Am I so old to you that you can't bring yourself to call me Slade? Or have you thought of me as the enemy so long that it's impossible to accept the goodwill of a friendly overture?"

"Not at all," she countered quickly, anxious to hide the fact that her pulse was acting erratically. "Slade is fine." She managed an ironic smile. "My mind is a little slow in making the adjustment, but I assure you that any friendly overture is very definitely welcomed."

"I'm glad that's settled." He heaved a sigh and shot her a look that begged forgiveness. "I'm sorry you had to deal with Dan Petrie, but if it gives you any satisfaction, you nailed his coffin this morning. He's out. And he won't be the only one to go, either."

A grim look of resolution settled on his face. "I'm going to have to rejuvenate Cordell Enterprises. It's got top-heavy. When it starts spawning men like Dan Petrie . . ."

His business life was all so totally foreign to Rebecca. She lifted her gaze to the curtains that hid the view of his world. But it was there, just behind them. That was his reality. She shouldn't have let him close those curtains. Somehow it had shifted the ground between them, closing a distance that was really unbridgeable.

He brightened again, sending her a smile that bridged all distances. "I'm like you, Rebecca," he said, the blue eyes projecting an intimate understanding. "We share the doubtful honour of being the last of our line. Except I don't have a grandparent left alive."

He wasn't like her, Rebecca told herself fiercely, and he had no right to be suggesting he was, no right to stir feelings in her that suggested possibilities that were impossibilities.

"You aren't married?" she asked. There had to be some woman in his life. A man like him had to have any number of city women hanging around him, even if he wasn't married.

His smile gathered a touch of smugness. "No attachment at all," he replied.

"Why not?" Rebecca demanded. It was unreasonable for him to be still single, a man in his mid-thirties. It wasn't as if he had no choice over whom to marry. *He* wasn't being forced by circumstances into a limbo state of loneliness.

He shrugged. "Perhaps I haven't found a woman I'd care to keep at my side."

Her green eyes mocked such a contention. "You must be a very demanding man, then."

"Yes," he agreed, looking at her with flattering speculation, subtly challenging her to be the one he would want to keep at his side.

Rebecca mentally recoiled from the flirtation. He was playing a game with her. As he probably did with any woman whom he found passably attractive. Rebecca was not interested in that type of game. It was cynical and heartless, particularly since he knew as well as she did that their lives couldn't mix. An interesting little affair—that was what he was contemplating, wanting from her. He would never stand at her side or be there for her when she needed him to be.

"Don't you want children?" she asked, more to probe his character than from any personal interest.

"I don't have a dynastic urge. If I die without having children—" a look of sardonic weariness dragged over his features "—what the heck does it matter? There are more than enough children in this world to be fed and cared for without my adding to the overpopulation problem."

Rebecca made no comment. Whether he was really concerned about the children of the world she could not

tell, but he obviously didn't care about having children of
his own.

"You look sad," he said softly.

Rebecca flicked her gaze to his. He had been studying
her again. "I'm not like you, Slade," she said, wanting
to establish that fact in his mind as well as her own.

Children were important to her... another generation. Paul knew that. Paul—an anguished sense of loss
twisted through her. She had shared her dreams with him,
shared everything with him, things that Slade Cordell
would never know or value.

Their lunch arrived, wheeled in on a trolley. As far as
Rebecca was concerned, it came none too soon. Slade
Cordell was a dangerous man, dangerous to her sense of
right and wrong. While a table was being set with the
meal, she worked hard at getting her mind fixed in a
purely business mode.

Slade Cordell was accompanying her to Australia. She
had to ensure it was for one purpose only, to push the
necessary restraints onto the management at Devil's
Elbow. She and her grandmother would extend him every
courtesy warranted in the circumstances. That was it. If
he wanted more, that was his problem, not hers.

Logic, however, was a poor force against the big
American's attractions. Apart from his strong physical
impact, which seemed to get stronger by the minute, he
was most attentive to everything she said, and occasionally there were those flashes of charm that begged a response from her. Rebecca struggled to fight off their
treacherous effect.

After lunch they travelled to Kennedy Airport in a
stretch limousine. Rebecca appreciated the extra room in
the stately car. It meant she could put some seat distance
between her and the man next to her. She found his
physical closeness intensely disturbing.

At least she wouldn't be sitting with him on the flight, she assured herself. Her ticket was for economy class and she was absolutely certain that Slade Cordell would never fly that way.

However, when they arrived at the airport, Rebecca found that she had underestimated Slade Cordell's "arrangements" for her. Her ticket was exchanged for a first-class one, at the expense of Cordell Enterprises. She could hardly protest Slade's argument that they owed it to her. And much more besides. The cost of her trip to New York would be reimbursed. He regretted that he could not make up for all the time wasted and stress caused by misdirected employees of his organisation. His apologetic concern appeared to be so genuine that even Rebecca's pride in her own independence was disarmed.

He was subtly but relentlessly moving in on her. Rebecca knew it. Yet she didn't seem able to stop him. There was nothing overt—a smile, a courteous touch on her arm, every word to her perfectly straightforward—yet she was beginning to feel hunted by a very experienced hunter.

Slade steered her to the first-class lounge to await their flight call, and Rebecca took the opportunity to escape his disturbing presence for a while. Having reclaimed her smaller bag from the luggage that had been waiting to be checked through, she took advantage of the luxurious amenities of the ladies' room to change out of her good clothes and into a more comfortable travelling outfit.

The stretch jeans, white T-shirt and denim jacket she had set apart for this purpose might not look first-class, but the need to impress anyone was past as far as she was concerned. Practical and comfortable, she thought, and a far cry from the elegant sophistication that Slade Cordell would be used to in his women.

Having packed away the coral suit and its attendant finery, Rebecca stood in front of the vanity and unpinned her hair. The thick black mass of it tumbled down her back. She brushed it out, gathered it with her hands, then slid a hair-grip around it at the nape of her neck.

She examined her reflected image, wondering what Slade Cordell saw in her. She simply couldn't comprehend why he would go so far to make a conquest of any woman, let alone a woman with whom he had nothing in common. Surely she had to be imagining his personal interest in her. Yet there was something in those compelling blue eyes that kept telling her she was not being fanciful.

Rebecca did her best to shrug off the disturbing speculation. She was going home—home to Wildjanna—and she had done what she had come to do in New York. With more success than she had ever believed possible. She didn't want Slade Cordell to be attracted to her any more than she wanted to feel attracted to him. There was no future in it. None at all.

Having steeled herself to keep a firm distance between them, Rebecca returned to the lounge. She was surprised to see Slade had also changed his clothes for a more casual outfit, although the soft supple grey leather jacket, crisp white sports shirt and beautifully tailored grey trousers were a long way from being off-the-peg garments. Rebecca suspected he would cut an impressive figure even in the cheapest, shabbiest clothes procurable. When he stood up at her entrance, she had the craven wish that he was someone other than who he was, someone who had been born and bred to share her kind of life.

She avoided meeting those dark blue eyes that were far too perceptive for her liking. She would have sat down and picked up a magazine to pass the waiting time except he stepped forward and forestalled her, one hand lightly grasping her arm, its warmth and strength seeping through her jacket sleeve and forcing her to look at him.

The expression on his face was grim. He looked older than she had previously thought, as though his years suddenly sat heavily on him. And his eyes, why were they probing hers so anxiously?

"Rebecca, a message has just come through for you from your hotel," he said quietly, his voice low and strained.

Whether it was the change in his manner or the beginning of a terrible premonition, Rebecca didn't know, but she felt an odd tightening of her heart.

"A message from my grandmother?" she asked. Some new trouble, she thought. Had Emilio broken the agreement?

"No, it's not from your grandmother, Rebecca. It's to say..." He hesitated, torn between the desire to soften the news and the knowledge that he was the last person in the world who could soften it. "You'd better read it, Rebecca."

He lifted his other hand, offering her the slip of paper he had held out of sight until now. Rebecca almost snatched it from him, impatient to know whatever it was she had to know. Her eyes leapt to the top of the printed message, expecting to read of some urgent problem on Wildjanna but the letters spelled out other words, words that hammered into her heart and broke something there.

Your grandmother passed away this morning.

She stared at the flimsy sheet of paper, her mind reading its message over and over again as though what was spelled out had to change into something else if she kept studying it, but it didn't change, and her mind finally had to accept the impact that had already broken something in her heart. Broken something and let in a searing sense of loneliness, bereftness, as if her whole world had disappeared and she stood on a tiny pinnacle on top of a terrible void.

"Rebecca ..." The soft call of her name reached her from a far distance.

She slowly lifted her gaze and saw a man looking at her with deep concern. Slade Cordell, her mind registered sluggishly. Slade Cordell of Cordell Enterprises. Gran had entrusted her with the mission of telling him what he had to be told. And here she was in New York—this terrible, soulless place—so far away, a world away from all that meant anything to her. While she had been here running around in futile circles, Gran...Gran...

It was *his* fault. But for this man and his damnable organisation she would have been home where she belonged. The drought would have been just another drought to be weathered. Gran would not have been so pressured or driven to expend so much of her strength in holding the peace. It was no excuse that he didn't know what was going on. He should have known. Should have stopped it. It was too late to make amends now. Too late ...

Then the mantle of Janet Wilder settled on her granddaughter's shoulders. Rebecca's spine stiffened. Purpose and resolution hardened the green eyes. Pain, no matter how bad, had to be endured, put aside until there was time to work through it. No matter what the rights or wrongs of the situation, there was a tradition to be upheld. Wildjanna needed someone in control. There were things that had to be done.

Slade watched the emergence of Rebecca Wilder from deep shock with a sense of awe. He had watched the blood drain from her face, the frightening, trancelike state that had followed. He desperately wanted to reach out to her, to help, to comfort, but he knew that any such gesture from him could only be rejected.

Then the blind bitter hatred he had feared—and probably deserved—had flashed out at him, brief, intense and firmly suppressed. The recovery of the woman, the burning inner strength that rose out of the ashes of nothingness was little short of incredible for one as young as she.

In the boardroom he had thought she was a woman of remarkable mettle, but even that had been an underestimation of her character. There was an air of majesty about her now, of a queen mounting the throne for the first time, girding herself for the task ahead, whatever that entailed.

An eerie feeling of premonition crawled down Slade's spine. His intuition about Rebecca Wilder had been right. She was capable of anything. Anything! He hadn't fully realised that potential in her.

She had thrown out a challenge that had excited him, fired his blood. The way she had attacked Dan Petrie, the almost primitive savagery of her spirit, the magnificent disdain for all he himself represented . . . Slade had never met that before. Never! The urge to tame her, to win her surrender . . . that, he'd been certain, would be an experience worth having.

Now he wasn't sure if in winning what he wanted, he might also end up losing more than he won. Yet somehow there was an even greater fascination in going on. The extra barrier of her grandmother's death made it a lot harder, but no, he couldn't back away now. He didn't want to back away.

"You've read this?" she asked, her ageless face strikingly set in lines of unbreakable strength.

"Yes. I'm sorry, Rebecca." He knew she wouldn't want his sympathy, but what else could he say?

"We have run out of time," she stated, her eyes clear and steady and determined. "If you care about your cattle I suggest you get a message through to your people on Devil's Elbow straight away. Tell them to keep their herd away from Wildjanna until we get there. It won't hurt the cattle to go thirsty for a day or two.''

"That's no problem," he assured her. "But why the urgency? We'll be there—"

"Emilio will take revenge," she cut in. "That's his nature. He'll be looking for any excuse to start blasting at your cattle or your people."

The green eyes looked through him, seeing a past or a future that Slade had no part of. "Emilio Dalvarez revered my grandmother. She ruled Wildjanna. And in doing so, she commanded his respect and forbearance. Those checks are now gone and his outrage at your people will be immeasurably deepened. He will feel justified in taking matters into his own hands. Only I can stop him now, and it will be at least another day before I can get home."

"Rebecca . . ."

Her focus snapped to him. "My grandmother is dead, Slade. You caused it. Indirectly it may be, but you and your organisation caused it."

There was nothing Slade could say to that. He nodded mute agreement, wishing he could take her in his arms, wishing he could offer her some comfort. He didn't dare try. Certainly she had felt an attraction towards him, but he was back to being the enemy again. Only time would make up the ground he had lost.

"I'll go and give the order. Make it top priority. They'll get the word at Devil's Elbow," he promised her. There was nothing else he could say to Rebecca Wilder at this point, but he was going to say one hell of a lot to his own people. *One hell of a lot!*

Rebecca watched him go to a small annex of the lounge where there were a number of telephones and fax machines. The pain and grief she felt welled up inside her, but she clamped down on them again. This was not the time or the place. She could not allow any sign of weakness. The tears and the deep sense of loss would come later when it was private and she could bury herself in her misery. There were too many things to be done first, too many things that had to be decided.

Beyond the shock and inner grief was also one driving certainty. It was the inexorable law of the land. After death came the regeneration, the inevitable cycle of life. No matter what Paul could or could not do, what he would or would not do, the death of her grandmother changed everything. From deep down in her soul Rebecca Wilder dredged up the one fundamental elemental decision.

There would be a fourth generation at Wildjanna.

CHAPTER FOUR

THEY BOARDED THE PLANE at the scheduled time, but takeoff was delayed so long Rebecca grew increasingly fretful. She hated flying at the best of times, and this was certainly the worst. Apart from which she didn't like the look of the plane, either. The first-class compartment seemed small and cramped.

She closed her eyes, sick with nervous tension, sick at heart. If only she had done things differently, she could have been home sooner. She might have been able to do something for Gran, save her from dying, or at least been there to... to just be with her, to hold her hand and tell her all the unspoken heartfelt things that were taken so much for granted.

She shouldn't have let all those people at Cordell Enterprises give her the runaround for days on end. She should have.... But it was no use feeling guilty now. It was too late to change anything. She could no more go back in time than she could push this dreadful plane forward in time.

They finally started to move. The noise in the cabin increased. Rebecca shut her eyes tighter and prayed that they would lift safely off the ground. The plane was still shuddering when a warm hand curled over her clenched grip on the armrest.

"It's all right, Rebecca," came the soft reassurance from Slade Cordell. "We're off the ground and it's all systems go."

His concern, his kindness tapped into the weakness she was desperately trying to keep at bay. She felt tears prick her eyes and kept her lids shut until she could manage to force the tears back. She wanted someone to hold her hand, to share the burden that Gran's death left upon her shoulders, to comfort the awful aching loneliness. Slade Cordell's hand was strong . . . but it would soon be taken away. To start leaning on him in any way would only sap the will she had to find to carry on alone.

He didn't care about her. Not really. Perhaps some sympathy for her loss, but she didn't want his sympathy. She opened her eyes and flashed him a hard look. She didn't want anything from Slade Cordell except that he do what should have been done by Cordell Enterprises a long time ago. This whole trip had been so wasteful.

"I'll feel a lot better when we swap over to Qantas at Los Angeles," she said tersely. She hoped she didn't sound too xenophobic.

He nodded, smoothly removing his hand from hers. "And I guess you want to be with your own people."

She didn't want to give offence, and it was pointless to state that Qantas was the second-oldest airline in the world, with the best safety record in the world. The last time there had been a serious accident was in 1947.

His mouth twisted into an apologetic grimace. "I guess you haven't had much reason to like anything American."

Rebecca felt a twinge of guilt at her manner towards him. For whatever reason he had chosen to do it, he was going to be on hand to solve the worst problem she had to face. She had to be grateful for that large mercy.

"I wouldn't make a blanket judgement from this trip," she said flatly. Then, because she wasn't ready to cope with any idle conversation, she turned away from him to stare out the window.

They had to fly across the continent of North America. Rebecca had no doubt that somewhere down there were people she would like, people who shared the same values as herself. In fact, most of the Americans she had met were very likeable. They were friendly, warm, hospitable people, extremely courteous and helpful—except those who had been ordered not to be helpful, and that wouldn't have been their fault.

No, she had no prejudice against Americans, only against those who worshipped at the shrine of the almighty dollar, and people like that could be found in every nation of the world. She had met plenty of Australians who were contaminated with the same disease.

The hours passed slowly. Rebecca rejected the meal offered to her. A movie was shown but she didn't bother with the earphones. There was no escape from the devastating reality of her grandmother's death. The picture on the screen was meaningless.

A continuous stream of passengers got up to use the telephones fixed to the cabin walls across from the galley. Rebecca wondered whom they were calling—business contacts, friends, family? I'm the last of our line now, she thought desolately. Just like Slade Cordell. But unlike him, she couldn't and wouldn't let it stay that way. Wildjanna demanded continuation. Too much of her family's lifeblood had been poured into it to let it fall into other hands.

Slade made no further attempt at conversation, perhaps recognising that there was nothing he could say or do. She appreciated his tact in remaining silent. It surprised her that he was sensitive to her feelings. Then she remembered how he had seemed to read her mind and realised that he was more perceptive than most people. It wasn't that he cared. He simply knew when to push and when not to push. She supposed that was one of the qualities a man had to have to head an organisation as vast as Cordell Enterprises.

Certainly, if he did have any designs on her personally, he knew this was not the time to push them. He was, after all, virtually a stranger. Not even a friend. Yet oddly enough, she was glad he was sitting next to her. Strong silent company was better than no company at all while she endured this long flight home. She knew she had his support, although she suspected there was a price to be paid for it . . . if he had his way.

They were held up again on the tarmac at Los Angeles, but at least this time they were sitting in the extended luxury cabin of a Boeing 747 and Rebecca was more philosophical about the delay. The first-class accommodation was more spacious on this larger plane, the seats more comfortable, the service more attentive, and she couldn't help feeling a gratified pride in the Australian national airline.

However, there were still another fifteen hours of flying to get through. It seemed to take forever before they left Los Angeles behind and headed out over the Pacific Ocean. Rebecca was about to wave away the offer of another meal but Slade interjected this time.

"You'll feel better—you'll sleep better—if you eat something, Rebecca. At least try it," he advised.

She privately acknowledged he had a valid point, so she forced herself to eat as much as she could, although she had little appetite for the fine food set before her. Afterwards she did feel better. She was even more grateful to Slade for the first-class seat since it allowed her to stretch out and rest comfortably. She slept for the rest of the way to Hawaii, and for the last leg of the flight to Brisbane.

She did not stir until the announcement that breakfast would shortly be served. They had crossed the international date line, which meant they had lost all of

Saturday, and it would be early Sunday morning when they arrived in Brisbane. Already Rebecca's biological clock was misfunctioning. She felt drained, tired and listless. It was more than likely shock had something to do with it, she reasoned, but the thought did nothing to revive her.

As she rose to go to the washroom to freshen up she noticed that Slade Cordell was clean-shaven and obviously ready to face the day ahead of them. She gave him a stiff little nod in response to his soft inquiry if she wanted a wake-up coffee. It was waiting for her when she returned to her seat and she sipped it gratefully.

"Rebecca, I don't want to distress you, but..." He looked searchingly into her eyes, looking for acceptance and finding it, although it was given with wary reservation.

"What do you want to say, Slade?"

He lifted an open hand in an appealing gesture. "I've organised a light aircraft at Brisbane Airport to fly me to Devil's Elbow. I don't know if you've made other travelling arrangements, but I thought, if you accompanied me, we could get things straightened out as soon as we arrive," he said persuasively.

The plan had been for her to take Monday's mail plane to get home, but that was no longer practical under the present emergency. An appreciative little smile hovered on her lips. When Slade Cordell moved, he certainly moved with efficient effectiveness. He was looking after her needs in a way that she wished... But it wasn't because he cared, Rebecca told herself sternly. It was simply his way of doing things. Control. Authority. A man used to being in command of himself and others. In deferring to her opinion, he was simply being tactful to suit the circumstances.

Rebecca nodded her consent. "Thank you. That will suit me fine."

"About your grandmother..." Slade hesitated, seeing the smile disappear and the sharp recoil in her eyes. He was wary of giving any offence. "I just thought...are there any arrangements I can make?"

She shook her head, poignantly aware of the medical and legal procedures that would already be in place. As with Pa, the flying padre would bring Gran back home to be buried on Wildjanna.

"We look after our own," she said simply.

There was a pattern to her life—a pattern to the land—that even Slade Cordell's power and authority couldn't touch. The thought of him confronting the Australian outback gave Rebecca a certain grim satisfaction. He would find her world as alien to him as she had found his. There he would be reduced to the same level as everyone else—a man who had to accept the terms the land forced upon him.

She wondered how he would stand up to it, then decided his stay would be so brief that it would not constitute anything more than a different experience. He could never be the one to stand at her side. For all his aura of being an invincible conqueror, he simply didn't know... what she knew.

An hour later the plane touched down on Australian soil. Rebecca was again grateful for the advantage of being a first-class passenger. She and Slade were among the first to disembark, and they moved through the arrival gates without having to queue. Their luggage appeared on the carousel at the second rotation, and again there was no queueing to get past the customs people. They were through the whole arrival process in half the time Rebecca had anticipated.

She was not expecting anyone to meet her. Her whole focus was on getting to Wildjanna. Slade was paged from the inquiries desk. As they moved in that direction, Rebecca's eye caught a wheelchair coming towards her.

That something broken in her heart savaged her again.
She couldn't bear to look at the occupant, to be reminded...

"Rebecca."

Paul's voice. Paul! She turned incredulously. Slade
Cordell was instantly forgotten. Her eyes fastened on the
face of the man to whom she had pledged her love, and
clung with a bittersweet mixture of despair and hope. It
had been a year since she had seen him, a year of dark
yearning for things to be different. But he had come to be
with her now, come for her in her time of need.

"Paul..." Her voice was a bare husky croak, shriven
by turbulent emotions that had burst from her control.

His sun-streaked hair had darkened from being in-
doors instead of where he belonged. His handsome face
was thinner, marked by suffering that he shared with no
one. The warm brown eyes were filled with painful compassion.

Rebecca moved towards him without a thought for the
man she left without a look or a word. Her hand slid into
the hand outstretched to her and gripped tight. Tears
blurred her eyes.

"You know about Gran?" she whispered.

"Milly called me," he answered quietly.

That was the housekeeper who had served her grandmother since before Rebecca was born, who had seen the
growth of the relationship between her and Paul, who
had shared its tragic outcome and wept over it with her.

"Your grandmother was a great lady, Rebecca. I know
how much you'll miss her. How much she meant to you.
I'm so sorry."

That was Paul, considering only her, never himself.
"Paul—" she swallowed hard, fighting to get some
steadiness back in her voice "—marry me, Paul. Please,
marry me. Reconsider..."

The flash of deep inner anguish she saw in his eyes silenced the words that still trembled on her tongue, aching to be said.

"No!" His thumb kneaded the back of her hand. "I realise you're tired, Rebecca. Overwrought..."

"It's not that! It's not!" She fell to her knees beside him, openly begging as she forced out the words that had to be spoken. "I need you now. Like I've never needed you before."

"No...no..." His head jerked away then snapped back again, his eyes as agonised as hers yet burning with fevered resolution. "It's not my life any more, Rebecca. You have to accept that."

"I need you, Paul," she pleaded.

"Rebecca..." He spoke her name as though it embodied the whole loss of every promise there had ever been, echoing into an irrecoverable past. He reached out his other hand and gently smudged away the tears that had spilled from her lashes. "I'll always be here for you when you need me, but I'll never marry you. Please understand that, Rebecca. Never."

Her mind sought frantically for some other way to reach past the barrier of his making, not hers. It wasn't fair! It wasn't right! She shook her head in helpless denial of what was happening to her.

"Don't look back, Rebecca," Paul said quietly. His hand slid down to her chin and tilted her face up to his. "Now, more than ever, you must look forward. You know you can always count on me to stand by you as a friend."

A friend! Rebecca bit her lips. She didn't want him as a friend. She wanted, needed to have him beside her always. Why couldn't he see that?

She stared past him blindly, still inwardly fighting Paul's edict. It came as a sickening jolt when she real-

ised that Slade Cordell was staring at her, his vivid blue
eyes ablaze with a stomach-twisting hunger.

Rebecca wrenched her gaze from his and struggled to
her feet, torn between the mortifying thought that Slade
had seen the baring of her soul and her need for Paul to
respond to it. Yet when she looked at Paul again, she
knew she had lost him. He had himself completely in
control, his eyes steady with purpose, his chin set with
determination.

"Milly also told me about the problem you're having
with Cordell Enterprises, Rebecca," he said earnestly.
"Don't worry about them. I'll put together a battery of
lawyers that will keep them in legal tangles for years to
come."

"No, Paul. I'm getting that problem sorted out." She
didn't want to introduce Slade to Paul. Somehow it didn't
seem right. Paul might look at Slade and see . . . Rebecca
wasn't sure what it was he would see, but Slade Cordell
was so much a man that it might make Paul feel less. And
that was wrong.

"I can help you financially, Rebecca," Paul assured
her. "I'm doing really well now. I can afford it. For the
first time last year our profits exceeded ten million dollars. We're going after the big time and we're going to get
it. . . ."

Money! What did money matter? Her eyes stabbed one
last desperate appeal. "Marry me, Paul, and come back
to Wildjanna!"

His gaze returned hers with resolute steadiness. "I've
got a new life. I know it's not yours, Rebecca. And yours
isn't mine any more. You are what you are, a worthy
successor to your grandmother," he said firmly, decisively. "You have a path to follow. That's given to very
few people in this world. I wish you well." He squeezed
her hand. "If you want me to come with you to
Wildjanna, to see you through . . ."

"No." That was too hard to accept, half a loaf that was no loaf at all. "I'll manage, Paul. I'm glad to hear you're doing so well. And thank you for coming to see me."

"That's what friends are for," he said softly.

"Yes. We're only friends," she whispered in painful resignation. He didn't love her. Not as she needed to be loved. He couldn't turn away from her now, when she so desperately needed him at her side, if he truly loved her. He had been separating himself from her ever since the accident, forging his new life without her, refusing to let her come to him.

"Always friends," he promised firmly. "Do you have some form of transport waiting for you?"

"Yes."

He nodded. "If there's anything I can do, call me."

"Thank you."

"Take care, Rebecca."

"You too, Paul."

She gave his hand a quick squeeze then turned away, walking blindly to Slade Cordell and the future that Paul would never share. He could have done it, if he'd wanted to enough. It simply didn't suit him any more. A different life, a different life.... The words hammered through Rebecca's heart.

She felt betrayed.

This was her darkest hour of need. She had been there at the hospital for Paul, offering him everything she was in his darkest hour of need. He had rejected her then and he had rejected her now. He hadn't been self-sacrificing at all in relinquishing his claim on her. It was Rebecca he had sacrificed, to follow a course that would fulfil his new needs. All this time, three years, and she had been yearning for something that was gone, that had never really been.

She had no one. No one but herself. She had to carry on alone.

"Does your friend need any assistance?" Slade asked, frowning over her shoulder.

"No." Rebecca did not look back. She knew that Paul would already be directing the wheelchair out of the airport terminal. A car, especially adjusted for the handicapped, would be waiting for him. He took pride in being totally independent.

She turned bleak, empty eyes to Slade Cordell. "There is a limit to what you can do with money."

It couldn't buy love. It couldn't mend what was irreparable. It couldn't buy back what was forever gone.

Gran was gone from her life.

Paul would only ever be a friend on the perimeter of her real existence.

That existence had begun and would end with Wildjanna. She had a path to follow and nothing—no one—was ever going to change that. It was imprinted too deeply on her soul. Paul had wanted to share it before the accident. He had said he loved her. But he couldn't have, Rebecca finally realised. Not deep-down love. Not life-commitment love. Because nothing should have changed. Just because he couldn't do what he had done before, he had sought a different life without her.

"You are what you are, Rebecca..." and he didn't want what she was any more.

A wave of tortured emotion swept through her, draining her of all strength. A hand clutched her arm as she swayed from faintness, a strong hand, giving her enough support to recollect herself.

"Would you like to sit? We'll have a coffee before—"

"No!" She forced herself to meet the concern in Slade Cordell's eyes. Temporary concern. It sickened her further because she needed so much more. So much, and

Slade wouldn't give it any more than Paul would. "We have to move on!" she said grimly.

Don't look back, Rebecca. You must look forward.

"Are you sure?"

"Yes. I'm sure."

You have a path to follow...

CHAPTER FIVE

SLADE'S ADMIRATION for Rebecca Wilder's strength of character was mixed with an even deeper frustration. He had felt acutely envious of that man in the wheelchair. The way their hands had gripped, the sharing of emotion that Slade himself had been excluded from. Not that he could expect anything else. Rebecca Wilder had no reason to like him, let alone...

He tried to shrug off the feelings she was stirring in him. He had to get her on the plane that was waiting for them, get her home. It was a hell of a thing to have happened, her grandmother dying at such a time.

He had known that terrible feeling of bereftness when Grandfather Logan had died, the sense of loss, of a void that could never be filled by anyone else. It took time to get over it, time Slade knew he didn't have. But he would make it. Somehow he would get over that hurdle. And every other hurdle, too!

He held onto Rebecca's arm as he led her out of the international terminal and signalled a taxi. Despite the fire of resolution in her eyes, she looked so pale and withdrawn that Slade didn't want to remove this minimal support. He was relieved that she didn't spurn it, yet it disturbed him that she no longer seemed to have any awareness of him.

She certainly had passion. He had been right about that. Although he hadn't liked seeing the intense naked emotion that had been drawn from her by that man in the wheelchair. Slade wanted to ask her about him. It was difficult to restrain the urge to find out where the man fitted into her life. But he had no doubt such personal questions would not be welcomed. Not right now, anyway.

He settled her in the taxi and gave instructions to the driver. It was only a matter of minutes before they were delivered to the section of the airport that handled light aircraft. The chartered pilot was waiting for them as arranged. After introducing himself he took charge of their luggage and led them to a six-seater plane, which had the stylish lines of a recent model.

A Piper Navajo, the pilot informed Slade, as he cheerfully stowed the luggage on board through a cargo door. He was obviously a talkative guy, and after the long silence Slade had maintained with Rebecca, it was something of a relief to chat innocuously with a friendly person.

Rebecca had completely withdrawn inside herself. Sensitive to her need for privacy, Slade once again quelled his mounting frustration and accepted the pilot's invitation to sit beside him in the cockpit. Perhaps after a couple of hours in the air Rebecca might submit to a conversation with him, but he was wary of pressing his company on her until he saw some chance of her accepting it.

That man in the wheelchair had hurt her. She had taken it on the chin and risen above it, but she had definitely been hurt. Slade fiercely wanted to fill the bleak emptiness he had seen in her eyes with something positive—positive towards him—but there could be no forcing anything from Rebecca Wilder. Anything he got from her would be hard won. Slade had no delusions about that. But he wasn't giving up.

"Have you ever flown to Devil's Elbow before?" he asked the pilot as they lifted off the tarmac.

"Never landed there, but I've been over it a few times." He threw Slade a friendly grin. "We get a fair few tourists who want to have a look at outback stations. The Channel Country is a good place to show them. The sheer size of those properties always boggles their minds. Thousands of square miles, homesteads that look like small towns..."

"Have you got a map that I can follow as we fly?" Slade was interested to know more about this country that had given birth to a woman like Rebecca Wilder.

"Sure thing!" The pilot happily complied.

The map was old and deeply creased and somewhat grubby. Slade spread it out and the pilot pointed out various features.

"First we go over the Great Dividing Range, then across the Darling Downs—best grazing lands in the world when we're not in drought—*they* sure need rain pretty bad right now." He dragged his finger across to the south-west corner of Queensland. "Here's Devil's Elbow. We've got a few hours' flying ahead of us."

Slade looked down at the tiny print that located his property, then found Wildjanna to the north of it. "Devil's Elbow was renamed Logan's Run four years ago," he said in ironic comment.

"Is that a fact?" The pilot looked surprised. "Well, I guess I'll just stick to the old name. It's got more local colour. See how the creek on it bends like an elbow? That's Windy Drop-Down Creek. For some geological reason the creek bed drops to a much deeper level on the adjoining property, and the water just dries up on Devil's Elbow when a big drought hits. But I guess you know all about that?"

"Yep. The situation is pretty bad," Slade agreed. "And I'm going to fix it."

He glanced at Rebecca but she was not listening to them. She was closed into some tight inner world that was hers and hers alone. The strange thing was, Slade reflected, she continually made him feel he was missing out on something terribly important. He didn't like the feeling of rejection she gave him.

What the heck, he thought, I'm going to change that. Whatever it takes, I'll do it!

Having reaffirmed that resolution, Slade turned his attention to watching the Australian landscape unfold below them. The populous coastal region was very quickly left behind, and once over the mountains, the country changed dramatically. Vast rolling plains stretched endlessly, and the sheer distance between townships surprised him. The further inland they went, the fewer signs of civilisation there were, and so much of the land seemed completely untamed by man. Signs of the long drought were everywhere, red earth bare of vegetation, scrubby trees more grey than green.

It was alien to any landscape Slade had seen before. Somehow it seemed imbued with an ancient timelessness and it was easy to imagine that it had not changed an iota since primitive man walked the earth. And primitive woman. He glanced at Rebecca. Perhaps that was the quality in her that tugged on something in his own soul. Untamed and elemental. Whatever it was, he wanted to explore it.

The pilot recalled his attention, pointing to a herd of kangaroos. "Pests to the graziers, particularly in times such as these. They've got to be culled to survive."

Slade watched them leap across the ground in a graceful flowing lope that held him fascinated. They were such a unique animal. "It seems such a shame," he protested.

"Nothing that can be done about it," the pilot said noncommittally. "It's a law of the land."

Slade repressed a feeling of horror. He hated killing of any kind. It seemed such a revocation of the very spirit of existence. Yet in a land like this, perhaps it did come down to the most primitive law of all, the law of survival. Was that why Rebecca Wilder was the way she was? Did that deep inner strength come from the continual fight to survive?

He looked at the kangaroos and wondered if the pilot was truly right when he said nothing could be done. Perhaps something could be done. Or was that thought the product of ingrained years of civilised living? He was a long, long way from New York. Did civilisation have any meaning at all here, in this country that Rebecca Wilder called home?

Slade was still musing on this idea when the pilot said, "There's a landmark coming up. That's Windy Drop-Down. And... Holy hell! What's going on down there?"

Slade saw it, too. A mob of cattle, the leaders standing up to their knees in water, the rest pressing forward, sprawling out behind, trying to get their drink. He saw one, two, three, four, five topple over and sink to their haunches. And it was not through weakness. They were being stopped dead by bullets!

Rebecca was suddenly between him and the pilot. She'd seen it, too. Slade felt a queasiness pass through his stomach. He knew without a doubt that these were his cattle, and they were infringing on her water rights. Even the horror of the killing going on could not outstrip the terrible sinking sensation that it was his fault. He couldn't bring himself to look at Rebecca.

"Pilot, get this plane down!" Her order was curt, imperative.

"It's not all that good a landing place."

"There's killing going on down there," she said tersely. "And it could get a lot worse before it gets better. I intend to stop it. Just get this plane down, pilot."

"Do as she says," Slade put in quickly, adding his support to Rebecca's command.

"Okay, lady. If that's what you want."

"And buzz them before you land."

"How low do you want me to go?"

"Clip their hair!"

"Right-oh!"

The pilot banked the plane and screamed towards the trouble area, levelling off only inches from the ground. Rebecca didn't even flinch. Without fear, Slade thought. She is completely without fear. Slade concentrated on giving nothing of his inner turmoil away. She's the one who hates flying, he thought. She should have been shaking in fear as they sped over the low contours of the ground, over a line of riflemen spread along the bank of the creek.

Slade saw more cattle being hit, their blood reddening the water. This was more terrible than he could conceive. But there was no sign of recoil from Rebecca Wilder.

"Put it down," she commanded in a steely voice.

"Where?"

"Close."

"Lady, far be it from me to advise you, but do you know what you're doing?"

"This is *my* land, pilot," she said fiercely. "And I will rule it!"

"Right! Fair enough! You'd better belt yourself in your seat, then. I don't guarantee a smooth ride."

Slade gritted his teeth. Back in New York—was it only yesterday?—he had idly thought he wanted an adventure. Landing a plane on rough ground and facing up to live bullets did not constitute his heart's desire. In fact, his heart was doing a lot of protesting. Along with his stomach. But a burst of adrenalin insisted that Rebecca Wilder was not about to find him wanting, not on her territory or any territory. It was a challenge to his manhood, and no way was Slade going to have his manhood diminished in the eyes of this woman.

The little plane shook as it bumped in its touchdown. It shook a lot more before it finally came to a halt. Slade heaved a very shaky sigh of relief and turned to Rebecca, who was already out of her seat.

"Open the door!" she called to the pilot.

It galvanised Slade into action. "Rebecca, you stay here. I'll go and sort this out."

"No way! I'm—"

He grabbed her arm to stop her. "You could get shot!"

The green eyes flashed scorn at him. "They wouldn't dare!" She tore her arm out of his grasp and leapt out of the plane.

He followed fast on her heels, driven by an overwhelming sense of urgency. He had to stop her, save her, protect her. "Rebecca!"

"You go and sort your lot out!" she threw at him contemptuously. "I'll deal with Emilio."

She sprinted off before he could begin to argue. She didn't even look back to see what he was doing.

I didn't intend to be a hero, Slade thought, but it looks as if I'm going to have to be one. He could hear the desultory crack of the rifles and felt dazed with disbelief. But it *was* happening! He shook himself into action and started making for the creek, chasing after Rebecca Wilder.

The soil was sandy and heavy going. Rebecca was running lithely over it, he noticed. Trainers on her feet. He was wearing the wrong darned shoes. He lifted his feet faster and moved into a better-paced jog.

He grinned. This was certifiable madness. If the executives Rebecca had faced in the boardroom could see him now. No wonder she had said they lived in a little eyrie high above the real world. If this was her world, New York would seem as unreal to her as this was to him!

I hope these gunslingers don't take me for a cow, he thought. The image of the man in the wheelchair flashed across his mind. What kind of courage could this girl inspire that you could risk ending up like that? Slade didn't know. All he knew was that he couldn't turn back, not even on that sobering thought. Wherever she went, he had to go. Or he'd never be able to look at himself in a mirror again!

He spotted the head of a man bobbing along above the bank of the creek. Slade quickened his pace. Rebecca still wasn't within his reach but he reckoned he could just about tackle her to the ground if some gun-happy cowhand started blasting his rifle in their direction. He almost hoped they would. He wanted to feel her body under his, to hold her, to stamp his domination on her.

The cattle, his cattle, were clearing away from the other side, panicked out of their thirst by the gunfire. He saw stockmen trying to round them up, bullwhips cracking around them. He started rehearsing the few choice words he was going to say to them when he got the chance!

Rebecca reached the edge of the bank, took up a belligerent stance and raised both arms in the air. "Cease your fire!" she yelled in a voice that roared command. "Emilio! Wherever you are, you'd better show yourself fast! This is my land! And don't let even one of your men forget it!"

"Hold your fire!" came the shout from farther along the creek.

Slade had just pulled to a halt at Rebecca's shoulder and those echoing words sounded pretty good to him. She set off striding towards the answering shout, completely ignoring him. Slade marched alongside her, determined on bolstering whatever argument she intended to put to Emilio, but uncomfortably aware that he would be regarded as the enemy until proven otherwise.

"You keep out of this, Slade!" Rebecca snapped at him as a group of men made their appearance some twenty yards away. "One word out of place and you're liable to get your head blown off. Just keep in the background until I'm ready to introduce you."

It made sense. He didn't like it, but reason insisted he should have some modicum of sense in this madness he had so recklessly embraced. He slackened his pace, letting her take the lead.

A tall, rangy man strode from the group to meet her. He swept off his hat as Rebecca took a confrontationist stand. His face was deeply tanned and weathered, his black hair liberally peppered with grey. Slade assessed his age at close to fifty but his lean hard physique wore none of the softness of civilisation. A tough adversary, Slade figured, feeling the fierce authority emanating from every inch of Emilio Dalvarez.

The hand holding the hat lifted to sweep accusingly at the other side of the creek. "They killed your grandmother!" he said in vehement tones.

"Killing cattle will not bring my grandmother back," Rebecca retorted just as vehemently. No backward step from her! Straight into counterattack! "It's the last thing she would have wanted, Emilio! And you know it!"

"They killed her!" he shouted in violent justification.

Slade's heart squeezed tight. Surely to God Emilio Dalvarez didn't mean murder. He couldn't mean . . .

"You think she would be dead if they hadn't kept pushing her beyond all reason?" Emilio argued passionately. "You think her heart would have given out if it wasn't stressed beyond bearing?" His other hand lifted with a clenched fist. "I tell you, Rebecca, they have to be stopped!"

Slade felt almost dizzy with relief. A heart attack had taken Rebecca's grandmother. He forgot Rebecca's instructions and stepped forward. "They will be stopped!

I give you my word on that, Mr. Dalvarez. Within a week, the herd on Devil's Elbow will be reduced to whatever numbers both you and Miss Wilder consider reasonable."

Emilio Dalvarez looked him up and down in studied contempt. "Who is this man?" he demanded.

Rebecca shot Slade a furious look before addressing her fiery neighbour. "You know why I went to New York, Emilio. You know it was my grandmother's wish that our problems with Cordell Enterprises be settled peacefully. And that is precisely what is going to happen, Emilio. This man is Slade Cordell himself, come to make amends for all the trouble his organisation has caused."

Emilio stared at Slade with narrowed eyes, measuring him again and not particularly liking what he saw.

"I regret to be making your acquaintance under such strained circumstances, Mr. Dalvarez," Slade said, resolved to clear the air as much as he could. "But I can assure you that I do deliver what I promise."

Emilio's mouth curled in cynical dismissal as he stared at Rebecca. "You believe him after all that's happened?"

"He's here, Emilio," she pointed out strongly. "If Mr. Cordell hasn't done what he claims he intends to do within a week, I'll review the situation. Meanwhile, I've come home to bury my grandmother."

She paused.

Emilio looked discomfited. "A great loss to you, Rebecca. A great loss to all of us," he asserted gruffly.

"Call your men off, Emilio. Take them home."

He shot Slade a hostile glare but the aura of violence he had carried to this confrontation had been appreciatively dimmed. "In respect for your grandmother, I will do as you say, Rebecca."

He jammed his hat on, swung on his heel and marched towards his men. Rebecca muttered something indecipherable under her breath, then, without even a cursory glance at Slade, she set off towards the plane. Slade quickly fell into step beside her.

"You said you'd send a message to your people," she bit out accusingly.

"I did! I don't know what went wrong, but I'm sure as heck going to find out," he assured her grimly.

Mistrust glittered in her eyes. "Your cattle should not have been there, Slade. It's your responsibility to get those carcasses out of my creek. And I want it done today."

"If I have to drag them out myself, it'll be done."

She said no more. She didn't have to say any more. Slade figured he was about as low as a rattlesnake in her estimation. So far all his words had been about as empty as a rattle, and it was well past time they gained a bit of substance. He had to make up the ground he had lost with her as fast as he could.

"Everything okay?" the pilot called to them as they neared the plane.

"It will be. When we get to Devil's Elbow," Slade replied darkly.

Rebecca said nothing until she was about to board the plane. Then she gave the pilot a tight little smile. "Thank you. That was a fine bit a flying."

The pilot grinned. "Oh, nothing like a bit of excitement to liven up a day! You're welcome, miss."

He was obviously as mad as everyone else out here, Slade thought. Maybe it was catching.

Rebecca nodded and climbed into the cabin. Slade resignedly strapped himself into the seat beside the pilot. No way was he going to win Brownie points by sitting next to Rebecca. She was one very tough lady. He wished he had known her grandmother.

It was a bumpy takeoff but Slade didn't care about bumps any more. What were a few bumps after what he had already been through? Oddly enough he was beginning to enjoy the feeling.

Whatever he made of the future, one thing was certain. He would make Rebecca Wilder concede to him if it was the last darned thing he did! The scorn in those glittering green eyes was going to change to something else before she saw the last of him!

CHAPTER SIX

FOR REBECCA, the next seven days seemed to pass by in a dream. She carried out all that was necessary with automatic authority, never once faltering in the role she had inherited on her grandmother's death. Everyone who lived and worked on Wildjanna was assured that nothing was going to change. The pattern of the past would continue into the future, a foundation on which to build. Only Rebecca knew how empty that future felt to her.

It was Sunday again. The mid-morning sun beat down relentlessly from a cloudless blue sky. The land was dry and parched, and what little grass remained was brown and brittle. The water in the creek was gradually creeping down to lower and lower levels. Would it last as long as they would need it?

Rebecca looked at the pitiless clear sky and knew the drought was not going to break today. She strolled slowly around the wide verandahs that skirted the whole homestead. Almost every room in the house opened onto them, but she had no desire to seek the cooler air closeted inside the wooden walls. As far as the eye could see in any direction, the land belonged to her, to Wildjanna. Normally she would have been filled with the pride of possession, the deep rich sense of belonging, but somehow that feeling evaded her.

She paused on the western verandah, looking out at the small family graveyard, trying to refire the purpose for which she had been born. In some strange way she felt detached from Wildjanna. It slowly came to her that this was caused by the aching sense of loneliness, the inner craving for a companion to love, and to be loved back. That unsatisfied yearning inside her was like a fog drifting between her and the solid realities of her life here.

Rebecca tried assuring herself that it was probably a weakness that time would eradicate. Losing Gran, facing up to the crushing of all hope with Paul... It had only been seven days, a week. A week in which Slade Cordell had certainly delivered what he had promised.

Rebecca's thoughts turned to the big Texan who had categorically proved he was as good as his word. He had laid all scepticism to rest from the moment he had first confronted the management at Devil's Elbow with their failure to carry out his direct order concerning the cattle. It was then discovered that, as a final act of revenge, Mr. Petrie had sabotaged the order sent from the head office in New York. Instead of "Keep all stock from watering at Wildjanna," the message had read, "Keep stock watering at Wildjanna."

Slade's ice-cold fury had been too awesome not to be believed, and the quiet steely authority that had characterised his leadership in the Manhattan boardroom had the men at Devil's Elbow shaking in their boots. He had demanded immediate action and there had been action aplenty at Devil's Elbow over the past seven days.

The carcasses of the dead cattle had been removed by tractors and buried by a bulldozer. From Monday there had been a steady stream of cattle trucks coming and going, shifting the excess stock to a glutted market. The price Slade received was abysmal, but he had sold without any regard for the cost to himself.

And Rebecca had to admire the way he had handled Emilio Dalvarez. It had been a master stroke of diplomacy to ask for Emilio's advice on station management, stock levels and on the sinking of artesian bores to the

water basin that lay deep beneath the Channel Country.
The bores were an expensive business, drilling through
layers of rock, and sometimes the subterranean water
tapped contained too`many minerals to be used for wa-
tering stock, but Slade was apparently intent on not
sparing any expense in implementing solutions to the
problems caused by the drought.

Established as chief adviser, the Argentinian's pride
had been well and truly salved. He had even reported to
Rebecca that Slade Cordell was a man of sense who saw
what had to be done and did it. Sanity at last prevailed.

Rebecca knew she should be relieved that the crisis was
over. And of course she was. Not only did it reduce the
problems caused by the drought to a manageable level,
but it meant Slade Cordell would soon be on his way
back to New York. And out of her life.

Better he go as soon as possible. He stirred needs and
desires that he would never answer, certainly not in any
permanent sense. The way he had stood by her side at her
grandmother's funeral, assuming the role of supporting
consort, looking after her…it was wrong. It should have
been Paul holding her arm, seeing that she had refreshments, finding a chair for her to sit down. It should have
been a man who truly cared about her, not one who only
wanted to get into bed with her.

That was what Slade wanted. He hadn't tried to hide
it from her. Every time she had met those compelling blue
eyes, she had felt it. He had somehow made her feel it, an
unwilling physical attraction that he would exploit if she
showed any response to it. But for the circumstances, he
might have acted a lot differently. As it was, he had been
sensitive enough to realise what an emotion-laden day it
was, and he had taken his leave without pressing her for
anything. She had not seen him since. Which was fine
by her!

She didn't want to see him. Slade Cordell was no answer to her personal needs. More likely than not he was planning his return to New York right now. There was no point in even thinking about him.

She stepped off the verandah and walked to the small burial ground where two generations of her family had been laid to rest. The picket fence that protected it had been freshly painted, one of the first orders Rebecca had given on arriving home. She opened the gate and stepped inside, seeking some solace for her miserable discontent.

The graves were all marked by headstones except for Gran's. A temporary wooden cross stood at the head of the newly turned earth. It would soon be replaced by a more fitting memorial for the matriarch of the family—the matriarch of Wildjanna.

Rebecca knelt to pick up a handful of loose soil. She watched it trickle through her fingers. The sands of time moved relentlessly on. She was twenty-six years old. At that age Gran had already given birth to her first son.

Emilio Dalvarez's manner towards her at the funeral had set Rebecca's teeth on edge. He had been altogether too gallant. It was obvious that when he considered a decent interval had passed, he intended to offer himself as a husband and partner. She was a young woman, in need of his manly advice and protection.

Rebecca wanted a fourth generation, but not through Emilio Dalvarez. Yet to have a child of her own, a child to love... If he gave her that, would it be worth overlooking the rest? Everything within her recoiled from accepting Emilio. He would take over any child she bore him, fighting her to assert his own kind of upbringing. If it was a daughter, he would expect her to do woman's work. If it was a son, he would do his utmost to mould him into his own image. Either way, the chances were that the child would become more a Dalvarez than a Wilder. Or be torn by the conflict between both parents.

No, Rebecca knew in her heart that she had to find some other answer. If only she could find someone like Slade Cordell to stand by her side for the rest of her life, to give her the children she wanted for Wildjanna...

A shadow fell across her grandmother's grave. Rebecca looked up. Her heart skipped a beat as she recognised the man who made the picket fence seem like an insubstantial barrier. The dark blue eyes begged her tolerance.

"Please forgive the intrusion," Slade said quietly. "I called at the house. Mrs. Hartigan thought you should be wearing a hat out here. So I—" he held out the wide-brimmed Akubra that Milly had given him to deliver personally to Rebecca "—hope you don't mind."

She straightened up, an ironic little smile hovering on her lips as she stepped forward to take the hat. "Milly's been fussing over me all week," she explained. "It's her way of...coping with things."

He cleared his throat. "I came to see you. To invite you to carry out an inspection of Logan's, er, Devil's Elbow. I hope that what I've done will meet your expectations."

"I'll take your word for it, Slade," she said, more in apology for her former mistrust than in rejection of his offer. "I'm sure you've done everything that's necessary."

He looked disappointed, vexed by her dismissal. "I'm going home in a few days," he said flatly. "I don't have much choice. There are a lot of loose ends I've got to fix up in New York. And a lot of people depending on me making the right decision at the right time."

It was what she had expected. It was patently absurd for her to feel deflated by the news that he was actually going back to his life in New York. Yet somehow it made her feel even more lonely. Nevertheless, even though Slade had nursed an ulterior motive for coming to Australia with her, he had been more than generous in his actions and with his time, so she dredged up a smile and aimed it fairly at him.

"I wish to thank you for all the trouble you've taken to get things sorted out."

He stared at her smile as if dazed by it. He took a deep breath and dragged his eyes back to hers. "Rebecca." He said her name in a soft yearning throb that seemed to curl around her heart and squeeze it tight.

Strong animal magnetism, her mind screamed. That was all it was. And he *was* going, leaving her world and returning to his city life. There could never be anything between them. Words spilled off her tongue in pure defence against the turmoil he was evoking inside her.

"It was good of you to come halfway across the world...and be here at this time. The integrity you've shown...your kindness and diplomacy...I'm sorry for my manner towards you at the beginning. Meeting you, knowing you has been the one pleasant thing that's come out of this mess. You've honoured all your promises and I deeply appreciate the way you've done it."

Her gaze fluttered down to the open-necked V of his shirt, denying the naked desire in his eyes. His broad chest rose and fell under the thin cotton.

"Rebecca!" he rasped, frustration gravelling over something like desperation. Then in one long passionate outburst he swept restraint aside. "Rebecca, you are the most *tantalising* woman I've ever met. Things between us would have been so different if events hadn't happened as they have. I know this is the wrong time and the wrong place, and you probably still blame me for your grandmother's death, so I'm the wrong man as well as everything else, but I don't know what more I can say, what more I can do..." His breath hissed out in a long ragged sigh.

"I don't blame you for Gran's death, Slade," Rebecca said quietly. She forced her gaze up to meet his, anxious to stop what he was clearly going to say, flinching at the raw wanting that glittered down at her. "Things couldn't have been different. You're the wrong man anyway," she said bluntly. "So it's best if we simply say goodbye and get on with our own lives."

"Give us the chance to get to know each other," he argued.

His voice was soft but his eyes were determined. There was not going to be any avoiding of what was on his mind, what was pulsing from him . . . and reaching her in debilitating waves. Rebecca stiffened her spine. She might feel weak but there was no way she would act weak. Her mouth curled into a deliberate taunt.

"Desire, Slade. Is that what you mean?"

His eyes bored at her with demanding intensity. "It's been there from our first meeting, Rebecca. Riveting, twisting, knotting sexual attraction. Call it desire if you like. But if you're honest, you'll admit it got to you, too."

Her chin lifted in angry pride. "All right. I admit you have a certain attraction for me. That changes nothing. I see no future in it. I'll never give in to it."

She turned away, wishing the subject had never been raised. It hurt. This whole scene hurt. She heard the gate creak. "No!" she cried, even as his hand fell on her shoulder.

"You're no frightened little wimp, Rebecca." He swung her around to face him, his eyes ablaze with purpose. "There's a steel in you that even I find daunting. And exciting. You don't run away from anything. When you want something, you go for it. And you want *me*. So don't evade the issue by talking about a future that neither of us can see right now."

The sheer force of his challenge punched through Rebecca's sense of discretion. Shaken by the physical power of his closeness, she broke away from him, stepped back and vehemently swung an arm out to encompass Wildjanna.

"This is my future! These are the graves on which it is built. This is my heritage. And the heritage of my children. Where do you fit, Slade?"

"Don't rule me out, Rebecca. You judged me once before, remember? And you were wrong!"

She shook her head and deliberately moved to the head of her grandmother's grave. She laid her hand on the top of the wooden cross. "You'll never be to me what Pa was to Gran. That goes beyond desire, Slade. It's the deepest commitment a man and woman can give to each other. A sharing of far more than bodies. I might have had that with Paul. Never with you."

"Why Paul?" Slade picked up instantly, demandingly, the challenge he projected in no way diminished. "Why not me?"

Hot colour flared into her cheeks. Her eyes defied him and the strong sexuality he emitted. "Because Paul Neilsen belonged here. He loved this land before..." Tears blurred her eyes. She swallowed hard, forcing down the lump of desolation that choked her throat. "You saw him at the airport. We were to be married...but he won't marry me now."

Resentment welled up in her as Slade simply stood there in grim silence, absorbing her words without comment, so blatantly virile that it hurt unbearably.

"You're the first man I've felt anything for since Paul's accident. It's been a year since... It's a physical thing that's beyond my control," she bit out angrily. "But I wouldn't go to bed with you to slake some sexual frustration, Slade. I'd make love with you for only one purpose, and that purpose would be to have a child."

The words had simply spilled out of the turmoil that had been going through her mind. Whether or not it was a mistake to have voiced them, it was impossible to determine. Somehow Rebecca felt cleansed, as though the very act of getting everything out into the open wiped away the grounds for Slade to persist in his desire for a brief fling with her.

Slade Cordell's face could have been carved from marble, totally inscrutable. "That's why there can never be anything between us," she said with decisive finality. "That's why I'll always reject you. I want more than you're prepared to give me."

Slowly his expression changed. The muscles around his mouth tightened. His eyes glittered. "Why tell me this, Rebecca? Why didn't you just use me? Why spurn me physically, when with the slightest little encouragement, and without me being any the wiser, you could have got me to serve your purpose?" he asked, his voice deep with dangerous undercurrents.

She gave a harsh little laugh, needing to break the tension that flowed from him. Her eyes filled with bitter mockery aimed at both of them.

"Perhaps I'm not as ruthless as you, Slade. To use someone to fulfil a need, use them intimately…and walk away afterwards. Perhaps I hope I'll find someone who'll fulfil all my needs, and who'll stand at my side for the rest of my life. Not for just a day. Or a night."

His dark blue eyes seemed to pierce her heart. Then his gaze lifted and swept out over Wildjanna. He turned away and walked slowly to the other end of the small graveyard. He stood there, his back rigid, his head tilted up, silent and totally motionless for several long, nerve-tearing minutes.

Rebecca watched him with glazed eyes, unable to bring herself to do or say anything. What he was contemplating she had no idea. She could hardly believe she had said as much as she had. The words had been torn from her very soul, and they had probably wounded his male pride, yet the truth was the truth no matter how unpalatable it was to him and his desires.

Paul had forced her to see the truth seven days ago. It put a stop to futile dreaming. Slade Cordell should thank her for not wasting any more of his time. He might feel frustrated about not getting what he wanted, but that would soon pass when he went back to his life in New York.

He turned and began to walk to her, pausing every couple of steps to read the headstones on the graves; her little brother, mother, father, uncle and finally Pa, who had carved out a life that had meaning to him, who had founded a family that would always have solid roots in a solid world.

Desire to fulfil his own needs was all it was with Slade, Rebecca thought dully. Yet when he lifted his gaze, and his vivid blue eyes locked onto hers, it was not desire but determination that burned from them.

"You want a child," he stated in that quiet voice that sliced to the heart of any issue. "I presume that's why Paul Neilsen won't marry you. Because he can no longer give you one."

It wasn't true. But pride held Rebecca's tongue. Slade had seen her on her knees, begging Paul to marry her. It was too humiliating to let him know the truth of Paul's rejection. It was less galling for Slade to believe that the man to whom she had given her love and loyalty had considered her needs above his own.

He was waiting for a reply. She stared back steadily and said, "That's none of your business, Slade."

A look of derision flitted over his face. His disturbingly direct gaze dropped to her grandmother's grave, lifted to the top of the wooden cross where Rebecca's hand still rested, her fingers almost white from the tight grip she had on it. His face seemed to sharpen, a conflict of interests warring across it, but when he lifted his eyes to hers again, they held a hard, relentless gleam.

"Don't you ever get lonely, Rebecca?" he asked in a soft insidious drawl that wound around her brittle defences.

"Perhaps that's why I want a child," she replied tersely, unable to deny what he so clearly perceived.

"Exactly." He bit out the word, then started walking slowly towards her, continuing to speak in that soft Texas drawl, his eyes holding hers in challenge. "Doesn't it seem wasteful to you to turn me away when I'm right here on your doorstep? On your own admission you find me attractive enough to consider the possibility of having a child by me. So why not take this opportunity, Rebecca? Why not go for what you want?"

He halted a bare half-step away from her. One hand lifted to cup her cheek, his thumb lightly caressing her tilted chin. Rebecca was so mesmerised by his words that she didn't even think to evade his touch.

"What's to stop you now?" he taunted softly. "I'm available, willing and able. And you won't be ruthlessly using me. I'm offering. The only thing preventing you from having the marriage you want with Paul Neilsen is the unfortunate fact that he can't provide you with the fourth generation for Wildjanna. If you become pregnant by me, you can go to him again, can't you? You can have it all, Rebecca. A child, the man you love, the future you want. All you have to do is take me first."

She stared at him incredulously. He was offering to father a child, and then to make no claim on it whatsoever! She could have a child of his to keep as her own. A fourth generation for Wildjanna. A child that might take after him, strong and indomitable, a worthy heir to a line of pioneers.

Slade's logic was falsely based, but every instinct Rebecca had was screaming that life didn't work by logic, anyway. The temptation he offered kept worming its way through her mind. His child . . . her child. She could not wrench her eyes from the hypnotic challenge in his. She could feel her heart hammering wildly against her chest. Her mouth had gone completely dry. She knew she should somehow deny all he said, but she could not find the will to take that critical step away from him.

"There are turning points in our lives where we are given a choice," he continued persuasively. "From that choice you can either forge your own destiny or be a cipher to the will of others. So much of what can be achieved is in the timing. You can tell me to go . . . or ask me to stay. Make your choice, Rebecca."

The web of temptation he had woven so powerfully clung around Rebecca's mind, making any clear thought impossible. Except what he offered had to be wrong. His whole argument was centred on her wants, her needs, the fulfilment of her future. What about him?

She remembered her strong impression of him in his New York office. Not a man of impulse, but a man who calculated every move. The question that had hovered in her mind then at last found voice.

"What do you get out of it, Slade?" she accused more than asked, and was mortified to hear her voice shaking.

He smiled, a slow smile that churned her stomach into knots. "I get to have you, Rebecca." The desire was back, simmering in his eyes. "That's what I want," he added unnecessarily.

Rebecca once again felt a treacherous warmth spreading through her. How he could evoke this response in her she didn't understand. She hardly knew the man. She didn't love him. Couldn't love him. In some ways he was totally alien to her. Yet she couldn't quite bring herself to turn her back on what he was offering.

"Is that all you want, Slade? Just to have me? You won't mind walking away afterwards?" she asked, torn

by the feeling that if she gave herself to him, it might not
be all that easy to see him walk away from her. There was
something irresistible about Slade Cordell, something
that made her feel he made his mark on everything he
touched. A permanent mark. She knew that if she gave
in to him she would hurt for the rest of her life.

"I'll go when you want me to go," he stated unequivocally. "You have my word on that. I won't linger around
if I'm not welcome."

What if she didn't want him to go? What if...? But the
situation forbade her to ask those questions. They were
too cold, too calculating. *Just for once, think with your
feelings, your emotions,* Rebecca urged herself. For
however short a time it might be, he would fill the emptiness and she wouldn't be alone. And if he left her with
a child, she would never be alone again. A child fathered by him...

Of course he would inevitably return to his life in New
York. That was too obvious to question. He had a vast
organisation to run, thousands of employees whose live-
lihoods were linked to his leadership. What he was offering her was a brief encounter that was supposed to satisfy
both of them. There was no hope of him staying with her.
No hope...

Perhaps he saw the uncertainties raging in her eyes.
Perhaps he wasn't sure that the seduction of words would
be enough. The hand that had been warmly curved
around her cheek suddenly shifted, softly raking through
the hair above her ear. There was a touch on her waist but
she didn't have time to think about that. His head was
bending towards hers. Rebecca raised a hand, which
fluttered ineffectually against the broad chest that was
moving closer, but she did nothing at all to evade the kiss.
Her lips tingled sharply as his mouth brushed softly over
hers, warm flesh against flesh.

It had been so long since Rebecca had been kissed that for the first few seconds she submitted to the contact with almost clinical detachment. Then the tantalising caress changed to a slow sensual pressure that sent tiny waves of sensation rippling through her whole body. Rebecca wasn't conscious of dropping her hat so that she could lift both hands to his shoulders. It was an instinctive reaction to what was happening to her, what Slade was making happen with a seductive expertise that coaxed her lips into tremulously parting. She felt his tongue tease the tip of hers, then in one smooth sweep of his arm he gathered her in against the pulsing heat and strength and power of his body.

An overwhelming awareness of his masculinity flooded through her. She wanted what he offered. The power of sexual attraction, so long denied, exploded into chaotic reality. She made a tiny sound of approval deep in her throat, and as if it was a sign that Slade had been waiting for, his tongue lashed over hers in movements that shocked her with their knowing intimacy, shocked and excited her in ways she had never before experienced, and desire was no longer a mental image or a disturbing feeling, but a tide of mounting sensation that was an intense physical need for fulfilment. The quick arousal of his body in response to hers gave her a wild wanton pleasure and a thrill of power. He held her hard against him as he moved his mouth to whisper in her ear.

"Ask me to stay, Rebecca." The words slid seductively across her mind while his tongue traced her ear, making her tingle at the sheer eroticism of the caress. "Ask me to stay," he murmured.

She said nothing, and Slade held her more firmly, his mouth meeting hers again and again, his warm breath fanning the flames in her cheeks, his hands caressing and moulding her closer to him, beguiling her more totally with every kiss and touch.

Again he said, "Ask me to stay."

Rebecca dimly realised that this was the end of the road. If she said no or remained silent any longer, he would take himself away from her and go back to New York. The choice had been offered. She had to make it.

CHAPTER SEVEN

REBECCA NEEDED what Slade offered her, needed it far more than he could ever know. For the moment, she was totally uncaring of where it might lead, as long as Slade stayed with her now.

"Yes," she conceded.

His hands stilled. She felt his chest expand. A long breath wavered through her hair. Slowly, very slowly, he eased himself back from her and lifted his hands to her face. Rebecca wasn't sure she wanted to open her eyes, to see what was written in his, but she had made her decision, given her word, and there was no evading any of the consequences.

She lifted her lashes, ready to meet a blaze of triumphant satisfaction, but the expression in the dark blue eyes was far more complex than that—an oddly poignant mixture of relief and appeal and a deep wanting that was yet to be satisfied.

"Let me take you away where we can be alone together," he said huskily. "And let it be for only you and me, Rebecca. Babies are for the future, not the here and now. There's so little time. I'll delay going back to New York as long as possible, but it can only be a week at most. You could leave Wildjanna for a week, couldn't you? Everything's running smoothly. Just a week, Rebecca. Just for us. Because of what we can be together."

Somehow his argument sounded twisted up, but as Rebecca took in the ramifications of what she was about to do, she realised it would be better if they did go away. Milly would probably be scandalised if they remained at the homestead, and Slade's staying with her—or her with him—would inevitably give rise to the kind of speculation she didn't want to answer. Not yet.

If she became pregnant there would inevitably be talk to contend with, but she would face that when and if it happened. And finally, since this brief encounter was all she would have of Slade Cordell, she didn't want the time wasted on anything else.

"Where?" she asked.

His smile made Rebecca feel distinctly light-headed. "We hold some real estate on a place called Forty-Mile Beach. It's within easy driving distance from Brisbane. There's a cottage we can use. Completely private. No close neighbours. It sounds like the kind of place I want to be with you."

It posed no problems as far as Rebecca was concerned. She had a weird sense of unreality about the seeming casualness of what she had agreed to. Yet her inner acceptance that there was no turning back from it was strangely beyond question.

"That's fine," she said cautiously, aware that she shouldn't allow Slade to make all the rules. She had seen his dominant personality at work and could not deny its power on herself. She could not afford to fall victim to it in any lasting sense. A week out of her life. Then she was on her own again.

He stroked her cheeks as though she was as delicate and precious as porcelain china. "I'll look after you the best I can, Rebecca."

It would be so easy to become putty in his hands, Rebecca thought. It was an effort to produce a dry little smile. "I don't need looking after, Slade. What I'm doing is dangerous...for me. I figure you're about as deadly as any man can get. I don't want to pay too much for the pleasure of knowing you.''

His face tightened into serious concern. "You won't get hurt, Rebecca, I promise you. I will look after you... And you're not to even think of having a baby...yet. Just give us time, Rebecca, so that we can both assess where we are and where we're going. You need to consider more deeply this matter of having a child."

An anxious note crept into his voice as he rushed on. "It's not easy being a single parent. A lot of people do it now, I know, but I feel there's got to be a better way than that. Whatever you can give a child at Wildjanna, and I admit there are natural advantages here, there will still be problems. Single parents have twice as much to do, twice the normal responsibilities..."

Single parent? Why was he suddenly assuming that outcome when he had argued she could use his child to get Paul to change his mind about marrying her? Not that she would...or could. But Slade certainly seemed to be backtracking, leaving Paul right out of her future.

"That choice is mine, Slade," Rebecca cut in, impatient with such unexpected scruples, which ran completely counter to the offer he had made. In any event, whether she had a baby or not was her decision and she would work out her problems her own way.

Slade took a deep breath, then spoke slowly, as though gingerly feeling his way. "We can only be together for a week this time, Rebecca, but I'll be back. I haven't finished with Devil's Elbow. There are things I want to do here. Which I *will* do as soon as I can make the organisational changes I need to make in New York. When I return—it will be in a few months—if you've really thought it all through and still want to have our child, we'll do it together."

A treacherous thrill raced through Rebecca, chasing the thought that this week would not be all she would ever have of Slade Cordell, and perhaps a much deeper relationship would become possible.

His hands slid down to grasp her arms and he spoke with urgent intensity. "Promise me, Rebecca, that you will leave the decision until then."

Another thought slid into her mind—a cold heart-twisting thought—what if he never came back?

In the four years Cordell Enterprises had owned Devil's Elbow, Slade had not had enough personal interest in it to even pay the vast property a flying visit. She couldn't imagine this past week had changed that attitude. It was quite plain now that he had come here because of her, and once his desire for her was appeased, it was far more likely that he would become submerged in his other interests again. It would be stupid to fool herself into believing he would ever change his life for her... or for the child he might father.

A gentle squeeze on her arm heightened his already strong physical claim on her. "You won't come back to New York with me, will you? You won't leave what you have here to be with me?"

A lifetime in that city, one of the biggest cities in the world? Rebecca's recoil from the idea was instantaneous and obvious.

Slade's mouth twisted in self-mockery. "No, I thought not."

She could not change her life, either. That was the reality. No matter what Slade made her feel—what he felt—after this week they would inevitably part to follow their own destinies.

"But I will return, Rebecca," Slade said softly, reminding her once again of his uncanny ability to pick up on her thoughts. "Don't doubt that."

She forced a smile. "One step at a time, Slade. I might change my mind about a lot of things by the end of our week together. As to when you return here, no doubt we'll both have had time to think more, and be sure of what we want."

Relief and satisfaction spread into his responding smile. "It will be a good week, Rebecca," he declared confidently, accepting her words as the promise he had demanded of her.

They were no such thing.

Going with him now was the first step. Rebecca was planning a great many more steps as she led him to the house.

Slade Cordell had already served one vital purpose. He had cast off the fog that had been drifting around her mind since Gran had died. Her life had meaning again, and her future path was suddenly very clear.

There was the children's project that she and Gran had discussed so often. That would most certainly become a reality, she silently promised her grandmother. And she would start on the new dam, which would become the lake they had envisaged. That would have to be done before the drought broke. The genetic breeding programme could wait a while, but there was much to be accomplished before she gave birth to a child, the child that Slade Cordell had offered her, the child she would have if the law of nature followed its inevitable course.

Rebecca now knew where she was heading and what she had to do.

The trip to Forty-Mile Beach was organised with what Rebecca was coming to recognise as Slade Cordell's forceful efficiency. A few calls made from Wildjanna and everything was set in motion. Her own arrangements were relatively simple. She told Milly she was going to Brisbane with Slade to settle some business, left instructions for her top station hand, packed a bag with the clothes she would need and made her departure. A plane was waiting at Devil's Elbow by the time they arrived there. A car was waiting at Brisbane Airport to take them the rest of the way.

It was early evening by the time they reached the cottage, a typical Queenslander structure built of clapboard with an iron roof and verandahs running all around it. Rebecca had no idea when it had come into the possession of Cordell Enterprises, but both the white-painted cottage and the grounds around it were well maintained.

A high hedge of hibiscus trees provided privacy from any passersby, except from the beach front. Clumps of palm trees added their tropical touch, and the sweet scent of frangipani trees in full bloom wafted on the air. A rather patchy but neatly cut lawn spread to the white sand that stretched around the coastline for as far as the eye could see in either direction.

The interior of the cottage was designed for casual living. The kitchen, dining and lounging areas were arranged in an open plan, taking full advantage of the beach view provided by a wall of glass doors. There was a large bathroom between two bedrooms. Slade carried their bags into the more spacious bedroom facing the sea. Rebecca noticed that the bed had been made up with fresh linen and clean towels had been laid out. The kitchen had also been fully provisioned, although to save the bother of cooking a meal tonight they had stopped along the way to buy fried chicken and salads.

As a lovers' hideaway, the whole place could not have been more ideal, but now they were here, Rebecca felt intensely awkward about the situation. Throughout the whole trip Slade had kept plying her with questions about her life, her family history, the various difficulties that had been overcome in establishing Wildjanna. His avid interest in knowing all she would tell him had not left her much time to think about how she would feel once they were alone like this. With Paul, nothing had ever really been calculated or planned. Lovemaking had been a natural progression of their feelings for each other. She simply did not know how to act with Slade. He was almost a stranger!

Afraid that he would perceive her inner tension, and inwardly cringing from appearing gauche to this sophisticated man of the world, Rebecca used the pretence of viewing everything there was to see before unpacking. She strolled out through the living room, opened one of the glass doors, crossed the wide verandah and leaned on the railing, ostensibly to breathe in the fresh invigorating smell of the ocean.

Part of her mind accused her of utter madness for making this choice. She was going to be hurt. It was inevitable. Because she did want more from Slade than he could or would ever give her. Another part argued that she had made the only pragmatic choice.

Her social world was very limited. She might never meet anyone she wanted to share her life with. The only man she had been attracted to since Paul was Slade. At least she would have a child, the child of a man she would have accepted as a mate if he had been born to her world.

She heard Slade step out onto the verandah. Rebecca hoped she looked relaxed as he joined her at the railing. She was intensely aware of him standing beside her, so aware that her skin prickled at his nearness and her pulse quickened to a wildly ragged tempo.

"There are very few places left in the world where one can enjoy something like this," he commented appreciatively. "There are no beaches, even in Hawaii, that could match what we have here. This has to be the best I've ever seen. To have an unpolluted seacoast that's not sur-

rounded by high-rises and cluttered with people, just un-
spoiled nature at its best . . .''

Rebecca slid him an ironic smile. "I guess it's not going to stay that way. Your company wouldn't have bought
this property for the purpose of conservation."

"No. I dare say it didn't. But now that I've seen it,
well, I like it the way it is. It would be a shame to spoil it
in any way at all. I'll keep that in mind when I do an investigation of all Dan Petrie's dealings." His brow
creased in concern as he searched her eyes intently. "If
you don't like it here, Rebecca, we can move somewhere
else. Anywhere. Any time."

"It's fine, Slade. Truly!" she asserted, surprised that
he should doubt her appreciation of the location.

He smiled his relief. "I just want you to be happy with
me. If there's anything—"

"I know. You'll wave your magic wand and it will be
done," she mocked lightly.

"It's not quite that simple!"

On that sighed comment, he turned her towards him,
gently drawing her into his embrace. She could not restrain an involuntary shiver as his hand stroked down her
back. Whether it was from apprehension or excitement
she wasn't sure. It was difficult to think straight with
Slade holding her close to him. She wanted, needed him
to kiss her again, to make her forget that she didn't really know him or love him. His mouth brushed warmly
over her temples and she tilted her face to his, but he did
no more than meet her eyes with a look that was strained
with repressed desire.

"I'm not going to rush you into bed, Rebecca," he said
softly. "I meant what I said about getting to know each
other. That's as important to me—more so—than any
other satisfaction might be. There's no hurry. You can
take your time. Nothing will happen until you're ready."

She stared at him, confused by a sense of disappointment and surprise at his sensitivity. She had thought him calculating and ruthless, yet he had shown tactful consideration towards her on the trip home from New York. As he was doing now. As he had done on the day of her grandmother's funeral. She decided that nothing about Slade Cordell could be taken for granted. He was indeed a very complex man, not easy to read at all.

"You said what you wanted was to have me, Slade," she reminded him questioningly.

"I will. When you're ready."

"I'm ready. As ready as I'm ever going to be," she insisted, willing her voice to remain perfectly steady and holding his gaze without the slightest flinch. The truth was she didn't want to get to know Slade Cordell too deeply. She was quite sure it was better not to. When it came time for the parting of the ways...

"You have no fear of anything, have you?" he said in a wondering, bemused tone of voice, and the admiration in his eyes emboldened her to take the next step.

She reached up and slid her hands over his powerful shoulders, around his neck. "You're not exactly a coward yourself, Slade." A wild streak of pride made her add, "I'm going to make certain this is as big an adventure for you as it is for me."

The sibilant expulsion of his breath fanned the hair at her temples. She felt the knot of tension in his body. Then he was crushing her to him, swinging her off her feet, moving with urgent purpose to the bedroom. He came to an abrupt halt at the foot of the bed, his chest heaving as he slowly set Rebecca on her feet. His face clearly bore the conflict of needs churning through his mind.

"Rebecca, are you organised for this?" he rasped. "Do you want me to take care of...?"

"I'm organised," she assured him quickly, letting him interpret that any way he liked. She spun away from him before he asked any more questions, pulling her shirt over her head as she walked towards a chair near the windows on the other side of the bed, hoping that the action would distract him from thinking any more about contraception.

It was clear to her that it wouldn't sit easily on Slade's conscience to return to his own life if he left her carrying his child. He did not want the responsibility of any consequences from what he desired of her. He wanted to walk free, and she would let him, but she was not about to be cheated of the choice he had given her. She *was* organised for that choice. Slade might or might not come back to Devil's Elbow. There was no guarantee that he would still desire her if he did. She had this week, and it was all she could really count on.

With her mind feverishly justifying her actions, Rebecca stripped herself completely naked. She tossed each garment on the chair with a deliberate abandonment that denied any nervousness over what she was doing. Only when she had nothing else to remove did she pause to work up courage for the next step. She had to turn around and she didn't know what Slade was doing, what he was thinking. She had never stood naked in front of a man before, not even Paul.

But this was different, she argued to herself. What was about to take place with Slade was an act of nature, not of passion. It was a continuation of the life cycle natural to all living creatures since time began.

Even as Rebecca told herself that, her hands instinctively lifted to undo the hair-clip at the nape of her neck. It joined the pile of clothes on the chair. She used her fingers to rake out the thick curtain of her long black hair, then only just resisted the impulse to pull it forward over her breasts. That would be a sign of weakness. She had made her choice.

She steeled herself with pride and purpose and turned to face the man she had chosen to be the father of her child, the man who would give her the fourth generation for Wildjanna.

CHAPTER EIGHT

SLADE HAD NOT MOVED. He still stood, as though struck to stone, precisely where she had left him. He was staring at her with an expression of dazed incredulity. If Rebecca didn't know better she'd have thought he had never seen a woman naked before.

She had no idea of how she looked to him. She thought her body was as feminine as most although she carried no excess flesh. Paul had once said she had perfect breasts, full and firm and beautifully shaped just for him. But that was lovers' talk. Her waist was naturally trim, emphasising the womanly curve of her hips. Her long legs were probably more muscular than those of women who led more sedentary lives, but they suited her well enough. She began to worry if she had turned Slade off by acting on her own instead of letting him take the initiative.

"Is something wrong?" she asked.

"No." The word came out huskily. He shook his head as though needing to clear it. She saw his throat work in a convulsive swallow. Even so, his next words sounded gravelly. "I've never met a woman like you before. No one remotely like you. Just...don't move, Rebecca. I want to look at you. I want to hold this image of you in my mind forever because I'll never see its like again."

His words, the admiring way he said them, sent a rush of prickling heat over her skin. "How long am I to stand before you like this before you're ready?" she mocked.

He was making her too conscious of her nakedness, and she hadn't come with him simply to be looked at.

His mouth curved into a bemused little smile as he slowly lifted his hands to begin unbuttoning his shirt. "You don't even realise how unique, how magnificent you are. I don't know what it is... What draws me so strongly... Perhaps that wild unreachable quality about you. All I know at this moment is that you make me feel privileged just to look at you. That may sound crazy to you...."

He took off his shirt, and Rebecca was instantly distracted by the strong maleness of his powerful physique—the breadth of his shoulders, the impressive delineation of muscles that had certainly never suffered from his supposedly sedentary occupation. He had the look of a formidable athlete in top condition, and Rebecca couldn't help wondering how he managed to stay so fit. Suddenly it didn't seem at all crazy to simply want to look at a person. She wanted to look at him.

"Whatever the reason—" his hands moved to unzip his jeans "—this is not something I want to hurry over."

She had given him time to think, Rebecca realised. The desire that had surged through him on the verandah was now under control, forged to his will. She had a few moments of panic as she wondered what he meant to do with her. But the end was the same, she hastily reassured herself. The means didn't matter.

"I want you, Rebecca," he said softly.

She wrenched her gaze up to meet his, her heart fluttering wildly at the thought of their coming together. She remembered how it had been with Paul and felt a painful stab of disloyalty to the love they had shared. But Paul had betrayed that love. Not she. And she couldn't deny the surge of arousal in her own body as Slade began walking towards her.

"I want more than a simple meeting of flesh with flesh," he said, his voice husky with a yearning that knotted her stomach. "I want to reach that unreachable part of you that keeps its own counsel. I want to know all the inner secrets of your soul. I want the whole essence of you, Rebecca Wilder, not just the substance." He stroked feather-light fingertips from her throat to the deep valley between her breasts. "I want to touch . . . more than your skin."

He wanted too much, much too much! Every self-protective instinct Rebecca had was shrieking in protest at the surrender he wanted from her. She couldn't give it to him. She couldn't let him take that much from her. It would make her too vulnerable to him, and when he went away . . .

Rebecca didn't stop to reason it out. All she knew was that what Slade intended was dangerous to her and she had to take the initiative of this act of intimacy away from him before he entwined her too deeply into his needs. She reached out, provocatively sliding her hands down his tautly muscled thighs.

"Don't make me wait, Slade," she said invitingly, her eyes open mirrors of her need for him. She moved, bringing herself into contact with the potent thrust of his body, the tips of her breasts brushing against his chest.

She felt the uncontrollable tremor that ran through him, knew he was strained to the limit of his will-power. "Kiss me?" she asked, needing to be submerged in the mindless passion he had evoked in her before.

He groaned her name in half-protest at her impatience, but the sound was stifled as his mouth crashed onto hers. There was no persuasive sensuality in the driving force of his passion to possess, and completely reckless in her desire to finish what had been started, Rebecca responded with an uninhibited wildness that she had not known herself capable of.

What followed was a savage kind of madness, like some primitive battle for supremacy that knew no boundaries. Slade's hands raked down her back, closed around the curved firmness of her buttocks and lifted her into more intimate pressure with his sexuality. Rebecca wound her legs around his thighs, enticing him to satisfy both of them. He swung around, tore his mouth from hers and strode for the bed, kneeling on it, kneeling over her as he laid her head on the pillows.

"No!" he breathed hoarsely, his eyes glittering into hers. "You won't have your way with me, Rebecca! I'll have more than that!"

He wrenched her hands from around his neck and pinned them above her head, silencing any protest she might have made with another plundering kiss, which she returned with all the violence of rebellion against his will. She used her feet to stroke the sensitive hollows at the backs of his knees. She arched her body to his, using all her feminine sexuality to deny him any control at all.

He was so strong, she had to be strong, too, as wilful as he was. Yet when he pushed himself down her body and his mouth closed over the sensitised peak of her breast, drawing on it with exquisite delicacy, she could not stop herself from crying out at the sweet agony-pleasure that pierced through her. Only then did he release her, freeing his hands to caress her into convulsive shivers of mindless pleasure.

And Rebecca gave up trying to fight him, trying to fight what he was doing to her. Her body seemed almost like an alien thing to her, producing reactions and responses and revelling in incredible waves of sensation, which drowned any coherent thought at all. Her arms felt heavy and drained of all strength. Her thighs quivered with uncontrollable excitement. She did not even know that her hands clutched Slade's head as he wrought this wild chaos inside her. She did not hear herself plead for the fulfilment of the craving that had built to an intolerable peak of expectancy.

But she saw his face when he moved to answer her need and knew that he had been caught up in the same sensual storm that raged through her. His eyes glittered with a feverish light. A harsh guttural sound of unbearable wanting broke from his lips as he drove himself deep within her. Rebecca arched up in a convulsive paroxysm of intense pleasure. His arms wrapped around her, clasping her body to his, imprinting the apocalyptic moment of absolute intimacy to the very depths of her soul.

He murmured soft comforting words that drifted through her mind without making any real sense. Then slowly he built a rhythm of spiralling delight, which was so intense that Rebecca felt she would die from it. Yet her body wantonly adapted to every exquisite movement he made, voluptuously inciting the eventual shattering of any last thread of control he held. The erotic pulse of his possession quickened into a fierce plunging need that swept them both to an explosive climax. And then there was only a sweet flooding warmth, a mindless desire to cling to each other as their inner lives merged and ebbed, sealing a union that took them far beyond any sense of self.

It was a long time before Rebecca even began to think. She felt so relaxed and drowsy and the languorous pleasure of simply lying in Slade's arms was an experience she wanted to savour. She liked the feeling of her naked flesh against his. She hadn't realised how deliciously sensual it could be to lie with a man like this without any barrier of clothing between them, and Slade certainly had a magnificent male body. He somehow made her feel more conscious of her own differing sexuality than she had ever been in her life.

She and Paul had never shared the erotic heights of lovemaking that Slade had brought her to. It didn't seem right that the most intense physical pleasure could be attained without love. But there was a vast difference between emotional satisfaction and sexual satisfaction. Slade was certainly an expert lover, but all he would ever give her was an experience...and she hoped a child would come of it.

A bleakness swept through her at the thought that this week would probably be all she would ever have of even this kind of loving. As for the other kind, she knew that what she had once had with Paul was over. It hadn't really been what she had imagined it to be—the lifelong commitment that nothing but death could break.

Strange, the desolation she had felt over that revelation was gone now. In making this momentous choice, had she put the lingering emotionalism of her relationship with Paul to rest?

Somehow that didn't seem right, either. She had loved Paul.... Or had she? Maybe she had simply clung to him because he was the only man who had ever offered her the chance of having the kind of relationship that Gran and Pa had shared. And after the accident, impossible to consider anything else; so she had clung on blindly, even though she should have seen Paul didn't want her kind of life any more. Perhaps she had despaired of there ever being anyone else for her...that Paul was the one chance. A mate. A partner. Someone to love her as Pa had loved Gran.

The actual truth was she felt a deeper tug of attraction towards Slade than she had ever felt towards Paul. As many times as she had told herself there was no future in it—and there wasn't—there was no denying Slade Cordell touched many deep chords in her. Deeper than Rebecca cared to examine.

Tears filled her eyes. What had to be done with Slade was done for now. She shouldn't be luxuriating in intimate togetherness that would make her long for it when it was gone. She had to keep things in perspective or she would end up in a wretched mass of confusion. She had never envisaged herself doing anything like this—giving herself to a man who offered her nothing of himself except his body.

She pushed herself away from him. The togetherness was a lie. They were destined to go separate ways. She had to keep that in the forefront of her mind as a defence against wanting more than she could have.

"Rebecca..."

Slade rolled onto his side, checking any evasion from him too fast for her to blink away the tears that clung to her thick lashes, and his keen blue eyes didn't miss them. The look of pained tenderness that crossed his face forced her to deny any real distress.

"Are you always that good with every woman, Slade?" she asked, a hard brittle edge to her voice.

His mouth twisted into a self-deprecating grimace. "Not good enough apparently," he murmured. Very gently he smeared the spill of moisture from the corners of her eyes. "You're thinking of him, aren't you?"

Slade was wrong about what was running through her mind. Although not entirely wrong. She had been thinking of Paul, and the general accuracy of Slade's perception stirred Rebecca to question it.

"Am I so easy for you to read?" she asked.

"No. But if you love him, it's only natural that you should be thinking of him now," he answered with an understanding that shook Rebecca even further.

She stared at him searchingly, yet found no resentment in his eyes. "You don't mind, Slade?"

"Yes. I mind," he said with a soft little half-smile. "I'd be less than honest if I didn't admit I'd prefer you to be thinking of me—us—and what we can have together."

She reached up and touched his cheek, deeply moved by his frank admission and driven to make an equally frank acknowledgement of what they had just shared. "I've never felt what you made me feel. I'll always be grateful to you for giving me that, Slade. Whatever else happens, at least I've known what it can be like. What it feels like to be...loved."

"Rebecca—" He sighed and shook his head. "Believe me, that was not like anything I've ever experienced either. You are what you are, and you answer something in me that I've never really known before. I guess that doesn't make much sense to you, and it doesn't really matter..."

It made sense. More than she would ever let Slade know, since it didn't really matter to him.

"In one way I feel very envious of Paul Neilsen," he mused wryly, "but not enough to change places with him. At least I have this much of you, and I imagine he would envy me, if he knew."

She flinched away from that thought. She wasn't at all sure that Paul would envy Slade at all. Not now.

"We all have to face realities, Rebecca," he said quietly. "You do that with an implacability that is completely beyond most people. So tell me about Paul Neilsen. Tell me what happened that resulted in his being tied to a wheelchair."

Perhaps it was the strange intimacy of the moment that drew her into recalling that terrible day. Or perhaps it was the compassionate understanding that flowed from Slade. In an odd way it was almost a release of her own deep guilt to talk about it. It also helped to deflect her growing awareness of what it might mean to her when Slade left to take up his real life. It was easier to recall the past than to contemplate the future.

"Paul flew helicopters. He loved their mobility—" her voice cracked a little as she thought of how much Paul's freedom of mobility was curtailed now...it was so wrong, so unfair "—and he loved the outback," she said with all her own deep passion for it. "He loved the space, the vastness of the country, the sense of being part of something bigger than more civilised forms of life. We always contracted him to help do the mustering from the outer boundaries on Wildjanna. He was especially skilled at that and enjoyed the challenge of getting the cattle on the move in the right direction...."

Her eyes dilated with the pain of remembrance as she continued. "I was at the mustering camp with Gran. I don't know to this day what spooked the herd of cattle Paul was driving in, but they started stampeding towards the camp. Paul saw the danger to us. He flew ahead of the leaders and brought the helicopter down in a low swoop to turn them away from us. He flew too low. The rotors clipped a tree and the helicopter spun out of control. It crashed into another tree. Paul's back was broken, his legs crushed, and—" She closed her eyes over another rush of tears.

"So he risked his own life to save you and your grandmother," Slade murmured.

She opened her eyes in bleak acknowledgement. "Yes. And the cost to him..."

Slade placed a silencing finger on her trembling lips, and the dark blue eyes bored sharply into hers. "It wasn't your fault, Rebecca. It was his choice. And life moves on in its own inexorable way. What does Paul do now?"

She swallowed the lump of emotion blocking her throat. Slade was right. She knew he was. But sometimes that didn't help to wipe out the misery that lay deep in her heart over what could never be changed.

"He was always good with machines. He's working on some computer technology for boats and planes. He's turned it into a business, which is going very well," she stated flatly. "He's... very successful."

Slade nodded. "A strong resourceful man. He couldn't be anything else."

"Why do you say that?"

"Rebecca..." He gave her a slow knowing smile. "They say that opposites attract, but it's far more common like attracts like. His strengths are your strengths. And you may not want to recognise it yet, but that's part of why we're attracted to each other. It's not completely physical. Not all of it."

She frowned, knowing it was not all of it, yet conscious they were poles apart in the way they viewed life. Just to show how obvious this was, she made a point of it.

"How old are you, Slade?"

"Thirty-six."

"I don't understand why it doesn't matter to you to have a woman you love at your side," she said questioningly.

His face hardened and a weary cynicism settled in his eyes. "I guess marriage can work for some people. It's most unlikely that it would ever work for me. That's the reality, and I'd be a fool not to face it, much as I might prefer it to be different."

"Why won't it work for you?" she persisted. "If you truly love someone—"

"What is love?" he cut in, his eyes sharply probing hers. "You say it's sharing everything. How do you get to sharing everything? I've had plenty of mutual attractions... but none stuck beyond the initial novelty."

Was that what she was to him? A novelty? Rebecca quickly crushed the wave of hurt, forcing herself to be ruthlessly practical. It didn't matter. She knew—she wasn't depending on it—that Slade Cordell wouldn't be part of her future. Only his child. If she conceived.

"Why didn't they stick?" she asked.

He expelled a heavy sigh and spoke in his slow Texas drawl. "One of the penalties of being what I am is that many people see me only as a figurehead of power. Economic power, corporate power, political power, power over people's lives, take your pick. It's true. I have all that. And it's been a large part of my attraction for every woman I've ever had. After a while I realise they're never going to see beyond that to the me I know. The me inside my head. The me that matters to me."

"Do you give them a chance to know the inner you?" Rebecca asked curiously.

His mouth curled in self-mockery. "Maybe not. Maybe no one has cared enough to try. After all, I have so much else. Why search for the soul inside a man when his bank account is as large as mine?"

"I don't care about your bank account," Rebecca said defensively, bridling against his cynicism.

"I know," he said softly. His eyes momentarily darkened with a hungry yearning. Then his mouth twisted in dry irony. "Nor are you out to use me in the usual way."

Rebecca realised, with a nasty jolt, that she was using him as a stepping stone to her own future. The discomfiting thought didn't sit well on her conscience. Slade was just as human as anyone else. He had feelings to be hurt, and she sensed that he covered a hurting emptiness with his cynicism. Yet this week ... It was not as if he was seriously involved with her. He was only after some *novelty*, wasn't he?

"You offered, Slade. If you hadn't offered I wouldn't be *using* you at all. You wanted me to use you so that you could have this," she said testingly, needing to confirm that she wasn't mistaken about his motives for wanting her with him.

She saw uncertainty flicker in his eyes, a flash of vulnerability that twisted her heart, then a quick firming of resolution. "Yes. I wanted this with you. Whatever I can have with you."

His reply relieved her mind to some extent, yet she felt a strong empathy for the inner loneliness it implied. She suddenly wanted, needed to give him as much as she could during their short time together. At least it would be some return for what he would give her, albeit without his knowledge. That was only fair!

"Slade..." She moved her hand to curl around his neck and draw him down to her. "Please kiss me again," she invited, her eyes warmer than they had ever been for him before.

It sparked a responding warmth in his eyes that quickly kindled into a blaze of desire. "You know I won't stop at kissing, Rebecca," he warned.

"I know." She smiled. "I don't want you to stop. I'd like you to tell me how I can give you more pleasure this time. I want to make this good for you, Slade."

His swift intake of breath was intensely expressive of the impact of her words. He hadn't expected to hear that from her after her earlier rejection of their intimacy. But she would make it up to him, Rebecca vowed to herself.

He wrenched his gaze from hers, ran it slowly down the outstretched nakedness of her body, then just as slowly returned it to her eyes. "You have one of the most provocatively sexy bodies I've ever seen, yet it's more the thought of you that excites me, Rebecca. If you didn't touch me at all, I'd still want you. Whatever pleases you will please me," he said, his voice husky with anticipation as he bent his head to hers.

There was no wild tempest of passion this time, yet in a totally different way their lovemaking was a much deeper sharing of themselves. There was a tenderness, a caring that had been missing before, a more conscious intimacy that was given and received with a fresh appreciation of each other. And when they finally lay entwined in the peaceful aftermath of contented fulfilment, Rebecca made no move to separate herself from him. It felt right and good to stay nestled in the warm security of Slade's embrace. She didn't feel alone.

CHAPTER NINE

FOR REBECCA it was a strange week. In one sense it was almost a fantasy come true. It bore no relation to what she thought of as her real life. There was no work to be done apart from a few household chores, which Slade shared with her. There were no responsibilities, nothing to plan except what pleasure to indulge themselves in next.

Each day was a hedonistic delight. They ate makeshift meals, swam in the crystal-clear waters of a brilliant turquoise sea, offered their bodies to the sun on the warm white sand and made love in so many erotic and gratifying ways that every experience made the next even more addictive.

She supposed it could be likened to a honeymoon, except for the sharp awareness that once it was over, it was over. There had been so little between herself and Slade beforehand, and there was certainly no promise of continuance after the week ended, yet they forged a kind of intimacy many newly married couples might have envied.

Rebecca wasn't even sure how it evolved, nor did she feel inclined to question it too deeply. She liked Slade's company. She found that his shrewd perception of people and understanding of them was far beyond her own experience. He opened up his world to her, and although the revelations on how he managed his business empire were fascinating in an objective sense, they made

Rebecca more convinced she would never want to be part of such a life.

Nevertheless that didn't stop her from respecting Slade's abilities, nor his command of all that had been achieved. He was a remarkable person, and Rebecca admired his strength of purpose and the talent and tenacity that had earned him his position as head of Cordell Enterprises. It had been no family sinecure. It was his place by right of his own dynamic intelligence and personality—a force to be reckoned with!

"Was it always your ambition to head the company your father founded?" she asked, wondering if it ran in his blood as Wildjanna ran in hers.

They were lying on the beach, Rebecca propped up on her elbow to watch Slade as he talked. She liked watching him, the lithe confident way he moved, seemingly never unsure of himself or what he was doing, the telling little expressions around his mouth, the powerful intelligence behind the vivid blue eyes that could be as sharp as razor blades, bright with sparkling amusement, dark with passion, soft with tender feeling.

They twinkled now with the knowledge that he was about to surprise her. "No. My first ambition was to be just like my grandfather. I was brought up on his ranch in Arizona. After my mother died, it was thought that I'd be better off with Grandfather Logan than in the care of nannies and housekeepers. You would have liked him, Rebecca. He was a cattle man through and through. No amount of oil riches was ever going to seduce him into a different way of life. When oil was drilled on his land, Grandfather Logan just moved from Texas to Arizona, set up another ranch and let my father deal with the oil business and everything else."

Slade shook his head in fond remembrance. "I really loved that old man. That's why I renamed Devil's Elbow for him. We bought that property just a few months after he died."

Rebecca hid a painful stab of disappointment Slade had not retained the ambition to be a cattleman like his grandfather. If he had... But that kind of wishful thinking had no place in their relationship. She now understood his concern over the cattle when she had confronted him in New York. It was a hangover from his youth. She told herself very firmly that the present and the future were in a totally different arena for Slade Cordell. She had no right to want or hope for anything from Slade after this week, yet...

"How old were you when you left your grandfather's ranch?" she asked, wondering if he had ever regretted not following in his grandfather's footsteps.

"Sixteen. My father thought it was time to start grooming me to take my place in the organisation he had built up."

"Did you want to go?"

"Yes," he answered without hesitation. "It seemed like an exciting new challenge. I wanted to see all that the big wide world had to offer. I guess I was ready to move on."

As he would move on from her, Rebecca sternly reminded herself. "You never went back?" she asked to put the matter beyond all possible doubt.

"Only to see Grandfather Logan. I don't go back now, although he left the ranch to me. It doesn't feel the same without him in his rocking chair on the porch. It's... empty, I guess."

As Wildjanna had been without Gran, Rebecca thought. But it wouldn't stay empty. Not with another generation.

"I guess you're happy doing what you're doing, running Cordell Enterprises," she said matter-of-factly, forcing herself to face that reality once again.

Slade didn't immediately agree with her. It seemed to Rebecca that Slade's face settled into a look of brooding discontent. Then she remembered the problems arising from Dan Petrie's enforced removal from the organisation. Slade had a lot of reorganising waiting on his plate. Then suddenly he relaxed and grinned at her.

"What I really wanted to be was an astrophysicist," he declared, his eyes twinkling at her startled bemusement.

"What's that?" she had to ask.

"Oh, someone who studies the stars, astronomy, the whole mystery of the universe. An astrophysicist tries to work out where we came from, where we are, what we are at and how the world and the universe will develop in the future." He gave a deprecating laugh. "If we're not all blown to bits by power-hungry politicians or some megalomaniac."

"That worries you?" It seemed a strange mixture of idealism and cynicism, hope and despair, and she wanted to know more about the way Slade thought.

"Where we are in five or ten billion years' time is fairly academic. But it does interest me and it does matter to me. Except for my father, and what he did, that's what I would have done with my life. I would have enjoyed tussling with the conceptual problems that are involved."

"And you can't do it now?"

He gave her a rueful little smile. "I'm probably more effective at making money. Cordell Enterprises funds a satellite doing basic research. That's as important as the work. Essential for getting the work done. Funds for such research are not easy to come by. Someone's got to provide them."

"But you're getting no personal satisfaction out of it."

He shook his head. "That doesn't really matter. It's that kind of work that's important. Human beings worry me. Why are we the way we are? Why do we fight? The wars, man's inhumanity to man..." He threw her a sharp look of irony. "Which, over the ages, has only been exceeded by man's inhumanity to women. I can't undo what's been done. But yes, it worries me, where we're all heading..."

He was a big man in far more ways than Rebecca had recognised. And a good man, as well. She could no longer believe he was a callous womaniser, or that he exploited anyone at all. A man who could be interested in the fate of the human race in five to ten billion years' time... She suddenly felt very privileged to know Slade Cordell, to have him share so much with her. She might not have much time with him but it was time well spent.

She leaned over and kissed him with a warm fervour that came straight from her heart. "That's for being what you are. The inner you," she said, smiling into his eyes. "And now I'm going to make love to you."

"Rebecca..." He said her name with a deep yearning that tugged at her soul, and the look in his eyes made her ache in anticipation of the loss that was inevitably coming.

She placed a finger on his lips, silencing the words that could not lead anywhere. All they had was now, and she began caressing him in the ways she had learnt gave him the most exquisite pleasure. When he could bear it no longer, she straddled him to take him inside her and felt both humbled and exalted by the look in his eyes as he watched her bring them both to an ecstatic fulfilment, which seemed more poignant than ever before.

THE LAST DAY FINALLY CAME, bringing with it a sharper appreciation of every moment left to them. Neither Rebecca nor Slade made mention of it. They didn't have to. A tension grew between them as the day wore to a close. Slade suggested a walk along the beach—their last walk together, although it wasn't acknowledged as such, not in words.

They walked a long way. Dying waves trickled around their feet. The footprints they made receded into the wet sand, wiped away by a natural force as surely and relentlessly as other forces were about to tear them apart. The sun that had shone so benevolently on them all week was a lowering yellow ball in a sky that was already gathering the shades of the brief tropical twilight.

It was Slade who stopped walking first. Rebecca halted a pace ahead of him, turned reluctantly, sensing the burden on his mind and knowing there was no answer to it. His eyes were dark with a turbulence that twisted her heart.

"I can't ignore my responsibilities, Rebecca," he said quietly.

"I know. I want to thank you for—"

"Don't!" The harsh command instantly cut off the speech that had been hovering on her lips. "You have nothing to thank me for. You've given me..."

He paused to take a deep breath. "Is it any use asking you to come with me?"

It hurt to say it but there was no evading the truth. "I have things to do, too, Slade," she said softly. "My life is here."

He nodded, looked out to sea for several nerve-wrenching moments, then slowly turned his gaze to her. "There is no hope, then, is there, Rebecca?"

It was a plea scraped from a need that she couldn't honestly fulfil. And if she tried, it would be a betrayal of herself. He knew that. It was written in his eyes even as he asked the question of her. It was more a statement, edged with despairing resignation, than a question.

"We each have our paths to take," she replied flatly. "I couldn't be happy in New York, Slade. It would suffocate me."

His mouth thinned as if forcibly holding back any further argument. His eyes seared her with barely restrained wanting. "I'll miss you." Short, punched-out words that thudded into her heart.

"I'll miss you," she whispered. And to herself she added, More than I can ever tell you.

"Tell me what you intend to do over the next few months," he said gruffly. "I want to know. When I think about you . . . I want to know."

"There's a project that Gran and I used to discuss a lot. I want to set it up and get it operational. It's an ideal, I suppose, but now that Gran has gone . . . It's like a legacy that she wanted to pass on. And I intend to do that."

She swallowed to clear the choking well of grief in her throat, then tried to explain the feelings that she had shared with her grandmother. "Most of the Australian population live around the coastline, and the outback is like a dream centre of tradition that few ever really experience. Yet I doubt there's one Australian who can deny at least a subconscious fascination with it, a wanting to be part of it for however short a time."

"Like our old American West," Slade murmured appreciatively.

"Perhaps. You know your country better than I do. Gran wanted—I want—to set up a programme where children whose lives have been limited, who, for one reason or other, only have a short time left to live, can come to Wildjanna and have that dream answered. This is something we can give, and Gran thought—I think—it might help those children. On Wildjanna, the cycle of life, the cycle of nature is so apparent. There's a timelessness that you become part of. The Aborigines understood it so clearly; the dream time; the melding of life and land; primitive, perhaps, but elemental . . ."

"Yes, elemental," Slade repeated, looking at her with eyes that seemed to attach that word and all its shades of meaning to her.

Rebecca's chest was suddenly so tight that it was a struggle to breath. She tore her gaze from his and looked out to sea—the vast shifting tide of water that supported and generated its own cycle of life, complementing the land.

"I have to make contact with medical—hospital—authorities," she said, forcing herself to ignore the pain inside her. "I know it will take time to make the availability of a stay on Wildjanna known to families who can benefit from it. And I have other preparations to make. The dam that Gran and I planned, just below the homestead. I've got to get it done before the drought breaks. It will become a large lake and attract all the wonderful birdlife of the outback, cockatoos, brolgas..."

She heaved a sigh and turned her gaze to Slade. "You've just seen the country at its worst. But after it rains, Slade, it's like a magical regeneration. The birds and wildflowers and animals that suddenly appear... It's as if God has waved His hand and performed another act of creation. To see it happen... If I could show that to children who have never seen life beyond the cities and will die in those godforsaken places without ever..."

She bit down on her tongue. Slade's life was citybound. She didn't want to be offensively critical, particularly when he was achieving things she could never achieve.

"I'm sorry," she whispered. "I didn't mean..."

"I know what you meant, Rebecca," he assured her, his eyes dark with a deep appreciation of what she was saying.

Encouraged, she went on. "Anyway, I want to get started on setting up the project. I'll need to arrange some kind of funding to alleviate travelling costs for the children and their families. After the drought breaks, when times are better, I'll be able to manage something myself, but..."

"Cordell Enterprises will supply the funds, Rebecca."

She stared at him, taking in the resolute purpose in his eyes, yet inwardly recoiling from it.

"Slade, I wasn't asking, wasn't hinting..."

"I know you weren't, but I want to do it. Won't you share this with me? If only for the children's sake?"

Put that way, it was impossible to refuse his offer. And at heart she didn't want to. In a deeply personal way, the project would be like a memorial of what they had shared together.

"Thank you," she said simply. "It will be money well spent, Slade. I'm sure of it."

He smiled. "So am I." The smile faded into a look of concerned consideration. "It's not easy to cope with suffering children, Rebecca. They need such special care. You will need medical equipment, trained nurses, perhaps even doctors on hand."

"I'll solve those problems when I come to them," she said determinedly. "Gran and I worked on how best to meet the situation. I'll cope."

He frowned. "What about yourself? It won't be easy on your emotions."

"I know." She sighed. She looked at the sun, sinking so quickly now, as it was sinking too quickly on so many people who didn't know how to cope with life because they had never had any understanding of the nature of it. "But when has anything worthwhile ever been easy, Slade?"

She turned to him with a resolute little smile.

His mouth slowly curved in response. "You have no fear, have you?"

She shook her head. "I have fears, just like everyone else."

"They don't show."

"I really hate flying," she admitted.

"But you do it," Slade said softly.

"I do what has to be done. We both do, Slade. We share that in common."

He stared at her for what seemed like aeons of time. Then he stepped forward and wrapped her in his arms, crushing her against him in a silent agony of need that dismissed everything else. His mouth swept over her hair again and again, trailing feverish little kisses through the thick silky tresses.

"Let's go back," he rasped. "We still have the night."

Although they barely slept at all, the dawn rushed in on them long before they were ready to face it. Packing their things and seeing that the cottage was left in reasonable order were mechanical tasks that added a sharper edge of sadness to their imminent parting. A car arrived to take them to the airport. They sat in the back seat, Slade's fingers laced tightly through hers, and neither spoke a word all the way. There was nothing left to say.

When they reached the airport, Slade turned to Rebecca, his face strained, his eyes roving hungrily over her face.

"Stay in the car, Rebecca. I'll instruct the driver to take you into Brisbane. Just tell him where you want to go."

"All right," she agreed, aware that the waiting for his flight to be called would be unbearable for both of them.

He curled one hand around her cheek, tilting her face to his, and he kissed her with such loving tenderness that she could barely hold back the tears.

"I'll come back when I can, Rebecca," he murmured, his voice rough with suppressed feeling. His eyes burnt fiercely into hers. His fingers stroked one last caress on her cheek. Then he opened the car door and left her.

She didn't watch him pick up his bag and stride away. She stared straight ahead, seeing nothing, forcing her mind to recite the steps she now had to take. She did not yet know if she was pregnant with Slade's child. Her child. Their child. She could only hope she was.

And for the first time she did not think of that child as the fourth generation for Wildjanna. More than anything else at that moment, the baby—if one had been conceived—was part of Slade Cordell, and she fiercely wanted it to be so.

CHAPTER TEN

SLADE CORDELL only half listened to Bert Hinkman expounding on what effect the latest tanker accident would have on oil prices. He was remembering the environmental tragedy resulting from the '89 accident when the *Exxon Valdez* ran aground, spilling two hundred and forty thousand barrels of oil into the sea off the coast of Alaska, blackening beaches, coating plant and marine life, killing....

A savage wave of revulsion swept through him. *What in hell are we doing to this planet,* he thought, *all in the holy name of keeping every machine running*? Human error, mechanical error, computer error...releasing forces of destruction that polluted the land and the sea and the air.

He rose restlessly from his chair behind the black marble desk and walked over to the wall of plate glass to stare broodingly at the man-made monoliths of Manhattan. Rebecca was right. This concrete jungle had no soul. Ambition, but no soul. The world was becoming more and more a godforsaken place, and where would it all end?

Rebecca...

The need for her ripped through him like a knife. He barely stifled a groan. As it was, Hinkman was probably wondering what he had said wrong to have provoked this impolite interruption to his dissertation. Slade recollected himself and turned to face him again.

Bert Hinkman was one of the best of the board members, not only efficient but completely dependable. He had been on the board in Blair Cordell's time and did his job with meticulous care. He liked it, took pride in his performance, and unfortunately for Slade had no ambition to move any higher. More than ever now, that high-backed leather chair in the boardroom felt like a millstone around Slade's neck.

His mouth moved stiffly into an apologetic smile. "Sorry, Bert. My mind wandered. Please go on."

"If you'll pardon my saying so, Slade, it's time you eased up a bit," the older man advised. "For the past four months, ever since you came back from Australia, you've been hard at it, revamping the organisation and setting up a new network of accountability. I won't say it didn't need doing, but you've been driving yourself to get it done."

He paused, then added in pointed concern, "When was the last time you had a full night's sleep?"

Slade gave a dismissive shrug and walked to his desk. He consciously tried to relax as he sat down again. Unless he knocked himself out with sleeping pills, a habit he did not want to fall into, he hated going to bed. It reminded him too painfully of what he didn't have—couldn't have.

"Quite frankly, you look like hell. Drawn and tired and—if I might be so bold—you're also uncharacteristically short of temper," Hinkman said with a telling little grimace.

"Getting a bad reputation, am I?" Slade asked wearily.

"No. I wouldn't say that," came the considering reply. "You're well-liked on the whole. And sometimes a short temper can move things along better than all the pleasant reasoning in the world. I merely mention it because it's given rise to some concern among those who know you. It's just not like you, Slade."

"I'll try to ease off, Bert." The trouble was, impatience was eating into him. He wanted everything running running smoothly as fast as possible. He wanted to go back to Rebecca. He wanted...

"Do you want to hear the rest of my report, or shall I—?"

"Yes, yes," Slade cut in, consciously softening the second yes as he heard the sharp edge on the first. "Please continue," he added gently.

But he couldn't concentrate on what his executive was saying. Not for long. He heard snatches of the report, enough to make intelligible replies to questions, but his thoughts kept drifting to an entirely different world—the one that held Rebecca.

He desperately wanted to be with her again, but was it the right thing to do? The question often tortured him in the middle of the night. She wanted a child. If he went back, could he deny her a child if she asked it of him? He had said that they would discuss it, but what kind of father could he be?

He'd be torn between both worlds, giving satisfaction in neither place. It wasn't fair to anyone, least of all to Rebecca—dropping in and out of her life whenever he could make the time. If he stayed away, maybe she would find someone who could give her the marriage she wanted, the kind of marriage she believed in.

But to stay away... Paul Neilsen had had the guts to set her free to tread her own path. But damn it all! Paul Neilsen couldn't give her what he could. Another month at most and he would have everything running in a responsible pattern. He could leave then. Take maybe as much as two months off to stay with her. If she let him set up a computer system at Wildjanna so that he could keep tabs on the figures coming in... maybe longer.

Was she feeling the same need for him or was she stronger than he was? Slade suspected she might be.

Implacable, he had called her, and he could well imagine her shutting all thought of him out of her mind. He had been so tempted to call her, to keep her thinking of him, remembering; but he recognised it as a selfish urge. Self-indulgent. Greedy.

She had given him what he had asked of her, and she had chosen not to come with him. He should have realised there could be no other choice for her right from the beginning. Implacable, like the land that claimed her.

Apart from which, she still loved Paul Neilsen, and that damned wheelchair would always keep her tied to him. Slade fiercely wished Neilsen had crashed doing something other than saving Rebecca's life. Because of that she would always love Neilsen—yet she had locked that love away in a separate compartment while she had given herself to Slade. Was he now locked away in another compartment while she got on with her life?

Slade was almost sure that she had come to love him that week, maybe not the same kind of love she bore Paul Neilsen, but it had been something special to her. He couldn't doubt that. Was it enough for her to want again, to always want, even though it only came from time to time?

Could she accept a marriage like that?

Was he prepared to commit himself to a marriage like that?

To have her, to know he could always have her... yet it was so impossibly impractical! Slade bitterly castigated himself for having started something that he couldn't finish right. But not to have known her as he had, even feeling the anguished need for her that he did now, Slade knew in his heart that he would do the same thing again, anything at all, just to have had that one experience she had given him. And he couldn't bear not to go back to her, no matter what. In three or four weeks...

Slade shook his head to clear it of the endless tread-mill of tormenting questions. He applied himself to listening to the end of Hinkman's report. As usual, it was succinct and penetrating. Slade gave the nod of approval to the recommendations offered and saw the older man out of his office.

Ease off, he recalled ruefully as he shut the door and turned towards the desk. It was well-meant advice but it was easier to bear the inner loneliness if he buried himself in work. Besides, there was so much that needed to be done.

Bert Hinkman had his responsibilities covered, but the rest... No, there was one other. Ross Harper, the new man on the board. He had promise. He definitely had promise. Sharp, efficient, one step ahead of the game. It had been the right decision bringing him in. New blood. Cordell Enterprises certainly needed an injection of that. If only Harper had more experience under his belt.

Slade heaved an impatient sigh. He couldn't expect too much too soon from a guy who was only just feeling his way, yet maybe Harper was a possibility for the future.

His mind drifted to Rebecca again, and her plans for the future. She had not yet applied to Cordell Enterprises for the funds needed for her project, but that didn't mean she wasn't busy with it. Such things took time to set up. He tried to picture where she would construct the dam that would become a lake. The drought had not broken, so she had certainly had the time to make the dam as big as she wanted it. He wished he had asked her more about it.

The telephone on his desk buzzed a summons, snapping him out of his musing. Get on with your own work, he told himself sternly, and strode over to snatch up the receiver. He hoped it wouldn't spew forth another problem that had to be resolved before he could leave.

"Mr. Cordell, there's a gentleman from Australia asking to see you. A Mr. Emilio Dalvarez. He says he only has today in New York—"

"Is he there with you?" Slade broke in, feeling as though a sledgehammer had hit his heart. Was something wrong at Wildjanna? Had something happened to Rebecca?

"Yes, sir."

"Bring him in immediately. I'll see him straightaway."

Slade paced the floor like a caged mountain lion as he waited for the Argentinian to be ushered in. Maybe the drought had caused more problems. Although if that was the case, Emilio could surely have communicated with him through the management at Devil's Elbow. During the week that Slade had spent there, he had neutralised all hostilities. He had left the man on friendly terms. There shouldn't be any problems that concerned Emilio Dalvarez enough to make a trip to New York.

A brief knock heralded the opening of his office door. Slade spun on his heel and moved swiftly to greet his unexpected visitor and offer an outstretched hand of welcome. "Emilio... it's good to see you," he said, hiding his inner tension as best he could, although instantly aware that the Argentinian was distinctly ill at ease.

A hard brown hand returned a tighter clasp than mere politeness required, but there was no assertion of superiority in it. Slade was sure it was more an expression of uncertainty, which disturbed him even further. Emilio Dalvarez was very much a man who would rarely be uncertain of anything.

"Mr. Cordell—Slade... I hope I am not imposing."

"Not at all. Please, come and sit down. We'll have a drink together. You can tell me all the news of what's been happening."

"No. No drink, thank you. I cannot stay long. I am flying on to Argentina this afternoon," Emilio stated. "The times have changed in my country. I'm allowed to go back for a short period. I am no longer an émigré. My father called for me to come. My mother is not well. I must go, you understand."

"Of course. I'm sorry that you've got problems," Slade sympathised. "I hope they are not too serious."

"Who is to know?" Emilio said philosophically. "My mother has lived a goodly span of years. Family is family. It is a long time since I have seen her. It is right that I go and be the son I am to her."

"Yes," Slade quickly agreed, then gestured an invitation to the grouping of sofas where Rebecca had sat with him so many months ago.

Emilio moved to one and sat with an air of great dignity. He wore a suit with considerable distinction, Slade thought, although his weathered face clearly denoted him as a man who worked outdoors. In his somewhat narrow way, Emilio Dalvarez commanded respect. He lived by his own lights, and Slade was not about to denigrate them. At the very least, Emilio had a sense of honour that was too rare a quality to be undervalued.

"This is a very impressive building," Emilio said, eyeing the plate-glass wall and its view over Manhattan. "I can now see that you have much to take into consideration."

It was a concession, but a concession to what? Slade decided it was up to him to take the bull by the horns. "Emilio..." He leaned forward from the seat he had taken opposite his visitor. "I realise your time is particularly valuable on this journey. As much as I am honoured by your visit, I feel sure you would not have broken your journey for idle chitchat with me. How is Rebecca?"

"As you left her!" came the sharp reply, edged with a hostile reproof that put Slade instantly on guard.

"What does that mean?" he asked, keeping his own voice steady and quiet.

"She is having your baby," came the unequivocal reply, stabbed home with a dark glare that expressed an angry frustration with the situation.

Slade was dumbstruck, dazed, his mind jagging between disbelief and the stark honest bluntness of Emilio's statement. His baby? The wonder of it. How had it happened? Why hadn't Rebecca rung him and told him?

"Rebecca Wilder is a proud independent woman. A strong woman," the Argentinian continued. "I hold her in high esteem, as I did her grandmother. She would never tell you, or ask anything of you. She will stand alone, that one." He glowered at Slade. "But to my mind, you have acted wrongly towards her. Badly wrong. To take such a woman, and not honour her enough to marry her. To leave her carrying your child—"

"Emilio, are you sure about this?" Slade broke in urgently. "I made her promise me she was protected..." But not all contraceptives were a hundred per cent failproof! And perhaps she had misled him. Or let him mislead himself.

Emilio snorted and stood up, drawing himself to his full height and looking down at Slade with contempt. "Are you denying that you are the father?"

"No!" Slade shot to his feet. "If Rebecca is carrying a child, it's mine. It has to be mine." He shook his head, still incredulous that it had actually happened. "I don't know how or why... you're certain that she is?"

"You are a man of the city," Emilio jeered. "There is no doubt in Rebecca's mind. What kind of soul do you have, to leave her like that?"

Had she deliberately lied to him? Slade's mind started reeling with implications. Had she told him what she knew he wanted to hear and cold-bloodedly gone ahead to use him for her own purpose? Was she that ruthless in forging her own destiny? Did she intend to go back to Paul Neilsen and...? Slade's recoil from that thought was instant and violent. Not with *his* child! No other man was going to be the surrogate father of *his* child!

Emilio had stalked over to the glass wall, taken in the panoramic view with a sweep of his eyes, then turned his back on it, his face sternly judgemental as he glared at Slade. "I would have married her," he declared. "I offered to do so. But Rebecca Wilder is an honourable woman. She told me why she could not accept my offer. She told me why she would not accept any offer. I respect her for her honesty. But you... You think you can take the best of both worlds without any redress? I—" he thumped his chest with vehement feeling "—I think you are despicable, and I wanted to tell it to you straight to your face."

It was clear that his own personal disappointment in regard to Rebecca had lent fire to his sense of injustice. Slade could no longer doubt that Emilio Dalvarez had not only told him the truth, but the Argentinian also felt passionately enough about it to break his journey home to his family.

Whatever motives or intentions Rebecca had, now was not the time for Slade to question them. This man was hurt, and Slade had contributed largely to that hurt, albeit unintentionally. How deeply Emilio's feelings for Rebecca went was impossible to tell, but it behove Slade to tread carefully and not add insult to injury.

"Emilio," he began softly, appeasingly. "This news has come as a great shock to me. It must have come as a shock to you, too, when you first heard it. I'm sorry about that. I didn't know that you had anything more than neighbourly intentions in regard to Rebecca.

Although even if I had known, in all honesty I could not have backed away from the attraction she holds for me.''

"I do not begrudge you that," Emilio fired at him. "She is a woman who could attract any man. She has the right to take whom she chooses. But for you to take advantage and then to leave her!"

"My relationship with Rebecca...that's a private thing, Emilio," Slade said more strongly, giving vent to some of the feelings he was trying to control. "But believe me, I did not come to it lightly, nor do I intend to let it go lightly. Even as you arrived, I was planning to return to her as quickly as I could. There is still some urgent business here. But now it's far more imperative that I go to her. And I shall be on my way to Wildjanna as soon as possible. Whatever has happened there, I'll do what's necessary to clean up the mess I left behind. You have my word on it."

"I hope so. I feel outraged."

"So do I," Slade assured him emphatically.

"You must have known what you were doing!"

"There are times when a man stops thinking, Emilio."

The anger simmered down to a grudging understanding, but there was still a lot of dark reservation in his eyes. "I hope your brains are now back in place," he said sternly.

"They will be by the time I get there. I appreciate what you've done, Emilio. I thank you, sincerely, for taking the time and the trouble to come to me. It is the act of a good neighbour, and I'll always be mindful of the service you've done me."

Emilio ruminated over those sentiments for several moments before giving an approving nod. "As a neighbour to both of you, it was my duty to speak to you."

"I couldn't agree more. I'm very grateful to you," Slade said with enough fervour to satisfy any of Emilio's lingering grievances.

In truth, Slade *was* deeply grateful to him, but he was anxious to get moving and he needed to get Emilio moving first. The sense of loss—that Rebecca had chosen not to share this with him—was intense and mind-shattering. He had to go to her. That it was his duty wasn't the issue at all. He wanted to go anyway. He needed to think. He realised he was still shocked, deeply shocked by Emilio's reservations. Somehow he had to find a way...

Filled with a tearing sense of urgency, he thrust out his hand, and was greatly relieved when Emilio took it with barely a hesitation. Slade ushered him to the door with a few more polite platitudes and they parted on terms of mutual respect.

His first call was to book a seat on the first flight to Brisbane. Then he called in his secretary and dictated at top speed. The man would have to come with him. He needed someone who was familiar with his work practices. He put out a few critical memos for each of his divisional managers as a holding action, particularising those areas that had not yet received his personal attention and demanding appropriate adjustments.

Until he could get back to New York he would have to trust others to fulfil the various criteria of responsibility outlined. His own personal feeling—barely suppressed—was that Cordell Enterprises could go to hell and he wouldn't give a damn, but an edge of sanity insisted that he couldn't desert the ship without any authority at all. As it was, he would be leaving it at a critical time for an indefinite period, but he had to go!

It was his child!

He had to know what was on Rebecca's mind. Why had she done it?

The pregnancy was a reality. Four months! A child on the way—halfway to being born. While Slade had never given having children a great deal of priority in his life before, somehow it was totally different now.

His son.

Or daughter.

His flesh and blood, and Rebecca's...

The rest of the world could go hang!

He was going to Wildjanna, and he was going to stay there and make sure everything turned out right. This was real life he was dealing with, not figures on papers or hypothetical reasoning. It was the life of his child! And he sure as heck was going to have some say in it! A great deal of say in it, if he got anything like his way at all.

Knowing Rebecca as he did, his say mightn't amount to very much. But one thing was certain. She was going to know that he was there to be counted!

CHAPTER ELEVEN

REBECCA LOWERED THE SCOOP of the bulldozer, changed gears and slowly reversed down the bank of the dam, the back edge of the scoop dragging over the loose dirt, smoothing the slope to a more eye-pleasing line. Then she trundled the bulldozer up to repeat the process.

The important part of the work had been done weeks ago. The structure of the lake had been carved out of the land. It could rain any time it liked and the massive banks would hold the water. What she was doing was purely cosmetic, but she wanted the end result to look as perfectly natural as possible.

The station hands had done the really heavy earth shifting and building. Rebecca had eased off her own workload once she was certain of her pregnancy, but for this hour each evening, after the heat of the day was passed, she liked to work on the finishing touches herself. Apart from the aesthetic purpose, it also served to tire her out physically before she retired for the night.

Memories tended to crowd in on her once she went to bed. Sometimes it was hard to get to sleep. She missed Slade—desperately missed all they had shared together—yet she didn't regret what she had done. Already the baby growing inside her had dispelled so much of the lonely emptiness that had threatened her personal existence. She looked forward to its birth with a wonderfully uplifting sense of joy.

Even Milly was not so cross-faced about it any more. Emilio, however, was another kettle of fish. Rebecca hoped that his trip to Argentina would take the edge off his disappointment. She hoped that while he was there he might even find another wife.

She reached the bottom of the slope again and changed gears to start the next run. She glanced up to position her line of approach to a neat parallel with the last grade and caught sight of a man jogging around the top of the bank, waving both arms above his head in an obvious signal to grab her attention. She put the machine on idle, waiting to find out what he wanted. She couldn't figure out who it was. He was too big to be...

Shock pummelled Rebecca's heart. Only one man she knew was that big; the towering height, the broad shoulders, the lithe muscular body, the long powerful legs eating up the distance between them. She whipped off her hat and then the goggles that protected her eyes from the dust the dozer kicked up. He was on top of the rise just above her now and there was no mistaking who it was. Slade Cordell had come back!

Rebecca sat there completely dazed by the sight of him plunging down the slope towards her. She hadn't really believed Slade would ever return. It had seemed far more logical that once back in his own world he would recognise that their week together was the fantasy it had been—time out of time for both of them. Anything else between them was simply not practical. Yet he was here! It was him!

Before Rebecca could recollect herself enough to greet him, or even move, he had swung himself onto the dozer, switched off the ignition key and was hauling her out of the seat, setting her feet on the ground, the vivid blue eyes dark with a turbulence of feeling that swirled around her, constricting her throat, her chest, so that all she could do was stare dumbly at him.

"What on earth are you thinking of, Rebecca?" he cried harshly, his hands squeezing her upper arms, fingers digging bruises in some terrible agitation of spirit. "Don't be such a fool! For God's sake! Consider the baby!"

The baby? He knew about the baby? But how could he?

He groaned and released her arms. He swept one hand around her waist to pull her none too gently against him. The other he lifted to her face, tremulously brushing away the untidy wisps of hair that had come loose from the tie at the back of her neck. I'm a dirty mess, she thought dimly, but Slade wasn't looking at her as though she were a dirty mess. His eyes hungered into hers with soul-stirring force.

"Say you're glad to see me," he rasped. "Say you missed me as much as I missed you. Say something. Anything, Rebecca."

It felt so good to be pressed to the length and strength of his body again. It felt wonderful to have him holding her, touching her. "Kiss me," she whispered.

His chest heaved against her tender breasts and then his mouth was on hers, feasting on hers, starving for the sweet devastating passion that flared so quickly between them. Rebecca responded with a fierce hunger of her own, wanting to drown in all the wildly pulsing sensations he aroused in her, wanting to obliterate all the hows and whys and wherefores, and exult only in the fact that he was with her again, giving her more of himself.

All these months she had forced up walls of logic to protect herself from yearning for such a moment as this, and now she didn't care that they came crashing down. She could build them again later. When she had to. But no way was she going to stint on this incredible reality. She revelled in Slade's kisses and clung to him in sheer boneless wanting. If it was madness, then it was a madness she willingly embraced.

He tucked her head onto his shoulder, keeping it gently pressed there as he fought the violent tremor that shook his body. His breathing was harsh and irregular, his arms still crushing her to him. His cheek rubbed over her hair in a soft mindless yearning as shaky bursts of words spilled from his heart.

"I've wanted you so much. I haven't stopped wanting you. Not for one day, one hour, one second . . . an agony of wanting. All this time, endless days and nights, waiting to get back to you. . . ."

Rebecca could not disbelieve him. His voice throbbed with the truth of what he was saying. His body throbbed its own confirmation even more convincingly. Her mind throbbed with the wonder of it.

"Slade," she whispered, for the sheer pleasure of saying his name.

"Why didn't you call me, Rebecca? Why didn't you let me know about the baby? I would have come sooner."

She sighed, realising once again that life didn't really work by logic at all. "You didn't want a baby, Slade," she reminded him softly.

He tilted her head back to search her eyes, his own reflecting an intense inner turmoil. "You must know I would care, Rebecca."

It was plain that he did care. Very deeply. Yet that first day in his New York office, he had given her the impression that having children was not important to him, that he could live quite happily without ever concerning himself over what a child of his own might mean to him. He had even offered to father one for her so that there would be no impediment to her marrying Paul. Although he had seemed to change his mind about that after she had given in to him.

"You did think that I wouldn't care," he said in a voice that sounded strangely hollow.

"Slade..." She reached up and stroked the taut muscles in his cheek. "It was my decision. And it wouldn't have been right for me to impose anything you didn't want on your life. Not something you'd never planned on doing."

"I said we'd discuss it, Rebecca," he reminded her, still deeply disturbed.

"You said a lot of things, Slade," she said softly. "And then quickly backtracked on them after I conceded what you wanted."

"No. You misunderstood."

She shook her head. "Maybe it changed for you in the week we had together. It did for me. But you held out something to me that day—over my grandmother's grave—and then you took it away, promising only a possibility in the future. I made my choice then, Slade, because I didn't trust you to come back and deliver what you'd promised me. And I gave you what you wanted in return."

The flesh beneath her fingertips contracted. "Was that all it was for you, Rebecca? A return for services rendered?"

"No. You know it wasn't." She smiled. "What am I doing here in your arms, kissing you like there's no tomorrow?"

"There is a tomorrow. We'll make a tomorrow," he said vehemently.

"Because of the baby?" Her smile slipped into sad irony. "How did you know about it, Slade? Did Milly blurt it out when you called at the homestead?"

"No. Emilio told me. He stopped off in New York on his way to Argentina."

That piece of news slapped into her face like a wet fish. Emilio confronting Slade in his office, puffed up with moral righteousness. Rebecca's insides deflated into a sick queasiness. Her arms limply withdrew from around Slade's neck. Her gaze dropped to stare miserably, sightlessly, over Slade's shoulder.

"I'm sorry. He had no right. No right at all," she said in bitter condemnation, knowing precisely how Emilio would have carried on, demanding that Slade make some reparation to the woman he had dishonoured.

Tears welled in her eyes. It must be the pregnancy making her weak, she thought. She hadn't expected Slade to come back. He had only come now in some stupid burst of guilt over the baby. If only Emilio Dalvarez had minded his own damned business...

She gave an anguished jerk of her head as Slade grasped her chin to turn it to him. "I'm all right!" she insisted blindly. "I'm fine! I don't need you, Slade Cordell! You didn't have to come. You're making this worse for me than it has to be."

She tore herself out of his embrace and lurched towards the bulldozer. A hand caught at her arm and she beat it away. "Don't touch me!" she hurled at him as she backed up against the machine and forced some stiffening down her spine.

Her shoulders squared to a dignified bearing. A bitter pride sparked through the moisture in her eyes. Her chin lifted in defiant rejection of her earlier susceptibility to Slade's physical magnetism. That her face and clothes were streaked with dirt made no whit of difference. She knew who she was. She knew where she was going. Her own rigid sense of destiny was stamped on every taut line of her face and body.

"Rebecca..." Slade stepped towards her, his hands raised in urgent appeal.

"No! Keep your distance, Slade," she demanded, steel spearing through the shakiness of her voice. "I won't have you using my—our—mutual attraction to mess up something that is completely clear-cut. I never counted on you turning up in my life again. If Emilio hadn't interfered—"

"I was coming anyway," he broke in vehemently. "Ever since I left you I've been working towards coming back to you. The only difference Emilio made was that I'm here sooner than I would have made it otherwise."

"How much sooner?" Rebecca pounced.

"A month, give or take a week," he returned impatiently.

"In that case, you just go back to your work, Slade. The baby and I are doing fine. We don't need you here. We don't need you to come back, either. A month will give you time to realise that you have no responsibility to this child whatsoever. I took full responsibility for it before it was even conceived."

"I'm supposed to ignore it, am I, Rebecca?" he asked in that soft-dangerous voice of his. "I'm supposed to leave you to your own devices and forget all about both you and the child? Is that it?"

The glittering determination in his eyes told her that his questions were purely rhetorical. It wouldn't matter what she replied, he was not going to be swayed from the course he had decided upon. She stared at him, recognising the same mesmerising force she had felt that day in the graveyard when Slade had issued his challenge, and it seemed that her world was collapsing in on her. He emitted waves of power that both threatened and tugged at her soul.

"Well, I can tell you this," he continued quietly. "Hell will freeze over first. You made the decision, but it's my child as much as yours. And I'm staying, Rebecca. We have offices in Brisbane and I've left my secretary there to set up a communications headquarters. As and when I'm needed to deal with business, I'll commute to Brisbane from Wildjanna. Or from Devil's Elbow if you're too stiff-necked to admit you want me with you every bit as much as I want to be with you."

He paused, inviting a response from her, but Rebecca was too amazed by his resolute organisation of his affairs to think clearly at all.

Slade pressed on, driving his points home. "Either way, Rebecca, I'm not going back to New York until we get our relationship sorted out. Somehow or other, there's going to be some giving and taking. The thing that's going to be sorted out is who are the takers and who are the givers."

Ruthless and relentless, Rebecca thought, yet strangely enough his declaration eased the sickening turmoil stirred by the knowledge of Emilio's unwarranted betrayal of her confidence. She felt a welling of pleasurable excitement that Slade so totally refused to be turned away. Nevertheless, the measures he had taken, and would take for the purpose of staying with her, could only be temporary. Apart from which, this time they could not put their separate lives on hold, as they had at Forty-Mile Beach.

"It won't work, Slade," she said bluntly. "You're a taker, and I'm not much good at giving. However, since you insist you want to stay, and you've gone to so much trouble about it, then stay. But have no expectations, Slade. It won't work for long. This isn't your life, and I won't accept you imposing standards and values on me that are not my own."

"I think it's up to me to decide what I want my life to be, Rebecca," he retorted, totally unshaken in his determination. In fact, the look in his eyes had intensified to a blaze of possessiveness. "There are two things I am sure of," he stated. "I want you in it. And I want our child in it. I haven't yet had time to work out the rest, but first and foremost I want you to marry me. That comes first, Rebecca. Then somehow we'll forge a new life."

"Because of the baby?" She shook her head incredulously, her eyes filling with scorn. "That's Emilio talking, Slade. You should know better. You should know me better. There's no way I'll marry you."

She couldn't afford to. If Slade wanted his child in his life, if she married him he would have a legal claim. He could take the child away from her when their marriage broke up under the inevitable pressures of their separate ways of life.

No way would she ever give him the power to do that. He had offered, she had taken, and she would fight Slade to the death if he tried to change his deal with her.

He moved towards her, each step slow and deliberate, and Rebecca had the strong sensation that nothing she said or did would hold him back this time. "That week we had together was the best week I ever had in my life. It wasn't just me, Rebecca. We shared something that few people even get near." His hands lifted and curled lightly around her shoulders, his eyes burning into hers. "Can you deny that?"

"No. But it doesn't change the situation we have now," she said forcefully, desperate to block the effect his closeness had on her. She was not going to waver over this. To give in would be a madness that encompassed far more than any brief physical or emotional satisfaction.

"I know it's not an ideal situation, but there are plenty of other marriages that survive long separations because of work. It makes the times together all the more special," Slade argued seductively. "It can be so with us, Rebecca."

She refused to let the idea take hold. It was a temptation she couldn't possibly nurture in any way. It could only lead to terribly destructive futures for both of them. And their child.

"You said marriage would never work for you, Slade," she fiercely reminded him.

"I'll *make* this marriage work. Whatever it takes."

"What you feel about the baby... it will pass. It's a *novelty* to you. Just as I was a novelty to you. If you'd ever really wanted a child in your life, you'd have made a way to have one before this. You're not thinking straight, Slade."

"I said those things before I really knew you, or myself, Rebecca. Don't hold them against me. Not now. Please, consider what I'm saying right here at this time."

Every instinct rebelled against any persuasion. Her voice was harsh with a violent clash of emotion as she replied. "No. I won't, Slade. I won't ever consider a marriage with you. We don't have enough together to consider a marriage. Not a lifetime marriage. You can't even begin to give me what I had with Paul. Stay with me as long as you like, but don't talk marriage to me. Let there be no feeling of obligation between us. That will sour our relationship faster than anything else. When you want to go, go."

His face tightened. His fingers dug into her shoulders. Then as if he realised what he was doing he made a savage grimace and pulled his hands away. Rebecca's heart dropped like a stone when he stepped back, swung on his heel and left her without another word spoken. He trudged up the dam wall and stood on the bank, apparently looking out over the whole expanse of the excavation.

As much as she ached to, Rebecca did not call out to beg him to stay with her, but her eyes clung to his dark silhouette, willing him not to go. It seemed to her there was a defeated droop to his shoulders and she grieved over hurting him. He had come to her in good faith—mistaken good faith—and in time he would see that her rejection of his proposal was no more nor less than solid common sense. However, that was probably no balm to his wounded pride right now.

It had taken every reserve of strength she had to reject his impulsive proposal. She wanted him so much. Wanted him with her for the rest of her life. But the reality was she could never have him like that. And she dared not risk giving him any legal right to take their child away from her.

Rebecca had to wait until her legs felt strong enough to follow him. He didn't move. He didn't even glance at her when she finally stood beside him. His face could have been carved of stone. Rebecca released a shaky breath and tried to speak in a calm voice.

"Milly will be preparing dinner. You're welcome to stay, Slade," she stated quietly.

"Crumbs, Rebecca?" He sliced her a tortured look that stabbed straight at her heart.

"Roast beef, more likely," she snapped reflexively. If he couldn't see that she was saving them both from intolerable stresses in rejecting his proposal, then he was unbelievably blind. "Please yourself," she added dully.

"Oh, I'll come," he drawled, the pain in his eyes overlaid with a dangerous glitter as he turned to her. "I'll take everything you offer me, Rebecca. I need some return for being used . . . once again."

The blood drained from Rebecca's face as she realised he was likening her to all the women in his past. "You got what you asked for, Slade," she justified weakly.

"Answer me one thing!" he answered venomously. "Do you intend to use my child to get Paul Neilsen to marry you?"

Nausea rolled through her stomach. "No," she choked out, fighting dizzying waves in her head. "It was you who suggested that, Slade. Not me. Never me."

"But you still love him," Slade said bitterly. "That's why you won't marry me, isn't it?"

"No. It's not. I'm sorry if you can't understand. I'm sorry." She felt herself swaying. "I have to sit down."

She dropped to the ground and had her head between her knees before Slade had time to react to her startling action. Black dots were dancing before her eyes, her face felt clammy, and the earth was whirling around, but she managed to stay conscious.

"Rebecca!" The sharp concern in Slade's voice penetrated the fog in her mind, and she was vaguely aware of him hunkered down beside her.

"Bit faint. That's all," she explained jerkily.

He muttered something savage but she couldn't make it out. Then she found herself being lifted up and cradled against his chest.

"Better on the ground," she protested.

"Better in bed," he said grimly, and started striding towards the homestead.

She managed to slide a hand around his neck and he hoisted her a bit higher so that her head rested comfortably on his shoulder. It felt so good to have Slade holding her again that Rebecca didn't protest any further.

"I'm sorry, Rebecca," he said in a pained voice. "I'm a darned fool, upsetting you like that. I came to take care of you, not..." A self-contemptuous sound gravelled from his throat. "Brains still in the wrong place!"

"Yes," she agreed.

He gave a harsh little laugh. "No. Not there. Not right now anyway. And I don't care if they're crumbs. Crumbs are better than nothing. Besides, I'll show you we've got more in common than you realise. You just wait and see, Rebecca Wilder. I'll show you. You're not going to get rid of me as fast as you think."

"Don't want to get rid of you," she mumbled, feeling snugly warm as her circulation surged back into action. She would take all he would give her, too. Crumbs. Anything. Until he left again. "I like you showing me things," she added as an afterthought.

"You're not to get into that bone-shaking bulldozer again," he said sternly. "You tell me what you want done and I'll do it."

"Can you drive a dozer?"

"I'll learn," he said grimly.

"Can you do any of the things I'll want done?"

"I'll learn," he said even more grimly.

Rebecca thought about that. She wasn't going to let Slade boss her around. On the other hand, as long as Slade stayed with her, she wouldn't have the problem of getting to sleep. She decided there was some compromising that would be acceptable.

"All right," she agreed. "I'll let you learn."

Slade breathed a satisfied little sigh.

Rebecca burrowed her face into the warmth of his throat and resolved not to think about the future. She didn't know and she didn't want to know how long Slade would stay with her this time. She would simply take each day as it came and make the most of it. At least they had got one thing settled. He didn't have to feel obliged to marry her any more. In fact, marriage was completely out of the question. She hoped Slade accepted that.

CHAPTER TWELVE

THEY HAD TWENTY-THREE incredibly marvellous days together. Rebecca knew exactly because she marked each day Slade was with her on the calendar in her office.

Not quite every hour was spent in each other's company. Slade needed an office also, and one of the spare rooms in the homestead was set up for this purpose. He had brought with him a teleprinter, a fax machine and a lot of other electronic communications equipment. Most days he was in touch with Brisbane, and occasionally he got up in the middle of the night to speak to his people in New York. These hours on his business became part of their routine and Rebecca did not interfere. Sometimes she fantasised that this arrangement was a permanent solution, but in her saner moments she recognised that as a pipe dream. It was only a Band-Aid solution, which could not possibly hold for long.

Milly, of course, looked down her long nose at the whole affair, until Slade told her categorically that it wasn't *his* fault they weren't married. Whereupon the wiry little housekeeper eyed him with much more favour and reserved her long-nosed look for Rebecca, who was not acting with the propriety that her grandmother would have expected of her. Rebecca happily ignored both Slade's claim and Milly's terse little reproofs. Each day was too precious to her to waste any second of it in argument.

Slade learnt to drive the bulldozer. Not very well, but well enough. She sat up on the bank and directed his labours, much to both their satisfactions. He wasn't too keen on her riding out to check the cattle on horseback, but he reluctantly conceded that there were places where a Land Rover couldn't be driven. He rode with her. He would learn how to check whatever she wanted checked. It was only a question of becoming more familiar with this land and its unique peculiarities. After all, he *had* been brought up on a ranch.

He suffered saddle soreness without complaint, declaring it was well worth it to have Rebecca rub liniment into him. In fact, he was perfectly content to invite soreness every night. It was getting to be mighty erotic. It gave him ideas he'd never had before, and sometimes Rebecca didn't finish massaging in the liniment before he had to show them to her. She didn't think it was worth protesting. Slade could make her forget anything when he set his mind on it. When they did eventually slide into sleep, they slept very well.

Whenever Rebecca stopped to think about what was happening, she only felt confused. Slade did not appear to be at all bored or discontented with the life they led. He really seemed to enjoy being part of Wildjanna. Yet she could not accept that it would stay that way for a lifetime. Whether it was simply another challenge for him, a complete break away from his other life, or perhaps a pleasurable recollection of his boyhood with his grandfather, she didn't know and she didn't want to ask.

However, she was all too poignantly aware that Slade was carving a deeper place in her heart with every hour he spent sharing her life. She was afraid to even think how she would feel when he left her to resume his real life. This was a fool's paradise, she told herself, but it didn't stop her savouring every moment of it.

Yet, as relentless as the sands of time, the end had to come.

And come it did.

As was their custom most evenings after the evening meal, they were sitting on the verandah, enjoying the peace at the close of the day. The air was completely still, not even the slightest waft of breeze. The landscape was drenched in the light of a full moon. No clouds. There hadn't been clouds for years. It didn't seem the drought would ever break. Rebecca looked at the excavated dam. Right now it was a stark wound in the ground, waiting for the water that would give it life. But one day...

Slade shifted restlessly in the wicker armchair that had been her grandfather's. He pushed himself out of it and stepped to the edge of the verandah. His head tilted as he stared up at the stars, a vast panoply of stars that shone more brilliantly in the outback than anywhere else in the world, as if the silence and lonely vastness of the land drew them closer, whispering the age-old message that this earth was part of them, part of the cycle of the whole universe.

The words that broke the silence were quietly spoken, but they not only shattered the peace of the evening, they also heralded in the hard inexorable reality that Rebecca had always known she would have to face.

"I have to go away, at least for a few days," Slade said, then turned to her, gesturing an apologetic appeal. "It's something I have to handle personally, Rebecca. If I could delegate it, I would. But I can't."

Rebecca sat very still, feeling a coldness creep through her body, a terrible tightness creep over her face. She had to force out the words that her lips didn't want to say. "You can come and go as you please, Slade. You don't have to consult with me. There's no obligation to—"

He muttered some savage imprecation under his breath, then threw his hands up in exasperated appeal.

"We've been together for nearly a month and you can still say that? What do I have to do to get through to you, Rebecca? It's not that I want to go."

He dropped his hands, shook his head and paced the verandah, pausing to shake his head again before swinging around to come back to her.

Rebecca watched the very deliberate air of his approach in bleak resignation, knowing this was the beginning of the end. Brisbane. Then back to New York. He would go because he had to go—there was no one else to take on his responsibilities—and then there would be pressures on him to stay longer than he meant to; he wouldn't be able to get away. He had probably neglected things to remain with her this long, creating problems that would require all the more of his attention when he was faced with them.

"Ever since we met I seem to have been fighting rejection from you, Rebecca," he threw at her with a violent edge of frustration. "You look on me as though I'm some temporary lover who can't be trusted with your full confidence. It doesn't seem to matter what I do or say. So why don't you give me the answer? How do I get you to believe in me?"

The idea came impulsively to Rebecca as she looked into his grimly determined face. At least it would guarantee that she would have him near her when she needed him most.

"There is something you can do, Slade," she said quickly before she could have second thoughts.

"Tell me!" he urged, his eyes glittering with a deep inner impatience.

"You can make the time to be with me when I give birth to our baby."

It was a purely rational challenge. If Slade truly wanted to share in her life and in their child's life, if he was deep-down genuine and this was not a passing impulse, a *novelty* that would eventually get buried under the weight of his other life, then one way or another he would make a point of being with her at the birth of their child.

"Of course I'll be with you!" he assured her. "I'll take you to the hospital, stay by your side the whole time. I want to be there, Rebecca."

She shook her head. "No hospital, Slade. This baby is going to be born on Wildjanna, just as I was, and my father and uncle and brother whose graves are also here at Wildjanna. This will be the fourth generation and I'm not going to any hospital."

He stared at her in total disbelief. "Rebecca, you can't be serious!"

"Never more so," she returned coolly.

The disbelief slowly changed to a look of appalled contemplation. "You have to have a doctor in attendance. You can't . . . you can't just have a baby by yourself," he protested.

"I'll call the Flying Doctor Service. Unless there's some known medical reason against it, most babies are born on the home properties out here, Slade," she explained.

"What if the doctor can't get here in time?" he argued frantically. "What if . . . ?" He had gone white in the face. He swallowed convulsively. "I have no experience in this kind of thing, Rebecca!" His eyes wildly challenged hers. "What if I'm away when it . . . when it starts happening . . . and the doctor can't come?"

Excuses, she thought, and dropped her gaze from his. She looked out over Wildjanna, her façade of calm composure hiding the painful pounding of her heart. "Nature does most of the work," she said tonelessly. "I'll manage by myself if I have to. You please yourself what you do, Slade. It doesn't worry me."

"Rebecca, I am coming back." There was a thread of desperation in the harshness of his voice. "It's just for a few days."

"Of course," she agreed, keeping her eyes fixed on the landscape. She gave a little shrug. "Whatever you want, Slade."

"I'll bring you back an architect. A builder. An interior decorator."

She looked at him as though he had taken leave of his senses. "What do you imagine I want them for?"

"To check over the additions to the house for the children's project," he replied with an air of triumphant satisfaction. "You want to get started on it, don't you?"

She had discussed her plans with several authorities and they had been met with co-operative appreciation. However, it had been pointed out that special amenities would have to be provided for children whose failing health could not bear any stress. The additions meant some structural changes to the homestead.

Rebecca had shown Slade the plans she had drawn up. He had examined them with interest, and made a couple of suggestions, which she had noted down. The topic hadn't been fully pursued because Slade had started playing with her hair and that had led to other things.

"I can't afford to build right now," she said decisively. "Once the drought breaks I'll be able to start thinking about it."

"I told you that Cordell Enterprises would supply the funds to do whatever was required. There's no need to wait," Slade argued.

Rebecca frowned at him. "Slade, I feel you're trying to buy me. This is my home. Whatever needs to be done to it, I'll do. The travelling costs and any medical equipment—that's different. I won't accept your paying out any money for additions to my home, Slade."

"It's not for you! It's for the children!" he retorted vehemently. "Besides, I intend to make this my home, too. If you have some objection to that, you'd better state it now. Otherwise, I'm bringing an architect, a builder and an interior decorator back with me."

He was right. She shouldn't let her pride delay anything when that meant depriving some children of what Wildjanna could give them. And she certainly had no objection to Slade making his home here whenever he could.

"Okay," she agreed. "Bring back whomever you want."

Slade heaved a sigh of relief. His voice dropped to a soft persuasive note. "Rebecca, you don't really mean that about having the baby here."

"Yes, I do."

Her eyes flashed her determination at him. She wasn't going to let Slade buy her off with his help for her project. If he wanted to be counted, let him stand and be counted when it was most important to her, not when he could make some convenient time for dropping in on her life!

His head jerked away, then slowly turned back. "I'll call you every day. At five o'clock. And I'll want to know all you've been doing, to make sure you've not gone wild and done . . . the things you shouldn't. Five o'clock," he repeated as though impelled to stamp it into her mind.

"As you like," she said flatly. "I may or may not be here to take the call. It will depend on what I'm doing. I won't spend my life hanging on what you do, Slade."

"I want you in my life, Rebecca," he said fiercely.

She pushed herself out of her chair, ruing the undeniable fact that her body was no longer lithe or graceful. She was into her sixth month of pregnancy and although she was still in fairly trim shape her balance was not as good as it normally was. Nevertheless, she threw her shoulders back and faced Slade with resolute pride.

"I made the baby. The rest of this situation was made by you, Slade. I didn't ask it of you. I can look after myself, and I want this baby too much to put its well-being at risk. Do what you have to do. I'm not stopping you."

Conflict warred across his face. "Whatever I have to do, whatever I have to accomplish, I'll win your love, Rebecca Wilder, if it's the last thing I ever do!" he declared vehemently.

It was the last thing she had ever expected to hear from Slade, and for a moment Rebecca was too stunned to make any reply to it. Desire, yes. The will to have his own way, yes. But to want her love.... He hadn't even believed in love. Did this mean he loved her?

"I hope so, Slade. I truly hope so," she said in a voice that shook with turbulent emotion, hopelessly aware that she already loved him.

Unaccountably tears pricked her eyes and she turned aside, not wanting Slade to misinterpret them as distress at his going. He caught her, his arms sliding over the tight bulge of the baby and gently pulling her against the vibrant tautness of his body. His warm mouth moved seductively over her ear. "I'll tame you yet," he murmured huskily.

"Do you really want me to be tamed, Slade?" she whispered, then swivelled in his embrace and kissed him with all the fierce passion that he aroused in her.

There was no more talking that night.

Slade left the next day.

A call came from him every afternoon at five o'clock. Although Rebecca berated herself for her growing dependency on that link with him, she could not deny herself the pleasure of some communication, however unsatisfied it left her.

There were seven long days before Slade returned to Wildjanna. With an architect and a builder and an interior decorator. Rebecca's reunion with Slade was constrained by the presence of the three visitors who had to be given most of her attention. They spent the rest of the day taking a lot of measurements and consulting with Rebecca, making sure they knew all her requirements and the requirements of the job. Rebecca readily agreed with the arrangements Slade had made for work to begin as soon as possible, and by the time all three flew off again in the plane, late in the afternoon, this part of the project was completely in their very capable hands.

"Satisfied?" Slade asked when they were gone.

"Yes, thank you," Rebecca returned lightly, unsure what Slade wanted from her.

There was a tense portending air about him, which stayed with him indefinitely, as though he was waiting for something to happen. Strangely enough, Rebecca had the impression that it was not entirely focused on her, yet she was mixed up in it. She wondered if she was supposed to express gladness that he was with her again, or if he expected her to give in and say she would marry him after all.

She did neither.

Her gladness was obvious anyway, and she was determined not to use any emotional pressure on him or take any from him. Their relationship could not survive that kind of strain. Unless they respected each other's rights to carry on their separate lives, the situation would fast become utterly destructive.

As it was, Rebecca couldn't see it lasting. Which was why a marriage between them couldn't even be contemplated. This minor separation would inevitably be followed by others, and, once the baby was born, they would probably become longer and longer. If they married, the time would eventually come when they spent so

little of their lives together that divorce was a foregone
conclusion. And then if Slade decided to fight her for
their child...

"No commitment unless it was a forever commitment," Rebecca recited firmly to herself, but as it turned
out, Slade didn't press her for anything. They resumed
their daily routine at Wildjanna as though he had never
been away, as though nothing had changed at all. Except
something had. Rebecca could not shake off the feeling
that Slade was waiting for something.

It was almost two weeks before she found out what it
was, and even when the first intimation came, she didn't
realise what it meant. They had just finished dinner one
night when Milly came hurrying into the dining-room,
her face reflecting a conflict of interests as she darted
anxious looks at both Slade and Rebecca before an-
nouncing that Rebecca was wanted in the office.

"What for?" Rebecca asked.

Milly hesitated, her answer curiously circumspect.
"There's a call for you. You have to take it."

"Who is it?" Rebecca demanded, slowly pushing herself up from the table.

Milly looked pained. She darted another anxious look
at Slade. "Mr. Neilsen," she gabbled quickly.

Rebecca's heart leapt in shock. "Paul? Paul is calling
me?"

Rebecca raced for the office, her mind awhirl with
disturbing possibilities. In the almost four years since the
accident Paul had never made contact with her at
Wildjanna. It had always been she who had called or
visited him. Something must have happened to him, she
thought, fighting down a sense of panic. He must need
her.

She grabbed the receiver and lowered herself shakily
into the chair in front of it. She forced herself to take a
deep breath, afraid that her voice would be trembling like

the rest of her. She owed Paul Neilsen her life. Anything he wanted of her she had to give.

"Paul? It's Rebecca," she announced as steadily as she could.

"I hope I haven't called you away from anything important, Rebecca." His voice sounded calm and warmly friendly.

"Not at all," she affirmed quickly, then, not believing there could be no particular import behind this extraordinary event, she pressed, "How are you?"

"Fine! Very happy!" he said, a little too heartily to Rebecca's ear. "I wanted you to be the first to hear my news, Rebecca. We've shared·so much together, been friends for so long—" The heartiness cracked a little. She heard a swift intake of breath. "And I know you'll want to wish me every happiness in my life, just as I wish you every happiness in yours. I'm getting married, Rebecca."

Married! Paul getting married to someone else! The shock of it left her speechless.

"Her name is Susan Hanley," Paul's voice continued brightly. "She's a wonderful person. She's been working for me for over a year now." He gave a forced little laugh. "She even anticipates my needs before I think of them."

Someone else fulfilling his needs as she had once fulfilled them before the accident. Paul had never loved her. Rebecca suddenly knew that beyond any doubt now. When the fantasy of running Wildjanna with her had come crashing down, he hadn't wanted the commitment of the marriage they had planned.

Paul's choice.

Slade's words came back to her, slowly relieving her of the long hangover of guilt over Paul's injuries. She was still grateful to Paul for saving her life, but the burden that had placed on her heart was no longer a heavy one.

He had found a woman who suited him better, a woman he wanted to marry.

"When are you getting married?" she asked, pushing a brittle brightness into her voice. Paul had known this Susan Hanley for a year, a whole year. No wonder he had looked so anguished when she had begged him to marry her at the airport that day. He was embarrassed even now. She could tell from the forced cheerfulness in his voice.

"Tomorrow."

She weathered this shock a little more cynically. Paul had put off telling her the truth until the last moment. Did he think she would make a scene? Another impassioned plea for him to change his mind? She supposed she couldn't blame him for thinking that. She had clung on so long. But he could have been more honest with her. All these years he had let her think his disaffection was because of his disabilities from the accident. Had he pitied her for clinging to a dream that he knew was over?

"I hope the sun shines for you, for you and your bride, tomorrow and always," she said, trying her best to demonstrate there was no ill will on her part. What they had had together was well and truly over. It had only ever been an illusion anyway. She truly hoped that Paul loved his Susan.

"Thank you, Rebecca." There was relief in his voice. "And I hope it rains for Wildjanna very soon."

"Yes. We sorely need it. Thank you for calling, Paul. I do wish you, both of you, every happiness."

"And I you," he added softly. "In your future life. Goodbye, Rebecca."

The finality in his voice was unmistakable.

"Goodbye," she echoed.

She heard the line disconnect and knew the last line had been spoken between them. There had been no suggestion that they could all be friends. That chapter of their lives was definitely closed. And in truth, Rebecca was content for it to be so. She wished she could see her future with Slade as clearly as Paul could see his with Susan Hanley.

Married . . . tomorrow.

Tears blurred her eyes and she hastily blinked them away. It was weak to cry. She had made her choice with Slade, and half a loaf with him was better than nothing at all. Besides, she would soon have the baby. Her hand went to her swollen tummy, gently caressing the mound of her child . . . Slade's child. She would always have some part of him, no matter what else the future held.

She didn't know how she knew that Slade was near, watching her, waiting. Some sixth sense picked up the force field of his presence. She looked around and he was there in the office doorway, grim-faced and emanating so much tension that Rebecca felt choked by it.

He didn't ask any questions. He didn't say a word. It came to her in a lightning flash of intuition that Slade knew what Paul's call had been about, not only knew but had known before she did. It was Paul's call that he had been waiting for ever since he had returned from Brisbane.

"You had something to do with this, Slade?" she asked, wanting to know precisely what he had done.

"Yes," he replied unashamedly. "I went to see him. You now know that he's never going to marry you. Never, Rebecca," he repeated, his face stamped with ruthless purpose.

What a strange meeting that must have been, she mused. The blackest of black comedies. Slade believing she still loved Paul. Paul believing the same. Both of them wanting the final severance of a relationship that didn't suit either of them. Poor Rebecca, they would have thought. But necessary to be cruel to be kind.

It was humiliating to think of them discussing her like that behind her back. Pride stirred. She didn't need them to decide her life for her. She could stand alone if she had to. If Slade thought this would change the situation between them, he was badly mistaken.

Her green eyes flashed steely determination at him. "That doesn't mean I'll marry you, Slade," she stated flatly.

A savagely determined glitter leapt into the vivid blue eyes. "Right now, I'll settle for something else. But we're going to make a family—you and I and our child, Rebecca. And one by one I'm going to hack away all your restraints from marrying me until you're left with no other choice. Then you're going to love *me*. Not him."

In that moment he wore the relentless air of a conqueror who recognised no barriers, and Rebecca felt her will crumbling under the strength of it. There was a stirring of response deep within her, a strange wanting to be his conquest, whatever the cost. Did he love her? she wondered. Or was this simply his need to possess, to stamp his domination on whatever he wanted, to win his way?

Rebecca didn't like to think of herself as a conquest. It was an alien feeling to everything she had ever lived by. Her destiny was her own to carve, not to be bent to Slade Cordell's will. She wanted a partnership, a mating for life. No way would she be Slade's woman unless he was her man . . . permanently.

"You can't make me marry you, Slade," she said quietly.

"I'll make it possible." His voice softened as he continued, becoming more appealing. "Your life and Paul Neilsen's crossed for a time. That time is over, Rebecca. Now it's our lives that are together. Paul recognised that immediately."

Her mouth curled in savage irony. "Yes. I imagine he did. With you telling him so, Slade."

He didn't so much as flinch. His eyes bored steadily into hers. "He doesn't love you, Rebecca."

She didn't flinch, either. "I know."

"He didn't want to share his life with you."

She shrugged and turned away. "I made a mistake," she said flatly. "Maybe I'm making another mistake with you."

"No!" He was across the room in a few swift strides, pulling her up from her chair, enfolding her in a tight embrace. She couldn't find the strength to resist. She sagged against the rocklike indomitability of his body and was soothed by his sharing it with her. She didn't want to be alone.

"This is our time, Rebecca," Slade insisted passionately, then kissed her with a driven need to impress that on her, to impress himself on her.

Rebecca didn't fight it.

She was content for it to be so.

For as long as it lasted.

But she would not marry him.

Apart from her own need to keep Slade's child, she had to safeguard the fourth generation for Wildjanna.

CHAPTER THIRTEEN

IT SEEMED a strange contradiction to Rebecca that although she and Slade spent less time with each other over the next two months, they grew closer together. Slade ritually went missing for at least two days a week, often at the weekends, flying off to Brisbane to deal with whatever business demanded his attention. He never failed to call her every evening he was away, and Rebecca was never left in any doubt that he would soon be with her at Wildjanna again.

She didn't mind these absences. Slade had to be free to do what he wanted, as she was to do as she wanted. The rapidly advancing state of her pregnancy meant that she had to leave most of the station work to the stock men, who readily carried out her instructions. Or Slade's, if he rode out with them, which he often did when he was home.

Slade invariably called Wildjanna home. He would get off the plane from his trips to Brisbane, give her a huge grin, sweep her into his arms and with a sigh of deep contentment breathe, "It's good to be home again." It was impossible to disbelieve him. Rebecca still refused to look too far ahead, but her own happiness in their relationship could not be denied.

Slade's pleasure in sharing everything he could with her deepened Rebecca's pleasure in his company. Work had begun on the additions to the homestead so she was not at all bored or frustrated from being restricted in the more physical work of the cattle station. Not only did she supervise every step of what was being done to her home, but there was a battery of correspondence to carry through, with letters to and from hospitals and the societies that dealt with the children who concerned her. Because of Slade's help, the project could be brought forward to almost a standby footing.

As soon as the baby was born and she was back to full working capacity, Rebecca intended to begin. If only the drought would break, everything would be perfect. It would be even more perfect if Slade could stay with her forever.

She had thought he might find her less and less desirable as her body swelled into an unlovely and cumbersome shape. However, far from being put off from the more intimate side of their life, Slade seemed to adore every aspect of her pregnancy.

Rebecca wondered if it was because this was a completely new experience for him. Another *novelty*. Yet he made her feel so loved and cherished that she didn't care why he did it, as long as he kept doing it.

He brought home bottles of beautifully scented body oil, which he gently rubbed into her tightly stretched abdomen. His eyes always reflected an awed delight if the baby moved while he was doing this. He made love more gently as time went on, mostly taking and giving a deep wondrous satisfaction in cradling her body spoon fashion against his, and embracing their child as well as Rebecca in their total intimacy.

He brought her books on prenatal care and insisted she practise breathing and relaxation exercises. After several weeks of determined coaching for the birth process, Slade finally broached the critical subject of the baby's delivery.

"First babies can be difficult, Rebecca," he warned her, clearly having done quite a bit of reading on it himself. "I know you have no fears about it, and you think it's all very natural, but you haven't had the experience and..."

He took a deep breath, his eyes pleading with hers in deep concern. "Please rethink about going into a hospital for the delivery. I promise you I'll be with you every minute. It's not that I want to shirk any responsibility. I just don't want anything to go wrong, either for you or the baby."

He was so deeply disturbed about it that Rebecca hesitated only a few moments before giving in. Although it meant their child would not be born on Wildjanna, Slade had given her so much that she could not feel it was fair to ignore his fears. The important thing was that their child be born safely, and she had no doubt that Slade would be with her.

In fact, she was almost ready to change her mind about marrying him. If he still wanted her to, after the baby was born, Rebecca was considering it. She was almost sure Slade would never intentionally do anything to hurt her. If he would agree to leave their child with her on Wildjanna—it seemed he might be content to do that, coming back to them whenever he could.

"All right. I'll go to hospital when the baby's due," she promised him.

"I'll make all the arrangements," he said in a happy burst of relief. "You won't have to worry about a thing, Rebecca. I'll take care of every possible contingency."

She accompanied Slade on his next trip to Brisbane and had a thorough medical checkup. The doctor declared that everything was coming along just fine, which was what Rebecca had confidently expected, but it seemed to set Slade's mind at rest.

They had a buying spree for all the baby's needs and ended up with twice as much as was necessary. Slade just couldn't contain himself, and it was such a joyful exciting outing together that Rebecca didn't have the heart to chide him for his extravagance.

He went completely wild in a soft toy department, ending up with an armful of adorable furry animals, some of which played nursery tunes, and when they returned to their hotel he lined them all up and sat listening to them with such a fatuous grin on his face that Rebecca couldn't help laughing at him. And loving him.

There was, however, one contingency over which Slade had no power, a contingency that the land had thirsted for throughout five long parched years. Rebecca's pregnancy was three weeks short of its full term when the clouds at last began to gather, huge black clouds that rolled over the sky, blotting out a sun that had ruled without pity for far too long. And the rain, the blessed life-giving rain, began to fall.

It started as a gentle sprinkle but did not remain that way for very long. Nor did the brief teasing shower that followed. It soon developed into a teeming downpour that beat at the ground, demanding entry. The dust was settled. Cracks in the earth swallowed their fill and closed. The water began running over the land, into the creek, into the new dam below the homestead. All the station hands on Wildjanna danced out in the pounding downpour and whooped for joy, soaked to the skin and loving every minute of it.

Any rainfall was good, but Rebecca prayed that this was not simply a passing storm. They needed days of rain before it could be confidently said that the drought was broken. By nightfall several inches had been measured and there was no easing of the torrential downpour. News reports on the radio stated that rain was sweeping right across central Australia. Some areas were already reporting flash flooding, and the drought was certainly eased, if not ended. The weather forecast for the following day was for more and heavier rain.

Rebecca and Slade lay awake in their bed for a long time, listening to the thundering beat of it on the iron roof. It was music to Rebecca's ears.

"I've never seen or heard anything like this," Slade remarked in wondering awe.

Rebecca laughed and snuggled up to him. "The outback is a land of primitive extremes, Slade. Nothing ever comes in half-measures. Drought, flood, fire...most times, all you can do is fight to survive the worst, then ride the crest of the best. It's both humbling and exhilarating, but always there is the challenge to keep pace with it. There's a harmony that has to be maintained, a link..." She heaved a deep sigh. "I don't know how to describe it."

"Elemental," Slade said, then grinned at her look of surprise. "I am not the blind city boy you think I am."

"No, you're not," she agreed, and sighed in contentment as his arm tightened around her.

She must have fallen asleep in an awkward position because the next morning Rebecca woke with a dragging ache in her lower back. Nevertheless, the nagging discomfort was quickly overridden by the excitement of hearing the rain still falling. Bubbling with high spirits, Rebecca pushed herself out of bed, dragged on a gown and hurried out to walk around the verandah and see how much change there had been during the night.

The new dam was already halfway to becoming a lake. The creek was rising fast and the ground was turning into a quagmire of squelching mud. It was a beautiful sight to Rebecca. As Slade joined her and slid an arm around her shoulders, she looked at him with sparkling eyes.

"I'm afraid you're not going to be able to get to Brisbane this week, Slade," she declared, smugly pleased that he would be forced to stay with her. "We'll be bogged in for quite a few days. No plane can come in or take off in these conditions."

"I didn't intend to go anyway," he returned with a funny little smile.

"No more problems for a while?" she asked lightly, hoping that would be the case until after the baby was born.

"Not for me."

The note of finality in his voice stirred her curiosity. She had made it a rule never to ask about his business, wary of being tempted to make demands that she had no right to make, but now she recalled that he hadn't spent any time at all in his office since his last trip away.

"Are you taking a vacation?" she asked, wanting to know how long this situation would last.

He met her eyes with a look of searching intensity, as though wary of her response to the answer of the question. "Something like that," was his rather obscure reply.

Rebecca was unsure whether to pursue the point or not. She was still hesitating over it when Milly called out that a news broadcast on the radio had said that the Diamantina river was in full spate. Rebecca's mind instantly turned to more urgent matters. The stock on Wildjanna had to be herded to high ground.

"If it floods, the Diamantina spills to a great lake, ninety miles across," she explained to Slade. "Windy Drop-Down Creek is a tributary. We've got to be prepared."

Slade frowned, then gave a slight shake of his head. "You mean ninety yards across, don't you? Not even the Amazon river..."

"No, Slade. I don't know about the Amazon, but in a big wet the Diamantina has been up to ninety miles wide." Her eyes danced at him as he shook his head again, not in disbelief, but in a bemused reaction to coming to grips with the realities of the outback. "You'll see it for yourself if the rain keeps up," Rebecca assured him.

"Ninety miles," he muttered. "No half-measures about that!"

Slade immediately got ready to ride out with the stock men, assuring her he would look after everything and see that the cattle were moved to higher ground. Rebecca watched him go from the homestead verandah, wishing she could go with him, but consoled by her pleasure in knowing that the drought really was ending.

So much had happened throughout its five-year course—Pa's death, Paul's terrible accident, the fateful meeting with Slade, which would never have occurred but for the necessity to conserve water, and then Gran's death and her own decision to have Slade's child. A new life, she thought happily, everywhere a new life. After the rain came the regrowth, losses to be recovered, breeding programmes to be initiated, a replenishing of the continuing cycle of nature.

Emilio Dalvarez would come flying back from Argentina, Rebecca thought with an indulgent sense of affection. He had always been a good neighbour and she could no longer hold any grudge about his interference in her personal affairs. Emilio had probably meant well, and his visit to New York had resulted in Slade coming to her a month earlier than he had planned.

She remembered her own visit to New York, the crossing point in hers and Slade's so vastly separate lifelines, and shook her head in bemusement over all that had eventuated from it. Slade had not concerned himself with the management of Devil's Elbow since then. There had been no need. They were running both properties as one, and now the rain would answer any problems that might have arisen.

Rebecca grew more conscious of the ache in her lower back as the morning wore on, but she attached no significance to it. The first rolling wave of pain came a couple of hours after lunch. It was not sharp enough to unduly disturb her. She had read that from the seventh month of pregnancy onwards it was not unusual to feel practice contractions. However, the second one, only an hour later, gave her pause for thought.

It couldn't be, Rebecca decided. There were still three weeks, almost three weeks, to go, and she wasn't ready to have the baby yet. Besides, with the rain coming down like this, she couldn't get to the hospital. A couple of pains were just a couple of pains, nothing to get in a fuss about. She was a normal, healthy person. There was no reason at all for her to give birth prematurely. Nevertheless, the nagging ache in her back was ominously constant. Rebecca checked the time, just in case she should.

Sure enough, almost to the hour, another pain rolled through her, lasting about thirty seconds. It was really happening, Rebecca thought in dazed wonderment. The baby wanted to be born. He or she was not content to wait for the normal timetable. Rebecca had to fight off a wild surge of excitement and force her mind to work along practical lines.

She had promised Slade that she would go to hospital for the delivery. A plane was out of the question, but a helicopter could lift her from Wildjanna. Slade wouldn't care how much it cost. She went into the office to make the necessary calls, then realised that even if there was a procurable helicopter, it couldn't get to Wildjanna before darkness fell. The weather conditions were hazardous for even daylight hours.

Nevertheless, she had to follow Slade's wishes. She called the Flying Doctor Service, informed them of her condition and asked for advice. The best they could do was to have a doctor on standby to give instructions should the birth occur during the night. Their information was that all air-rescue helicopters were out on missions to pick up people in danger of being drowned in the flooding. Rebecca made several more calls but they only served to confirm what she had already surmised. An imminent birth was not as critical as an imminent death, and she had no hope of being picked up before morning.

She bent over as another contraction made itself felt, automatically employing the breathing technique that would minimise the discomfort. The office clock confirmed that the time elapsed from the last one was only forty-five minutes. Rebecca figured the baby was following its own schedule and was not about to wait on anyone's convenience. Maybe it wanted to be born on Wildjanna. Maybe it knew it was the fourth generation.

The thought brought a blissful smile to Rebecca's lips as she hugged her cumbersome body. *It will be all right,* she told her baby. *I know what you're doing and I'm going to help you all the way.*

Slade got back to the homestead just at dusk. He came in wet and muddy but spreading cheer with the news that the cattle had all been herded onto high ground. He seemed enormously satisfied with his day's work, and grinned happily as he recalled that he didn't have to stint on water tonight. He was going to soak in a full hot bath for at least an hour, and Rebecca could reward him for his labours by soaping his back.

Rebecca suppressed her own news until he was stretched out in steaming water and thoroughly relaxed. "I've been labouring, too," she said, her eyes dancing with her inner knowledge as she lathered soap over his chest.

"Mmm..." It was half a question, half a sound of sensual pleasure.

"Our child is on its way into the world."

Slade's eyes flew open. His body jackknifed into a sitting position. "Rebecca, you don't mean now!"

She nodded, then quickly explained that there was no way she could get to hospital in time for the delivery—she had tried—and they would have to manage the birth themselves.

Slade fought the waves of panic that pummelled his stomach and made a useless mash of his mind. Rebecca had no fear. He must not show fear. He recited that thought over and over in chaotic desperation. His worst nightmare was coming true, but showing fear was the worst possible thing he could do. He was not going to fail her. He was going to make her believe in him. And please God, he prayed wildly, don't let anything go wrong.

The host of expressions that flitted across Slade's face went too fast for Rebecca to identify, but it was determination that finally settled on it. "I can do it, Rebecca. You're not to worry or be afraid. I can do it," he assured her. "I've got everything we need stored away in my office. Have you told Milly?"

"Not yet. I didn't want to panic her."

"I'll need her help. But you're not to worry. I'll explain it all to Milly and get her organised."

Rebecca shook her head in bewilderment. "What have you got stored away in your office?"

"The midwife equipment." He surged out of the bath and started drying himself, all his movements brisk and purposeful. *It's just a case of mind over matter,* he told himself. Hadn't he always prided himself on his competence? A little baby wasn't going to beat him. *Except it's my baby,* his mind screamed. *Rebecca's and mine! And everything's got to go right!*

Rebecca stared at him in sheer astonishment. "How do you come to have midwife equipment?"

He gave her a rueful smile. "I learnt how to do it in case something like this happened. I said I'd look after you, Rebecca, and I will. I've done a midwifery course, watched deliveries . . ."

"But you said I had to go to hospital!"

He sighed. "Rebecca, the more you learn, the more you become aware of what can go wrong. It's not much of a risk. Most deliveries are straightforward. So you're not to worry. I can handle it," he insisted earnestly.

Another pain surged through Rebecca, putting reality ahead of theory. Slade instantly sprang into action, gently rubbing her lower back as he coached her breathing.

"How long since the last one?" he asked when the pain had receded.

"About forty minutes."

"Okay. Try to relax now. We'll go and tell Milly and start getting prepared."

Apart from the few contractions, which required her complete concentration, Rebecca was in a constant state of amazement over the next two hours. Slade had Milly so busy sterilising basins and preparing one of the bedrooms that the housekeeper quickly recovered from her initial shock over the news and did his bidding with an air of incredulous fascination. Which echoed Rebecca's own feelings.

Slade might well have been a doctor himself, he was so knowing and confident and meticulous in his preparations. Everything was accomplished with a calm efficiency that inspired the utmost confidence in his claim that he knew all about handling a home delivery.

Rebecca was both mortified by the lack of faith she had once shown in him and exalted that he had gone so far to prove that she could trust him and depend on him. Few husbands would do so much for their wives, and she had refused to marry him, not only refused, but couched her rejection of him in the bitterest terms by comparing him to Paul.

Slade was a far finer man than Paul, far stronger, far more caring about her needs, far more loving. Shame burned through Rebecca, such deep shame that she felt driven to confess the truth of her feelings for him. She hadn't been fair to Slade. She hadn't been fair at all.

"I thought you went to Brisbane on business," she began, pained now by the reservations she had kept harbouring, the reservations that had forced Slade to such lengths in order to prove she could trust him. "I had no idea you would...would care so much. I just wanted you with me when the baby was born. I thought Cordell Enterprises would take you away from me and—"

"It never will, Rebecca," Slade said, his eyes gravely promising that truth. "Believe me, this means more to me than anything else in my whole life."

"I believe you," she whispered, her own eyes filling with emotional tears. "Having you with me . . . it means a lot to me, too, Slade. More—more than I can ever say. And doing all this for me . . ."

"Lucky I did. I'm not sure how well I would have coped otherwise." He gently wiped away the spill of tears on her cheeks. "You're doing fine," he said softly. "Just think about having the baby, Rebecca. We made it together and we're going to bring it into the world together. Okay?"

She nodded and quickly sucked in her breath as another pain started. He was so good to her during each contraction, encouraging her to lean on him or take up any position she found most comfortable for riding it through. She didn't want to lie down. Milly brought her drinks when her mouth and lips got dry from all the shallow breathing. Slade held her hand and told her heartwarming stories about the births he had witnessed during his midwife course.

The time between the contractions kept lessening and the pain grew progressively stronger. By midnight they were only five minutes apart, barely enough pause to recover from one before the next started. Rebecca had to lie down.

Milly sat on the chair beside the bed and held Rebecca's hand tight while Slade carried out a full examination. He reported that the baby was in the right birth position. Everything was going by the textbook, Slade assured himself, but textbook data—not even the few deliveries he had seen were anything as harrowing as this.

He felt utterly helpless, trapped within a situation over which he had no real control, unable to take Rebecca's pain upon himself, unable to make the baby come faster. The only relief was in knowing that everything was normal. So far. If anything started to go wrong... But he had to keep thinking positive, help Rebecca, make it right!

The next half-hour was wave after wave of continual agony. Rebecca coped as well as she could but she couldn't help crying out. Slade grew so distressed he wanted to give her an injection, but Rebecca refused to have it, insisting that she wasn't going to interfere with the natural process in any way. Slade helped her onto the pillows and lifted her knees up, sure that she was about to move into the second stage of labour, and no sooner did he have her positioned than the membranes ruptured and she had a blessed feeling of release as the forewaters flooded down.

"Okay, Rebecca, we're ready to move," Slade told her, trying his utmost to keep his voice steady and all that he had learnt clear in his head. "When you feel the urge to push, push," he instructed. "Go with the contraction. Don't fight it. And don't panic."

"Won't panic," she gasped as the compulsion to bear down began.

There was a terrible maelstrom of panic circling Slade's mind but he refused to let it in. Rebecca had suffered so much. He was not going to fail her when she needed him most. He was not going to fail her!

The pushing part was not so bad, but the pain in between had Rebecca breathing hard. Slade kept encouraging her, telling her that everything was going fine. The steady conviction in his eyes helped. Her eyes clung trustingly to that conviction. Slade wouldn't let her down, she thought. He had never let her down. He had done all he said he would do, and now he was standing by her in her hour of need. Standing by her as few men would or could. So strong. So steadfast. Looking after her. Loving her. He had to love her. No man would do all this for her unless he loved her.

"You're doing great! Just one or two more pushes, Rebecca," Slade soothed. *I'm ready,* he told himself. *I'm ready to do all I have to do to make sure our baby is born safely. Only another few minutes. My hands are shaking. I've got to stop my hands from shaking. Concentrate . . .*

"Milly, hold the cleaning towel and bunny rug ready," he commanded.

Rebecca pushed.

"The head is coming now," Slade cried excitedly. The miracle of it . . . a beautiful, perfect head. He had it in his hands. Their child . . . "Keep pushing, Rebecca. Shoulders . . ."

She felt a slithering release accompanied by more water, then heard her baby's first cry. What a wonderful sound it was!

"My child . . ." The awe and wonder in Slade's voice billowed through Rebecca's mind.

"Is it a boy or girl?" she asked, too exhausted to move but so exhilarated she wanted to do so much more. She wanted to feel her baby, touch it tenderly.

"Rebecca, I reckon you've just given birth to the first female president of the United States." Slade's voice was bursting with relief and pride and joy as he quickly placed his child—her child—over Rebecca's stomach, her head hanging down over Rebecca's waist to stop her from inhaling any fluid. "Or, if not that," he raved on, grabbing the cleaning towel from Milly to wipe the wetness from the tiny body, "I guess she'll make the finest astrophysicist in the whole world."

He'd done it! He'd done it right! Their daughter was safe and sound! Born to them this night—born to both of them—they'd made her together and brought her into the world together, their very own child, alive, healthy, perfect! It had been the most frightening experience of his life, but the reward, the ultimate reward of it, a new life! Thank you, God! If You're out there watching over us, thank you . . . thank you . . . for this new life!

"I think you're forgetting Wildjanna," Rebecca said indulgently, her eyes feasting on the unbelievable perfection of their baby.

"Never," Slade said with deep conviction. "Wildjanna is her home. It will always be her home, no matter where she goes or what she does."

The fourth generation.

Are you looking down from somewhere, Gran? Rebecca thought wistfully. Do you know I've kept the faith that you and Pa brought to this land we call home? This is your bloodline, mine, fathered by a man who is strong enough to stand beside me, Gran. The mission to New York, your last command, it took me to him, brought him to me . . . and now the line will go on with this child who was born on Wildjanna tonight.

Slade passed Milly the cleaning towel, took the bunny rug, then with tender loving care wrapped his daughter up warmly and gently put her on Rebecca's breast. The feeling as her baby started sucking was unbelievable. She was so tiny, so beautiful . . . Rebecca cradled her in her arms and looked at Slade with blissful tears in her eyes.

"Thank you . . . thank you," she whispered.

It was all she could think of to say. She saw that there were tears in his eyes, too, and when he bent and kissed her, her heart was so full she thought it would burst with love.

"Got to clamp the cord now," he said huskily, and set about doing so. There was more to do, more to get right. He had to look after Rebecca, make sure he didn't forget anything. She was depending on him. She believed in him.

"What time is it?" she asked.

"Five past two," Milly answered, her voice uncharacteristically indulgent.

With an overwhelming sense of relief Slade followed through each step that completed the birth process, knowing that nothing, nothing at all had gone wrong. He couldn't stop smiling at Rebecca. She looked as though she was lost in a beautiful dream, looking down at their child at her breast. A couple of times Slade had to blink back tears. A grown man crying... It was absurd, yet surely there was nothing in the whole world—the whole universe—that could match the miracle of birth. And to see Rebecca like this...with their baby.

Time had lost all meaning for Rebecca. She had her long-awaited child, safe and sound in her arms. Then Slade brought in the baby's bath, and together they carefully washed their new little daughter and dressed her in the clothes they had bought.

The wonder of her choked both Slade and Rebecca into silence, but their daughter had no sense of awe at all. She loudly protested the whole bathing process, demonstrating a voice that was going to demand a lot of say in her life. But once she was snugly wrapped in a bunny rug again, she went straight to sleep.

The bassinet was ready for her, but Rebecca was loath to let her out of her embrace. Milly announced that she was off to bed. Her usually stoic face shone with warm benevolence as she dropped a kiss on Rebecca's forehead and ran a caressing finger down the baby's soft cheek. She gave Slade an approving nod, then left them alone together.

Rebecca smiled at Slade. "You must be tired, too."

He smiled back. "I'm too exhilarated to be tired."

"Yes. So am I." She shifted to the side of the bed. "Lie down with us, Slade. Hold me. Share her with me."

He heaved a deep sigh of contentment as he wrapped his arms around them both. Rebecca turned her head towards his and looked into his eyes, deep blue eyes that returned all that she felt. Perhaps even more.

"I've never loved anyone as much as I love you. And the child you've given me, Slade," she said softly. "If you still want me to marry you, I will."

"Rebecca ..." He made her name sound like a long echoing dream of wanting and fulfilment. "I can't remember when I first knew I loved you. But this I know. You'll always have my love. As will our child, and any other children we have."

"Oh, Slade ..." She was so choked with emotion she could barely speak.

He meant it. She knew he did. And she knew their lives were now irrevocably entwined. If Slade had to go away on business for Cordell Enterprises, it wouldn't change anything. The bond went too deep. Soul deep. They had made a family. She would never let anything destroy that. She would never let it be taken away from them.

CHAPTER FOURTEEN

NEITHER REBECCA NOR SLADE saw any necessity for her and the baby to be airlifted to a hospital. They both agreed that a medical checkup could be postponed until after the big wet. Slade informed the Flying Doctor Service that everything was fine and under control, mother and baby doing well.

The torrential rain eased off, but heavy showers continued to fall over the next ten days. The drought was well and truly ended. The dry red desert stirred from its long sleep and began to bloom, sprouting the green of fresh grasses. The great pendulum of life swung once more, transforming the landscape with vegetation that would be gradually consumed as the cycle moved on.

"In a few weeks, the plains will be covered in a riot of yellow daisies and purple parakeelya flowers," Rebecca informed Slade with shining eyes. "It's so stunningly beautiful..."

He chuckled. "I believe you. I'm starting to get used to all the surprises this land keeps dishing out to me." He shifted his gaze pointedly to the new lake where a black and white pageant of pelicans stretched around the far bank.

The previous morning they had been woken by the corellas' dawn chorus. A flock of galahs had swept in, their rich pink breasts rosier in the morning light, and two yellow-billed spoonbills had joined them, strutting a stately progress around the edge of the water, which reflected their white plumage.

"We'll be mobbed by budgerigars and zebra finches next." Rebecca laughed, then heaved a great sigh of satisfaction. "I'm so glad we excavated that dam. My only regret is that Gran isn't here to enjoy it."

Slade hugged her shoulders and dropped a kiss on her hair. "Her great-granddaughter is, and I reckon she'd be content with that."

Janet Logan Cordell, as she would be christened, suddenly decided she wasn't content, and gave a lusty yell to tell them she had woken up from her morning sleep and wanted to be lifted out of her lonely bassinet. Which Slade was only too happy to do. He was totally besotted with his baby daughter, who seemed to reciprocate the feeling. Any crying always ceased as soon as she was cradled against his broad shoulder. It was as though she instinctively knew that her father would make everything right for her. She hadn't yet learnt that not quite everything was within his power.

But Rebecca had been giving a lot of thought to that. She couldn't imagine that Slade could keep running Cordell Enterprises effectively from Brisbane. Sooner or later he would have to go back to New York and make his authority felt. The example of Devil's Elbow showed how management could get out of hand if it wasn't kept in check. Slade felt his responsibilities too deeply to let that happen again.

As much as Rebecca recoiled from the thought of living in New York, she figured she could stick it out without complaint for at least a month or two. She would have the baby to help keep her occupied while Slade was at work, and when they were all together . . . almost any sacrifice was worth that. It wasn't as if Slade would ever ask her to give up Wildjanna. She could always return when she wanted to, and Slade would come back to her as soon as he could.

He had done all the compromising in their relationship so far. Not that he seemed at all unhappy about it. In fact, there was no doubting his obvious contentment in their life at Wildjanna. But as his wife—and she did want to be married to him, if only to confirm the sense of family for their daughter—Rebecca felt it was only fair to offer Slade some return for all his generosity.

They had decided to make a big day of their wedding at Wildjanna. All the property owners in the Channel Country would be invited and they would make a triple celebration of the occasion, a marriage, a christening—both to be performed by the flying padre who serviced the outback—and a grand party to mark the end of the drought.

Slade was going to ask Emilio to be his best man. They had received news that the Argentinian was on his way home with a new wife, and Rebecca decided it would be a nice welcoming gesture if she asked Emilio's bride to be matron of honour. But that was all weeks ahead, when everything had settled down after the rain and people could afford the time away from their properties to relax and make merry.

Since Slade made no mention of having to leave Wildjanna before then, Rebecca assumed he had organised a long vacation to cover their baby's birth. They were so happy together it was all too easy for Rebecca to leave the matter of her accompanying him to New York in abeyance. That was a future thing that she would meet when they came to it.

However, as it turned out, other circumstances prompted her to tell Slade what she had decided. The rough clay airstrip finally dried out enough for the mail plane to resume its weekly drop at Wildjanna, and Slade eagerly raced off in his Land Rover to meet it as it came in to land. He returned with a bundle of letters and newspapers, which he handed to Rebecca.

"There's something else, too," he informed her, with a great grin on his face. From the back of the vehicle he unloaded an old rocking chair, made of American oak and marked from many years of use. "It was Grandfather Logan's," Slade explained as he set it down on the verandah. "Just my size," he added as he settled into it and started it rocking. "I've been looking for a comfortable chair like this for quite some time."

That statement didn't make much sense to Rebecca but she couldn't help smiling at his smug air of satisfaction. "You had it brought all the way from America so you could rock here at your ease?" she laughingly teased.

"Grandfather Logan would approve. He was right all along. This will be the life for me," Slade declared.

"When you do have to go back to New York, I'll come with you, Slade," she said impulsively. "After all, our daughter should have a taste of your world, too. And besides, we both want to be with you."

The chair stopped rocking. The vivid blue eyes locked onto Rebecca's with an expression she couldn't read, but it made her heart flutter with gladness that she had made the offer. He came out of the chair slowly, took the bundle of mail from her hands and set it on the wicker table. Then he drew her into a gentle embrace and spoke in a voice that throbbed with deep emotion.

"Thank you, Rebecca. I appreciate how much it would cost you to live in a city such as New York, so far away from here. I know how much a measure of your love for me your offer is. And we will go, for short visits occasionally, just to make sure my financial interests are being looked after, and to give Janet—and any other children we have—the benefit of knowing both worlds. But I'm not tied to Cordell Enterprises any more, Rebecca. My life is now here with you. It always will be."

She stared at him, not comprehending how that could be so. "But you're chairman."

"Not any longer," he said quietly. "I made up my mind to put someone else in that position before I spoke to Paul."

The shock of his total commitment to her drained the blood from Rebecca's face. "You gave all that up . . . for me?"

His smile was softly ironic as he lifted a hand to her cheek in a tender caress. "It wasn't so much to give up. The problem was in finding someone to take over from me. Someone who would be good enough. Over the last few months one man proved himself capable of handling everything I threw at him. A guy named Ross Harper. He's probably chairing a board meeting right now, and relishing every moment of it."

Slade called her fearless, but Rebecca had known many moments of intense fear in her life. This one was as paralysing as when she knew Paul's helicopter was going to crash. What Slade had done was just as irreversible, and again it was all because of her. Making a sacrifice of years of leadership and achievement, throwing it away. And if she failed him . . .

"I wish you hadn't done that, Slade," she said in a strained little voice.

"I wanted to," he assured her. "We're going to have a lifetime marriage, Rebecca. Nothing less would satisfy me, and I know it's what you want, too."

A lifetime marriage . . . They were her words. If she had given in to him when he had first asked her to marry him, he wouldn't have felt forced to go to such lengths as to sever all his responsibilities to Cordell Enterprises. It was her stubborn independence that had fed Slade's obsessive determination. And he would surely regret what he had done in years to come. How could anyone give up ruling an empire and be satisfied with simply being a husband and father? Eventually he would get bored and feel frustrated and end up hating her.

"You shouldn't have done it. It won't work," she protested, sheer panic squeezing her heart.

"Yes, it will," he answered calmly.

She shook her head in helpless despair. "I wouldn't have given up Wildjanna for you, Slade."

"I know. I knew from the time you faced me over your grandmother's grave that you and Wildjanna were inseparable, Rebecca."

He stroked her cheek with loving tenderness. "Don't be distressed, my darling. I'd been discontented with being chairman of Cordell Enterprises for some time, long before I met you. Then you burst into my life—I was feeling particularly restless and frustrated with everything that day—and you attracted me so much I wanted to pursue the attraction."

His smile held not the slightest twinge of regret. "Best decision I ever made. And when I heard you were carrying my child, I sure as heck knew what I wanted. If I needed any confirmation of my feelings, that first month here with you was more than enough. Apart from which, I really enjoyed working on Wildjanna. It was more solid and real and satisfying than sitting in an office toting up figures and listening to reports. And the stars at night, the clarity of the sky..." He cocked a quizzical eyebrow. "You won't mind if I build an observatory here, will you, Rebecca?"

She shook her head, dazedly hoping she was wrong to worry about their future together.

Slade grinned. "I figured on asking you that *after* we were married. Not that I thought you'd object. I've just been distracted—very happily distracted—by being a new father. In fact, I'm going to give myself a lot of time for such distractions. Astrophysics will be a fine hobby on the side."

Rebecca's inner tension eased a bit more. Slade had always wanted to be an astrophysicist. Maybe he wouldn't miss being the head of Cordell Enterprises after all.

"You know, all the stars we see are only five per cent of what's out there," he went on, the eagerness of an enthusiast in his voice. "Scientists call the other ninety-five per cent the dark matter. I'm going to work on that dark matter, Rebecca. I'd be happy to spend the rest of my life on that. Just think of all the mysteries of the universe waiting to be uncovered!"

The light of mission in his eyes convinced Rebecca that this was something he really wanted to do.

His focus sharpened on her. "And another thing! We can offer the children who come here for a visit a look at the universe through my telescope. It will round off and complement all that Wildjanna can offer them."

He was right. It would be a marvellous experience.

"You know what else I thought?" Slade continued, his eyes twinkling with the surprise he had in store for her.

Rebecca shook her head again, not trusting herself to speak until all her turbulent emotion had calmed down.

"That day we had to shift the cattle to high ground, it would have saved us a lot of time if we could have tracked them all first by satellite. Once I've got my computers installed in the observatory and hooked in to our satellite, we can always find out where the cattle are, even the most wayward stragglers."

"Our satellite?" Rebecca croaked incredulously.

"Yep. I did tell you Cordell Enterprises financed one, didn't I? The infrared sensor devices are so accurate they can track a moth at a distance of a thousand miles. And I haven't severed all connections with the old firm, Rebecca. We still hold fifty-one per cent of the shares. Who knows? We might have a son who takes after my father. Myself, I reckon I've got more of my grandfather in me."

Yes, she'd like a son, Rebecca thought dizzily. Slade was still going too fast for her to take everything in. "Where have you put this satellite?" she asked.

"Right overhead," came the cheerful reply. "It's in geosynchronous orbit, revolving with us at the same speed as the earth rotates every day. Of course, the sensors are only part of the story. You still need the stock men to round up the cattle and do all the physical chores that have to be done. But there are all sorts of applications to station work we can do on the computer. We can use all the land on Wildjanna and Devil's Elbow much more efficiently, Rebecca. We might even buy out Emilio's if he wants to go back home to Argentina. I reckon we can run the greatest cattle station in the world."

Rebecca started to laugh as all her worries were comprehensively chased away. Slade was already staking out another empire. A new challenge. With her. And there was no doubt about it now. He was not a city man. He had pioneer blood, too.

He gave her a mock frown. "Have I said something funny?"

"No." She sighed. "I have this vision of you running a vast cattle station . . . from your observatory."

"I don't mind doing the physical work, too," he protested.

"Infrared sensors have to be the ultimate in laziness!"

He was smugly unashamed. "Grandfather Logan would have been proud of me."

Rebecca laughed, then wound her arms around his neck and kissed him. "Feel like giving me the benefit of some more brilliant ideas?" she asked, moving her body against his.

Slade's response was gratifyingly instant. A low sexy growl gravelled from his throat as he swept her off her feet and strode for the bedroom. They passed Milly along the way and the housekeeper asked if anything was wrong.

"No. I've just got this uncontrollable urge to make love to the mother of my child," Slade tossed over his shoulder, not pausing in his step.

"Well, at least you're not doing it in front of the horses," Milly snapped back at him.

Which convulsed Rebecca with giggles.

Slade paused at their bedroom door. "That wasn't nice, Milly."

"Huh!" the housekeeper scoffed. "Nothing you could do would shock me any more, Slade Cordell. You get off about your business. I'll keep my eye on the babe."

"Milly, there's no telling how long this will take," Slade lobbed back, then quickly stepped inside the bedroom and closed the door.

It took every second of a full hour for Rebecca to show him how deeply, wildly, passionately, tenderly, totally she loved him. Slade had precisely the same idea. It was such a beautiful time together that when they heard their baby demanding to be fed, Rebecca threw on a gown, hurried to fetch their child from Milly and carried her back to Slade so that they could all be together.

It always fascinated him to watch his daughter latch onto Rebecca's breast and suck so knowingly and greedily. "Nature sure is a marvellous thing," he murmured as the tiny rosebud mouth found its target with unerring instinct once again. "She's just like you, Rebecca."

"In what way?" Rebecca asked, her eyes adoring the big American who had given her everything she had ever dreamed of. Such a big man in every way—mind, heart and soul—the inner him even bigger than the outer him.

Dark blue eyes lovingly caressed her and the baby she held to her breast. "Elemental," he murmured, and heaved a sigh of contentment.

Slade knew he had won more than he had ever dreamed of. Others might look at what he had done and wonder at the losses he had taken in order to have what he had now, but he knew what he had won. This woman who had answered the long questing in his soul...this woman at his side for the rest of his life. And he counted himself a mighty big Texas-size winner—all the way!

THE SEDUCTION OF KEIRA

CHAPTER ONE

KEIRA MARY BROOKS wriggled her bottom. It was not
a sensual wriggle. It was not a provocative wriggle. It
was a desperate wriggle. Anything to ease the back-
breaking, mind-numbing ache of being crammed into
an over-small, over-hard, economy-class seat on a
twenty-two-hour international flight that the travel
agent had promised would save her a fortune.

Keira had known it was a mistake right from the
beginning. How can you save a fortune when you
don't have a fortune in the first place? The travel
agent's spiel was obviously based on faulty logic. On
the other hand, Keira had not exactly been over-
loaded with choices. The price was right for her limited finances. She did feel, however, that the travel
agent should have explained that the price was for the
very worst seat in the Boeing 747.

She was jammed, literally jammed, in the middle
seat, in the middle row, in the middle of the aeroplane; crammed between one elderly gentleman, so big
that he had to be a retired wrestler, and one very
overweight lady who, Keira mused darkly, would have
had no problem getting accepted for a job in a circus.

Keira eased herself onto her left hip, gained some
relief from the pressure on the base of her spine, felt

eyes watching her, lifted her own to meet them. She had to lift her gaze a fair way because the watching eyes belonged to the big elderly gentleman on her left and her head only came up to his shoulder.

He looked stiff and staid. A walrus moustache added interest to his fleshy face. From the few words Keira had heard him speak over the past twenty-two hours, he had a British accent. He continued to stare. From the glazed look in his eyes, Keira figured that the long journey had broken down the famous British reserve and he no longer gave a damn whether or not it was rude to stare. Or perhaps his bottom was hurting, too, Keira thought sympathetically.

In any event, she was used to being stared at so it didn't worry Keira. In countries where people were generally dark in colouring, her hair had been the main object of fascination. For some genetical reason, it incorporated every shade variation from almost pure white to a deep yellow-gold. Its long, silky fairness was woven into a single thick plait over her shoulder at the moment, but it still seemed to strike people as something worth looking at.

By rights, Keira's eyebrows and eyelashes should also have been fair, but they were a light ash-brown, which tended to add an intriguing smoky emphasis to her green eyes. The retired British wrestler stared at her eyes for a long time before his gaze slid down her neat straight nose and fastened on her mouth.

Keira had a rather wide full-lipped mouth. It balanced up her high cheekbones and her squarish jaw line so she didn't mind it being a bit on the wide side, although she sometimes thought her face was all teeth when she smiled. She had noticed people seemed to get distracted by her smile. She tried to remember not to smile too much, but most of the time she forgot.

As she did now. The poor man had to be suffering, probably much more than she was, so Keira smiled sympathetically at him. He was holding a cup of coffee in his hands. Out of the corner of her eye, she saw the hot liquid spill over the rim and trickle onto his fingers.

"Sir, your coffee," she warned kindly.

The coffee slopped more alarmingly. The big man grabbed at his lap, emitting a cry of pain. He stood up, heedlessly dropping the cup on the floor as he brushed wildly at himself. He trod over people in his hasty plunge to the aisle, then charged towards the nether regions of the aeroplane.

"Sorry," Keira whispered, but in his anguish he didn't hear her.

It was an unfortunate fact that these nasty little incidents seemed to follow her around like a black cat, blighting the general happiness of her life. Keira heaved a deep sigh. She genuinely regretted what had happened to the big man. On the other hand, his abrupt removal gave her room to think without being distracted by the anguish in her bottom.

Keira stretched all her limbs, relieving her cramped muscles before luxuriously spreading herself across both seats. Thought was imperative. There was barely thirty minutes to landing, and the "fortune" the travel agent had saved her only amounted to the coins necessary for one telephone call and the fare for a very short taxi ride. One block at most, which wouldn't get her very far, and would leave a lot of walking at the end of it.

The telephone call was reserved for Justin. He was her cousin, an accountant, and a very cautious, conservative man. By Keira's standards he was also very wealthy, and in this particular situation her only chance of being saved from immediate penury.

He also needed careful handling. He was happily married, no children as yet, and Keira hadn't seen him for five years. But she knew his habits. He liked to get sheets of paper, write down figures on them, add them up, then draw conclusions from them about which he lectured her interminably.

Keira's view was much more simple. Family always sticks together through thick and thin. Blood is thicker than water, and a lot thicker than nasty little numbers on a page. At which stage, Justin would run his fingers through his thinning hair and growl. The problem with Justin was that he wanted family and numbers to add up correctly all the time. And they just didn't. Not with Keira, anyway. Justin had a lot of difficulty coming to terms with that.

Like the time he sent her the money to return home for his wedding. Keira would have gone—family first above everything else—but she had been on safari through Kenya, which was where she had met the sheikh, who had kindly invited her to Morocco, and by the time the post with the invitation and the cheque caught up with her, the wedding was over. What was the point in flying to Australia when Justin and Louise were already on their way to Fiji for their honeymoon? They never would have met, so there was no point at all! Only Justin didn't seem to understand that.

Keira had posted the cheque back to him with profuse apologies, explanations and congratulations, but communications between them had definitely been strained by the incident. Although he hadn't written it straight out, Keira had been left with the forceful impression that Justin considered she had let him down. From then on he only sent dutiful birthday and Christmas greetings, with the somewhat sarcastic postscript, "Are you still alive?"

Keira had regularly assured him of her continued survival with postcards from every country she visited. Which brought her to the problem of how to approach the conversation when she made her all-important telephone call. The opening phase of communication could be decisive. After all, Justin thought she was still in Reykjavik, Iceland. *He would be surprised.* And Justin didn't react well to surprises. So perhaps...

The big man reappeared from the nether regions of the aeroplane. His face was fixed in an attitude of interminable suffering. With a rush of true compassion for him, Keira relinquished the extra space. This kind of travel, she thought, was the end.

Which went to show it *was* time to come home, or she wouldn't have thought that. A few years ago she would have happily camped on the deck of a tramp steamer to get somewhere new. Now she longed for a bit of home comfort. She hoped Justin would provide that for a little while until she got on her feet again.

The No Smoking sign flashed on. Fasten safety belts. Ten minutes to landing. Keira recollected that she hadn't decided how to handle Justin. She shrugged. Perhaps it was best to simply leave it in the lap of the gods. Play it all by ear.

From her disadvantaged position in the middle of the aircraft, she caught only glimpses of Sydney as the plane banked to make its approach into Mascot Airport. Even so, the distinctive features of her home city triggered a ground swell of feeling that caught Keira by surprise.

It's true, she thought. There's no place like home. Over the past five years she had travelled the world and left bits of her heart in many places, but when it came right down to the bone, she was a born and bred Australian and her native land claimed first and last place in her soul.

The plane landed and the long flight was finally over. Disembarking was an exercise in enforced patience, but Keira was soon able to stretch her legs on the walk through the tunnel into the terminal. Having collected her backpack and duffle bag from the baggage carousel, she had to suffer another long queue at Customs.

At last she was free to find a telephone and call Justin. It was six-thirty in the morning. Thursday morning. He should be home. Keira dialled his number, then felt a nervous kick of anticipation as the click of a lifting receiver cut off the call pattern.

"Justin Brooks," came the gravelly grunt of displeasure at being wakened. The tone clearly implied that any decent upstanding working person deserved his full rest, and whoever was calling had better have a damned good reason for it.

Keira grimaced an apology, which unfortunately he couldn't see, and pitched her voice to a soft croon of appeasement. "Dear darling Justin, it's Keira, your beloved wayward cousin."

Incredulous silence.

She pitched her voice to what she hoped would be sympathetic appeal. 'I'm sorry if I woke you...."

"Time differential," he muttered. Then with a note of urgency, "Where are you? What part of the world?"

He actually sounded concerned about her. She hadn't expected that. "I'm home, Justin. At least, I'm here in Sydney. At Mascot Airport."

"Thank God! Don't move an inch! I'll be there straight away!"

Keira was dumbfounded. She had hoped for a response, prayed for a response, but this example of cousinly love was more than she had expected ... or ever experienced before.

"Are you sure, Justin?" she asked uncertainly. "I mean, I can wait—"

"No!" Explosively positive. Or negative. Keira felt a bit confused until he added, "Don't you dare move! I'm coming straight away. I'm out of bed already. I'll be there in thirty minutes maximum. You are not to go haring off somewhere. Do you hear me, Keira? For once in your crazy wandering life, stay put!"

Things were really looking up. Perhaps Justin's idea of family loyalty had changed for the better. "Well, if you insist—"

"I do! Promise me you won't move!" he commanded.

Thirty minutes was a long time to stay absolutely motionless, and her mouth felt like a desert. "Am I allowed to have a cup of coffee at the cafeteria?" she asked cautiously, not wanting to put him off his stride.

"Good thinking! I'll find you there. Sit down and don't move. Oh, and Keira—" the bossy voice wavered into anxious uncertainty "—you haven't got fat, have you?"

Strange question! Her eyebrows shot up. "No. I don't think so. What's the matter, Justin? Have you got a skinny car now?"

"Checking. Just checking. It has been five years. Am I going to recognise you?"

"Same as I ever was," she answered breezily.

"Great!" A huge sigh of relief. "I need you, Keira. You can't let me down."

"Oh, I wouldn't do that, Justin," Keira assured him fervently. "I—er—need you, too."

"Perfect!" A smug note there.

"Perfect for what?"

"I'll fill you in when I see you."

The receiver was decisively slammed down. End of conversation. Keira hung up her receiver in a state of bemusement. Justin had never needed her in his life before. In fact, he had always seemed to find her a disturbing or disruptive force. She was almost sure he had resented her intrusion into his family household when her aunt and uncle, his parents, had taken her in after her own parents were killed in a car accident.

Keira had been ten then, Justin fourteen, and even in his teens he had liked everything orderly and predictable. He had always acted the responsible big brother, but the truth was, they had never shared a common wavelength, and Keira suspected Justin regarded her as a cross he had to bear for the sake of family. Now that she was twenty-six and he thirty, things might be a little different, but somehow Keira doubted it.

Whatever the reason, it was lucky Justin needed her, because she certainly needed him. It was indeed a perfect resolution to her temporary problem. She didn't understand why it was perfect for Justin but no doubt he would soon enlighten her. Meanwhile a cup of coffee would go down well.

As Keira headed for the cafeteria, she couldn't help wondering what fat had to do with anything. Justin certainly wasn't thinking straight. How on earth would she get fat trekking around the world on a slim budget? She was in great shape. Quite a few men privately agreed with her as she went striding through the terminal.

Their eyes were caught by the fascinating jiggle of her full breasts, which turned her man's cotton shirt into an incredibly provocative garment. Their heads swivelled as she passed by, drawn inexorably to appreciate the way her stretch denim jeans moulded the trim, taut, cheeky femininity of her bottom. Keira was still trying to work out the numb ache, and the rolling movement she used was positively mesmerising.

That, in turn, drew attention to her long, lissom legs which should have been sexily encased in high-heeled calf-length boots. Her sturdy army boots, so practical and comfortable for walking long distances, earned disapproving frowns.

Keira, however, was blithely unaware of these cursory appraisals. Her mind was filled with the blissful thought that she could afford a cup of coffee with a clear conscience. All was temporarily right with her world. Justin would certainly feed her and put a roof over her head if he needed her.

Having found the cafeteria and paid out the last of her hard cold finances on a steaming cappuccino, Keira settled at a table and considered the situation. First she would oblige Justin with whatever he needed her for. She hoped he would be suitably grateful enough to lend her the money to visit his parents, who had retired to the Gold Coast of Queensland. Then she would look around for a job.

She wondered what Justin's wife was like. He hadn't mentioned Louise on the telephone, but no doubt she was now warned her cousin-in-law, the prodigal one who had missed the wedding, was about to descend upon them and mess up the neat orderliness of their lives.

Maybe Louise was ill, and that was why Justin needed her in such a hurry. Or maybe his mother or father was ill and they needed a helping hand. Keira worried about that for a while. Auntie Joan's last letter had assured her that all was well at home, but it was not in Auntie's nature to worry anyone. Keira automatically discounted the idea that Justin needed her himself. That was totally beyond the realms of even her inventive imagination.

Suddenly she spotted him, hurrying towards the cafeteria. Her eyes widened in shocked surprise. Justin hadn't stopped to shave! Unbelievable! Appearing unshaven in public indicated a crisis of maximum proportions. Though he had managed to dress in conservative grey trousers and a conservative white shirt. On the other hand, he probably didn't own any other colours.

His forehead was a little higher on account of his light brown hair having receded a little farther. From her seated position, Keira couldn't see if it was any thinner on top. His face looked more or less the same. It was actually a good-looking face and Justin could even be called handsome when he smiled, but his smiles were very rare, and right now he wore a harried anxious expression. There was no flab on his tall well-proportioned physique. Had he developed a fastidious obsession against fatness? Keira wondered.

His face positively lit with relief when he saw her. It was almost as good as a welcome. Keira gave him her warmest smile. His brown eyes beamed approval at her. *Approval* from Justin? This meeting was getting curiouser and curiouser by the second.

"Am I glad to see you!" he enthused as he arrived at her table.

"Likewise!" Keira replied brightly. "Am I allowed to move now?"

He pounced on her backpack and duffle bag as though they were hostages for her continued good behaviour. "Yes," he said. "Best if we get going."

She stood up and planted a cousinly kiss on his raspy cheek. It really was nice to see him, even though their minds worked on different wavelengths. It made her feel even more at home.

"It's so kind of you to come and collect me like this, Justin," she said with sincere gratitude.

His face went grim. "These are desperate times in which we live."

"Precisely," she agreed with feeling.

He frowned at her. "Are you tired, Keira?"

"How far away is the car?"

"It's just across the road in the car park. No great distance. Maybe a hundred metres."

"Lead on," she invited. "I am suffering a broken backside but I can get myself that far."

He watched her walk beside him for several anxious moments, checking that her mobility was not too impaired.

"Are Auntie Joan and Uncle Bruce all right?" she asked, wanting that worry settled.

"Mum and Dad?" he said distractedly. "Same as usual. Fine as far as I know."

No problem there, Keira thought in happy relief. She was very fond of Justin's parents. They had never understood her, but they had never criticised her, either. Their attitude towards her was one of benevolent tolerance. Occasionally they likened her to her father who apparently had nursed a wanderlust when he was alive.

"Will you be right for tonight?" Justin suddenly asked.

"For what?"

A look of black thunder passed over his face. "A man," he said, and there was no benevolence at all in his tone of voice.

Keira had the forceful impression that the man in question did not bask in Justin's favour. "What kind of man?" she probed warily.

His mouth curved into a sly little smile. "No one you'd object to, Keira. Most women seem to find him charming. You might even feel attracted to him. He's reported to be a very eligible bachelor."

Interesting, Keira thought. "What do I have to do?"

The smile turned into a smirk. "Oh, be yourself. As much as you can."

There was something fishy about that smirk. Justin was never comfortable with Keira being herself. Her attitude to life offended his sense of precision. "Is that all?" she asked suspiciously.

He cast her a stern look. "You definitely *must* forget that you're my cousin. That is essential."

Keira didn't care for that idea. After all, it was essential to her that Justin remember he was her cousin.

"Apart from that," he continued, "all you have to do is try your best to seduce him. I want him compromised. Past the point of no return."

She couldn't believe this! "My God, Justin! What do you think I am? You actually want me to seduce a man?"

Justin nodded with smug satisfaction. "That will certainly turn the tables." Then he had the thick hide to offer her a sympathetic look. "I'm sorry about your broken backside, Keira, but you have all day to rest and get some sleep. You should be fit by tonight."

She took a deep breath. Maybe all the rushing around so early in the morning had made Justin light-headed. "You really want me to seduce a man I've never met?" she asked, still not believing he could be serious.

"You've had enough practice," he said glibly. "Shouldn't be difficult for you."

Keira's jaw dropped. She gasped at him. A surge of indignation effected a fast recovery. "I have not! I've never done such a thing in my life!"

He slanted her a wise look that denied any belief in her protestation of innocence. "Well, see if you can get some practice tonight," he advised.

Keira shut her mouth. This was not the time for confrontation. She certainly wasn't going to seduce anyone, not for love nor money, but it wasn't at all practical to say no right now when she still needed Justin's help and support. Appeasement, Keira thought. She'd sort out what was going on eventually, then wriggle out of it somehow.

"I don't think I understand this, Justin," she said in a befuddled tone.

"It's quite simple." He threw her a knowing look. "Fight fire with fire. Elementary. I'm doing the fighting. You're the fire. Couldn't be more perfect, really."

Keira shook her head. "I'm sorry, Justin, but this sounds like you're stretching family obligations past a reasonable point."

"Not at all, Keira. This is family. All family," he argued with considerable vehemence. Almost passionate vehemence! "Do this one simple thing for me and I'll be obliged to you all my life. Longer. For eternity. That's family!"

His brown eyes stabbed encouragement at her. "Do you want me obliged to you all your life, Keira?"

It certainly had its attractions. As a backup for emergencies, to have an ever dependable support like Justin was not to be scoffed at. Even so, Keira wasn't about to sell her body for the sake of security.

"It would be nice," she answered cautiously. After all, they weren't quite out of the airport yet. They were only crossing the road to the car park. She didn't want Justin to dump her bags and leave her flat.

"Then do it!" he concluded decisively.

Keira temporised. "I think I need a few more details, Justin. I mean, if I'm to get this right for you...."

He sighed, putting on his lofty superior face. "Keira, there's no point in explaining the details. You can't follow a simple budget let alone a complex equation. This is much more difficult. Just do precisely what I say when I say it."

He gave her a hard, warning look. "You are you. I recognise that. But for the next few days you are not to let things happen to you, Keira. You are not to improvise, or ride along with some tide of opportunity. This is a perfectly planned military operation. I'm the field marshal. You're the private. I give the orders. You go out and die for honour, glory and happiness."

Dying was definitely out as far as Keira was concerned. No one's honour, glory or happiness meant that much to her. "This all sounds pretty one-sided to me, Justin," she said pointedly.

"Do you want my eternal gratitude?"

He dumped her backpack and duffle bag on the pavement behind a Daimler. Justin had owned a Ford Falcon five years ago. Now he had a Daimler. His stocks had definitely gone up in the world. A lot of home comforts flashed across Keira's mind.

"Yes," she said.

"Then that's settled. You're the private. I'm the field marshal."

Keira allowed the field marshal to stow her baggage in the Daimler's boot, then see her settled into the beautifully comfortable passenger seat. Her bottom was very appreciative. Lovely luxury, she thought. Being a private was not entirely bad, but obeying orders—Justin's orders—was a highly questionable area.

She waited until he had the car on the road, then asked, "Are you sure the plan is going to work, Justin?"

"That's my worry. Not yours," he said with pompous authority.

"But you will be grateful for my help."

"I promise."

"Grateful enough to give me a loan?" This was very definitely the time to introduce the practicalities of life.

Justin winced. "How much?"

Keira did some quick figuring, then tripled the amount for good measure. Justin bared his teeth at her, then divided the figure by six and came up with five hundred dollars.

Keira winced. "Justin, that would hardly keep body and soul together for longer than—er—a few days."

"The rest on delivery," he said with a look of triumphant satisfaction.

Nailing her down to his orders, Keira thought in disgust. No trust at all. So much for *his* family feeling!

"What am I to deliver before I get the rest? This man's head on a plate?" she asked sarcastically.

"That would be eminently satisfactory," he said, without so much as cracking a smile. He looked as though he meant it.

"So I'm supposed to be a modern-day Delilah?"

"Exactly."

"Why?" she demanded to know.

There was a rush of blood to his head. His face went a dark red. He glared at her. "Because I want my wife back! And you're going to help me do precisely that."

Shock rippled through Keira's mind. It was followed by a burst of clarity. Louise had obviously run off with another man. Poor Justin *was* in a crisis. She certainly had a family obligation to help him.

"After all," he argued hotly, "if you can take off with an Arab sheikh and miss my wedding—"

That still rankled.

"—you can take off with an Australian playboy and save my marriage!" he finished triumphantly.

Keira smothered a sigh. Justin was upset. He wasn't thinking straight. For one thing, he really did have the wrong idea about her association with the sheikh, which had had nothing whatsoever to do with seduction. And *his* campaign to get his wife back was sure to be disastrous. It was perfectly clear that she would have to sort it all out for him. Men simply didn't understand women. And they never really listened to them, either.

Subtlety, Keira thought. Justin didn't have any appreciation of subtlety. No point in arguing. She would have to show him. Maybe after *his* plan failed, he would begin to listen to her and really see, for the first time, what she could do.

CHAPTER TWO

KEIRA DID NOT let Justin down.

She did everything he told her to do.

She even accepted the alias Delilah O'Neil. Justin was adamant about that. He wouldn't accept anything else. In Keira's opinion, this was stretching cousinly love to its outermost limits. However, Justin argued that Louise knew he had a cousin called Keira, and Delilah O'Neil was a name he could remember. At all times. It was also rather unusual, he said, and would draw attention to her.

She accompanied him to a dreadfully overcrowded party, hung on his arm, looked adoringly at him as ordered, showed him how to loosen up with several new dance steps no one else seemed to know—inadvertently stirring considerable interest amongst onlookers—and generally fulfilled the role of the blonde Biblical bombshell that Justin required of her.

He refused to point Louise out to her. Louise was to be ignored. Keira began to suspect Louise wasn't at the party at all, because Justin didn't point out *the man* to her, either. This gave Keira much secret relief because she really didn't know anything about seducing a man, not deliberately anyway, and she couldn't go along with that part of Justin's plan.

Then it happened.

The big moment.

The one she had given up believing would ever happen to her. She had travelled the world, met thousands of men, but never once had any one of them awakened any special recognition in her heart.

She didn't see him coming. There was a voice behind her, low, soft, seductive. "Please don't spoil the magic for me. Tell me you're intelligent as well as stunningly beautiful."

She looked around, drawn by the voice, unsure if the words were spoken to her or someone else. And there he was, blue eyes twinkling at her, blue eyes dancing through her brain, tripping her heart, sending a zing of excitement through her veins.

He was half a head taller than Keira, over six feet tall. His hair was midnight black, a stylishly tamed mass of waves and curls that gave a rakish air to his handsome face. A devilishly handsome face, darkly tanned and composed of sharp planes and angles that were distinctively masculine and intriguingly attractive. Black eyebrows were lifted in a wickedly challenging arch. His sensual mouth was pursed in teasing invitation, slowly widening to a dazzling white smile.

He held two glasses of champagne in his hands and he offered one to her. "I know your escort is at the bar. I know we haven't been introduced. I know I am intruding on what is forbidden ground. But there are no rings on your fingers and the thought came to me that someone should look after that. So I beg your indulgence. If necessary...your forgiveness...for this intrusion."

He was playing with words. There was no hint in his eyes of needing forgiveness. Self-assurance surrounded the man like the aurora borealis. Keira dazedly took the glass he offered her. Their fingers brushed. Something like an electric charge ran up her arm.

"Speak to me," he commanded. "I need to hear your voice."

Keira smiled. She couldn't help herself. "You've been saying the same thing to every attractive female you've met since . . ."

She dropped her gaze to measure a suitable height from the floor. He wore an open-necked shirt of fine white linen, pintucked and expensively tailored. Black trousers hugged his lean hips and muscular legs. Somehow his body emitted a raw sexuality that was all male animal. The physical impact of the man was like nothing she had ever felt before. Keira almost forgot her train of thought. She belatedly fixed her gaze at mid-thigh, surveyed the area intently, then looked up at his vividly inviting blue eyes.

"Er—I'd say, since you were five years old," she concluded.

He laughed, warming her with his pleasure and delight. "You know me so well already. I must offer you every opportunity to further your knowledge. Ask anything you want of me. Whatever is possible, or impossible, shall be granted."

"That's a rare offer. Perhaps a little rash? You don't know me. I might ask for the moon and the stars."

"Then you'd have them. From me. With compliments."

"How?"

"I'd take you away from this maddening mass of people to somewhere private, personal, quiet and peaceful, and open to the sky...a yacht, a beach house, a mountain chalet. You choose," he invited. "Whichever you want can be yours."

She laughed. The sheer fantastical extravagance of his offer appealed strongly to her own sense of spontaneity. "You can conjure such places up with your Aladdin's lamp, can you?"

"I don't have to. I own all three," he assured her with such arrogant confidence that Keira was inclined to believe him.

It gave her pause for thought. She lifted her glass and sipped the champagne while she reassessed him. Her heart and soul were engaged. They were pulsing with very positive messages. He was THE ONE. But there had been a lot of women in this man's life. Did he recognise her as the one for him? Was he seriously attracted to her, or was he simply throwing her a line, having decided to sample someone new?

"You must be a very wealthy man," she remarked.

"Very," he agreed nonchalantly, but there was a flash of hardness in the blue eyes.

"You think I can be bought?" she challenged, pitching her voice to light mockery.

One eyebrow lifted quizzically. "Can you?"

She lowered her long thick lashes as though for private thought and consideration. She secretly enjoyed making him wonder before she answered with a flat, "No."

He smiled...slowly, lazily, winningly. "Then I don't think it."

Keira's heart pitter-pattered all over the place. She took another sip of champagne to settle the palpitations. It failed to achieve that purpose because he lifted his free hand and trailed his fingers through the long tress of hair that had fallen forward over her left shoulder.

"Spun silk," he murmured. "I've never seen anything like it before."

Justin had not allowed Keira to rest the entire day. At four o'clock he had taken her to a hairdressing salon to have her hair shampooed and blow-dried and any ragged ends trimmed to the one shining length that flowed to below her shoulder-blades. He had insisted that she leave it loose, which was a nuisance for dancing, but suddenly Keira felt Justin had got something right. His judgement wasn't all bad. Not all the time.

On the other hand, she wasn't just a head of hair, and when its admirer lifted a swath to his lips, Keira experienced such a frightening tide of sensual excitement that she voiced a protest. "You take a liberty, sir."

He breathed in its scent before allowing it to slide from his fingers. "Guilty as charged. I'll accept any punishment from you except banishment," he replied, his eyes wickedly daring her to make some outrageous claim on him.

"If I say you're not to touch me again?" she challenged, unable to resist testing him.

"Unacceptable. That is banishment."

"Do you always make the rules?" she asked.

"I spend most of my time breaking them."

"Not a conservative man."

"No more than you're a conservative woman."

"Why do you say that?"

His eyes simmered with a heat that curled right down to Keira's toes. "I watched you dance." He took the champagne glass from her hand, placed it on the mantel behind her, transferred his to the same place, then curled his fingers around hers in a possessive grip. "Come dance with me. I'll show you we're made for each other."

He didn't wait for her consent, but began leading her through the crowd.

She shouldn't, Keira thought. She shouldn't move from where Justin had left her while he got them drinks from the bar. She shouldn't be letting any of this happen at all. Justin had laid down the law. No riding a tide of opportunity.

But this was the big one, Keira argued to herself. The king tide! It wasn't her fault that Justin had messed up the love of his life. He couldn't really expect her to pass up what might be the love of *her* life. That was totally unreasonable. Not even Justin could be that unreasonable, could he?

She looked back, trying to spot him, wanting to catch his eye with an apologetic appeal, but she couldn't see him. Only one dance, she told herself, needing to appease an uncomfortable stab of guilt. She had promised not to let Justin down, and she wouldn't—but one dance couldn't hurt too much. And then... Well, she would have to wait and see.

Besides which, if Louise and her man weren't here, what harm could this little desertion of duty do? It was only one dance.

She allowed herself to be led out to the huge tiled patio that spread from the main entertainment room to the swimming pool. Keira didn't know whose house this was, or why the party was being held. Those items were not on Justin's need-to-know list. But it was a magnificent home and ideal for entertaining on a large scale. Justin's social circle had apparently zoomed up with his stocks.

Music was supplied by quadraphonic speakers set around the patio. A track from Michael Jackson's *Thriller* was being played. The strong hand holding Keira's pulled her closer as the man to whom it belonged turned to face her.

"Make your own rules," he invited, the blue eyes glittering warm anticipation. "I'll follow."

Every instinct warned Keira that this was dangerous. He was not a follower. He did not ride along with opportunity. Nor did he let it pass by. He seized it and made it his. Yet the sense of danger only served to heighten the excitement he stirred in Keira. She wanted to know how well he could dance, whether he could match her.

To give Justin his due, he had tried, but he didn't really feel the rhythm. He was too inhibited to let his body flow with it. Too uptight. Too conscious of his dignity. Too civilised. But Keira knew intuitively there would be no holds barred with this man.

She moved back to give herself space. He watched her, waiting, his body poised, ready to respond to any movement from hers.

Keira was wearing her little black dress, a designer original she had picked up very cheaply from a second-hand shop in Paris. It was made of some magical fabric that could be rolled up into nothing and stored in a pocket of her duffle bag. Keira had worn it innumerable times. It was ideal for any special occasion and perfect for dancing.

The style was very simple. The close-fitting bodice was cut on the bias, moulding the fullness of her breasts in such a way that a bra was unnecessary. Shoestring straps supported a low heart-shaped neckline. Around her trim waist she wore a gold chain. The plain circular skirt fell from just below her hips, giving her legs free mobility. High-heeled black sandals were strapped securely around her slim ankles.

He was waiting for her to start fast, Keira thought, as she let the rhythm beat into her mind and through her blood. She decided to completely throw him, if she could. She raised her arms to shoulder height and started the slow shimmer she had learnt from Moroccan belly dancers. Slow was always more difficult than fast. It took masterly control.

He was quick to catch on, swaying his body in a complementary pattern while he wove his hands through movements that captured the essence of Eastern dancing. His eyes held hers, mesmerising in their intent, forcing her to acknowledge that he had matched her.

She switched to jazz steps she had picked up in New Orleans. He was instantly on his toes, loose-limbed, lithe and dangerous, stalking her every move, pivoting, lunging, inventing an increasingly provocative reply to everything she initiated.

He didn't touch her, but Keira was aware that he was deliberately heightening the sexual element. His body language became more and more aggressive, and the hot challenge in his eyes goaded her to remain tantalisingly elusive, exulting in the teasing game and so intensely caught up in it that the ring of spectators applauding their performance barely impinged on her consciousness.

Suddenly he caught her to him. "Let's try some dirty dancing," he murmured, his powerful thighs thrusting hers into an intimate sequence of intricate steps, one strong arm keeping her body pinned to his, searing her with his animal heat.

"You said you would follow," she reminded him.

"I warned you I break rules."

He arched her back over his arm, pressing her lower body into his, making her aware that he was very much an aroused male intent on satisfaction.

"You go too far," she said breathlessly as he swung her up again and whirled her through a dizzying number of pirouettes that necessitated a fast juxta-position of their legs.

"You incited it," he retorted. "Tell me your name."

It was on the tip of her tongue to say Keira when she caught sight of Justin watching them. Shame burned through her as she realised she had completely forgotten her cousin and his crisis. "We have to stop," she gasped, feeling her control slipping as the body directing hers asserted more and more dominance over what was happening.

"Tell me your name first," he insisted.

"Delilah," she choked out, hating having to use the alias Justin had demanded, but a promise was a promise. "Delilah O'Neil. And you must stop now. This has gone too far."

"Not nearly far enough," he murmured in her ear as he whirled her around one last time. "You know it. I know it. Why stop?"

"I came here with someone else. I must go back to him."

"Make your excuses. Leave him. Come with me."

"I don't even know your name."

"Nick Sarazin."

"Then please, Nick. I owe my companion loyalty."

His eyes blazed their command into hers, but Keira believed in loyalty. He might have captivated her body, but not her will. She was far too conscious of Justin's need to callously ignore it. If Nick Sarazin was truly attracted to her, he would make another time and place for them to meet.

Frustration momentarily tightened his face and hardened his eyes. "Very well," he said, bringing their dance to an abrupt but graceful halt. "Go back to him. When you change your mind I'll still be here, waiting for you."

The arrogant assumption pricked her pride. She stepped back from him, her green eyes meeting his in cool challenge. "I think, Mr. Sarazin, you've had your own way with women far too easily for far too long.

Wait, by all means, but *I* shall not come to you. If you want me, you'll have to find me. Thank you for the dance.''

The surprise on his face was intensely satisfying to Keira. She smiled at him, then swung on her heel and headed towards Justin, who was still standing where she had seen him.

Very conscious of having wavered off the plan, Keira quickly wiped off her smile and constructed an apologetic expression. It was difficult. She could feel the blue eyes of Nick Sarazin boring into her like laser beams. She couldn't resist swinging her bottom, which was now free of its cramped ache.

Nick Sarazin was the one, all right. Keira still felt his heat in her blood, like an intoxicant or a fever. But falling in love was a serious business. Nick Sarazin had to be taught that. Keira did not intend to be taken lightly. To her mind, there was a proper way of going about things, and while she loved spontaneity, she strongly disliked rude disregard for other people's feelings. There had to be giving as well as taking.

It was not as if Justin was some casual escort who meant nothing to her. Justin was family. Not that Nick Sarazin knew that, but he hadn't bothered to find out, either. He simply hadn't cared about anything except having his own way with her. His self-assurance definitely needed dinting. A bit.

Oddly, Justin wasn't looking at her at all. His gaze was fixed on a point over her shoulder, and far from appearing vexed or in any way upset, he was projecting a nonchalant confidence. He gave her a warm smile of approval as she joined him.

"Marvellous dancing, Delilah. You seem to have met your match," he remarked while handing her the drink he had been holding for her.

"Thanks, Justin." She looked at him quizzically. "You don't mind?"

"Not at all. I think I'll have to learn how to dance like that."

She frowned. "I meant about him. He—er—kind of carried me off."

A sly little smile tilted her cousin's mouth. "He looked as though he wanted to do a lot more than that."

Keira flushed. "Well, the truth of the matter is he fancies me."

"And do you fancy him?"

"Yes, I do," she confessed. "Rather a lot. But I won't let you down, Justin."

"Oh, don't let me stop you from following your heart's desire."

She looked at him incredulously. Such generosity of spirit from Justin, against his own interests, didn't seem like him at all. Keira wondered if he'd been sinking more drinks than was good for him, but he didn't seem to be at all pie-eyed.

"What about your plan?" she reminded him.

Sheer unholy triumph glittered in his eyes. "The plan, my dear Delilah, is working perfectly. You already have my eternal gratitude. Louise doesn't know what to think. The mat has been whipped out from under her feet. The tables are already turned. Just look at me adoringly for a few moments."

Keira tried to oblige but it was difficult. She felt very confused. "I don't understand, Justin," she said as she did her best to adjust her body language to express what she didn't feel for her cousin. "What about the man you want seduced?"

"The natural order of things is now in progress. You don't have to worry about it."

Keira breathed a sigh of relief.

Justin's eyes narrowed. "In fact, I now suspect that Louise was using him as camouflage to get me to change my mind."

"About what?"

He gave her a stern look. "That is our private business. But the plot gets thicker and thicker, the intrigues deeper and deeper. Louise can be a very tricky fighter, but she's met her match in me. Oh, yes! I'm more than a match for my wife!"

He paused to savour that thought, then beamed happily at Keira. "What we can be sure of, at this point in time, is that I'm winning. And winning well. Which is the main thing."

Keira sighed. She was sure she could be a lot more helpful to Justin if only he'd tell her what was going on. Apart from which, now that she had Justin's permission, she very much wanted to follow her heart's desire. Except that course was not viable at the present moment. She had just spiked it with her retort to Nick's arrogance. She actually needed to stay with Justin to force Nick Sarazin into an appraisal of his manners and expectations.

Consoling herself with the thought that at least she didn't have to pretend an interest in some other man,

Keira resigned herself to a continuation of the Delilah role. "So what's next on the menu, Field Marshal?" she asked, hoping to get a glimmer of what was in Justin's mind.

"Just keep projecting adoration," he said smugly. "You do it very well."

"Thank you. But I'm not too sure my heart's desire is going to like that, Justin. I don't want to put him off."

Her cousin gave her a wise look. "Trust me. That's precisely what will make him even more determined to take you away from me. I promise you he'll make another move before the night is out."

"Why do you think that?" Keira asked, hoping it was true.

"Instinct." He grinned. "And the way he watched you come to me. The fire is alight. We have to keep it burning. So we'll walk slowly across the floor, ignoring everyone else, totally immersed in our love for each other."

He tucked her arm around his and looked fatuously at her. They walked . . . slowly . . . and Keira did her best to follow Justin's lead. She examined her cousin's eyes as she had never examined them before. They were a nice brown but she found herself craving blue. Besides which, she wasn't absolutely sure Justin was right about this. She didn't want Nick Sarazin to start thinking she was seriously attached to Justin. On the other hand, that hadn't stopped him from approaching her in the first place.

All the same, Keira couldn't help feeling that feeding a fire was a very dangerous thing to do. Fires could get out of control. Fires could destroy. She had a strong urge to back off.

"This is getting to be a bit of a strain, Justin," she warned him. "I don't know how long I can keep it up."

"Not much longer, Keira."

"You forgot to call me Delilah."

"Damn! Delilah, Delilah, Delilah. I never was good with names."

"That's because they're not numbers."

"Which reminds me, you didn't slip up with your dancing partner, did you? You told him you were Delilah O'Neil?"

"Yes. But I didn't like it, Justin. I might get serious with Nick Sarazin."

"No problem," Justin pontificated. "If it doesn't get serious it won't matter what your name is. It it does get serious, he won't care about such a triviality. Take my word for it. A man doesn't care about names. It's the woman that counts."

"Is that how you feel about Louise?"

His fatuous look tightened into grim determination. "I wouldn't have married Louise if she wasn't the woman for me. The only woman. And by God, she's going to stay my woman!"

No doubt about it, Justin felt very deeply about Louise. Keira hoped Louise felt the same way about him and that their differences would soon be sorted out. She very much wanted to get on with her own life and she fiercely hoped Nick Sarazin would be part of it. A big part.

"You must stay Delilah O'Neil until I tell you everything's okay," Justin commanded.

Keira sighed compliance. "As you wish, Field Marshal." She couldn't very well upset his plan if it *was* actually working, but if his judgement was wrong... Keira shook her head. That didn't bear thinking about.

"Now we shall circle the room and make a spectacle of ourselves," he instructed. "Show the world that Justin Rigby Brooks need never have any trouble with women."

"Are you sure this is not going over the top, Justin?" Keira demanded critically.

"Think of the loan you need from me," he reminded her.

He did have a point.

Keira managed a fair show of adoration for about ten minutes, but the strain was getting to her facial muscles. She desperately needed a break so she excused herself to go to the powder room. Justin didn't mind giving her this consideration and pointed her down a hallway to the bedroom at the end of it, which, he said, had an en suite bathroom.

There were two women touching up their make-up in front of the dressing-table mirror in the bedroom. They assured Keira that the bathroom was free. Keira dallied in the bathroom for a while. She was beginning to feel very tired. Jet lag catching up fast, she thought, and splashed water over her face in an attempt to keep the draining fatigue at bay for a little while longer.

She desperately hoped she hadn't put Nick Sarazin off with all this adoration aimed at Justin. Yet if her cousin was any yardstick about how a man felt about the right woman, Nick Sarazin would find a way to win her, no matter what. If he truly did think they were made for each other.

When Keira emerged from the bathroom, a slim dark-haired woman was pacing the bedroom floor in tense agitation. Keira instantly felt a twinge of guilt for having dallied so long. The woman looked quite distressed.

Keira made an apologetic gesture. "Sorry..."

If looks could kill, she would have been reduced to dust on the spot. Dark brown eyes stabbed violent murder as the woman spoke in bitter accusation.

"Just what do you think you're doing with my husband, you...you brazen hussy?"

CHAPTER THREE

KEIRA'S INITIAL SHOCK from the verbal attack faded into the realisation that this woman surely had to be Louise. Justin's wife of four years—a wife who had walked out on him for reasons unknown—a wife who had flaunted another man under Justin's nose.

A curious fascination gripped Keira as she appraised her wayward cousin-in-law. Louise had a neat professional look about her. Justin would like that, Keira realised. Her thick black hair was cut into a short stylish bob that suited her round face. It was a pretty face, dominated by large dark eyes flashing jealous fury at Keira.

She was short and petite, and Justin would like that, too. It would make him feel very manly and protective. She wore a yellow silk dress with black polka dots and a fancy black patent leather belt. The effect was smart more than sexy, but there was certainly no doubting the curvaceous femininity of Louise's figure.

Whatever the bone of contention that ruptured their relationship, it was apparent Justin had succeeded in lighting an extremely passionate fire in his wife. She was certainly not indifferent to him. Which meant their marriage could be saved, given the right help.

However, saving a marriage was very tricky business. The utmost tact was called for. When all the problems were resolved, Keira wanted to be friends with Justin's wife, so her first priority was to defuse the violent enmity that was presently aimed at her.

She offered an open, friendly smile. "Are you Louise?"

It provoked violent rejection. "You sly bitch! You know exactly who I am."

Keira tried sweet reason. "How can I? We've never met before."

"Don't act the dumb blonde with me or I'll tear the skin off your face!" Louise sniped viciously. "I know you're not dumb."

"No, I'm not dumb. But I do feel rather at sea with this situation," Keira said soothingly. "If you care about your husband, why did you leave him?"

Louise moved so fast that Keira didn't see the hand coming. It hit her a ringing blow across the face. "How dare you think you can interfere with my marriage? Mind your own damned business!"

Keira dazedly lifted a hand to her stinging cheek. She had never been physically struck in her whole life. She abhorred violence of any kind. Yet, in a way, she couldn't blame Louise for being upset, considering the provocation Justin had masterminded. Keira began to suspect there would be repercussions when Louise found out who the brazen hussy really was, and how she had been tricked.

One thing was certain. She could hardly fight with Louise, and she didn't want to. She edged warily away. Louise seemed to be working herself up for another assault. Keira tried to present a logical point of view for her cousin-in-law's more sober consideration.

"If you leave a husband, it implies you don't want him any more. That makes him fair game for other women," she said pertinently.

"You dirty, devious witch! He's not fair game!" Louise shrieked. "He's mine!"

Perhaps not the right time for logic, Keira thought, but decided it might be worthwhile to push one more point. "Then don't you think you should do something about keeping him?" she advised, backing further away as Louise advanced on her.

She saw the doorway out of the corner of her eye. Keira decided this was Justin's problem, not hers, and she was better off out of it. If she could make her escape until the madness of this situation was resolved . . .

"You sneaky, wicked slut!" Louise screamed.

"I'm not!" Keira defended.

"If you don't keep your eyes off my husband, I'll tear them out!"

"There's no need for that," Keira said hastily. "There is an explanation. . . ."

That seemed to inflame Louise even further. "I'll give you an explanation! Written in blood on your face!" Her hands were lifting like talons. She meant it.

Keira backtracked fast. "I'm fond of Justin," she said defensively. "But that's all. You see—"

Louise sprang at her, bloody murder glittering in her eyes. Keira turned and ran. She was out of the bedroom and a couple of steps down the hallway when her hair was caught from behind. The yank nearly took her head off. I'm going to be scalped, she thought.

"Justin!" she yelled, needing him to get here on the run. A very fast run. He had a lot of quick explaining to do to douse this fire. He *had* gone too far. Things were totally out of control. And she was the one about to be destroyed!

"Hussy!" Louise screamed, pulling on Keira's hair so that she was dragged around to face Louise.

Keira could see the satisfaction and triumph in Louise's eyes as she disentangled one hand and raised it to claw down her face. Keira threw up an arm to defend herself and cried out again, more desperately.

"Justin, Justin, Justin!"

Louise's hand slashed down. It didn't reach Keira's face. It was arrested only millimetres from striking. Thank God Justin had got here, Keira thought in shaky relief. But it wasn't Justin.

"Oh, I say!" came a very British voice as a big brawny arm swept between the two women, forcibly separating them, giving Keira some much-needed room away from Louise.

Keira drew back her head as Louise's fingers loosened from her hair. She looked up gratefully to her rescuer. Her eyes met a walrus moustache and she stared in startled surprise at the big retired wrestler who had sat next to her on the plane.

"Surely there has to be a better way," he started to chide Louise, but got no further.

Louise turned on the instant, her black fury switched to him. Keira had to hand it to Louise. She had fast reactions. Without so much as a pause she kneed him violently in the groin. The poor man didn't have time to look surprised. His face went white. He emitted a tortured groan of pain and doubled over.

Louise glared at Keira over the poor man's stricken body. "Keep away from my husband or you'll get worse than that! I'll kill you!" she threatened. Then she tossed her head in the air and marched off into an admiring crowd who politely clapped.

It must have looked like a David and Goliath contest, and little David, the underdog, had won. Keira instantly knew that everyone was going to be against her. She was cast in the role of the bad woman. The marriage breaker. I've done nothing, she wailed inwardly.

Two faces seemed to leap out at Keira from the mass of people in the immediate vicinity.

Justin, beaming absolute delight.

Nick Sarazin, looking darkly and doubly frustrated.

Then the heaving groans of the retired British wrestler demanded Keira's attention. She bent to help him, her hand sliding over his shoulders. "Are you all right?" she asked sympathetically.

"No," he moaned. "Not all right at all."

"I'll get you onto a bed," she suggested.

"Finished," he said. "I'm finished."

Keira saw action was imperative. She quickly tried the nearest door, found it opened to a bedroom, then urged the poor man towards it.

"You need rest," she told him comfortingly. "I'm so sorry you were hurt. Please tell me if there's anything I can do."

"Just finished." He tottered a couple of steps, saw the bed, looked at Keira in anguish. "I beg you, leave me. Please..."

"But there must be something..."

"No! No!" he cried, looking quite distressed. "There's nothing you can do. You—you're dangerous. Totally dangerous."

"No, I'm not," Keira assured him.

"Please. Leave me. I'll be all right. Just finished."

"Nothing more can happen to you," Keira promised.

"Go away!" he begged. "I don't want to be beaten up by some jealous husband. Go away."

Oh, dear! Another nasty incident, Keira thought. "If you're sure..." she said uncertainly.

"Yes, yes," he urged desperately. "Never been more sure. Leave me alone with my pain."

"I'm sorry," she said, and saw relief pass over his face as she backed away. He lurched into the bedroom and shut the door behind him.

Keira heaved a deep sigh. Just because things seemed to happen around her, it wasn't all her fault, was it? He had spilled the coffee all by himself this morning. And tonight... Well, it had been his choice to be the gallant gentleman. For which Keira was truly grateful. She should have thanked him. Somehow she didn't think he would appreciate her thanks right now, so she decided it was better not to press the matter. Perhaps she would do so if she ever ran into him again.

Keira wondered what he was doing here. It seemed an odd coincidence that both of them should have come to the same house on their first night in Sydney. But it was a small world, she reflected, shrugging off any further speculation. The retired British wrestler was irrelevant to the immediate problem.

One thing had been made very clear. Louise was far from indifferent to Justin. And she certainly wasn't indifferent to Keira. Passions were running very deep here, and it was time to wipe that smug look off her cousin's face. Fighting fire with fire had elements of extreme danger, and Keira passionately hoped Justin knew how to put the fire out. Otherwise Louise was going to make life very difficult for Keira in the future.

Apart from which, Keira felt very unhappy about Nick Sarazin having witnessed that nasty little scene. Somehow it made all her role-playing with Justin seem sordid. She was not a marriage breaker. She had been doing her best to be a marriage saver. But it hadn't looked that way. If Justin's strategy had lost her a chance with Nick Sarazin... A lump of lead dragged at Keira's heart. It didn't bear thinking about.

She braced herself for the fray and made her way through the crowd to Justin, who was looking far too cocky for his own good. He needed to be brought down to earth with a good thump.

"This job as a private soldier is finished, Justin," she said. "That's the end!"

"Ah... Delilah, Delilah, Delilah, I adore you," he crooned sickeningly. Then grinned. "Great little fighter, my wife. As feisty as they come. She was going to kill you. Sorry about your hair, but it does demonstrate how much Louise has been kidding me. Everything is going marvellously well.''

''It's finished!'' Keira repeated emphatically. ''You tell Louise the truth.''

''Never.''

''Then I'll tell her!''

He frowned at the determined defiance flashing from her green eyes. ''Be serious, Keira.''

''I am serious. Deadly serious. I am not going to die for your honour or glory or happiness, Justin.''

''Look,'' he said appeasingly, ''there's more to this than meets the eye.''

''Then you'd better start explaining it to me,'' Keira demanded, taking a very firm stand.

''Not here. It'll spoil everything. Just hang in a little while longer.''

''No.''

''Until tomorrow.''

''No.''

''A few hours more.''

''No.''

''I'll double the loan. And I won't demand payment of any interest on the money.''

Keira could hardly believe her ears. She had never known her cousin to be so free with his money. Except when he had sent her the airfare to come to his wedding. Which she had missed. He must be absolutely convinced that this plan of his was going to save his marriage. But Keira had her doubts. Serious ones, at that!

''I'll triple the loan to keep the plan strictly between us until tomorrow,'' Justin pressed keenly.

Keira frowned hard at him. She had no need for that much money. All she had wanted from him was a reasonable loan to tide her over until she could get a job. Money was not that important to her. Not as it was to Justin. Either he was completely nuts or he was desperate for her not to interfere in what was, whcn all was said and done, *his* marriage and *his* private business. She just hoped he knew what he was doing.

"All right," she conceded reluctantly. "But not for love nor money will I be persuaded to let you use me falsely beyond that, Justin. And I'm not going home with you tonight. I won't have Louise thinking I'm committing adultery with her husband. You've got to tell her the truth about me pretty darned quick or you won't have a marriage to save."

"I will. As soon as I get the right opportunity."

"Promise!"

"I promise. In the meantime, I take your point about spending the night with me, so what are we going to do with you?"

"A room in a hotel."

"Okay."

"A suite."

"What do you need a suite for?"

"Bodily comfort. After all I've been through—"

"Suites are expensive."

"Consider it danger money. And proof of how eternally grateful you are."

She had him over a barrel. He conceded handsomely. "Whatever you want. But you've got to stay Delilah until tomorrow."

"The sooner you tell Louise the better, Justin," she warned. "I'm going to find a telephone right now and book a nice big safe suite for my well-being. And I'm going to stay there until you've cleared my name with Louise. You owe me that."

The cost of maintaining her in a suite should clear his mind about when to tell his wife the truth, Keira reasoned. Having thrown down her ultimatum, she marched off in search of a telephone, determined to hold Justin to his promise.

Nick Sarazin found her first.

All of a sudden he was in front of her, blocking her way, his blue eyes flashing a hard challenge. "He's no good for you, Delilah," he stated with firm conviction. "If you didn't know before, you know now. He's married."

It was one thing getting Justin to sort out the problem with Louise. Nick Sarazin was a completely different kettle of fish. Keira owed him nothing, and his demanding manner got under her skin, scraping over her recently lacerated pride. Not only that, he was making assumptions that he had no right to make.

"Justin has been very good to me," Keira said loftily. "So you don't have anything to worry about. And I happen to be rather fond of him." Which was the truth. She *was* rather fond of Justin, although after what had happened with Louise that fondness was rapidly diminishing.

Nick Sarazin's jaw line tightened. It made him look very aggressive, like a warrior about to fight to his death. The blue eyes glittered with repressed anger.

"You were well named Delilah," he grated. "Very accurately named."

Keira found her pulse beating faster. Nick Sarazin had definitely got the wrong idea about her. She wondered how she could correct this misinterpretation. She couldn't very well reveal what she had assured Justin she would not reveal. But her sense of loyalty was wearing perilously thin.

Although Justin had been right about Nick.

He had made another move on her, and he was certainly burning.

Her cousin had next to no understanding of women, but it did seem he had an understanding of what went on in men's minds.

Once again, Keira tried to soothe troubled waters. "I guess my family had reasons for bestowing that particular name on me, just as your family had reasons for bestowing yours on you," she said reasonably. "You have to live with yours, with its satanic overtones, just as I have to live with mine."

"Are you always so callous to other people?" he demanded, his sympathies obviously with Louise.

Keira's chin lifted. Her green eyes held his in cool challenge, refusing to give him any quarter whatsoever, not on the grounds he had raised.

"No," she stated flatly. "Most of the time I'm just me. If you don't like that, Mr. Sarazin, just step out of my way and let me get on with my own business. After all, it's you interfering with me, not the other way around."

His hands shot out and gripped her wrists, determined that she stay...at least until he had finished with her. Another liberty, Keira thought, but since she didn't mind, she didn't say anything. She liked him holding her and was glad that he wanted to, but she was not about to take any disparagement from him.

"What do you find so attractive about him?" he demanded to know. "Dammit! You can't find him attractive!"

Keira had to admit to herself she didn't find Justin all that attractive, but she certainly wasn't going to admit that to a stranger. Family was family. She searched her mind for a reply and found one she thought suitable.

"He's the kind of man who always takes care of me once he gives me a commitment. It's a quality I value. Perhaps you'd like to tell me your rating on that, Mr. Sarazin," she invited mockingly.

"I could give you more love in a minute than you'd ever get from him in a lifetime," he retorted fiercely, his voice throbbing with raw passion, his eyes searing the coolness from hers. He looked hard at her, hotly assessing. "Make that time factor *one hour*."

Keira's heart flipped over. Once again she felt a fierce tug on her soul, and a treacherous excitement flooded her veins. The thought of experiencing his promise almost eroded all common sense, yet a thread of sanity insisted this might be a line he threw at all women.

"You really believe you can deliver on that?" she asked doubtfully.

His hands left her wrists and started sliding around her waist. He moved closer, deliberately heightening his physical impact on her. His eyes simmered with

memories of the more intimate contact they had already shared with his brand of "dirty dancing".
"Certain," he said with absolute conviction.

"Maybe we only dance well together," she suggested defensively, refusing to admit the chaos he wrought inside her.

"We're compatible," he said gruffly.

"You don't like me," she protested.

"What has liking to do with passion?"

"You feel passion?"

"Very definitely." His eyes burned into hers as he spoke in a low intense voice. "I want your hair on my pillow. I want to bury my face in it. I want to ravish your mouth and know all its dark inner secrets. I want your body entwined around mine in the most primitive dance of all. I want your wild earthy rhythm pulsing through me. And I promise I'll take you where you've never been before. We were made for each other, Delilah."

It was as if his words had a life of their own, writhing through her in seductive temptation, stealing her breath, squeezing her heart, knotting her stomach, sending quivers of weakness down her legs, tingles through her toes. What woman in her right mind could resist such an offer?

Was this how it was—a want, a need, a desire that overrode everything else? But what about trust and caring and loving—weren't they more important? Why did she feel that he was the one? Was there any real choice, or was it all preordained through some physical chemistry neither she nor he had any control over?

She suddenly felt a strong empathy for the passion that had driven Louise to such violence. It ran through Keira's mind in a wave of almost unbelievable ferocity that if Nick Sarazin took her and walked away she would want to kill him. Yet not to experience what he offered her was another kind of death, a rejection of what could be.

"I want you," he said. "I want you to walk away from him right now. Forever. And come with me."

Somehow Keira found voice enough to ask, "Why are you so impetuous? Let's give it some time. I'll think about it."

"No time. No thinking. Now or never, Delilah. It's as simple as that. Make your choice."

The tension emanating from him tore along Keira's nerves. Nick Sarazin was not a conventional man. He was gambling the lot on one throw, and demanding that she do the same.

Keira wasn't afraid of taking risks. She had never been interested in a safe life. Safe meant limited and she refused to be limited to anything. Nevertheless, she was not rash and not about to take a leap into the unknown.

"Where are we going?"

His eyes glinted with satisfaction. He relaxed enough to smile, sensing his victory. "Away from Sydney. Away from everything. You can choose wherever you want. But we're going."

Oh, dear, Keira thought. He was going to make it difficult for her to exert any control over this particular outcome. What was bound to happen was almost inevitable. Did he view relationships in terms of easy come, easy go? she wondered. On the other hand, perhaps she would be able to convince him that he didn't want to let her go. Ever. The fact that he hadn't wanted to let her go tonight, despite all that had happened, gave Keira some reassurance that there was a chance of a future with him.

"The beach house?" she suggested. After the cold of Iceland and Europe, she really fancied some hot Australian sun. If he gave her time to enjoy it.

"Fine!"

He scooped her hard against him, and before Keira could have any second thoughts about her decision, he was pushing through the crowd towards the front door, sweeping her along with him.

"Nick, I have to speak to Justin first," she protested.

"No. He's married. You don't owe him any loyalty and you don't speak to him again."

"You're putting demands on me already. I don't like that, Nick."

"I'm saving you from yourself," he said grimly.

"But Justin's got my things."

"I'll buy you whatever you need."

"I don't want you buying me stuff. It would make me feel bought. I never like to feel bought. In fact, I resent it."

"Send for whatever you need tomorrow."

"Justin will worry about me."

"You can call him on my car phone."

"You'll listen in."

"Most certainly."

"Why can't I speak to him before we leave?"

"Because you're finished with him. Because you've made up your mind. Now stick to it, Delilah. Remember at all times that he doesn't count any more."

Jealous. And possessive. And so far he had nothing to be jealous and possessive about. Maybe he was just plain demanding. Yet there were very positive signals of passion, Keira thought, so she didn't protest too much.

"Haven't you ever heard of politeness, Mr. Sarazin?"

"Yes. And I've also heard of double-dealing."

Keira thought about that highly questionable remark as they went down the front steps to the driveway. "You don't trust me," she accused.

His eyes glittered mockingly in the semi-darkness. His face had taken on a satanic look. "Not one iota."

"You're well named, Nick."

He grinned wickedly. "So are you, Delilah."

"Devil!"

"Seductress!"

The irony of the situation suddenly descended upon Keira. She wasn't a Delilah, nor a seductress, nor a woman hankering after a married man! And twenty-four hours ago she had been sitting beside the retired British wrestler with the walrus moustache, unaware of Justin's crisis and unaware of Nick Sarazin's existence!

"I don't think this is going to work out," she said limply. There was too much misunderstanding at this early stage.

Nick paused in his step, looked at her, then hoisted her in his arms and clutched her tightly against his chest. "Just stay put," he commanded, "and let me worry about that."

He strode along the driveway as Keira tried to catch her breath. Her arms automatically found their way around his neck. It was a very strong neck. He was a very strong man. He made Keira feel very feminine.

"Why are you carrying me?" she asked huskily. Her voice was melting. Her brain told her she should be protesting very firmly. Nick Sarazin had no right to seize control like this, taking away her choices. But somehow the messages from her brain were getting quite muddled by a lot of strange and strong sensations.

"Because I feel like it," he said in a harsh, gravelly tone.

Keira decided she didn't really mind him taking this particular liberty. As long as he didn't make a habit of taking liberties without any consultation with her.

He didn't carry her far. A black two-seater Jaguar sports sedan was parked outside one of the garages at the side of the house. He reached the passenger door and let her feet slide to the ground, but she was still held fast in his embrace. She wasn't sure if it was his heart thumping so hard or hers, but when he lowered his head towards her upturned face, Keira felt an exultant leap of anticipation through her whole body.

Because of their heated exchange, she had expected him to kiss her with passion, yet his lips moulded slowly, sensually into the fullness of hers. He tasted them exquisitely, seducing them into opening further and further with an escalating range of exciting sensations.

Then he was exploring the full intimacy of her mouth, weaving erotic dances with his tongue, stirring dimensions of feeling that sent bursts of wonderment through Keira's brain. A hand stroked her long neck, wound its way through her hair, took hold, and suddenly there was an explosion of passion, a wild, plundering drive for total possession with a ravishing stream of kisses that came so hot and fast that Keira was barely aware of one ending before another began.

Waves of excitement flooded through her body, and it seemed that he absorbed the very essence of her so that she floated weightless, her legs a useless support, his arms supporting her, his body a hard solid raft in a shifting sea of turbulent sensation. So intense were the feelings he evoked that Keira moaned in bereft protest when he finally lifted his head away, leaving her with an unforgettable imprint of the kind of loving he was capable of giving her.

And he was far from unaffected. He was as aroused as she was, breathing hard and fast as he lifted his hand to cup her face. He stroked his thumb lightly over her tingling lips as his eyes glittered into hers, piercing the daze of mindless wanting.

"Remember that when you speak to Justin Brooks," he commanded in a harsh rasp.

Then he unlocked the car door, opened it and eased her onto the low-slung passenger seat. Keira could barely think, let alone comprehend what had just happened to her. If that was a minute or two... what would an hour of Nick Sarazin's loving be like?

Her limbs were like water. It didn't occur to her to fasten her seat belt. Nick did it for her. Then he was beside her in the driver's seat. The powerful engine of the sports car throbbed into life. They shot down the driveway, out into the street and away from the party.

Nick punched out some numbers on the car phone, picked up the receiver and told whoever answered to take care of the house, look after the colonel's needs, he would be back in a fortnight or so, and he wanted to speak to Justin Brooks, who was one of the guests. Then he handed the receiver to Keira.

The blue eyes bored into her, hard, hot and demanding. "Tell him you're with me. You're finished with him and you're staying with me. Permanently."

CHAPTER FOUR

PERMANENTLY?

A wild rush of elation danced through Keira's brain. Nick must think she was the one for him!

Then a niggling little voice whispered this might only be an emphatic expression to drive home the point that Justin was to have no more relevance in her life. Which, of course, she couldn't agree to at all. Justin was family.

Besides which, Nick had no right to order her around. He didn't own her. He had no claim to exclusive rights on her, either. They weren't married yet.

That last thought gave Keira pause for consideration. Was she going to marry him if he asked her? It might be very difficult to settle down to a humdrum existence after all her footloose years. On the other hand, she couldn't imagine Nick Sarazin leading a humdrum life. And she couldn't imagine wanting any other man but him.

All the same, he was not going to order her around. He was going to have to temper this demanding habit if he wanted to be her husband. It was not a quality she valued. In fact, it was decidedly negative to her way of thinking. Taking care of her was fine, but taking care of her against her will was definitely a no-no.

"Justin Brooks." Her cousin's voice.

Keira took a deep breath. Nick was listening. She had to get this right to avoid any more misunderstandings that she couldn't explain away.

"Justin, this is Delilah. I've taken off with Nick Sarazin. You might remember him. He's the man I danced with. So you don't have to worry about me any more. I'm calling you from his car phone and we're on our way to..."

She looked questioningly at Nick. "Where is your beach house?"

Blue eyes locked with green. "I don't want him coming after you."

Keira sighed. If only she could tell him the truth, she could dispel that notion in a second, but... She spoke into the phone. "Justin... Nick doesn't want you coming after me. You won't do that, will you? Tell him that whatever Delilah decides is fine by you. I'm passing the receiver to him."

She held it to Nick's ear and they both heard Justin give firm assurance that Delilah had his every blessing to live her life as she saw fit. She smiled triumphantly at Nick and resumed her conversation with her cousin.

"Thank you, Justin. I knew I could rely on you to say that. And I know I can rely on you to send my bags by special courier to... What's the address, Nick?"

He conceded it with a dark brooding look.

She passed it on and waited until Justin wrote it down. "I want them tomorrow, Justin. Without fail," she said firmly. "And I also need the payment you owe me, so please include that with my bags. I won't be happy if it's not there, Justin. In fact, I don't know what I'll do if it's not there.''

"It'll be there," he promised. "And Delilah..." He said her name with pointed emphasis. "I understand that you're finished with our mutual project, and that's fine by me, but I've still some way to go, so the cat stays in the bag until tomorrow. Okay?"

She sighed in resignation. "Okay. Tomorrow. Goodbye and good luck, Justin."

"And the best of luck to you, too, Delilah," he said with uncharacteristic fervour. It must be because he's so grateful, Keira thought, because she had never known her cousin to be overly demonstrative with good wishes or affection.

She hung up with a feeling of deep satisfaction. The rift was definitely healed. Justin had forgiven her for taking off with the sheikh and missing his wedding. However, there was the difficulty with Louise to overcome before they could all be a happy family again. She hoped Justin's plan covered that because Keira didn't like being cast as the bad woman. She wasn't bad at all.

"What's on tomorrow?" Nick demanded suspiciously.

Keira threw him a vexed look. This not trusting her one iota was distinctly tiresome. "I'm getting my bags," she stated patiently. "And the money Justin owes me."

"I suppose you're used to twisting any man you like around your little finger," Nick remarked in a savage tone.

Keira's vexation with the situation deepened. *He* still thought she was bad. She hoped he wasn't going to be a slow learner about her character or she would run out of patience with him.

"I get the impression that *you're* used to twisting any woman you like around *your* little finger," she retorted, determined to give him tit for tat until he started to get reasonable.

His mocking smile had a grim edge. "But not you."

"I'm a free spirit," she said, which was a fair assessment of the truth.

She thought that the right man, if he used the right kind of rope, could tie her down, but she wasn't going to be bound or gagged if she didn't want it to happen. Nick Sarazin had to learn that, and he might as well start learning now.

"What did Justin Brooks owe you payment for?"

Keira threw him a look of reproof. "Just because I let you get away with listening in on a private conversation, it doesn't give you any right to know my private business. What I've done with my life up to this point in time is absolutely no business of yours. You'd do much better if you simply take me as you find me, and stop reading all sorts of nasty things into my words and actions."

She paused, then pointedly added, "I don't like it. In fact, it could wear out my passion pretty darned fast."

His mouth twitched into a conciliatory smile. "I beg your pardon. I was merely curious, not thinking nasty things about you." He raised an appealing eyebrow at her. "Am I not to know anything of your life?"

"That depends," she said cautiously. She was mollified by the smile, but she still had to watch her step because of Justin's plan.

"On what?" Nick asked.

"What you tell me about your life," Keira answered lightly.

"It's an open book. Ask away as much as you like," he invited.

"The house where the party was held, that's yours, too?"

"Yes. That's my Sydney residence."

Which made Nick the host of tonight's party. Therefore he must know Justin, if only as an acquaintance. And he probably knew Louise, as well. Since all three had some connection, social or business, Keira could understand why Justin wanted her to retain her alias with Nick until everything was settled.

"What was the party for?" she asked. "I mean, was there any special reason for it?"

He gave her a quizzical look, then shrugged. "It was in celebration of the successful launch of a new product."

"Something you make?" she asked curiously, wondering where all his opulence came from.

The quizzical look was slightly harder this time, blue eyes sharply probing hers. "Don't you know who I am, Delilah?"

She returned her own puzzlement. "How could I? I only met you tonight. You told me your name, but you didn't tell me anything else about yourself."

He frowned, as though not quite believing her. "And my name meant nothing to you?"

"No. Why should it?"

He shook his head. A self-mocking little smile played over his lips. "Why, indeed?" he murmured.

"Are you famous or something?" Keira asked.

He gave a dry chuckle. "Apparently not. Though I had imagined most people would have heard of me. I've run a high-profile business for a fair number of years."

"What kind of business?"

He grinned knowingly. "Advertising. The Sarazin Advertising Agency."

He said it as though that had to mean something to her. But it didn't. "Well, it's nice for you it's been so successful," she said.

He looked incredulously at her. "You can't mean you've never heard of that, either?"

She shrugged apologetically. "Sorry."

He simply couldn't accept it. "Don't you ever watch television?"

"Not much. I travel a lot."

"Where?"

"All over."

"All over what?"

"All over the world. I've been out of Australia for a number of years," she explained. "And before then...well, I was in out-of-the-way places. Television wasn't important."

This time he looked at her with sharp curiosity. "What *was* important?"

"Oh, seeing things. Finding out things. Meeting people. Talking to them." She smiled. "Call it a long journey of discovery."

His eyes lingered appreciatively on her smile for several seconds before he turned his gaze back to the road. Then he slowly shook his head, a bemused expression on his face.

"You must have done some travelling, too," she remarked.

"Why do you say that?"

"Few people would pick up that kind of Eastern dancing unless they've experienced it first-hand."

He nodded. "I knocked around the world for a couple of years when I was younger."

"How old are you now?"

"Thirty-three. And you?"

"Twenty-six."

"What kind of job do you hold?"

She laughed. "I don't hold any kind of job for long. I move on, you see. I guess you could call me a Jill of all trades. A rolling stone. I've been everything from a shoe sales person to a hair model for shampoo. I was even nanny to a sheikh's son for a while."

"A sheikh," he repeated in dry amusement.

"Mmm, in Morocco. Very educational. I once thought being an archaeologist would be the most exciting job in the world, but it's not, you know. A lot of hard grind for very little reward."

"Where did you do your archaeology?"

"In Egypt. It wasn't a successful dig but it was an experience. I learnt a lot about Egypt."

"What has been your most exciting job?" he asked curiously.

She yawned. She couldn't help herself. Fatigue was washing over her in an overwhelming tide. She had only had short snatches of sleep in the last forty-eight hours. Even today, although she had spent several hours on a very comfortable bed, she hadn't had a long, restful sleep. Her biological clock was totally out of whack.

"I don't know that I could pick out a most exciting one," she replied, too weary to really think about it.

"Being a model?" he suggested.

"That was very boring. Good money, though."

"Not enough to keep you in it?"

"I had other things to do." She yawned again. "I'm sorry, Nick. I'm dreadfully tired. Would you mind very much if I dozed while you drive?"

"Go right ahead. There's a knob to the left of your seat if you want to lower the back rest," he said, flashing her a kindly smile.

"Thanks."

He was heart-wrenchingly handsome when he smiled like that, Keira thought. She adjusted the back rest and nestled herself into a more relaxed position. She closed her eyes and felt very content to be with him, not caring where they went, or how long it took them, as long as it was together.

"One last question, Delilah," he said softly.

"Mmm?" She didn't bother opening her eyes. Her lids felt very heavy.

"Do you do this kind of thing very often?"

"What?" Her mind was getting foggy.

"Take off with a man you don't know."

"Never before."

"Why are you doing it this time?" he asked her sharply.

She stirred herself enough to answer him, but her thoughts were drifting into a deeper haze. "You're the one...."

"The one... what?"

"King tide..."

"I don't understand."

It's very simple, she thought, but the words didn't reach her lips. They were lost as sleep overtook her, dragging her into dark oblivion.

Nick Sarazin glared at her in deep and mounting frustration. Who the hell was she? What was she? Where had she come from? What did she know? Who had sent her?

Her last words were utter gibberish, yet they had to have some meaning. She was certainly intelligent. As well as being so damned beautiful and alluring that he had been on fire for her from the moment he had seen her dancing.

A Delilah who had seduced her way around the world? So many question marks she raised.

Yet her face in sleep was as smooth and as innocent as a babe's.

And that hair! Was it real? He shifted uncomfortably in his seat. Just the thought of it made him stir. Everything about her made him feel more aroused than he could ever remember, as if somehow she embodied all that a woman should be or could be....

A fantasy, he thought mockingly. That was what she was. A siren from mythical legends. Green eyes like the sea. Maybe those words, king tide, did have some relevance. And if he didn't watch himself, he could drown in it. On the other hand, that might not be a bad fate.

The image of a mermaid swam into his mind. Ridiculous... absurd. He glanced at her long shapely legs. The loveliest legs he had ever seen. The way she could move them—the speed, the grace, the command—the sheer provocative sensuality of her body.

He'd got her. That was the main thing. Yet the question continued to tease his mind—what exactly had he got? The speculation began to irritate him and he leaned forward to switch the radio on. A Mozart concerto. He turned the volume low so as not to wake her.

From his Sydney home at Hunter's Hill, it was barely a two-hour trip to Forrester's Beach on the Central Coast. He liked the house he had bought there. It was simple. Comfortable but unpretentious, suitable for casual living. Of course, he had it serviced, but it didn't require live-in staff, and it gave him a sense of privacy, something that was becoming more and more precious to him these days. Once he had hankered after fame and wealth, but having achieved both, there was a price to pay. Nevertheless, having enjoyed economic freedom for years now, he would never want to give that up.

A free spirit. He looked at her face again. In some ways it was a strong face. Unusual bones, more delineated than most. Smoky eyelashes. How were they that colour if her hair was real? Yet how could a hairdresser achieve the variations of shade between white and deep gold? She was a strange contradictory creature.

Not many women defied him these days. Or challenged him, as she had. No fawning or flattery from her. He was beginning to believe that what he had achieved was totally meaningless to her. It had been a long, long time since he had felt uncertain of a conquest, and even now he wasn't sure she was a conquest. *A free spirit...*

But she would be his.

He'd make her his.

She was still fast asleep when he brought the car to a quiet halt in the driveway of the beach house. He alighted quietly, unlocked the house, switched on lights as he strode through it to the main bedroom. There he opened the sliding glass doors to let in fresh air and the sound of the ocean with its endless rolling surf. She would probably feel at home with that, he thought whimsically.

The sweet haunting scent of frangipani blooms wafted on the sea-breeze. An image floated into his mind. The soft velvet of fragrant petals shading from white through cream to deep gold. It brought a sensual smile to his lips.

He went to the linen cupboard, took out a sheet, walked quickly to the veranda and spread it on the double sun lounger. He leaned over the veranda railing and gathered as many blooms as he could reach from the huge frangipani tree that graced the north side of the house. He sprinkled the blooms over the sheet. All the elements, he thought, water, air, earth and the fire burning between them. It gave him a deeply primitive satisfaction in his arrangements.

He took one small spray of flowers with him to the kitchen where he paused long enough to put the kettle on to boil. Coffee seemed like a good idea. He wanted her awake, alert and responsive. Apart from needing his desire for her satisfied, Nick felt a sense of urgency about getting rid of that elusive quality Delilah O'Neil emanated. He wouldn't feel content until he had her precisely where he wanted her... in his arms, joined to him.

He returned to the car. She hadn't stirred. He opened her door, leaned down to unfasten her seat belt. His hand brushed over the soft fullness of her breast, lingered a moment, then dropped to the seat belt buckle. He wanted to touch her, but he wanted her knowing he was touching her.

Keira was awakened by an arm sliding under her legs and another burrowing around her shoulders. She opened her eyes, saw the darkly handsome face hovering over hers. The recognition in her heart was instant and electric. She smiled at her man.

"Are we there?" she asked.

"Yes," he said gruffly, and lifted her out of the car.

Keira wound her arms around his neck and nestled her head onto his broad shoulder. She breathed in the strong male scent of him and sighed in happy contentment.

Nick pushed the car door shut behind him and headed for the house.

Keira could hear the dull roar of the ocean, and there was a smell of salt in the air. The Pacific Ocean, she thought, half a world away from the Atlantic. She was home . . . home in many senses. It felt so right to have Nick Sarazin holding her like this.

He carried her through the house to a very large bedroom before setting her on her feet. His lips brushed over hers with what felt like loving tenderness.

"Are you all right, Delilah?"

"Mmm . . ."

He trailed soft little kisses around her face. "I've put the kettle on to boil. I'll go and make us some coffee. Okay?"

She'd prefer him to keep kissing her, but he had had quite a long drive and probably craved a cup of coffee. "Okay," she agreed.

He lifted a hand to her cheek and gently swept her hair from her face. She looked into his eyes, so vividly blue, enveloping her in their intensity.

"There's an en suite bathroom through that door." He nodded towards it. "How do you like your coffee?"

"Black."

"Sugar?"

"No. Straight black, thank you."

He smiled as he stroked her cheek in a soft salute. "Don't go back to sleep on me."

"I won't," she promised. Her skin was still tingling from his touch, and the feel of his body had aroused hers out of its lethargy.

He moved away to a row of wall cupboards, opened a door, pulled out a drawer, withdrew a cellophane packet. "I keep a supply of *yukatas* for guests," he explained. "They're—"

"Japanese lounging robes. Evolved from samurai ceremonial garments," Keira finished for him, smiling at his surprise. She walked over to take the packet from him. "I did tell you I've done a lot of travelling, and a lot of learning. Thank you, Nick. It will be handy until I get my things."

"Keep it if you like," he offered.

The practicalities of the situation had snapped Keira out of her trance. She looked searchingly at Nick Sarazin. Had he really meant permanent? There was a wary reserve in his eyes, as though he was uncertain of her, or uncertain of her reactions.

"There's a supply of shower caps in the bathroom, if you want to make use of one," he added.

"Thank you." Her green eyes flashed with a sharp stab of inquiry. "You're well prepared . . . for your guests."

He shrugged and gave an offhand smile. "A matter of hospitality."

Convenient hospitality? she wondered. She had acted on instinct, choosing to come with him, but she suddenly felt very unsure about his feelings for her. How deep did his passion go?

She recollected his question to her and decided that this was an appropriate time to toss it back at him. "Do you do this kind of thing very often? Taking off with a woman you don't know?"

He met the challenge in her eyes with hard self-mockery. "No. Never with women I don't know. But then I've never met a woman like you, Delilah. You are . . . exceptional. Therefore, like you, I make an exception—for you." One eyebrow lifted in sardonic inquiry. "Is that what you wanted to hear?"

"Only if it's the truth."

He gave a soft little laugh. "Take my word for it. You'll never hear a truer truth."

A bubble of happiness lifted her doubts away and she burst into a smile. "I think you're exceptional, too, Nick. Very arrogant, too dominating, too demanding, but definitely exceptional."

The blue eyes danced with amusement. "How am I supposed to respond to being chastised and complimented in the same breath?"

"Oh, you've got a few things to learn about me, Nick Sarazin. In fact, you're going to have to be a very fast learner," she advised pertly.

"I intend to be," he promised . . . or threatened.

There was suddenly an aura of intense purpose about him, and Keira once again felt a sense of danger. She knew intuitively that this man could hurt her as no one else could—deeply, irrevocably. Warning messages slid across her mind—passion, fire burning out of control. And fire could destroy.

"I think I'll take a shower," she said.

"I'll go and make the coffee," he said.

And so they separated . . . for a while.

But Keira knew what was coming, as surely as night followed day. Nick Sarazin was not about to hold back. In coming with him, and in responding to his kisses as she had, Keira knew that Nick had every reason to be complacent about her consent. He was not to know, and probably would never believe, that sharing a bed with a man was not a common feature

of her life, despite her twenty-six years. In fact, it was
extremely uncommon. Which was probably why she
was beginning to feel intensely vulnerable about it.

The timing was far too premature in one sense, yet
Keira didn't believe time would make any difference to
how she felt about Nick Sarazin. This inner certainty
that he was the one had to be acted upon. However,
going too far too soon might be a mistake. She might
end up getting very badly hurt. The problem was . . .
how could she tell if she was the one for him?

CHAPTER FIVE

THE PLEASANT BEAT of warm water washed the lingering fatigue from Keira's body. As she dried herself with a soft fluffy towel, her gaze drifted around the well-appointed bathroom. A lot of home comforts here, she thought appreciatively. Luxury and every possible convenience, even to a hairdrier and a specially magnified make-up mirror attached to the tiled wall beside the vanity bench.

Keira thrust her arms into the loose sleeves of the *yukata*. The light cotton garment was a sea-green colour, splattered with a navy-blue twig-style pattern. Nice combination, she thought, as she wrapped it around her and tied the belt. Then she whipped off the shower cap and shook her hair loose. For a few moments she examined her reflection in the mirror, wondering why Nick thought she was exceptional.

She knew he found her hair attractive, but hair was only hair. He surely wouldn't break his personal rules for something as superficial as that. Of course, there was the physical attraction, which had been quite close to explosive when he had swept her into his "dirty dancing". Did he feel a sharper desire for her than he'd felt for any other woman? Was it all sexual with him, or was there more? Did he feel engaged in the same way she did? Only time would sort that out, Keira told herself.

She left the bathroom and found that Nick had not yet returned to the bedroom. She laid her clothes on a cane armchair. She liked the white and lemon and lime-green furnishings of the room. Bright and beachy, she thought. The floor was of polished wood, although there were several mats for softness underfoot.

Her gaze kept shying away from the bed.

It had a bad effect on her nervous system.

Keira never liked to feel pressured. She instinctively resisted such a state of affairs. Her feet automatically took her across the room to the sliding glass doors. Stepping to the veranda railing gave her an immediate sense of relief or release. Being closed into a room, or a situation, was not a good idea, she decided. It encroached on free choice.

A light breeze wafted through her hair. The sound of the surf crashing onto the beach seemed very close. She lifted her gaze to the night sky, searching out the constellation of the Southern Cross, another sign that she was home.

"I give you the moon and the stars," came Nick's voice behind her.

She turned, laughing. He stood in the doorway, a mug of steaming coffee in each hand. Keira's laughter choked in her throat as she was assailed by the overwhelming impact of his strong masculinity, which the casual garb of a scarlet *yukata* seemed to emphasise . . . dramatically.

Apparently there was a second bathroom in the house because his hair was a mass of tight damp curls from showering. The loose cotton robe gaped almost to his waist, revealing the firm delineation of flesh and muscle and a sprinkle of black curls arrowing down from the base of his throat. Scarlet and black. The colours of the devil, Keira thought. But there was nothing satanic about Nick's face. The blue eyes promised heaven. His jaw was shiny from having been freshly shaven, and a tangy male scent drifted from his skin.

Keira had never felt heart-wrenching desire before. She had been mildly attracted to quite a few men, but she had never before experienced the heart-pounding, mind-blasting desire to know a man's body with absolute intimacy, to feel it, taste it, merge with it to the exclusion of all other considerations.

She felt it now with mesmerising force. She was struck speechless, motionless, caught in a thrall of intense fascination, staring at him.

He stepped onto the veranda, moved to her side, placed the mugs on the wide railing. As though he emitted a magnetic force she turned towards him, drinking in his profile, which seemed carved out of stone in the moonlight. Until he threw his dazzling white smile at her.

"Is this what you wanted, Delilah?" he asked softly.

"It must be," she whispered, then wrenched her gaze from his face and lifted it to the stars again. She wanted more, of course. Much more. But if the fates were kind, that would come. This intense physical response to him, this compelling recognition that no one else had ever evoked, was the beginning. For anything to develop there had to be a beginning. From there it would expand like the universe, for good or ill. She saw a falling star and wished on it. Let it be good. . . .

"What did you mean by king tide?"

Her heart jolted at this voicing of her private thought. Her gaze dropped sharply to the probing inquiry in his. "I said those words?"

He nodded. "Just as you were falling asleep in the car."

She frowned. She wished she hadn't said them. They were too revealing. The thought of explaining the concept behind them made Keira feel even more vulnerable. If Nick was not in sympathy. . .

Better to shrug it off. "Time and tide waits for no man," she said glibly.

"And?" he prompted.

"And what?"

"And I think there's much more to it."

He was too perceptive. She picked up her mug and began sipping the coffee. Her skin was prickling with sensitivity from her very nearness to him. If she let things proceed as Nick clearly meant them to—if she rode this king tide she felt building inside her—would he love her? Could he be as good as he said he was? Would it lead to the ultimate fulfilment she craved?

He was waiting for an answer. Keira suddenly realised that the best way of finding out how closely they could come together was to reveal her innermost thoughts. There was no point in holding back. If Nick's response revealed they were not mentally attuned it was better to know now, before she plunged in too far.

"Things happen. Sometimes suddenly. Unexpectedly," she mused softly. "Circumstances create an opportunity that is written in sand. Often it's not recognised until it's too late. The chance is gone. It evaporates. Or you misread the situation. And it's still gone. You must have experienced it yourself, the sense of time and place, of opportunity never to be repeated."

"Yes," he agreed quietly. "I've found that in my life, too."

Keira smiled, deeply pleased that he had understood. She turned her gaze out to sea, remembering the lines she had learnt so long ago. "The idea comes from a speech in Shakespeare. Nothing to do with nature, Nick."

"Tell me the idea," he urged.

She flicked him a teasing look. "You really want me to quote Shakespeare?"

He smiled. "An adman takes quotes from any source that can spread the message most effectively."

She eyed him uncertainly. "You might misinterpret it."

"Then you can correct me."

Because she wanted to share with him, to understand him and be understood, Keira decided to chance it. Her gaze automatically returned to the ocean as she spoke the words that had influenced so many of the choices she had made in her life.

"There is a tide in the affairs of men,
Which, taken at the flood, leads on to fortune;
Omitted, all the voyage of their life
Is bound in shallows and in miseries.
On such a full sea are we now afloat,
And we must take the current when it serves,
Or lose our ventures."

There was a long silence before Nick spoke. "You think coming with me will lead on to fortune?" he asked in a flat, toneless voice.

Disappointment stabbed her heart. His thinking was cynically twisted by the power and position his wealth had given him. "I don't think Shakespeare was using the word fortune in the way you're using it, Nick," she said with dry irony. "There is more to fortune than gold. There's happiness, well-being . . ."

"Besides which, you can't be bought," Nick cut in with an apologetic grimace. "Sorry . . . wrong note. I stand corrected once again. And I beg your pardon for the lapse into shallow judgement. I should be learning faster."

Keira shrugged. "This isn't a matter of learning. You either feel it or you don't. Besides, a neap tide can either lift up or destroy. I don't know what's going to happen. I don't know which you will do to me, Nick. That's up to you."

She gave him a crooked smile. "But if I hadn't come with you, I'd never have known. I guess I had to find out. I wasn't going to spend the rest of my life wondering what I might have missed."

He cupped her face, keeping it tilted to his as he searched her eyes long and hard. "I don't know what to think of you," he said at last. "But I'm glad you're here."

He took the coffee mug from her and set it on the railing. Then he gently took her by the shoulders and turned her to face him. Was it going to happen now? Did she want it to? Keira's pulse leapt into overdrive as her heart began to pound erratically. Her breathing became fast and shallow. She had never been involved in anything like this before.

But he didn't draw her into an embrace. There was a smile in his eyes, a soft curve of sensual whimsy on his lips. He dropped his hands from her shoulders, and from the pouched looseness of the *yukata* above his belted waist, he withdrew a sprig of frangipani flowers.

"They make leis of these in the Pacific Islands," he said, presenting the fragrant cluster to her. "They're flowers of greeting, for happiness and well-being and for celebrating momentous occasions... and for lingering, loving memories. They're the flowers of love."

Either he was a very fast learner indeed, tapping into the needs pulsing through her, or he was expressing what he thought and felt. Keira desperately hoped it was the latter. It had to be. Or she would never have the confidence to follow her instincts again.

He plucked one of the perfect blooms and positioned it over her left ear, winding a long silky tress of her hair around it to fasten it there. He took another bloom, positioning it higher, then another and another, outlining her face with flowers in such a slow,

deliberate way that it seemed like a reverent ceremony, as though he were dressing her as his bride.

The heavy fragrance surrounded her, so sweetly intoxicating that Keira felt she was floating on a full
sea, buoyed by currents of exhilarating happiness and
glorious well-being. She watched Nick's dark handsome face, so intent on what he was doing, so brilliantly lit with satisfaction when he completed the halo
effect with a flower over her right ear and his eyes
roved over his handiwork.

"And so it is," he murmured, half-wonderingly.

And so it is. Keira's heart pounded. Because it had
to be!

Then he smiled at her as he took the stripped frangipani sprig from her hands, plucked the last bloom
from it and tossed the empty stalk away. "I want you
to remember the scent of this flower all your life," he
murmured, brushing the soft petals over her lips, under her nose, around her face, gently closing her eyelids, as though he was anointing her skin with the
velvet perfume.

His voice whispered its caress into her mind, tones
deeper than normal. "Remember how I loved you this
night, with the moon and stars overhead and the roll
of the sea beating its eternal rhythm."

She opened her eyes, not seeing the moon and the
stars, only him. Not hearing the sea, only the thunderous drum of her heart and the sweet echo of his
words of love, inextricably mixed with the sweet,
heady smell of the frangipani.

He curved his hand around her cheek, tilted her chin
up, bent and kissed her lips, lightly, softly, meaning-

fully. Not fierce demanding passion—Keira knew that would come later—but a touching, a tasting, a reaching out . . . a beginning.

The tug on her soul grew stronger, irresistible. She tasted him, needing to know more of this man who could simultaneously project unlimited passion and exquisite restraint. She felt her lips swell with sensitivity against his, heightening the contact, the movement, the awareness, the sensation of being one with him.

His mouth moved away from hers, grazing up her cheeks, over her eyes, her temples, her forehead. She wanted to press into the warmth she felt emanating from his body, to touch him, yet the desire to reach out was entangled with the fascination of savouring what he was doing to her.

His hand slid under her hair to the nape of her neck and tilted her head back. His eyes locked onto hers, dark and turbulent, seeking answers from her. "Is this how sirens enslave men's souls, simply by being?"

"It's you enchanting me, Nick," she replied huskily. "Is it possible . . . ?" Her mouth dried up. It was so important, so critical.

"Anything is possible," he assured her, a deep indomitable throb of conviction in his voice.

She swallowed hard and cast caution to the winds. "Is it possible to fall in love at first sight, Nick?" she asked.

His expression softened as his gaze roved around her face. "I think it must be," he whispered.

He trailed his hand down her throat, feathering her skin with the lightest fingertip touch, grazing slowly down the deep valley between her breasts, narrowly parting the loose edges of her robe to her waist. Keira held her breath—whether in fear or anticipation she didn't know—but he made no attempt to undress her.

He took her hands, which were still clasped in front of her, and spread their palms over the bare heated flesh below his throat. She felt his chest rise and fall as his breathing quickened. He began stroking her arms, her shoulders, her back, drawing her closer and closer to him. She could see the pulse at the base of his throat beating fast, beating for her, and any doubts Keira might have had about Nick's feelings for her were drowned in a wave of blessed certainty.

This wasn't lust. It was loving. Beautiful, caring loving. Keira moved her hands, sliding them under the loose covering and over his strongly muscled shoulders. Her man, she thought fiercely, and knew she had reached the point of no return. Until now she could have stopped. That was no longer possible.

As though Nick sensed her surrender to him, he enfolded her in his arms, heating her flesh with his, crushing her against him. His mouth sought hers, and the urgency that had been missing before burst into wild hungry kisses. Keira thrust her hands into the thick black curls above the nape of his neck, revelling in the tempestuous rush of his need for her.

It was right. Yes, it was right, she thought exultantly. Her senses seemed to have taken on a supernormal quality. His hard muscular body was imprinting itself on hers and it felt so good, as though she had been formed precisely for this, to yield her softness to his moulding. The taste of him was as heady as the perfume that clung around them. She moved her face so that Nick could kiss her throat, her neck, behind her ear, laying warm sensual trails with his tongue as she undulated in his arms, wantonly making herself available and vulnerable as he found one fresh target after another for his sultry, warming, intoxicating kisses.

He found her mouth again and stayed there for a long time, passion giving way to a slow deliberate sensuality, to a mesmerising contact where their lips were barely touching, yet her awareness of him had been fanned to such a fever pitch that it was like an exquisite, almost ethereal floating, a hazy cloud of harmony and pleasure.

He drew open her *yukata* to reveal her breasts to the heavy atmosphere of the night, to the moon and the stars and the scented breeze from the sea. Then he pressed them to his own hard heated flesh, claiming them as his possession, denying them to the rest of the world. Keira hugged him so tightly that his hands were free to find erotic spots on her back, her long-limbed thighs. She trembled under his every touch, wanting more, her whole body alive with anticipation for all that could happen between them.

He pushed the sleeves of her *yukata* from her arms, shrugged out his, and both garments fell at their feet. Then they were together again, totally abandoned in their nakedness, claiming each other like pagan entities in the moonlight, their bodies exulting in the sharper, more compelling intimacy, slithering, sliding, dancing to a mounting inner rhythm that could not be denied.

Keira knew that meaningless incoherent sounds were breaking from her lips as Nick kissed her almost senseless. Her thighs trembled against the power of his. The aggressive maleness of his body excited her beyond anything she had ever known, igniting some mysterious chain-reaction of responses in her that seemed to melt her bones.

The thought ran through her mind that she would never be the same again. And she didn't care. She knew only Nick, felt only for him, lived only for him. If she was his pleasure, then he could have all of her, for always and forever.

He swept her with him onto a wide lounge, and there seemed to be flowers all around her. Nick scooped them up over her breasts, caressing her with them, following their perfumed trails with his lips. She writhed in ecstatic pleasure at the sheer eroticism of his lovemaking. She felt, time after time, that there could be no more exquisite pleasure than this, but then he would excite a new crescendo of sensation, and all Keira could do was cling to him in helpless surrender to his control.

The greatest satisfaction came when at last he entered her, and the full heavy surge of him inside her was the ultimate answer to all the feelings he had evoked. Keira moved slowly, rhythmically, undulating under his fierce insistent pressure, her pleasure being heightened in continuous waves. She was not just melting around him. Her body was doing something that she had had no idea it was capable of. It was as if her blood was thickening and every cell in her body was fusing into something else entirely, like a metamorphosis that radiated from Nick's possession of her.

We are becoming one, she thought, then all thought disintegrated with everything else, and Keira found a languid peace that went beyond peace. She was in her own private valley, a world of contentment and sunshine where nothing ever went wrong.

But Nick had held himself back for her sake, and the desire for absolute completion urged her to help him fulfil his desire. She wanted him to savour the full joy of what had happened between them, and she encouraged him to surge into her to his fullest limits, stroking him, kissing him, mumbling meaningless words until with a harsh animal cry he attained the blissful release that let him join her in the valley of peace.

He held her close to him for a long time after, his breathing slowly returning to normal. The heavy musky scent of their lovemaking mingled with the heady perfume of crushed frangipani blooms, permeating the night, creating a memory that would live on for the rest of Keira's life.

She felt so languorously content that she could have stayed where she was forever, idly looking at the stars, listening to the sea shifting the sands. So it was written, and so it has come to pass, she thought, savouring the warm, loving reality of holding the man of her dreams in her arms. She could not have imagined anything more wonderful, more perfect.

When Nick levered himself up to look at her, she smiled, her eyes luminous with happiness, her face glowing with the knowledge of a new life, a new dimension of living. He kissed her softly, lingeringly.

"I think your name should have been Lorelei, not Delilah," he murmured, smoothing strands of hair away from her face.

She wanted to tell him her name was Keira, but now was not the right time. This was too perfect. She recoiled from the thought of explaining about Justin being her cousin, and the problem with Louise. Any talk about anyone else would be far too intrusive on the intimate mood of this moment. She would do it first thing in the morning.

A look of something like pain crossed Nick's face. He rolled onto his back, carrying her with him so that she lay with her head tucked under his chin, her cheek pressed over his heart. He held her there tightly for several long moments, then slowly relaxed his embrace and began to stroke her hair.

"What will I do with you?" he mused softly, as though she were a conundrum he couldn't figure out.

"Love me," she answered with a sweet sigh of contentment. "Love me always."

His chest rose and fell in a much deeper sigh. "Perhaps I will," he murmured. "Perhaps all the rest is irrelevant. And it is only you that matters."

Keira smiled to herself. It was what she wanted to hear. And tonight's experience was only a beginning. The future shone very brightly in her mind's eye, much brighter than the moon and the stars, and full of glorious warm sunshine. The promise that he had held out to her had been fulfilled. It could only go on. And get better.

She fell asleep under the slow enchantment of his entrancing, caressing hands. She was vaguely conscious of being carried and set down against soft pillows. Her body moved instinctively to snuggle against the lovely warmth of his, and her forehead puckered in protest as a wrong name whispered into her ear.

"Delilah."

Keira . . . it should be Keira.

But the long journey to this moment took its toll, dragging her into a deep, fathomless sleep that knew nothing of the man beside her, the man who was savagely wishing she wasn't what she appeared to be.

CHAPTER SIX

NICK WAS GONE from her side when Keira woke in the morning. She felt bereft until she saw the note propped on the bedside table. The sense of relief when she read it was deep and intense.

"Gone for provisions. Back soon."

She wished he had signed it, "Love, Nick," but it didn't matter. His actions and words last night were enough to hug to her heart. Heaven, she thought, and stretched luxuriously in the king-size bed. Nick's bed. Which she would share with him from now on. Forever and ever.

A crumpled flower caught her eye. She picked it up and brushed the soft petals around her face, remembering, exulting in the memory. She breathed in the heady scent and felt her body clenching with other memories. Nick had been right. He had given her more love in an hour than any other man could give her in a lifetime. Keira had no doubt about that.

Morning sunshine was streaming in through the glass doors. It was going to be a beautiful day, Keira thought. The best day of her life. She rolled off the bed and headed for the bathroom, eager to be ready for Nick's return.

There were still flowers tangled in her hair, their petals browning at the edges now. She carefully removed them. She had a sudden fancy to cast them into the sea and let them float on the current. She did not want these special flowers thrown into a rubbish bin. To her, they were like a bridal bouquet.

Having showered and freshened up as best she could, making use of a new toothbrush from a supply that Nick obviously kept for guests, and a comb that looked equally unused, Keira wandered into the bedroom and took the liberty of looking into the wall cupboards for something to wear. She wanted to go down to the beach. Her little black dress wasn't suitable for that, and she wanted something shorter than the *yukata*. She didn't think Nick would mind if she raided his wardrobe this once.

A row of T-shirts caught her eye. She chose a green one. It made a sloppy mini dress with her gold chain belt cinching it in around her waist. She also borrowed a pair of stretch underpants. There was something terribly intimate about wearing Nick's underpants. And deliciously sexy.

Keira laughed at herself. She didn't normally have this kind of awareness, but this morning was different. Her whole life was different. The focus of it had changed dramatically. Everything circled around Nick Sarazin.

She found a straw hat, scooped the wilting flowers into its crown and was at the glass doors leading onto the veranda when it occurred to her that she should leave Nick a note in case he returned before she did.

She quickly retraced her steps to the bedside table and added her own message to his.

"Gone down to the beach. Back soon."

The double sun lounger on the veranda bore no trace of last night's lovemaking. Nick must have swept everything clear while she slept this morning, Keira thought, and felt vaguely disappointed. She would have gathered those flowers, too, if they'd still been there.

A flight of steps at one end of the veranda led down to a lawn that spread to the sand. It was barely twenty metres across the beach to the water. The surf was relatively gentle this morning, no huge crashing waves. Keira waded in, enjoying the swirl of the water around her ankles and calves.

She had finished casting the frangipani blooms on a receding wave when she saw a larger one beginning to swell. A big dumper, she thought, and realising it might swamp her makeshift dress, she turned quickly and ran for the safety of the beach, laughing with sheer joy in the morning, the sunshine, the water and sand.

Then she caught sight of Nick, watching her from the veranda, and waved at him in happy greeting. He looked so athletic and devastatingly handsome in white shorts and T-shirt.

"Stay there! I'll join you!" he called out, returning her wave.

He turned into the bedroom before Keira found breath enough to answer. She didn't particularly want to stay where she was. She had done what she had come out to do—the flowers were all adrift—and her stomach felt very empty. Breakfast seemed like a much better idea.

She ran up to the house, thinking of cooking a stack of bacon and eggs if Nick had thought to buy them. She expected him to be in the bedroom, changing into swim gear, but he wasn't. Then she heard his voice talking to someone and followed the sound down a hallway to a well-equipped kitchen. Nick had his back turned to her, a telephone receiver nursed against his ear as he spoke in sharp, clipped tones.

"I assure you, it's fixed. You have nothing more to worry about on that score."

A business call, Keira thought, and waited quietly and patiently so as not to interrupt his train of thought. Taking off with her, as he had last night, was undoubtedly causing a few problems. However, that idea was totally shattered when Nick next spoke, his tone one of mounting exasperation.

"Louise, I promise you she won't be having anything more to do with Justin."

Keira froze, the words and implications too frightful to relate to herself. Yet it had to be. Nick listened for a moment, but his next words put the issue beyond doubt.

"It was *my* bed she shared last night. Not his. And I expect to keep her with me. In fact, I made damned sure she'll have no inclination whatsoever to stray from my side. I don't lose a woman until I want to, Louise. So stop being hysterical. And just for once, do something constructive about patching up your marriage. Have the baby, for God's sake! I've done what you asked me to do. Now you do what you have to do, because I'm finished with your schemes.''

Keira clutched at the door jamb as she felt the blood draining from her face. Her mind whirled in sickening circles. Justin asking her to seduce a man away from Louise... Louise asking Nick to get "the brazen hussy" away from her husband, to eliminate any possibility of her returning.

Nothing to do with love.

Cold-blooded, calculated seduction.

Nick Sarazin had never thought—not for one moment—that she was the one for him. There had been no sincerity in anything he had said and done. All a performance, a beautifully contrived performance, an evil, satanic performance!

Keira shuddered in revulsion. Never had she felt so despoiled, so ravaged, so cheated and betrayed. Even her own cousin had let her down, knowing she was going with Louise's *man*.

Nick Sarazin, the Australian playboy, notching up a Delilah on his belt of conquests.

Her stomach churned. Bile rose in her throat, and perhaps she made some stricken sound choking it down. Nick suddenly spun around and saw her. They stared at each other, the horror of realising what she had overheard stamped on his face, the horror of having been his victim stamped on hers.

Keira knew then what Louise had felt last night. She wanted to claw out his deceiving blue eyes and disfigure his darkly beautiful face. She wanted to maim and kill and destroy until there was nothing left of him to remind her of the man she thought he had been. The violent passion that flooded through her was such a frightening, alien thing that it spurred her into flight.

She ran blindly. Anywhere away from him, anywhere. She stumbled down the hallway, through the bedroom, onto the veranda, down the steps. And behind her he called that hated name. "Delilah! Delilah!" Hoarse and urgent and demanding that she stop.

Demanding. So much he had demanded of her, and taken and used, abusing her feelings for him with such callous disregard. A devil, uncaring what hell he sent her to, uncaring as long as *he* got *his* way!

She staggered through the sand towards the water. The tide was going out. Her flowers were gone. Gone like her love. And there was black despair in the heart she had opened to him, desolation in the soul she had opened to him, betrayal in the mind she had opened to him.

"Delilah." He was coming after her.

"No!" she screamed, shaking her head in anguished denial. "Keira! Keira!"

He didn't stop.

She couldn't bear him near her. She plunged into the water, welcoming the cold buffeting of the waves. A glance over her shoulder showed Nick ploughing in after her. Damn him to hell forever! she thought savagely. Didn't he know it was time to stop? Couldn't he see that nothing could be gained by pursuing her now?

Then a wall of water crashed on top of her. Caught off guard by the dumper, Keira was swept off her feet and tumbled into a maelstrom of sea and sand. Hard biting hands gripped under her arms and hauled her out of the churning turbulence. She was coughing and spluttering too much to put up any fight. Then she was dumped again, on warm dry sand this time, and her hated rescuer sat himself beside her, breathing hard.

Keira did some hard breathing herself once she had retched up all the sea water she had swallowed. Control was what she needed—iron-clad control. Nick Sarazin could talk himself blue in the face but she wouldn't let him get to her. Never again!

"Are you okay?" he rasped.

"Yes," she bit out. "Go away."

"Not until I explain."

"There's nothing to explain," she sliced at him, then turned her head away in contemptuous dismissal.

He was not deterred. "Louise works for me."

Keira didn't want to hear a whole stack of self-serving lies. "I hope she's good at her job!" she sniped.

"And she had a problem—"

"Which is very certainly your problem now!"

"—with her husband. I was trying to sort it out."

"You have succeeded admirably."

"Won't you please listen?" he demanded in exasperation.

"No!"

"Why not?"

"Because I know perfectly well what you've done. You seduced me."

"I did not!"

"Yes, you did!"

"Only a little bit. The rest of it was—"

"Too despicable to contemplate!" she blazed at him, her green eyes stripping him of any defence through the dangling rats' tails of her hair.

"It was beautiful!" he protested angrily. "You were beautiful! The whole thing was beautiful!"

Beautiful lies, she thought savagely. Even to saying "always," deliberately lying so she would have "no inclination to stray from his side." He probably made every woman he wanted to seduce believe that he was the one for her. *Made for each other!* Keira would never forgive him for that. The passionate hatred welled up again.

"Yes, well," she drawled. "I expect an adman knows all about setting a stage and creating an effect." She raised her hand in savage mockery. "I salute you! You're the grand master of the game! I now appreciate why you've been so very, very successful."

He looked darkly furious, the blue eyes glittering daggers at her. "You tell me, what point is there in destroying what we've got together? It's plain stupid, Delilah!"

Keira rose to her feet. Her legs felt shaky and she knew she looked a total mess, but she disdainfully ignored the sagging wet T-shirt now coated with gritty sand. She raked back the long strands of hair that clung to her face and neck like lank seaweed, tilted her chin high, looked at him in towering scorn and delivered her judgement. "We've got nothing!"

"The hell we haven't!"

"And you can stop calling me Delilah! My name is Keira!" she flung at him. Having delivered the ultimate exit line, she turned and started marching along the beach, seething at the crass arrogance that expected her to overlook his rotten manoeuvring.

"Where do you think you're going?"

He had jumped to his feet and fallen into step beside her. The demand in his voice was typical. Keira's resentment of his attitude reached new heights.

"Away," she snapped.

"Where?"

"The last person I'd tell that to is you."

"Will you stop being so damned unreasonable?" he yelled at her. Then he dragged in a deep breath and lowered his tone to one of soothing persuasion. "This is ridiculous. Let's go back to the house. We'll have a shower together. I'll wash all the sand off your body, dry you off with a big fluffy towel. Then we can relax on the bed and I'll tell you in detail just how reasonable I've been."

If the arch-seducer thought he could wheedle a repeat performance with her, he was a very slow learner. She favoured him with a look of acid contempt. "Pigs might fly!"

He glowered at her. "Why did you say your name is Keira?"

"None of your business."

"But it's not Delilah, is it?"

"No."

"You were out to seduce *me*, weren't you?" he accused.

"Now that *is* ridiculous!" she retorted in seething bitterness. "I'd never dream of being so hard-hearted, calculating, mean and despicable. Not like some other people I could mention."

His laugh was a derisive bark. "I bet you thought you were seducing me and that's why you're in such a huff. A little dent to the female pride."

She pulled up for a breather. It was heavy going through the sand. Besides, it gave her the opportunity to slap Nick Sarazin down, metaphorically speaking.

She looked him straight in the eye and said, "I think you're stupid."

"What?" His disbelief in such an idea was written all over his face.

"I think you're stupid," Keira repeated emphatically.

An angry flush tinged his cheekbones. The blue eyes blazed with a turbulent mix of emotions. Paramount seemed to be self-disgust. "You're damned well right! I am stupid! For falling in love with a woman like you!"

This clenched-teeth declaration gave Keira pause for thought. But only for a moment. It was another one of his lies to keep her with him. "I'm leaving," she stated determinedly.

"Because I'm falling in love with you?" he demanded incredulously.

"Because I don't trust you one iota!"

"Ha!" he scoffed. "You've got the roles reversed. I don't trust you. Remember?"

"Too bad!" Having caught her breath, she set off again, determinedly ploughing on, away from him.

"What's your relationship with Justin Brooks?" He was beside her again, stubbornly persisting in being demanding.

"Since you're on such good terms with Louise, get her to ask him," she advised sarcastically.

"You're impossible!"

No, just badly hurt, Keira thought. And he was frustrated because he wasn't getting the pleasure he had anticipated out of his successful seduction. He was losing a woman before he chose to. And, of course, she might go back to Justin and that would mean Nick Sarazin losing face to Louise. A *huge* dent to *his* pride!

"You can't go anywhere looking like that!" he argued, obviously deciding an appeal to common sense might work.

"Yes, I can," Keira retorted, not giving an inch.

"You don't have any money," he said triumphantly.

"Then I'll have to get by without it."

"You are *bloody* impossible!" he yelled, reduced to swearing by her intransigence.

"Yes," she agreed calmly. "To you I always will be."

Something like an animal growl issued from his throat. "We'll see about that," he muttered fiercely.

He moved so fast that Keira could not take any evasive action. He turned on her, tackling her like a rugby forward and hoisting her over his shoulder.

Keira kicked and beat at him in total disregard of her firm belief in non-violence. Nick Sarazin totally ignored any damage she might do to him. Holding her in a relentless grip, he strode manfully up the beach to the house, determined on having his way with her.

"I hate you!" she screamed.

"Hate is the reverse side of love," he replied with infuriating smugness.

"I'm not staying with you." She wished she could kick *him* in the place it hurt most.

"That's okay. We'll work it the other way. I'll stay with you."

"No, you won't!"

"You're not going back to Justin Brooks. He's a married man."

"Put me down, you rotten bully!" Keira cried bitterly, finding some outlet for her rage in thumping Nick Sarazin's buttocks as hard as she could.

"Would you like to claw my back? I find that exciting, too."

"Oh!" She tried twisting so she could cuff his head, but couldn't quite make it. "I'll get you for this!" she cried in frustration.

"That sounds even more exciting."

"You're enjoying this, aren't you? Playing a big bully caveman," she raged.

"It has its moments."

"It won't get you anywhere. I can promise you that."

"On the contrary. It's got us both back to the house." He started up the veranda steps. "In another minute or two we'll be in the shower together. And then I'm going to kiss you senseless, since I can't talk common sense to you."

"You just try it, Nick Sarazin!" Keira threatened, premeditated murder in her heart. "I'll bite your lips. I'll bite your tongue. I'll claw your skin off. You'll be bleeding like a stuck pig by the time I'm through with you. And don't count out other more painful damage, either," she added as he crossed the bedroom floor and she caught sight of the bed she had shared with him.

"On second thought," he said, pushing open the bathroom door, "I think I'll simply leave you here to cool off for a while."

"A very wise decision," she said sarcastically.

He turned on the taps in the shower, tipped her into it, sidestepped her swinging fist and went off laughing, shutting the door with a triumphant bang after him.

Keira fumed with mountainous outrage. If Nick Sarazin thought he'd won anything with his brute tactics, he had a big surprise coming. She would show him he couldn't tell her what she could or could not do. She could do any darned thing she set her mind to!

She left the taps running, marched out of the bathroom, through the bedroom, along the veranda, down the steps, around the side of the house, reached the street and set off for the far, far distance, for the great stream of humanity, for a world without Nick Sarazin!

Brutally unshackled from the ties of a false love, she was a free spirit again. Above everything else, Keira Mary Brooks was a survivor, and she would survive Nick Sarazin, too!

Given enough time to put the soul-destroying experience behind her.

CHAPTER SEVEN

A BLACK JAGUAR SPORTS sedan pulled up at the side of the road ahead of her. Keira had no idea how far she had walked, or in what direction she was going, or how much time had passed since she had left the beach house, but she had no doubt about the owner of the car even before Nick Sarazin stepped out of it.

He was clean and spruce in stone-washed black jeans and a white sports shirt. Expensive Reeboks on his feet. Even his casual clothes reeked of money and class, confirming his playboy status, Keira thought savagely. He rounded the car, opened the passenger door and stood waiting beside it with his arrogant brand of self-assurance.

"This has gone far enough, Keira," he said sternly when she stopped dead and turned away from him, pointedly waiting for a car to pass before crossing to the other side of the road. "Get in the car and I'll take you wherever you want to go."

"I don't get into cars with strangers," she sniped at him.

"I'm not a stranger," he grated.

"Yes, you are. Your mind is totally alien to mine," she retorted fiercely.

"If you don't get into the car, I'll pick you up and put you there," he threatened.

Her green eyes blazed a promise of quick and sudden death. "Do you want your car smashed?"

He thumped the hood in exasperation. "For God's sake! Be reasonable. You can't go walking around like that. You might as well be naked."

"It's *my* skin," she hurled at him, then set off across the road, leaving him swearing and cursing.

However, his comment about being naked did sink home. In her distraught state of mind, Keira had forgotten how revealing a wet T-shirt was. When she reached the other side of the road, she tried picking the clinging fabric away from her breasts, but it only flapped and stuck to her skin again when she let it go. It would dry eventually, she told herself, but she felt extremely conscious of the problem as she trudged along.

The black Jaguar pulled up in front of her again. He must have made a U-turn, she thought, as Nick Sarazin leapt out of the driver's side and planted himself in her path. Keira looked across to the other side of the road, wondering how often she was going to have to zigzag before her erstwhile lover got the message that he was dead as far as she was concerned.

"All right!" he said, holding up his hands in an appeasing gesture. "I was wrong. And stupid. I'm not going to manhandle you again. I'm just concerned about you, Keira."

"I don't want you concerned about me. I can look after myself," she argued coldly. "I've been doing it for twenty-six years and I'm very good at it, thank you. If you'd just go away and get out of my life, I'll get on very well by myself."

He didn't like that idea one bit. In fact he was beginning to look quite anxious and desperate. It gave Keira considerable satisfaction to see his self-assurance cracking. Time he learnt he couldn't have everything his way.

"How can you keep on doing this to yourself?" he demanded. His gaze dropped to the clearly delineated shape of her breasts. Looking at them seemed to increase his anguish. He wrenched his eyes up again. His hands sliced the air in agitation. "Without money or—"

"I've been in stickier situations and got out of them," Keira informed him scornfully, folding her arms to stop him from looking at her body.

He didn't like that thought, either. "Would you mind telling me how?"

"All I've got to do is keep walking until I find a policeman. Or a policeman finds me. One or the other always happens. The police are always kind and helpful in situations like this. Particularly when I tell them in detail what you did to me. Not only will they look after me, but they'll keep their eyes open for *you*. One false step..."

"Oh, great!" he muttered angrily. The blue eyes blazed fierce resentment at her. "And what do you propose to tell them? That you've escaped from a mad rapist?"

"What a good idea!" she agreed with acid sweetness. "How clever of you to think of such a thing.

However, I don't think I will use it. My aim, at this point in time, is to forget that you ever existed."

An angry red slashed across his cheekbones. The blue eyes glittered a fierce challenge at her. "That's not what you felt last night, Keira," he rasped.

Pain stabbed into her heart and welled into her eyes. She hastily looked away, blinking rapidly, mortified that his words had slipped past her guard. "If you had any feelings you wouldn't remind me of that," she muttered fiercely.

"I'm sorry." He sighed. Deeply. "I truly am sorry. I'm desperately sorry that you feel so hurt. I'll make amends. Please give me that chance, Keira."

She shook her head, far too disillusioned with him to take any more chances. "You're not the man I thought you were."

"You're not the woman I thought you were, either," he said softly. "Is Keira another alias, or is it truly your real name?"

She supposed that was fair comment but it didn't make any difference. "Only the person counts. Not their names." She turned weary washed-out eyes to his. "Last night you pressured me into a decision. Now or never. You've had the now, Nick. This is the never." Her mouth curled into a smile of bitter irony. "The tide wasn't a king tide after all. It ebbed very suddenly this morning."

He took a deep breath. His face sagged into grim lines. The blue eyes begged forbearance. "It sounded bad, Keira. That was all. What I said to Louise was for a purpose—"

"Everything you've said to me, Nick, was for a purpose. I understand it all," she said with quiet, but pointed emphasis. "You and I are *not* made for each other. We have different values. So please, do the decent thing for once."

"Which is?"

"Let me go."

He paused, reflected, considered. The blue eyes questioned the judgement in hers for a long time. Keira's gaze remained steadfast. There was not the slightest wavering in her resolution to put this encounter with Nick Sarazin behind her. Eventually he reached a decision.

"I can't let you go like this, Keira. Not this way," he said with disturbing intensity. "You're a walking invitation for trouble, with a capital T. And I do happen to be concerned enough to want to prevent it. Tell me where to take you, and I'll take you there. When I'm sure you're safe and well looked after, I'll let you go."

She considered the proposal. Nick looked sincere, sounded sincere, but she knew he couldn't be trusted. Nevertheless, she was footsore, tired and hungry, and the alternatives to trusting him were not exactly attractive.

"Would you take me to Justin?" she asked.

His grimace was followed by a sigh of grudging resignation. "Yes. Even to him. If that's what you want."

"He's got my things," she explained. "I'll have to ring him."

Nick gave her an ironic smile. "The car phone is at your disposal."

Still she hesitated. "Do you swear this is a genuine offer?" she asked suspiciously.

"Why would you doubt it?"

"You told me you break the rules."

"I never break my word." He moved to the passenger door and opened it for her.

Keira paused for a moment. "I'll make a mess of your car," she warned, all too aware of her wet, gritty state.

"Since I seem to have made a mess of everything else, that is the least of my concerns," he replied.

She was suddenly very weary of fighting. With a dull sense of fatalism she pushed her legs forward and entered the car, oddly uncaring that it was stupid to trust Nick Sarazin in any shape or form. Somehow it was no longer important. Nothing seemed to be important. She felt lost in a way she had never felt before, as though her sense of direction had been taken away.

Again he fastened her seat belt for her, because she didn't think of it. He didn't chide her for her negligence. He didn't say anything. He started the car and drove at a relatively sedate pace. Whether it was the events of the morning catching up with her, or whether it was because she was sitting still instead of walking, or simply from delayed shock, Keira didn't know, but she started shivering and couldn't stop.

Nick turned the air-conditioning to warm, but the rise in temperature made no difference. Even her teeth began chattering. When they reached East Gosford, Nick pulled the car into a shopping centre.

"Stay here. I'll get you a coffee and something hot to eat," he said in a kindly tone.

"Thank you," she whispered gratefully.

"I'll be as quick as I can," he assured her.

She nodded, tears blurring her eyes at his consideration. She was a mess, physically, mentally and emotionally. Any kind of control seemed to have slipped out of her grasp. She concentrated hard on getting it back. She had to call Justin and stop him from sending her bags to where she wouldn't be any more.

She took several deep breaths, picked up the car phone and dialled his home number. He was probably at his office, she thought distractedly, and tried to remember the number for information, but it eluded her. She had been out of Australia for too long. Luck, however, was on her side. Justin had not gone to work. He answered her call, much to Keira's relief.

"Justin, you haven't sent off my bags already, have you?" she asked shakily.

"Keira? Is that you?" He sounded unsure.

"Yes."

"It doesn't sound like you," he said, a frown in his voice.

"It's me. What have you done about my bags?"

"Everything's set," he assured her. "I've put five hundred dollars in cash in an envelope in your handbag, plus a cheque for the balance. The courier should be arriving here to pick them up any minute now."

"Cancel the courier, Justin. I don't want them sent. I'm on my way back to you."

"Here? You can't come here, Keira," he said anxiously. "Louise has agreed to have dinner with me tonight and I..."

"Justin, please." Her voice broke as tears rushed into her eyes. "I've got nowhere else to go," she sobbed.

"Keira?" He sounded incredulous. "What's happened? Why are you crying?"

"You should have told me, Justin," she burst out in bitter grievance, "that he was Louise's man. I did my best to help you. You should never have let me go with him, knowing who he was. You had to know."

"Keira, you liked him. You wanted to go with him," he justified himself vehemently.

"He only carried me off to get me away from you, Justin. Louise asked him to and he..." She couldn't go on. She broke down and wept uncontrollably. "I need you," she sobbed. "I need your help, Justin. Please..."

"What the hell did he do to you?" he burst out angrily.

"Enough," she choked out.

"I've never known you to cry about anything before!"

"Justin..." She gulped hard, trying to recover some control of her voice. "Can you book me into a hotel? Get my bags there for me? I'll stay out of your way. I you could do that for me."

"Come home to me, Keira. We'll have to try and sort things out with Louise! If she put that guy onto you—"

"No! No, I don't want to make trouble. A hotel. Please, Justin. No trouble. I don't want to be involved any more."

"Keira..." Troubled uncertainty.

"Please don't argue. I couldn't bear it."

"I'll kill the bastard!" he muttered fiercely, then forced himself into more productive thought. "A hotel. I'll get the best for you, Keira. A suite at the Regent. I'll send your bags over there right now. They'll be there waiting for you. All you'll have to do is give your name at the desk. Now what about getting there? Where are you?"

"Gosford."

"Do you want me to come and—"

"No. I can get to the Regent. Thank you."

"Family is family," he said strongly. "Don't worry, Keira. I'll look after you."

His support broke the dam again and Keira burst into another flood of tears. "Thank you," she choked out and fumbled the phone down. She never cried. Justin was right about that. She had always prided herself on being able to rise above such a show of weakness. Yet for some stupid reason she couldn't seem to stop crying. It was as if she had no say in it at all. Her body wasn't obeying any edicts from her mind.

She was even more of a shuddering wet mess when Nick Sarazin opened the passenger door. He muttered something savage under his breath, leaned across her, undid her safety belt, lifted her out of the car, set her on her feet, wrapped a soft mohair rug around her, then hugged her in a tight embrace.

"Did Justin Brooks let you down?" he asked gruffly.

"No." She snuffled.

He heaved a deep sigh. "Keira, I saw you talking on the phone."

"He's booking me into the Regent. Will you...will you take me there?"

"Yes. I'll take you there. If that's what you want," he added in a flat, unenthusiastic voice.

"It's what I want," she said.

"Then why are you crying, Keira?" Nick asked softly.

"Because..."

"Because why?" he prompted.

"Because I hate weak women."

"You're not weak, Keira." He tightened his embrace and his lips moved warmly over her temples.

Against all she knew to be true, Keira's heart kicked over, and she felt a terrible temptation to lean her head on his shoulder and surrender to whatever he wanted to do with her. Somehow she summoned up enough backbone to say, "You shouldn't be holding me like this." It came out very shakily.

"Why not?"

"Because—"

"I want to."

"—you don't mean it."

"Then why would I do it, Keira?" He rubbed her back in a gentle, comforting circular movement and kissed her some more, soft warm kisses that transmitted a soothing tenderness.

"I don't know," she quavered weakly. "You gave your word that you'd let me go."

"Yes. I did. But that doesn't mean I want to," he murmured huskily.

"You have to," she protested, beginning to feel painfully confused.

"If you say so," he agreed. His chest heaved and fell in another deep sigh. Then he helped her into the car and fastened her seat belt for her again. "The food should be ready by now. I'll be back in a minute," he said.

He closed the door and disappeared. Keira still shivered, but only in convulsive little bursts, not continuously. And it was a different kind of shivering, shot through with memories she had promised herself not to remember. Nick Sarazin wasn't the one. He shouldn't be able to affect her like this. Not now. She simply couldn't afford to be weak and stupid. It could only be destructive.

The mohair rug had a new smell about it. Nick must have gone and bought it, she reasoned, because he hadn't had it when he left the car. It was kind and thoughtful of him. Caring, too. But he couldn't really care. Maybe he felt guilty about what he'd done. He might have realised she wasn't a Delilah. She had certainly been mistaken about him, so she probably shouldn't judge him too harshly for being mistaken about her.

The whole situation was a mess.

She hoped Justin and Louise would get back together again.

At least one good thing should come out of it.

The door on the driver's side opened. Nick leaned down and held out two take-away cups of coffee. A plastic bag hung from his wrist, and the smell of hot fish and chips wafted from it. "Mind holding the coffee while I get in?" he asked.

She took the cups and he settled into the driver's seat and closed his door. Then he produced three cartons from the plastic bag, placed them on the console and opened them before retrieving his mug of coffee from her grasp.

"Prawn cutlets, fish pieces and chips. Help yourself," he invited with a warm smile that did nothing to settle Keira's equilibrium.

"Thank you," she murmured.

They ate in silence. The food was hot and freshly cooked and tasted very good to Keira. When they had finished, Nick produced paper napkins from the plastic bag to wipe their hands, then stacked the empty cartons and cups into it and slung it on the back seat.

"Feeling better now?"

She nodded. "Much better, thanks."

Again he smiled, doing another lot of damage to Keira's peace of mind and heart. It was because he was handsome and attractive, she told herself. Nothing more than that. Any man with those looks would make a woman's heart flutter a bit. His mind, however, was certainly not in tune with hers, and that was what counted.

He started the car and they got on their way again. "Have you known Justin Brooks long, Keira?" he asked, his tone one of idle curiosity.

"Yes," she answered briefly.

"How long?"

There seemed no point in not telling him the truth. "All my life. Our families were very close."

"Not any more?"

"My parents have been dead for quite some time."

"Do you have any brothers or sisters?"

"No."

"That must be rather lonely for you," he remarked in a sympathetic tone.

"I guess you don't miss what you've never had."

The bitter sense of betrayal came sweeping back. He had given her the sense of being loved with a performance that probably no other man she ever met would match. She wished now that she'd never had it. He had left her with a false measure to judge others by, deliberately going out of his way to implant it in her memory. Ego on his part, no doubt. Perhaps he was intent on building a reputation as a legendary lover. A born and bred adman, promoting himself as an artist of the bedroom.

"Do you have any family?" she asked, wondering what had made him the kind of man he was.

"I'm the youngest of four sons. And my parents are still alive," he answered easily.

"Do they approve of the way you live?"

He sliced her a hard, questioning look. "Do you seek approval from anyone for the way you live, Keira?"

"No," she had to admit. Although she privately added that she didn't make a speciality of seducing people, despite Justin's wild ideas about her.

"I guess they consider me the black sheep of the family," Nick confessed wryly. "My brothers are all in staid respectable professions. Law, medicine and architecture. They responded properly to my parents' expectations of their sons. I, being the youngest by several years, was allowed a little more leeway."

"You mean you were spoilt," Keira commented drily.

He grinned at her, totally disrupting the regularity of her pulse. "Maybe they grew tired of setting goals for their children. Anyway, I was always inclined to go my own way. From time to time, they lined me up and chastened me with dire predictions about my future, but I guess, in a way, I was a free spirit, too. I wanted to try my wings. Which I did, to the tune of more dire predictions."

"But you eventually proved them wrong."

"Mmm, in some ways," he said consideringly. "I've ended up making more money than my brothers, but perhaps they've achieved more in a personal sense than I have."

"What do you mean?" Keira asked, curious to know what he found lacking in his life.

He shrugged. "They're all happily married with families."

"You envy that?" She couldn't keep the disbelief out of her voice. With his looks and wealth he could have had his choice of any number of marriageable women.

"Sometimes." He gave her a twisted little smile. "Sometimes they say they envy me my freewheeling life-style, but I suspect if they had it, they wouldn't feel comfortable with it."

"But you do." Of course he did. An accomplished seducer would never feel content with possessing only one woman.

"Do you, Keira?"

She frowned, not quite comprehending his question.

"I mean are you comfortable with your life?" he elaborated. "Do you feel you're missing out on something?"

The pain came back again. "Yes," she answered dully.

"What?"

What you offered me last night and took away this morning, she thought, and a wave of wretched misery swept away any further interest in the conversation. "Someone I could share my life with. Someone to love me," she answered flatly, then turned her head to the side window. "If you don't mind, Nick, I don't want to talk any more."

The tears welled again, but she was able to fight them this time. She stared unseeingly at the passing scenery, and after a while her eyelids grew heavy. She closed them and slipped easily into sleep. When she woke, feeling hot and flushed and unpleasantly sticky—the air in the car was very warm—they were already in Sydney, but she didn't recognise precisely what suburb they were travelling through, and they were not on a main thoroughfare.

"Why aren't we on the highway?" she asked.

"Less traffic this route," Nick answered.

Keira grimaced. Typical male. Women invariably stuck to a highway to get anywhere. It was the simplest, most straightforward route. Men always seemed compelled to find short cuts that proved them smarter than everyone else. Or perhaps it was some innate desire to beat the system and come out a winner.

In any event, the parting of the ways was fairly imminent, and the thought of never seeing Nick Sarazin again, never being with him again, suddenly brought a leaden weight to her heart. Simply the loss of a dream, Keira told herself. It had been such a beautiful dream last night. But she mustn't think about that. Maybe, some time in the future, she would be able to think about it without it hurting too much, but not now.

The car slowed. Keira frowned, not understanding the reason for it. There was no car slowing ahead of them, no red traffic light to halt them. Then they turned into a driveway she instantly recognised. Nick Sarazin's Sydney residence!

He was taking her to his home, not the Regent. He had promised Louise to keep her with him, and he was keeping his word to Justin's wife, not to her. He had lied to her again. Deceived her again. Seduced her with his pose of concern and caring.

"You have to be the most hateful man I've ever met, Nick Sarazin!" she seethed, jabbing at the seat belt release button and trying to struggle free of the rug. "I'll never believe another word you say!"

He threw her a look of soft appeal, the blue eyes as insidiously winning as she had found them last night. "I can't take you to the Regent looking as you do, Keira," he reasoned. "I will take you, I promise. After you've cleaned up."

Her heart galloped in frantic protest. She couldn't trust him. He would find another excuse and another excuse not to take her, and keep playing on the attraction he knew she felt for him. Just as he had when he'd wrapped her in the rug. It had been so weak of her to let him hold her and kiss her. Hopelessly weak!

There was only one thing to do. The moment the car stopped, Keira was out and running, hurling the rug away from her to free her legs from any constriction.

"Keira! No!" he shouted, and she heard his feet crunching the gravelled driveway as he started to run after her.

She cast a frightened look over her shoulder. She had about a five metre start on him. If she simply ran to the next house, would the people there help her? But if no one was home...

"Colonel! Stop her!" Nick yelled.

Keira instantly swung her gaze forward, alarmed at the thought of meeting some other opposition to her leaving.

She couldn't believe her eyes.

The retired British wrestler who had sat next to her on the plane, who had saved her from Louise's clawing, was right in front of her, the huge bulk of his body blocking her way, legs and arms spread in readiness for catching her.

CHAPTER EIGHT

"YOU!" HE CRIED, as startled as she was.

His walrus moustache quivered. His arms dropped, his hands instinctively moving to protect himself from a repeat of his previous encounters with Keira.

Although it hadn't been her fault either time, Keira thought. She could have run past him then, but her step had faltered at being confronted with the big man.

His gaze was drawn to her breasts, still clearly outlined by the damp T-shirt. His eyes goggled for a moment before he dragged them to her face in urgent pleading. "Don't hurt me," he begged. "I've got nothing to do with it, whatever is happening."

"I'm sorry. Truly I am," Keira said sincerely. "If you'll just let me go around you..."

However, before any action could be taken, the mohair rug enveloped her again and Nick Sarazin's strong arms were around her shoulders and waist, holding her immobilised. He pinned her against his body, making her sharply aware of his powerful muscularity.

"Thanks, Colonel," he panted gratefully.

The big man's relief was enormous. He straightened to a more dignified stance, puffing his massive chest out as though he had actually done something.

"Colonel, you can't let him do this to me," Keira pleaded. "He carried me off and seduced me and—"

"No, no!" The big man firmly shook his head, then looked at her knowingly. "Mr. Sarazin wouldn't do such a thing. Something else must have happened. You're a very dangerous young woman."

"Thanks for the understanding, Colonel," Nick said with considerable relief.

"He's abducting me now," Keira explained frantically. "He's keeping me with him against my will. Please do something, Colonel."

"Keep you out of trouble," the colonel approved. "You can't walk the streets—" he harrumphed "—as you are. Not without the rug. There's no telling what might happen. Or who might get hurt. Terribly dangerous."

"I deeply appreciate your vote of confidence, Colonel," Nick said with sickening gratitude. "Maybe you can talk some sense to her. Between the two of us we might be able to convince her to be reasonable. All I want is to give her the opportunity to get cleaned up and into some fresh dry clothes so she'll look decent."

"My word, yes!" the colonel agreed with fervour. "Most essential. Too dangerous the way she is." He eyed Keira sternly. "You may not mean to cause a lot of damage, young lady, but you've got to think of others." He wagged a reproachful finger at her. "The least you can do is minimise the impact. You don't want to cause loss of life. Which is possible, looking the way you do."

"Colonel, you won't help me?" Keira pleaded.

"Not in the way you mean."

"Would you call the police?"

"Definitely not! They're very busy people and—"

"Colonel, are you staying here with him?" Keira asked anxiously, seeing one possible way out of this hopeless impasse.

"Yes, I am," he affirmed. "Mr. Sarazin has kindly offered me his hospitality. Very generously. Very generously indeed," he repeated emphatically.

"If I get cleaned up and look decent, will you make sure he lets me go?" she pleaded.

The colonel frowned, looked over her shoulder at the man holding her in tight constraint.

"I assure you, Colonel, I will take this young lady wherever she wants to go, when she's fit to be seen in public," Nick said fervently.

The colonel nodded in satisfaction and returned a stern gaze to Keira. "You have his word. Mine, too. You don't need any more than that."

"I might, Colonel," Keira said with deep feeling, her large green eyes fixed imploringly on his. "Can I trust you to keep to your word?"

His big face went bright red. "Absolutely!" He harrumphed again. "Better get moving. Can't stand out here all day."

Satisfied that she had at least won this point, Keira twisted her head around and shot Nick Sarazin a hard, bitter look. "You don't have to hold me any more. I'll come quietly. For cleaning up purposes only."

"That's all I intended, Keira," he said softly. His blue eyes apologised for the distress he had given her.

He withdrew his restraining embrace and stepped back, gesturing an invitation towards the house.

Keira felt painfully confused. Had she misjudged him? Could he be trusted now? If he had a guest in his house, he could hardly have meant to keep her at his side by force. And he must have servants, as well. At least a housekeeper for this huge residence. He had spoken to someone in his employ last night, giving instructions. She simply hadn't been thinking straight. The shock of finding herself here instead of at the Regent had completely thrown her.

A self-conscious flush heated her cheeks. "I'm sorry," she said impulsively. "I guess I was behaving like a fool."

"I should have explained better," he replied, generously taking the blame for the misunderstanding.

She searched his eyes, desperately unsure of how she felt about him. How could he have been so hardhearted and calculating, when now he seemed genuinely kind and caring?

"I don't mean you any harm, Keira," he said softly. His mouth twisted in rueful irony. "I never did, believe it or not."

Her heart lifted immeasurably and she heard herself say, "I believe you."

He smiled a dazzling white smile that danced through her mind and her heart and her soul. "At least that's a step in the right direction," he said in a tone of deep relief and pleasure.

He *is* the one, Keira thought, then didn't know if she was going mad under the stresses of the day.

Nick gently grasped her elbow. "Come inside now. A shower to wash the sand and sea off, then a spa bath to take away all the tension, and you'll feel much more ready to face the world."

"Yes," she agreed dazedly.

"Dangerous," the colonel muttered in a tone of grim foreboding.

He was right, Keira thought, as she moved ahead at Nick's urging. She couldn't be sure Nick Sarazin hadn't simply changed tack to seduce her again, suiting his manner to the circumstances. But at least this was no longer a now-or-never situation. She could walk away from it, and if Nick genuinely wanted to pursue a relationship with her he would come after her.

As he had been doing all day, Keira suddenly realised. But there were other reasons for that, not necessarily the kind of strong attraction that never wanted to let go. When, or rather if, Louise and Justin got back together again, Keira could begin to feel more certain of what Nick Sarazin felt towards her, but she no longer thought it was quite so imperative to thrust him out of her life and shut the door on him.

He led her through the house to what she suspected was the master bedroom suite. It was too large to be a mere guest room. Besides, the royal blue and off-white and red furnishings were manly enough to indicate that this was Nick's room. A king-size bed, she noticed, and opposite the bed a large unit containing a television set and speakers for whatever music facilities were behind the cupboard doors. There was also a heap of magazines on the bedside table.

Nick did not pause in the bedroom. He opened a door that led into an incredibly spacious and luxurious bathroom, and set about turning on the taps to fill a spa bath, clearly designed to accommodate two people. Keira wondered how many women Nick Sarazin had invited to bathe with him over the years, then sternly told herself it was none of her business. Except he was certainly very skilful in the art of seduction, and she had better watch her step very carefully.

The spa had a wide marble ledge around it and Keira sat down there, watching Nick as he sprinkled bath salts into the water from an elegant onyx jar. The smell of the salts was fresh and invigorating rather than heavily perfumed. The running water turned them into a foam that looked inviting.

Nick opened a mirrored cupboard, took out a folded towelling bathrobe and a blow-drier for her hair, then laid them on the vanity bench, ready for her use. "Anything else you need?" he asked, clearly intent on pleasing her.

"A comb, please," Keira said.

He opened a drawer and added a comb to the pile. "I'll have some clothes for you by the time you're finished in here. Take as long as you like, Keira. There's no hurry, is there?" The blue eyes flashed at her in persuasive appeal.

"No. I guess not," she said uncertainly.

She was clutching the rug tightly around her, waiting for him to leave her alone. Somehow being in this bathroom with him was generating a sense of intimacy that she wasn't sure she welcomed. Nick Sarazin was too vital a man to be ignored, and she was far too aware of everything about him—the corded muscles of his bare forearms, the lithe economical way he moved, the tight springiness of his black curls, the masculinity of his buttocks, the denim of his jeans stretching tightly over powerful thighs when he bent down...

As though he sensed her unease, he flicked the switch that started the spa action in the bath, then gave her an encouraging smile. "I'll leave you to it then. Just turn that switch off before pulling the plug. Okay?"

"Okay." She gave him a somewhat shaky smile. "Thank you for looking after me, Nick."

"My pleasure," he said warmly, making a graceful exit.

It felt good to slip the gritty T-shirt and underpants off. It was even better to stand under a hot shower and wash the sand from her hair and body. She shampooed her long tresses twice to make sure all the salt water was rinsed away. Then she wrapped her hair in a towel and slid into the soft foam of the spa bath.

This was sheer heaven, she thought, as the spurts of water from the nozzles hit her skin and tingled over it. She lay back and whimsically decided she could stay here forever. The air bubbles massaged her muscles, releasing the fatigue and the aches and the pains, and Keira felt at peace with herself for the first time that day.

A knock on the door startled her into sitting up. "Who is it?" she called suspiciously.

"Mrs. Patterson. The housekeeper, dear. Mr. Sarazin thought you might like a nice cool drink while you were enjoying your bath."

"Oh, yes! Thank you! Come in."

She slid her body under the bubbly foam as the door opened to reveal a middle-aged woman of plump proportions. Her pepper-and-salt hair was neatly permed. She wore a blue dress and a friendly smile on an open, friendly face. Her brown eyes twinkled curiously at Keira as she carried a tray containing a long glass of orange juice.

"This is very kind of you," Keira said to cover a sudden embarrassment at being in Nick Sarazin's bath.

"Not at all," the housekeeper demurred. "I always look after Mr. Sarazin's guests. That's part of my job. Is orange juice all right?"

"Lovely, thank you." Ice clinked in the glass as Keira lifted it off the tray. The smell of freshly squeezed oranges made Keira's mouth water. She hadn't realised how thirsty she was.

Mrs. Patterson bent and picked up the rug and the damp gritty clothes. "I'll take these out of your way," she said.

Keira flushed. "Sorry they're such a mess, Mrs. Patterson."

"So long as you're all right, dear. That's the main thing. And not to worry. Mr. Sarazin will look after you," the housekeeper admonished kindly, then bestowed another friendly smile on Keira before leaving with the bundle of washing.

It made Keira wonder what story Nick had concocted to explain her arrival in such a bedraggled state. Probably that he had saved her from drowning, she decided. A waif of the world with nowhere to go. Which was close enough to the truth. Although she didn't need Nick Sarazin to look after her. On the other hand, the idea of him looking after her permanently was definitely seductive.

Eventually Keira pulled herself out of the bath, deciding she couldn't stay there forever. She turned off the switch, lifted the plug, then dried herself thoroughly before wrapping the towel around her to form a makeshift sarong while she dried her hair.

She felt lethargic after the long bath, and her arms ached from holding the hairdrier by the time she was finished with it. However, her hair was a long, clean, gleaming mane again, spilling over her shoulders like finely spun silk. Keira put on the bathrobe, tied it securely, then ventured out to the bedroom. There were no clothes set out for her that she could see, so she decided to walk through the house until she found someone.

The colonel was seated in the large living-room, which faced onto the pool and patio. On seeing her, he rose instantly from his leather armchair and waved her to another chair on the other side of a long coffee table.

"Come sit down. I'll go and tell Mrs. Patterson you're ready," he said.

Keira did as she was bid, somewhat surprised that it was the housekeeper and not Nick Sarazin who was to be summoned to take care of her. Maybe Mrs. Patterson was preparing some clothes for her, Keira reasoned.

The colonel returned and bestowed an approving smile on her. "That's better, isn't it?" he said in an avuncular tone.

"Yes," Keira agreed. "Where's Mr. Sarazin?"

"Gone to get you some suitable clothes. Back soon," he informed her. "Mrs. Patterson is bringing us some afternoon tea. Marvellous woman, Mrs. Patterson. She understands all about afternoon tea."

He was very British, Keira thought with a little smile. "Is this your first trip to Australia, Colonel?" she asked.

"Yes. First trip. And I must speak to you about that," he said on a note of urgency. He leaned forward in his chair. "You see, British taxes are ruinous. People think I make a lot of—er—money, being who I am, but that's not so. Not so at all. Only a bit player. A small-time character actor. Nothing big. And taxes take most of it—"

"Here we are, Colonel Winton!" Mrs. Patterson announced as she wheeled in a trolley. She beamed at the big man as she started unloading a plate of Devonshire scones and a plate of little sandwiches onto the coffee table.

"You are a treasure, Mrs. Patterson." The colonel beamed at her.

As all the tea things were set out, Keira was privately amused by the fact that she had been hopelessly wrong with her idea of the colonel being a retired wrestler. Looking at him now, she could see he would make a marvellous character actor.

As soon as the housekeeper left them, the colonel leaned forward confidentially. "I've come out here to feature in a series of TV advertisements that Mr. Sarazin wants to make. I was supposed to fly first class, but there's a big difference in the fare between first and economy classes. Thousands. So I thought I'd save the money. Taxes, you know. Very hard to get around taxes."

"Yes. I expect it is," Keira said drily. She'd never had to worry about such a thing herself, never having flown first class and never having paid taxes, but clearly it was of great concern to the colonel.

"So I thought, just between us, you don't have to tell Mr. Sarazin that I didn't fly first class, do you? I suffered a great deal to save that money."

She gave him a sympathetic smile, remembering all too well her own suffering to save money. And she hadn't spilt boiling coffee over herself. "I promise you, I won't say a word about it, Colonel." It was the least she could do to make up for the incidents that had happened around her.

"Ah!" He beamed happily. "A remarkable young woman. Remarkable! Are you in the acting field, as well?"

"No. I'm just a travelling girl," Keira replied simply.

He looked surprised. "I thought, well, with your face and—er—figure, and being with Mr. Sarazin..."

"That's something personal," she said dismissively.

His face went bright red again. "Oh, ah, yes, understandable, of course." He recovered from his confusion and plucked up an avuncular smile. "Beastly long flight, wasn't it?"

"It certainly was." She laughed as she added, "I thought my bottom would never recover."

"From what?" Nick Sarazin's voice inquired pleasantly from behind her.

The colonel leapt in before Keira could answer. "From sitting so long. All those hours from London. Miss—er—Keira and I were on the same flight out. We were commiserating with each other over the discomforts of travelling so far in one hop."

"You were on the same plane?" Nick asked, the blue eyes sharply probing Keira's as he joined them.

"Yes. I was flying economy class, which is a lot more cramping than first class," Keira said to ease the colonel's concern over a possible gaffe.

Nick frowned. "You only arrived here yesterday morning?"

She nodded. "A bit past five, wasn't it, Colonel?"

He nodded, too. "Frightful hour." He leaned forward. "Shall I pour the tea for you, my dear?"

"Thank you."

Nick placed some carrier bags on the armchair next to Keira's. "I hope something fits," he said in a distracted fashion. Then he settled on the armchair next to the colonel's so he was facing her.

Throughout afternoon tea, Keira could feel Nick reviewing everything that had happened, assessing, drawing conclusions, all from the fact that she had arrived in Australia only yesterday morning. He of-

fered little conversation, only answering questions
when asked. The blue eyes rarely strayed from Keira,
and she grew more and more conscious of all the
things he would be adding up in his mind. She hoped
he wasn't like Justin, who added things up all the time
and thought life should be answerable to numbers and
logic.

What would be obvious to Nick Sarazin was the fact
that she had known Justin all her life and their families had been close.

The fact that her bags had been at Justin's house.

The fact that she had been Delilah for Justin last
night.

The fact that Justin owed her a payment.

Nick would undoubtedly realise that there was no
affair between her and Justin, and that last night's
adoration was all pretence for Louise's benefit. The
act had worked only too well, resulting in consequences that were totally disproportionate to what had
been a well-meant deception.

The colonel polished off a prodigious amount of
scones and sandwiches, adding to his already impressive girth. Neither Nick nor Keira ate much, but
nothing was left of all Mrs. Patterson had provided.
The colonel rubbed his bulging stomach in blissful
contentment and beamed at both Keira and Nick.

"If you two good people will excuse me, I think I'll
have a little nap before dinner," he declared.

They excused him.

The tension in the room instantly rose.

Keira worried over whether Nick had reached the
idea that she had set out to seduce him away from

Louise at Justin's urging, and felt a yawning pit in her stomach despite the afternoon tea. If he tried justifying what he had done on that score, they had very definitely reached the end. What she had felt with him last night had nothing whatsoever to do with Justin or Louise.

If he didn't leap to conclusions, if he decided to question her or invite her to explain the situation, Keira decided she would tell him the whole truth. There was no longer any obligation to keep silent for Justin's sake. Whether Nick would understand how it had all come about was, of course, rather critical to any future relationship between them. If there was to be one. Which was still highly questionable, given his motives for seducing her.

"There is more to you than meets the eye," he said slowly, mildly, consideringly.

"Not at all," Keira defended. "What you see is what you get."

He chewed on that for a few moments.

Keira kept stewing over what he thought of her. Did he believe she was a Delilah who played fast and loose with any man she found attractive, or did he now realise that she was not given to light impulsive affairs? If she hadn't thought he was the one . . .

"What are you going to do after I—er—leave you at the Regent?" he asked.

Keira's heart plummeted. He was letting her go. He didn't want to keep her any more, not for Louise's sake nor his own. He had added up the facts and decided she was no threat to Louise's marriage, that her relationship with Justin was one of old acquaintances, strictly platonic. There was no need for interference. No need for any further seduction.

Which left her to herself again.

No point in hanging around in Sydney. Justin didn't want her messing up any reconciliation he could effect with Louise. Best to make her way up the coast to Queensland, she thought dully, yet inwardly she recoiled from the prospect of having to be bright and cheerful for Auntie Joan and Uncle Bruce. She needed time to get herself together again, time to put all this behind her. Somewhere cheap where no one would bother her.

"Have you ever heard of a place called Boomerang?" she asked, her green eyes mocking his supposed interest in her future plans.

"No. I've never heard of it," he replied.

"Never been there?"

"No."

That was good. Easier to wipe him out of her memory if they shared no ground in common. "You have no idea where it is?" she asked to make doubly sure of that.

"No."

"Then," said Keira decisively, "I think I'll go there."

The skin between Nick Sarazin's eyes furrowed as he fiercely concentrated. The pieces of the jigsaw puzzle presented by Keira were falling into place. Of course, there were a few pieces missing, but he hoped he now had most of the overall picture. If he was wrong... That didn't bear thinking about. He had been wrong too many times already today, and he had only recovered this far by the skin of his teeth. Keira was something outside his experience. One thing was certain. He couldn't afford another mistake.

"You really can't get rid of me fast enough, can you?" he probed softly.

Her chin came up. The green eyes flashed with pride. "I'm glad that perception is starting to sink in." Then with a touch of scorn to cover the hurt lurking behind it, "You're not a very fast learner, Nick."

She was right. He had let himself be blinded by Delilah and not seen Keira fast enough. There was no way he could undo the damage at this point. He knew he needed a symbol. A few of them, in fact. People always thought he was gambling when he did these sorts of things. But Nick knew he wasn't gambling for the simple reason that he always won. He crossed his fingers. I hope I'm not making the biggest mistake of my life this time, he thought. But I'm getting nowhere here. The situation has to be changed.

He rose to his feet.

"Well, if that's the case," he said agreeably, "I think I'll oblige." He gestured towards the carrier bags. "If you'll go and get changed, I'll take you to Justin. And the Regent."

He saw the shock of disbelief flash across her face. At least he had got rid of the idea he was keeping her at his side for Louise's sake, he thought with satisfaction. But the satisfaction was short-lived when he saw the sharp recoil of hurt in her eyes. His heart squeezed tight and he began to doubt the course he had set himself.

"Very well," she said and slowly, wearily, pushed herself up from the chair, her beautiful face shadowed by bleak disillusionment.

She stepped to the adjacent armchair and picked up the carrier bags without so much as a glance inside them to see what he had bought for her. She simply didn't care about such things, he thought. Totally meaningless to her. Which was something he'd never met in any other woman.

Nick had no doubt that she'd spoken the absolute truth when she'd said he couldn't buy her. There had to be another answer for the payment from Justin. She hadn't played Delilah for money. Out of friendship? Caring for his happiness? Owing him a favour? Wanting to help save his marriage?

She paused, looked up at him, her sea-green eyes luminous with the Lorelei look that swam into his soul and tugged at something there...and he had the spine-chilling sensation that a king tide was going out and he was being left behind.

The urge to wrap her in his arms and hold her tight was so strong that he could barely restrain it. To do so would be wrong, very wrong. If he didn't force himself to let her go, she would never accept the trust he wanted to share with her.

"What's holding you back?" he asked, his voice harsh and rasping in his need to control the rampant desire churning through him.

The light in her eyes clicked out, replaced by a hard glitter of pride. "Nothing," she snapped. "Absolutely nothing."

She marched away from him, head high, back straight, her silken hair swishing around her shoulders.

Nick watched her until she was out of sight, fighting the desire to follow her, to take her as he had taken her last night, to share with her everything they could share until she was forced to acknowledge that nothing else mattered.

But force would never work with Keira. He knew that beyond all reasonable doubt. She was a free spirit who made her own choices. If he didn't respect that he didn't have a chance in hell. Nick Sarazin always maximised his chances. He would treat Keira differently from every other woman he had ever known.

He wandered out to the patio where he had danced with her. Was it only last night? He felt he had lived through lifetimes since then. Seeing her run into the sea as though she preferred that world to any holding him, finding her gone from the shower, trying to get her into the car, trying to get her into this house . . .

He shook his head.

He had to treat her differently.

The seduction of Keira required the utmost delicacy, a far more mental process than a physical one, and letting her go was the first step.

But he would get her back. He would chase her to the ends of the earth. Wherever it was necessary to go. Whatever it took. He was not going to accept ''never''.

CHAPTER NINE

KEIRA TIPPED THE CONTENTS of the carrier bags onto Nick's king-size bed. A couple of expensive bras and matching panties in silk and lace, two different sizes; two pairs of white sandals; a tangerine gaberdine skirt with an elasticised waist; a white crocheted top with little tangerine knobs worked through it. The price tags had been cut off the clothes, but Keira knew that none of them was cheap.

She hated having to take anything from Nick Sarazin, but since it was *his* choice that she be properly cleaned up and dressed before he took her to the Regent, she was not responsible for the expense he had gone to. She certainly hadn't asked it of him. She hadn't known he had meant to buy her clothes. Something from a jumble sale would have done her just as well.

However, she had no heart for arguing the toss at this point. The sooner she was dressed, the sooner she could get away from him. She had been right about his mind being alien to hers. How could she have been so mistaken about him? At least the confusion he had stirred was slowly clearing. There could be nothing meaningful between them. When he dropped her off at the Regent, that was that.

She forced herself to put on a set of the underwear he had provided, and found the process repugnant. They were the kind of things a man would give to a Delilah. Keira knew she would never wear them again. In fact, she would tear them off the moment she was safely in her room at the hotel.

She didn't mind the skirt and top so much. They didn't seem so personal. She managed to fit her feet into one pair of the sandals. They were a bit tight across the toes, but she didn't have to wear them for very long. She would take all these things to a charity shop tomorrow. No doubt Nick Sarazin could afford such a donation to the poor and needy.

She left the extras on the bed and walked to the living-room, where she had left him. He was standing on the patio where they had danced together. Was it only last night? Could one come alive and die within less than twenty-four hours? She stared at him and felt a numb passivity. No hatred. No love. No passion either way. He was not the one. He was a stranger who had walked into her past and out of her future.

He turned and saw her, then walked briskly inside. "Ready?" he asked.

"Yes," she said.

Those were the only words they spoke from leaving his residence at Hunter's Hill until they arrived in the city.

Keira had never been to the Regent before. It stood in a commanding position on Circular Quay. Justin's definition of the best was not necessarily the same as everyone else's, but as Nick pulled his Jaguar to a halt in the private driveway Keira took one look through the huge glass doors and decided Justin probably knew what he was talking about this time. The luxurious foyer spelled class with a capital C.

She could now understand Nick's reservations about delivering her here in her former state. Not that she would have cared. She could have weathered a few lifted eyebrows with no trouble at all. Too many people lived their lives by what others might think of them. That was not for her. She knew what she was inside and she was comfortable with herself. That counted for more than what others might think. If Nick Sarazin didn't care for how she thought or what she was, they were better apart.

She released her seat belt as he switched off the engine. She looked directly at him and said, "Thank you. Goodbye and good luck, Nick." Her hand was already opening her door so that he need not get out at all.

"I'm coming inside with you, Keira," he stated decisively. "I want to be certain you are safely looked after."

She threw him a hard, cold look. "I don't need you looking after me."

He returned a look of grim determination. "For my own peace of mind."

Keira paused to consider that. Maybe he did have a conscience, which was giving him considerable unease. She looked away. He opened his door and slid out, cutting off any further argument.

With a vexed sigh of resignation, Keira alighted from the car and resolutely ignored Nick Sarazin's presence beside her as he accompanied her into the hotel. She did not pause to appreciate the marvellous ambience of the foyer, which rose to the height of three podium levels. Having to postpone the moment of farewell made her feel uneasy. Nick Sarazin liked having his own way too darned much. She marched straight to the enquiry desk. Thankfully, a member of the staff gave her instant attention.

"How can I help you, ma'am?"

"Mr. Justin Brooks was to book a room for me here. Could you please check to see if he's done that?"

"Was the room to be in his name or yours, ma'am?"

"I don't know."

"Your name, ma'am?"

"Keira Mary Brooks," she said with a touch of defiance, conscious that Nick was listening.

The desk attendant smiled. "I'll check the computer."

If Nick Sarazin showed any reaction to her full name, Keira did not see it. She kept her gaze fastened on the desk attendant, who quickly confirmed that the booking had been made.

"Can you please check if my bags have arrived?" Keira asked.

"Certainly, ma'am. Just a few moments while I call the baggage room."

Keira steeled herself to turn and face Nick for the last time. His face was stamped with grim determination, yet the blue eyes seemed to have a sick, hungry look as they met hers. She wasn't sure if it was her tension or his that made it difficult to speak, but she finally forced the necessary words out.

"You can go with complete peace of mind now, Nick."

His mouth twisted into an ironic smile. "Oh, I wouldn't say that, Keira. I'll let you go. That was my promise. Try to keep out of trouble."

"I'll be fine, thank you," she said stiffly. Without him she wouldn't have *been* in any trouble, and her eyes mockingly told him that.

"I hope so," he said softly and turned away. He moved a few paces, then swung around, the blue eyes stabbing at her. "You really did play me for being a dummy, didn't you, Keira Mary Brooks?"

"Don't be a fool, Nick," she answered softly, her heart and soul suddenly throbbing the message that this was a man she could have loved forever, if his mind had been more in tune with hers. "Even though I was under a promise of silence, I didn't once lie to you. It's not my fault that you couldn't recognise truth," she added sadly.

His eyes lingered on her, sweeping over her in one final glance before he turned away again. He took a step, then ran straight into Justin.

"I want a word with you, Sarazin," Justin said in a low, threatening voice. "A lot of words."

His face was flushed with anger. His body projected the fact that he was in a fighting mood—legs slightly apart, chest puffed out, hands clenched, shoulders squared, chin out, mouth grim, brown eyes blazing.

On the other hand, Nick's tension of a few moments ago instantly relaxed into a non-threatening pose. "Go right ahead, Mr. Brooks. I am fascinated to hear what you have to say," he drawled.

"I want to know what you did to Keira," Justin demanded. "As far as I'm concerned, she's my *sister*."

"Your sister?"

"As good as," Justin declared vehemently. "Keira has been in our family since she was ten. We're close. Very close. I've always regarded her as my little sister." He raised a hand and poked a finger in Nick Sarazin's chest as he added, "And you made her cry!"

Keira was so astonished at this big-brotherly display from her cousin that she simply stood riveted to the spot, seeing Justin in a totally new light.

"Feeling a bit guilty about your part in this, are you, Mr. Brooks?" Nick taunted softly.

Of course, thought Keira. That accounted for at least some of Justin's aggression. But all the same, he was family sticking up for family, and Keira felt fonder of her cousin in that moment than she had ever done before.

Justin's face went a darker red. "A man has a right to save his marriage. Any way he can. Particularly from people like you. You tried to do the wrong thing by Louise. You did the wrong thing by Keira...."

"Oh, hell!" Nick Sarazin groaned, a look of anguish on his face. His misdeeds were obviously getting the better of him.

Justin's finger poked again. "Now that you've failed with Keira, don't think you can come back to Louise. If you try that..." He looked Nick Sarazin up and down, saw the difference in physique, knew he was at a disadvantage, but went on. "If you so much as look at Louise again, I'll knock the brains out of your head!''

"No need for that," Nick retorted coolly. "I have never had anything but a friendly and professional relationship with Louise. Never intended anything else. I'm sorry that things have worked out the way they have. Might I recommend that you and your wife sit down and talk to each other, instead of involving other people in your stupid games.''

"Games!" Justin said scathingly. "Who started it, eh? Who went on with it last night and hurt Keira so much she cried?''

"I've had nothing whatsoever to do with the dispute between Louise and yourself, Mr. Brooks," Nick replied in a calm, soothing voice. "I wanted to talk to you about that last night. Louise has been very wrong and very foolish to use me as a tool in her argument with you. I want that cleared up.''

"Oh yeah," Justin jeered disbelievingly.

"Yes!" Nick affirmed. "It was you who upset the apple cart. You chose to turn up with your Delilah, which turned Louise into a hysterical madwoman. I might add that my perception of Keira was influenced by the fact that she was with a married man. Which was your fault, my friend.''

"Oh, sure!" Justin's mouth curled in contempt. "Everything is someone else's fault! Everybody blames me, including Louise. A very convenient shifting of cause and effect so that you don't have to feel responsible for anything." His fists balled. "I ought to smash your face in.''

"Do so, if it makes you feel better," Nick said flatly. "I'm well aware that I should have treated Keira differently. That blame is certainly mine."

Justin glared black murder at him. "You and your playboy games! I've never known Keira to cry before in her life. She breezes through everything. But you had to do it, didn't you? You had to carry her off and have your way with her. In the old days they had it right. You ought to be made to marry her—"

"Justin," Keira protested sharply. Then in a quiet appeasing tone, she added, "I did go willingly. I thought..." She flushed painfully. "Never mind what I thought. It's over now. Please let Mr. Sarazin go, Justin. There's no point in this."

"He shouldn't be allowed to get away with it," Justin argued. "Shotguns," he added fiercely. "That's what we need. Plenty of shotguns."

"If it's any satisfaction to you, Mr. Brooks, I didn't enjoy making Keira cry," Nick said in a tone of quiet sincerity. "I regret it very deeply. I've done all she would let me do to make amends. I would suggest that you stop haranguing me and start taking care of her."

Justin's brow furrowed in concern as his eyes darted over her. "What can I do, Keira?" he asked.

"I'd like to go to my room," she said wearily.

"Right!" he agreed, the steam going out of him as he looked fretfully at her. "I'll get the key and take you up." Then he cast Nick one last belligerent look. "You keep out of our family, Nick Sarazin. I've had enough of your interfering ways!"

"Mr. Brooks—" Nick's voice dropped to a low note of urgency "—make sure Keira has everything she needs. She won't take any more from me."

"Neither she should!" Justin rushed out angrily. "I'll look after her."

Nick's hand shot out and squeezed his arm. "Take good care of her!"

The action and the delivery of those words carried an ominous threat. Keira couldn't see Nick's face, but his body suddenly looked as tense as a coiled spring. Justin looked startled, but before he could react Nick removed his grasp and strode away without a backwards glance.

Justin stared after him with a dark frown on his face, shook his head, then came over to Keira, his brow still puckered in thought. "That guy didn't want to let you go, Keira."

"You made him feel guilty. That's all, Justin," she said dispiritedly. "Let's move. Since you're here, I'd like to talk to you. In private."

"Of course," he agreed, his eyes searching hers in a troubled fashion. "Did he hurt you physically, Keira?"

"No." A sadly ironic smile curved her lips. "He actually looked after me very well once he accepted that I wouldn't stay with him."

Justin cleared his throat and looked relieved. "That's all right, then," he muttered, then stepped over to the desk and took charge of getting her and her bags to the suite he had booked.

A porter accompanied them to demonstrate all the features and facilities for guests' enjoyment and comfort in the apartment, which he called an executive suite. It comprised a bedroom, lounge and dining-area, plus a luxurious bathroom. He opened the curtains along two walls to reveal a magnificent view of Sydney Harbour, pointed out the telescope in the corner for more detailed viewing, explained how to operate the television, the lights and the telephone, wished Keira a pleasant stay and finally departed.

"This must be costing a fortune, Justin," she remarked ruefully, sinking into one of the leather lounges.

He shrugged and slanted her an apologetic smile. "I'm sorry I got you into this, Keira. If I'd had any idea that Sarazin wasn't genuinely taken with you, I would have told you about his connection with Louise. But the way he looked at you..." He heaved a deep sigh and settled onto the opposite lounge.

Keira didn't want to talk about Nick Sarazin. That episode was closed, as far as she was concerned. "Have you told Louise about me yet?" she asked.

Justin frowned. "I planned on doing that tonight. I hadn't figured on this happening. Do you think Sarazin will tell her before I do?"

"No. I think he's wiped his hands of the whole affair. But, Justin, it must be obvious to you now that Louise loves you very much and doesn't want any other woman to have her husband. She didn't leave you for another man," Keira said pointedly. "There's something else behind this. What's actually going on?"

Justin's face took on a sullen look. "It's time we started a family. I'm thirty, you know. I don't want to be an old father."

Typical Justin, Keira thought. Life by numbers. "Doesn't Louise want to have a baby?" she asked softly.

"She agreed about having a family before we were married," Justin argued, looking even more sullen. "Four years I've waited. That's long enough. And now that she's finally pregnant, she says she's going to abort the baby. My child!" He rose to his feet in towering outrage, gesticulating his disgust. "Just because she reckons she's not ready, she wants to get rid of our child! No way in the world am I going to go along with that!"

Keira was shocked that Louise would even suggest such a thing. She couldn't imagine wanting to get rid of a child conceived by a loved husband. It felt all wrong. "Why did Louise let herself get pregnant if she wasn't ready?" she asked, trying to understand why this was happening.

A guilty flush darkened Justin's face. He avoided Keira's questioning eyes. He made an awkward dismissive gesture. "Louise kept putting it off and putting it off. I—er—mucked up the contraceptive thing. I thought if she happened to get pregnant she would accept it and we wouldn't be arguing about it anymore. As it turned out, that wasn't one of my best ideas."

Men! Keira was swamped by a wave of resentment. Why did they think they had a God-given right to take free choice from women? Blindly intent on having their own way no matter what!

Having suffered through Nick Sarazin's bullying, Keira found herself a lot more sympathetic towards Louise's cause, although she still couldn't sympathise with the idea of an abortion. She took a deep breath and tried to talk calmly about a woman's point of view.

"Justin, Louise is the one who has to bear the pregnancy. And all the changes it will make to her. A baby doesn't interfere much with a man's life-style, but if Louise enjoys her job and her freedom..."

"Keira, we agreed on having a family!" Justin justified himself strongly. "I'm not asking for a whole brood of kids. Only two. Preferably a boy and a girl. I'm trying to organise that. Now surely that's not too much to ask of the woman I've married. The woman I want to have my kids. She said she wanted them, too."

"All right," Keira soothed. "So the deed is done and Louise is pregnant, and she found out you tricked her into it."

"She's twenty-eight, for heaven's sake!" Justin cried in exasperation. "Statistics say that a woman has a better chance of having healthy babies before she's thirty. After thirty, the percentages start going against you. That's the figures, no matter how you look at them."

Numbers again, Keira thought with a heavy sigh. And outdated attitudes. These days women in their thirties were having perfectly healthy babies. She took another deep breath and tried getting down to the nitty-gritty of the situation. "In any event, Louise is now pregnant, and you want her to come home to you and have the baby," she stated slowly.

"Yes!" Justin affirmed. "But she's fighting mad, saying I had no right to abrogate her rights. She uses a lot of other fancy words, as well. And she said she would find another man who respects her and her rights."

"She doesn't really want someone else, Justin," Keira assured him. "You've got to start giving her a lot of extra considerations since you've forced this baby on her. If you want her back and you want the baby, why don't you offer to hire a nanny so that Louise can keep working if she wants to? If Louise has a solid career going for her, she must earn more than you'd have to pay a nanny, so you'd certainly be able to afford it."

He looked disgruntled. "Why can't she be content to stay home and be a proper mother to our child?"

"Justin, you can't have everything your own way," Keira said sternly. "It's not fair on Louise. If that isn't her choice, you can't force it. You're in this situation because you tried forcing. Doesn't that teach you something?"

She paused to let that sink in, then added, "As it is, Louise's hormones are probably all upset from being pregnant. You should be cosseting her and looking after her. Enveloping her in love. Wooing her all over again. She's the one who's making the sacrifices to have your child. You have to make it worthwhile for her. And that's going to take a lot of loving and indulgence from you. Particularly in the circumstances.''

He paced up and down, chewing over that advice as though it was sour to his taste. Eventually he seemed to swallow it. "You could be right, Keira. A nanny," he said consideringly.

"Yes. And a promise that you will share in all the chores related to having a baby and not leave everything to Louise."

"Won't a nanny do that?" he asked.

"Nannies do have days off, Justin," Keira pointed out.

"Oh! Right!"

"And make a big fuss of Louise while she's pregnant. Give her flowers. Take her out a lot. Assure her that's she's still desirable to you when she starts to lose her figure. A lot of women feel very insecure about that. You've got to show her you love her all the more for carrying your child."

"Mmm..." He beetled a frown at Keira. "How do you know all these things? You've never had a baby." His eyes suddenly widened as an idea struck him. "Or have you? Is that why you stayed away—"

"No, Justin." She rolled her eyes in exasperation. "I was travelling around. That's all. But I have worked as a nanny and I know about pregnant women. Believe me, you're going the wrong way about this if you want to keep Louise and keep her happy. Stop talking about your rights and start working on solutions."

He grimaced, but he looked ready to start making concessions. "So you think if I take her out and give her flowers and promise her a nanny that—"

"It would be a start in the right direction. But you've also got to tell Louise about me, Justin. Tonight. Without delay. You've made her feel very insecure about you. You won't get anywhere until she feels secure again. Tell her you did it in desperation because you love her so much and you were out of your mind."

He looked affronted. "I was not out of my mind. It was a perfectly planned military operation to make her jealous."

"Well, you certainly succeeded," Keira said bitterly. "And your ignorant private soldier paid the penalty for it."

His affront crumpled into acute discomfort. "Things didn't work out exactly as I planned, Keira."

"Just get it sorted out with Louise. Tonight!" Keira demanded.

"I will. I swear I will. I'll do all you say. See if it works. There might be something in your ideas."

"Don't expect instant miracles," Keira said drily. "You've got a lot of making up to do. The trouble with men is they don't know how to think like women. It's a dreadful fault."

"Well, how can men think like women?" Justin argued with perfect logic. "If they did that, they wouldn't be men."

This sounded like a circular argument. "You could try listening with an open mind," Keira said pointedly.

Justin wasn't listening any more, Keira thought. His eyes were boring into her from underneath another beetling frown. "I know how men think," he said triumphantly.

"Yes, I suppose you do," Keira answered wearily.

"Do you know what I think?"

"No."

"Louise asked Nick Sarazin to get you out of the way, Keira, but that's not why he did what he did. Nor why he wanted to keep you with him. He was well and truly gone on you last night. Stricken is how I describe it. Lovesick. Call it what you will. When he left us down in the foyer it was perfectly plain to me that he was still carrying a torch for you."

She threw him a pained look. "Justin, I'd prefer not to talk about—"

"Okay," he agreed soothingly. "You're probably well rid of him anyway. It's just that I know how men think."

"You may be right," she said cynically. She didn't believe him. Easy come, easy go.

He glanced at his watch. "I'd better get going. Got to buy some roses. How many?"

"I think twelve is a good number," Keira said helpfully.

"Yes. Twelve. Will you be okay, Keira? Got everything you need? I have to move fast. Get Louise back into a state of matrimonial bliss."

"Yes, do that, Justin." She gave him a grateful smile and gestured around her. "Thanks for the suite. I don't know what I would've done without you."

He responded with a funny self-conscious smile. "Well, hell! You are my little sister. Not that you ever needed me around. And you're a holy terror to pin down to anything. The way your mind works is totally unfathomable."

"But I'm family," she finished for him. "And you're family to me, Justin. I may not seem to need you, or appreciate you, but it's always been comforting to know that you *are* around if I do need you. And not because I always need you for a loan. I truly am sorry I missed your wedding. I would have come..."

"Oh, I guess I only wanted to show you off to Louise," he said, good-naturedly shrugging off the grudge. "After all, not everyone has a beautiful eccentric cousin who runs off with sheikhs and leaves trails of devastation behind her."

"Trails of devastation? How can you say that? I never have! I do not!"

"Oh, no?" His mouth quirked into a teasing grin. "I reckon you've caused more accidents than any other hundred women put together. Just by being you. I remember kids on bikes having all sorts of smashes because they were gawking at you. And that was when you were only a teenager. I bet you've left havoc all around the world. It's a wonder you haven't been sued for being a public nuisance."

"Justin!" she protested disbelievingly. "It's not like that. I haven't done anything."

"You don't have to. But I know why Louise wanted to tear your hair out. It's a lethal weapon. Not to mention a few other weapons in your armoury. In short, I have no trouble believing that Nick Sarazin would fight like hell to keep you. But I won't talk any more about him. You obviously don't want to talk about him."

"No. And you'd better start treating Louise right," she reminded him tersely.

"I'm going. I'll ring you in the morning with the news."

"Good luck, Justin. And do try listening," she urged, wanting everything to work out for both him and Louise.

"Thanks, Keira. And try being good for once," he admonished. "Don't go wandering off until I call you."

In a sudden rush of affection for her absurdly number-minded, but reliable cousin, Keira rose from the lounge and pressed a warm sisterly kiss on his cheek. Justin's face turned red again. She thought she heard him mutter, "Dangerous," as he hurriedly let himself out of the suite.

Keira relaxed onto the soft cushions, idly drinking in the panoramic view of Sydney Harbour. There was no other place in the world like this, she thought. Her memory clicked through a host of sights she had enjoyed and marvelled at, but this was home, and perhaps that was what made it so special to her.

Her mind drifted over the years she had been away, the countries she had travelled through, the people she had met, the friends she had made. Much of what she had seen and done had been shared with others, but no one person had shared everything with her. She wished . . .

She closed her eyes and the image of Nick Sarazin was sharp in her mind. Her heart clenched. Her soul cried out in yearning. Why couldn't he have been the one? It wasn't fair that they had seemed so close last night. It wasn't fair that she had felt so sure.

A sense of terrible loneliness crept through her. Maybe she would never meet the one. Maybe she was destined to always be a traveller through life, alone, never sharing with one particular person above all others, never doing everything with one constant soul mate.

That appeared to be an unattainable dream.

CHAPTER TEN

NICK SARAZIN sat on the beach at Boomerang, fore-arms propped listlessly on his knees, the lowering afternoon sun beating warmly on his bare back. He stared out to sea, wondering if Keira had deliberately misled him about coming here.

Another day almost gone and she hadn't arrived. It was a week since he had left her at the Regent Hotel. Seven days of waiting and watching out for her, and God knew how many hours of worrying over what might have happened to her in the meantime. His hands clenched in a spasm of frustration. He shouldn't have let her go.

What other choice did he have? his mind taunted, and the answer came back—none that was viable! He forced himself to relax again. She would come, he told himself for the umpteenth time. He remembered the bitter satisfaction in her eyes when he had confirmed he didn't know where Boomerang was and had never been there. She wanted somewhere totally free of him. Therefore she would come. It was simply a matter of waiting out the interim.

Maybe she had been caught up in the battle between Justin and Louise, and that was holding her up. Maybe he should have stayed in Sydney and kept a watch on things there. He shook his head, vexed at himself for indulging in purposeless speculation. He had decided on a course and he would stick it out for at least another week before reviewing what he should do.

If he hadn't come ahead of her, he wouldn't have been able to scout out the situation and set up his best chances. Paying the rent on the caravan next to his and preparing the park manager ensured that Keira would be placed where he wanted her. Close to him. And he now knew all the best places to take her. If he could persuade her into accepting his company.

There were a lot of ifs in his scenario, Nick acknowledged with a sense of barely controlled impatience. He craved action. He needed reactions to hit off so he could manoeuvre—tell her the things she needed to be told. It was this damnable waiting that was driving him around the bend.

He pushed himself up, brushed the sand off his board shorts, then tramped up over the dune to the national park, which was basically all Boomerang was. It hadn't been hard to find, nor hard to get to. When Keira had flung the name Boomerang at him, he had imagined it would probably be some tiny settlement in the Red Centre of Australia. A national park on the north coast of New South Wales had come as a pleasant surprise.

Certainly it was a long way from being a flourishing tourist resort. The place was little more than a camping site, a dozen caravans, a general store, bushland and beach. Primitive and peaceful.

Except Keira's non-appearance was nagging away at any peace that Nick might have found here.

He trudged towards the shower block, pausing now and then to exchange small talk with a few of the campers. There was no formality about Boomerang. People chatted to each other and casually invited anyone to join in activities. On the other hand, if you wanted to be left alone, you were left alone.

Out of habit and hope, but not with any real expectation, his gaze automatically swept up the road that led down to the park. A hiker was coming around the last bend, backpack strapped on, duffle bag hanging from the shoulder, a khaki cloth army hat dipping over the forehead, blue and green checked shirt hanging loose, faded jeans, army boots.

Definitely not Keira, he thought with a stab of disappointment, yet there was something about the hiker that kept him watching—the easy fluidity of movement, a kind of jauntiness that suggested pleasure in walking, a lithe roll of the hips above long shapely legs.

His heart suddenly catapulted into a wild thumping.

A thick flaxen plait hung over one shoulder.

Not even the loose shirt could fully hide the provocative jiggle of full feminine breasts.

He wanted to laugh. He wanted to shout for joy. He wanted to dash up the road and swing her into his arms and never let her go again.

Better judgement prevailed.

Nick headed for his caravan, happily secure in the knowledge that he had not waited in vain.

IT HADN'T CHANGED AT ALL, Keira thought with a surge of pleasure. Of course, Boomerang was off the general tourist track, and the five kilometres of road from Foster were so steep and winding that few motorists would bother taking that particular drive, which was little short of dangerous.

Quite a few tents were pitched in the park but it was far from crowded with campers. Enough for some company if she felt like it. The easy camaraderie at Boomerang was one of its attractions to Keira. Several people gave her a friendly wave of welcome as the manager showed her to the caravan she had rented for a week. Even the rental had remained relatively reasonable compared to what she had paid six years ago. In a way, it was like stepping into the past.

A shower first, she thought, once the manager had left her to her own devices. She laid her bags on one of the bunks, tossed her hat on another, then sat down on the double bed to remove her boots. She eased her feet out of them. Then there was a knock on her door. Some friendly soul come to offer her something, she thought with a smile. Maybe a freshly caught fish for her dinner. People were like that at Boomerang.

The smile was still lingering on her lips as she went to greet her visitor. She opened the door and there he was, blue eyes twinkling at her, blue eyes dancing through her brain, tripping her heart, sending a zing of excitement through her veins.

He offered her a long glass of orange juice that tinkled with ice. "I thought you might be thirsty," he said, flashing his dazzling white smile. "And I wanted to say hello to the woman I've been waiting for all week.''

She shook her head dazedly. A thousand questions pummelled her mind. One found its way to her tongue and spilled from her lips. "Why?"

"A chance to begin again," he said softly. "Without any misconceptions this time." He nodded to the next caravan. "I'm over there. We have barbecue facilities between our separate accommodations. Will you have dinner with me this evening if I cook it for you?"

Keira was plunged into utter confusion, mental, emotional and physical. She had not expected to see Nick Sarazin ever again. All week she had been trying to bury the memory of him, filling her mind with other things, keeping herself as busy as she could. Yet his impact on her a few seconds ago had been exactly the same as when she had first seen him, despite all that had happened between them.

She took the cold drink he had brought her as she struggled to get her thoughts into some sort of coherent pattern. "Thank you," she said huskily. Her throat had gone very dry.

"Does that mean my invitation is accepted?" he asked lightly. "I'm very good at barbecues. I can cook you a fine steak, tomato, onions, bacon, banana, pineapple. I'll toss in a side salad of greens. Bought some fresh bread buns, too. How does that sound?"

His vitality swamped her with tingling life. Keira found it impossible to reject him. "It sounds...good," she said, uncertain of any ground with him.

Justin had been right, she thought. Nick hadn't wanted to let her go. But where did he see this leading to? Another seduction that went his way? Whatever his aim was, he had to be very determined about it to have come here and waited for her all week.

"I know you'll want to unpack and get yourself settled," he said quickly. "Come and join me when you're ready."

Keira didn't know if she would ever be ready. "That would be fine," she heard herself agree.

His grin of delight sent a shaft of warmth right down to her toes. "I'll do my best to please," he said, then raised his hand in a friendly salute and left her to return to his caravan.

Keira stared after him, still struggling with a sense of disbelief. He wore a pair of brilliant orange board shorts, topped by a loose royal blue singlet which had an orange sunset above purple waves printed on the back of it. He was bare-armed, bare-legged, bare-footed, and in the casual surfie gear he could have been a beach bum. Certainly he didn't look out of place at Boomerang. Yet somehow he still retained the air that said the world was his oyster. Which he could open when he willed, and consume at his leisure.

There was a buoyancy in his step, a firm assurance in his powerfully muscled legs, a confident strength in his broad shoulders, and the curly black head seemed to be tilted high as though nothing could ever bow him down. He could go anywhere, do anything, be anything he wanted to be.

The desire to have a man like him walking beside her for the rest of her life ripped through Keira with devastating force. It shook her so much that she hastily closed her door, shutting out the sight of him, trying to shut out the needs that Nick Sarazin evoked. Didn't she know that he couldn't be trusted?

Yet that wasn't entirely true, Keira amended quickly. Nick had kept his word about taking her to the Regent, and she could hardly complain about his kindness and consideration for her needs once he had given his word. In hindsight, he had been very good to her. And generous.

She took a sip of the chilled orange juice. It was delicious. A thoughtful and generous gesture, Keira acknowledged, as was his offer to cook dinner for her. She suddenly recalled Colonel Winton's enthusiastic praise of Nick's generous hospitality. It had to be part of his nature, not simply an act put on to influence her opinion of him.

If she let herself think about it, Nick Sarazin had been a very generous lover, as well. Not selfishly demanding or uncaring of her pleasure. He had made it beautiful for her. More beautiful than she could ever have imagined any man making love to her.

If Justin was right, if the seduction had had nothing whatsoever to do with Louise's request, if it was because Nick had truly fallen in love at first sight, as she had with him, then maybe he was the one after all.

After the strain of battling to put Nick Sarazin behind her, the enormity of this thought and what it might mean to her set off a trembling reaction. She almost spilled the drink in her hand. Keira set the glass down on the small dining table and slid herself onto the nearest bench seat.

A memory sliced into her mind, something Nick had said as they lay together under the stars. *"Perhaps all the rest is irrelevant. It is only you that matters"*. If that had been his feeling then, his true feeling, then surely there was a very real chance that this could be a new beginning.

A surge of wild happiness made Keira feel positively dizzy. She finished the drink Nick had given her, tried to steady the extremes of emotion that could lead her astray. Hope and desire did not constitute the most sensible approach to a man like Nick Sarazin.

The wisest course was to keep her distance, take the time to feel her way with Nick, make sure he was the one she wanted him to be. This evening's date with him was not a now-or-never situation. It was simply an opportunity to explore the possibilities of a new beginning.

Keira held on to this common-sense thinking right up until six o'clock. It did not stop her from fossicking through her bags for her best pair of shorts—which were a practical sage-green—and the matching shirt that tied at her waist. Nor did it quell a rush of very physical memories while she soaped her body clean in the shower. Nor did it have any influence whatsoever on her decision to unplait her hair and brush it into a free-flowing mass of crinkly waves. Nor did it assert any control over the excitement throbbing through her heart.

It was common-sense thinking that said it was silly to hang around inside in her caravan when she could be helping Nick set up for the barbecue. She could hear him outside, getting the fire going under the hot-plate, whistling to himself. A happy smile curved her lips as she recognised the tune—"Amazing Grace".

She opened her door and stepped onto the small patio. "Do you play the bagpipes, too?" she asked laughingly.

He threw her a grin, which promptly died on his face. He stared at her for several long nerve-tingling moments, and Keira felt he was absorbing every detail of her reality, savouring it as though he had hungered for it too long. Her own light-hearted amusement died under the intensity of his gaze and she was conscious only of the thunderous beat of her heart. She saw him drag in a quick breath and slowly release it. Then he stretched his mouth into the grin he had lost.

"I'll do anything you want," he said softly.

Keira felt the tug at her heart. It was the same feeling as when they had first met, the force of an inevitable attraction pulsating magnetically between them.

"My judgement of you was wrong," he said even more softly.

Keira felt the pain and the pride behind that admission. She heard the sincerity behind the words. "I made mistakes, too," she said huskily.

Her feet were tumbling off the patio, propelling her towards him. Somehow—Keira had no real awareness of how it happened—she was inside the circle of his arms and he was hugging her against his chest in a very possessive fashion. An excitingly possessive fashion. She felt his breath waft warmly through her hair and could not repress an impulsive urge to bite his shoulder.

"I don't think I like you, Nick Sarazin," she mused in a muddled-up sense of positive desire and caution.

"Forget what happened in the past," he murmured, the low throb of his voice intensely persuasive. "From the moment I first saw you, you were *the one.* No one else. You know it. I know it. That's how it happened."

"Louise..."

"Forget Louise. She had nothing to do with it. You were *the one.*"

Keira's heart skittered around her body and came to rest somewhere in the vicinity of her throat. She looked at this man, her eyes glowing in the soft light of the setting sun. So much a stranger, so much *her man.*

"Are you speaking the truth, Nick Sarazin?"

"As true as Tara," he said enigmatically, but the blue eyes were alight with a blaze of convincing fervour. "As true as my mother gave birth to me. As true as... you're Keira. *My* Keira."

"I was the one for you?" Keira asked. Her voice was way off key because of the choking position of her heart.

"You were *the one!*"

"You really felt that?"

"I swear it. From the moment I first saw you," he affirmed with passionate emphasis.

Her heart danced to its proper place, having made up its mind about how matters stood. However, the brain in Keira's head dictated that she should still have doubts about where all this was leading. Her brain dictated that she shouldn't be so easy to get this time, after all the bad things he had thought about her.

"I'm glad you said that," her heart declared. Her mind then added, "I might be able to find it in my heart to forgive you. Someday."

He pressed her closer, using the persuasive power of his aggressive maleness to instantly evoke a flood of awareness that shook the female core of Keira to her tiniest bones. With the skill of an artist who knew the value of contrast, he spent tender little kisses over her hair.

"You'll forgive me," he said softly. "I'm sure of that."

"Why should I?" She didn't want him to be too sure of her or too sure of having his own way with her. It might make him demanding.

"Because you're you," he replied huskily. He lifted her chin and planted floating kisses over her lips, punctuating a few more reasons. "Because you're a warm person, a loving person, a concerned person, and most of all a caring person. You have a giving heart, Keira. You are a loving woman. A jewel. You're the woman I want in my life."

That all sounded wonderful, but how could he know those things about her? Maybe he was just making them up to seduce her with words. "You're an ensnarer of women, Nick Sarazin," she said, letting him know he had a bit of proving to do.

"Only for you, my darling."

He scooped her up in his arms, cradling her tightly against his chest. This is getting to be a habit, Keira thought, but since it was a great improvement on being slung over his shoulder, and she secretly liked him showing her how strong he was, she let him have his way.

Before she knew it, her arms were wound around his neck—without shame or pride, she thought—and her face was so close to his throat that she had an irresistible urge to press her lips to it. Which she did. And it was very satisfying.

In case he became too encouraged, she warned him, "Forgiveness is not an easy business."

"I know," he replied with suitable solemnity. "Which is why I have to show you what I feel so it will become easier."

"How are you going to do that?" she asked suspiciously. He was carrying her towards his caravan. She could get into big trouble there if she wasn't careful.

"A surprise," he said, smiling at her so warmly and lovingly that he was at the caravan door before Keira gathered some wits.

"What surprise?" she demanded, but somehow the demand turned into an excited purr of anticipation. Bodies were terribly treacherous things, she thought.

"Close your eyes." He closed them himself with soft butterfly kisses on her eyelids.

Negotiating the step into the caravan and through the doorway was not an easy task with her in his arms. Keira helped by pressing herself as close to him as she could. There was something intensely satisfying about feeling her breasts squash into the hard, warm wall of Nick's chest. They tingled with delicious sensitivity.

The door banged shut behind them. "Am I allowed to open my eyes now?" Keira asked, an irrepressible smile on her lips. She already knew what the surprise was from the fragrance around her.

"Not yet." He carried her to the double bed and gently laid her on it. "Now!" he commanded.

The caravan was festooned with flowers of every conceivable kind. Wildflowers from the Australian bush, exotic flowers from the tropics, hothouse roses, orchids. Keira gazed around in heart-pounding wonderment, then finally plucked up the courage to meet and question the blue eyes that she knew had never left her face, blue eyes dark with need, hungry for all she could give him.

"Why, Nick?" she asked softly. "Why did you do this?"

"Because you're my flower girl," he answered simply. "Every moment of every day I thought of you, I thought of flowers. I had to have flowers in case you came. All my life I've been growing towards something, a branch out here or there, each year a fresh lead, but never feeling complete, always some part further to grow—until I met you. Then I knew, Keira. You were the bloom that had been missing, the flower I'd been growing towards, the fragrance of my life."

His words were a sweet caress on her soul, a seductive balm to the doubts that fretted her mind, a velvet glove squeezing her heart. They wound around her, through her, and Keira's free spirit suddenly quivered in a weird little panic at the sense of being shackled to him before she was ready, before she was sure that this was what she wanted, before she knew beyond all reasonable doubt that it was right.

Instinctively she sought delay, wrenching her eyes from his and sending them around the flowers again. "How on earth did you get them?" she asked.

"I went in to Forster and bought every flower they had. I had them imported. I went into the national park for the wildflowers, and every time I picked one of them, I said to myself, this is for Keira...."

Every word he spoke seemed to tighten a hoop around her chest. He sat down beside her, hemming her in on the bed, his hand reaching out to fan the long tresses of her hair out on the pillow. She tried to lighten the atmosphere, tried to smile at him teasingly.

"Oh, Nick! I hope it didn't make you feel unmanly being seen to pick flowers."

The blue eyes bathed her in love. "Not when they were for you, my darling. Why on earth should I feel *unmanly* when I'm doing something for you?"

The hoop squeezed even tighter. Keira scooped in a deep breath. Her eyes accused him of deliberate, knowing, tactically perfect ensnarement, but somehow she couldn't drive much conviction into her voice. "You're a terrible man, Nick Sarazin."

"Yes," he admitted.

She sighed. "I think I'm weakening."

"I hope so." He moved his legs onto the bed and rolled his body next to hers.

Keira's heart leapt into her throat again. "Aren't we supposed to be cooking a barbecue?" It was a ragged little protest, without any fire at all. There was a terrible amount of weakening going on inside her.

"This could be more important," he murmured, reaching across her to pluck a flower from the far pillow. It was a frangipani bloom. He gently stroked the velvet petals down her cheek.

"I am the one, aren't I, Nick?" Even Keira could hear the fear of the empty void in her voice, the black chasm that would open and swallow her up if he was deceiving her.

The blue eyes met hers with searing intensity, intent on burning away any last lingering doubt. "You're *the one,*" he assured her, his voice deep and vibrant with passion. He tucked the sweet creamy flower behind her ear. "Remember, forever, the fragrance of love," he murmured, his lips brushing softly over hers.

"Promise me, no deceit, ever," she whispered, barely stopping her lips from clinging sensuously to his.

"I love you," he promised and showed her, with his mouth and his hands and his body, how very much and in how many ways he loved her, and Keira surrendered to the passion of his embrace, surrendered herself into his possession, and came once more into the sweet valley that was so full of warm blissful sunshine, a valley of glorious contentment because *her man* was beside her, inside her, around her, sharing it all with her... and she was not alone.

Eventually they stirred themselves and barbecued a dinner of sorts. The fine steak was somewhat charred, tomatoes collapsed into soggy messes, onions were fried almost out of existence, the bananas were completely underdone and the pineapple was forgotten. It was the best meal they had ever eaten. The bread buns were perfect.

After they cleaned up, they went for a stroll along the beach to look at the stars and enjoy the sight and sound of the sea. They talked of other beaches, other seas, other stars, sharing their feelings about the places they had been in years gone by, sharing their minds and spirits and finding chords of empathy that deepened and broadened their pleasure in walking side by side.

But the need for a more physical expression of intimate bonding grew stronger and stronger, and in mutual accord they returned to the flower bed in Nick's caravan. They made love and talked and laughed and slept intermittently for a few hours. In the grey pre-dawn light, Keira suggested that it would be nice to watch the sunrise from the headland at the end of the beach. Nick agreed it was a fine idea.

It was quite a stiff climb up the steep rock surface, but their feet were light and sure this morning, and there was a sublime confidence in their togetherness. They made it to the top in good time. Shafts of gold from the rising sun were just beginning to send glittering streaks across the sea and into the sky. Nick slid his arms around her waist and pulled her against him as they watched the dawning of a new day...a new beginning.

Keira sighed in deep contentment and dropped her head against Nick's shoulder. "Tired?" he asked, rubbing his cheek over the silky softness of her gleaming hair.

It was funny, Keira thought, but being in love seemed to stop you from being tired. "A bit," she said, so he would keep cuddling her.

His arms pressed her into snuggling closer to him. "I've never felt more alive in my life," he mused softly, his breath wafting through her hair with a sigh of deep pleasure.

"Me, too," Keira whispered.

"You feel it also?"

The strangest feeling of shyness came over her. "Yes," she breathed, wondering why someone like her who had been everywhere, done everything—well, almost everything—should suddenly feel shy with someone with whom she had shared the deepest intimacy.

Movement caught her eye and she instantly pointed to it in excitement. "Look, Nick! Dolphins!"

"A whole school of them," he cried in delight.

"Aren't they beautiful?" Keira breathed.

"Yes, very beautiful."

The deep throb in his voice somehow made the comment personal. Everything this morning seemed personal, as though it was all made just for them to share and enjoy. There was a long harmonious silence as they watched the wondrous animals of the sea cavort over the waves, as if they, too, were greeting the new day with a joyous sense of life.

"Justin is not always wrong," Nick suddenly declared.

Keira frowned at this jarring note. Keira wasn't sure about that. Maybe Justin *was* always wrong. But family was family. She owed her cousin support. "No, he's not always wrong," she said stoutly.

"In fact," Nick amended, "at times he can be astonishingly right."

Keira couldn't see where this was leading. Although she was loath to move from her nestled position, she twisted her body a bit so that she could look at Nick's face. He smiled at her but the smile was a little crooked and strained. The blue eyes seemed intensely watchful as they held hers.

"Don't you agree?" he asked.

"Mmm." A non-committal course seemed wisest.

"Then I suppose we should do what he said," Nick pressed lightly.

Keira's mind was not overly keen on accepting numbers and military operations, which was a fair summary of anything Justin put forward. To get a better grasp of what Nick had in mind, she asked, "What do you think Justin said?"

"He said something about us getting married. If I remember correctly, shotguns were to be used."

"No, Nick." No one was going to pressure her into marriage, with or without a shotgun. The decision for or against such a relationship was definitely a matter of free choice.

"Try saying yes," Nick suggested, smiling his way into her heart again.

Was he being serious? "No, Nick," she said, wondering why he should feel so urgent about it.

"Why not?"

"We hardly know each other," she pointed out.

"We know enough. All that really matters," he argued.

There was definitely a serious gleam in his eyes. "I'll think about it," Keira said cautiously.

"I love you."

Her heart pounded its response. "That helps," she conceded.

"You're *the one* for me," he said with strong conviction.

"That's a lovely thought, Nick," she encouraged.

"Think of spending our lives together, getting to know more and more about each other, a surprise every day, and gradually learning to adjust so we fit together better and better."

"It could be exciting," she mused.

"More exciting than anything we've done before," he persuaded.

"Yes." She nodded, perfectly happy to be persuaded.

"People call me a gambler, but I'm not. When I decide to do something, the dividends can be enormous."

"I'm starting to believe you."

He moved her within his embrace so that she was facing him properly. "Try kissing me this way," he suggested.

"Okay." Keira was perfectly amenable to this kind of trial.

Nick kissed her, long and slow and erotically teasing. "What did you think of that?" he asked.

"Try it again, Nick. Just to be sure," she said dreamily.

He did, adding a few sensational refinements that were positively dizzying. "Marriage is the only answer," he said deviously.

"Perhaps you're right," Keira said, offering her lips to his again. "You need a woman."

"A special woman." He pressed the words onto her tongue. It was wicked what he could do with his tongue.

"I might be able to do the job," she gasped.

"You're the only one who *can* do the job," he insisted, teasing her some more.

Her nerve endings were shrieking out to be fed as only he could feed them. "I must be going slightly crazy—"

"I've never seen anyone more sane."

"—but I think I might marry you."

"Which goes to prove how eminently sensible you are," he said passionately, and his next kiss sent all her nerve endings into a wild dervish of wanton excitement.

They made love on top of the headland with all the world stretched out below them.

Am I dreaming this? Keira thought. Her mind told her she must be dreaming because everything was too exciting and beautiful and perfect to be true. She hugged Nick closer as wave after wave of pleasure suffused her body.

"Keep me dreaming," she whispered into Nick's ear. "Keep me dreaming all my life."

CHAPTER ELEVEN

A DAIMLER MOVED OFF the Pacific Highway, taking the turning to Forster through which it had to travel before making its way to Boomerang. The guiding hand on the steering wheel belonged to Justin Rigby Brooks. Beside him sat his wife, Louise. Spread comfortably on the back seat was Colonel Winton.

Keira was heavily on the minds of Justin and Louise. A rapprochement was in order, now that everything had been sorted out. And who was to know where Keira might disappear to next if they didn't catch her in Boomerang? Justin had decided that they couldn't count on his cousin being predictable for more than a day or two. Best to strike while she was still within striking distance.

The colonel's mind automatically shied away from the thought of approaching that dangerous young lady. Impossible to avoid this one last meeting with her, but an hour or two should not constitute too much of a danger if he was careful and kept well away from her. He knew enough, now, to avoid the worst situations.

He immersed himself in viewing the incredibly foreign countryside. Totally different from England, he kept thinking, but the natives were very friendly when they weren't being violently aggressive. Louise Brooks was really charming, and the offer of this trip up to the Gold Coast of Queensland was certainly a handsome apology for the injury she had done him. Of course, the colonel was aware that her working for Nick Sarazin had contributed to her concern over his welfare, but that was only right and proper and he had no complaints at all about this interesting compensation.

Neither Keira nor Nick had any premonition that a visitation was about to descend on them. In their own good time they came down from the headland, their appetites well sharpened for breakfast. They demolished a heap of bacon and eggs, changed into swimming costumes, then lay on the beach to soak up some sun.

"You didn't tell me where you've been since I dropped you at the Regent," Nick remarked in mild curiosity. Now that Keira was here, it was of no consequence, but he was interested in everything about her. "I thought you'd come straight to Boomerang," he added, smiling to show her he meant no criticism of her movements.

"I meant to, but I got a bit sidetracked," she explained. "I thought I'd come through the wine district of Pokolbin, and I met some people there who worked for Balloons Ahoy. They were short a helper and oddly enough one of the things I've never done is go riding in a balloon. Have you been up in one Nick?"

"Mmm, one New Year's Eve party, greeting the new year."

They talked about the pleasures of sailing silently along in the early morning sky, and found total agreement once again. Nick thought about the fatal tragedies there had been from ballooning in recent times and thanked his lucky stars Keira had arrived safely at Boomerang.

He knew he could never stop her from doing anything she wanted to do, but he decided then and there that if it was anything dangerous, he would be glued to her side, and if they got killed, they got killed together. He did not expect life would ever be dull with Keira.

Which, of course, made her even more *the one* for him. What he had to do was get her married to him very fast, so he could always be by her side to take care of her. Now that he'd found the flower of his life, he was not about to lose her or let her be injured in any way. Not if he had anything to do with it.

Every so often, Keira obeyed a compelling urge to run a hand over a part of Nick's anatomy. This was to reassure herself that the dream was still going on and acquiring a definite feel of reality. Nick smiled a lot. There was no part of him that Keira didn't find attractive. Eventually he suggested they have a swim. The water was closer than their caravans. It helped to lower their burning temperatures.

Having decided they had had enough sun and sea for a while, and that a long cool drink was in order, they walked hand in hand up the sand-dune to the park.

Keira's yellow costume was a classic one-piece racer, cut high on the hip, with a scooped neckline and secure straps over the shoulder. The thin nylon stretch material enabled it to be packed into the size of a pocket handkerchief. It was a perfectly practical swimming costume, and relatively modest . . . when it was dry. Wet, it tended to emphasise Keira's rather lush femininity, faithfully outlining form, shape and curvature.

Colonel Winton, seeing her come over the dune from the beach, wandered slightly off the path towards the caravan that had been pointed out as Keira's. He tripped over a tent-peg, crashed into a camp stool, rolled off onto a metal bar and received a significant and painful injury.

His companions gave him no assistance. Justin and Louise had both stopped dead in their tracks, amazed at the sight of the man who held Keira by the hand. Nick Sarazin was the last man on earth they had expected to see with Keira.

"Oh, hell!" Nick said slowly. He had seen Justin and Louise first. His hand tightened around Keira's. "Here's trouble!"

Keira glanced up and instantly identified what Nick was talking about. Her lateral vision picked up the body of Colonel Winton rolling on the ground. "Louise has been at it again," she murmured, wondering if it was Louise's warlike nature that appealed so deeply to Justin and his military mind.

"Will we make a run for it?" Nick suggested. "See if we can escape?"

It was an attractive idea, but family was family. "I think we have to face the music, Nick," Keira decided.

"Yes," he agreed with a sigh of resignation. "I guess we have to."

His heart didn't appear to be in it. Neither was Keira's. Justin she could handle, but Louise was a fairly scary prospect. Colonel Winton was struggling to his knees, his forehead bent to the ground as though in the deepest prayer to be delivered from all further suffering. At least he couldn't say it was her fault this time, Keira reflected with some relief. She hadn't been anywhere near him.

"What are we going to say?" Nick asked her.

"That it's all your fault?" Keira suggested hopefully.

"That might not be the wisest course," Nick said grimly. He, too, had picked up the contorted figure of Colonel Winton grovelling on the ground.

They made their approach in gloomy silence. A face-to-face confrontation could not be avoided, but at ten paces from her cousin and his wife, Keira's feet limped to a halt. So did Nick's. Both of them had good defensive instincts. Room to manoeuvre was essential if battle was to be joined.

Louise's expression was not projecting peace in our time. It was reserved, stern-faced, unsmiling. Justin was looking confused, suspicious and disapproving. However, he was the first to take the initiative, thereby demonstrating that military minds dictated that moves should be made to resolve sticky situations.

"This is a little embarrassing," he managed to grind out.

"Yes," Nick agreed, just as solemnly.

"Don't be a fool, Justin," Louise said airily, her head tossing high. "Why should it be embarrassing for me to meet Keira for the *first* time?"

A smile lit her face. She advanced on Keira, her arms outstretched in every appearance of a welcoming gesture, her dark eyes flashing what looked like delight in this meeting.

Keira darted a nervous glance sideways, looking for an escape route. Louise could be deceptive. Keira had seen how fast she was capable of moving. There could be a lot of pain for her in this encounter.

Louise gave her no chance. She threw her arms around Keira, embracing her warmly. "Oh, it's so wonderful to see you at last! After all this time!" she gushed with bubbly enthusiasm.

Keira was not slow to catch on. She hugged her cousin-in-law in warm response. After all, Delilah had not been Keira, and there was absolutely no need to remind Louise that this was the *second* time they'd met.

"I'm so sorry about not having made it to your wedding," Keira offered with sincere apology.

"I understand," Louise said firmly.

"It was a sheikh," Keira explained limply.

"Unavoidable in the circumstances," Louise agreed.

"Thank you for being so understanding," Keira said with deep gratitude.

"That's what family is for, isn't it?" Louise asked. She stepped back and gave Keira a firm smile.

"Oh, yes. Definitely. Very definitely," Keira agreed.

"I'm pregnant," Louise confided to them and the world in general.

"Is that—er—good news?" Keira asked diffidently.

"Oh yes," said Louise. "That is definitely good news. Isn't it, Justin?"

"Yes, dear." Justin stepped forward very smartly and put his arm around his wife's shoulders. "The very best news," he added with intense fervour.

"This year," said Louise, "I'm devoting myself entirely to good news. Aren't I, Justin?"

"Yes, dear. Only good news. This is the year you only hear good news."

"Ah," said Nick. "I've got some good news."

The colonel staggered around from behind a caravan. "Dangerous," he said. "Totally, recklessly, foolhardily dangerous. Should be banned."

The good news people ignored these unharmonious comments.

"Keira and I are going to be married," said Nick.

Louise's eyes flashed brightly.

"This had better not be some kind of joke," Justin said belligerently.

"It's no joke," Nick said hastily, and turned to Keira for support. "Is it, Keira?" He put his arm around her shoulders to emphasise *their* togetherness.

"It's not a joke," Keira agreed.

"Then," said Louise with determination, "that's good news!"

"Recklessly dangerous," said the colonel, but the good news people did not hear him.

Peace and harmony had been established.

Justin was shaking Nick's hand and welcoming him into the family.

Keira, having privately given Louise top marks for diplomacy, had reached the conclusion that Justin had certainly met his match in his wife. He was saying how lovely Louise looked, and how she was obviously going to be one of those lucky women whose beauty was enhanced by pregnancy. Which, of course, was good news.

IT WAS THREE MONTHS before the wedding took place. Keira had been in no rush. In her own mind she was certain what her feelings were for Nick, but she wanted to be certain that Nick was certain, too. If he wanted to change his mind, he could. No pressure, no obligation, free choice.

Nick didn't want to change his mind. He appeared quite impatient with what he considered was a very long delay. However, as Keira pointed out, she had been away from home for five years, and she wanted to give Auntie Joan and Uncle Bruce some family time before taking off with a husband.

Besides, there was the important business of meeting Nick's family and being accepted by them. "They might not think I'm respectable enough for you," she said doubtfully.

"Since I'm not respectable either, they'll think we're perfectly suited," Nick declared with confidence.

He was right. They all seemed to think she was the one for Nick. Their thinking, Keira decided, was probably influenced by Nick's obsessive devotion to her. He never shifted from her side, which was fine by Keira. That was precisely where she liked having him.

They invited Colonel Winton to stay for the wedding, but having done what he had come to Australia to do—the TV advertisements were all on film—he declared he had to go home to England. In fact, he intended to retire to a small and ancient fishing village on the Cornish coast. There he could close the door on the world and never come out again. It was far too dangerous.

Keira had a quiet word with Nick, and, true to his generous nature, Nick ensured that the colonel had a first-class seat on his flight to London. The colonel's parting words were that he hoped that nothing unseemly would happen at the wedding, and he wished Nick all the luck in the world—all the *good* luck—because he was definitely going to need it.

Apart from a few photographers falling over each other, nothing untoward occurred at the wedding. The church was filled with flowers. It was a happy occasion. A memorable occasion.

The family on Keira's side wondered how matters would finally end up, Keira being Keira, but she certainly made a stunningly beautiful bride this once, and they were very proud to own her as one of them. Although, as Justin said, no one else—to their knowledge—had ever made Keira cry, so Nick Sarazin might do the impossible and make her happy enough to settle down. But one simply never knew with Keira. Totally unpredictable.

Everyone on Nick's side of the family nodded knowingly as he spoke the words, "Till death us do part.'' Nick always did what he wanted to do and he certainly had no intention of ever letting his bride go anywhere without him at her side. That was totally predictable.

Nick smiled as he slid the gold wedding ring on Keira's finger. Her sea-green Lorelei eyes swam up at him. His blue eyes promised her that the world was their oyster, and they would ride the king tide together for the rest of their lives.

Keira smiled back.

She knew how it would end up.

She had her man.

Nick Sarazin was the one.

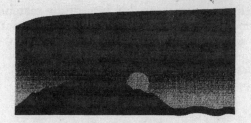

MILLS & BOON®

Next Month's Romance Titles

♡

Each month you can choose from a wide variety of romance novels from Mills & Boon®. Below are the new titles to look out for next month from the Presents™ and Enchanted™ series.

Presents™

THE PRICE OF A BRIDE	Michelle Reid
THE VENGEFUL HUSBAND	Lynne Graham
THE PLAYBOY AND THE NANNY	Anne McAllister
A VERY PRIVATE REVENGE	Helen Brooks
THE BRIDE WORE SCARLET	Diana Hamilton
THE BEDROOM INCIDENT	Elizabeth Oldfield
BABY INCLUDED!	Mary Lyons
WIFE TO A STRANGER	Daphne Clair

Enchanted™

HER OUTBACK MAN	Margaret Way
THE BILLIONAIRE DATE	Leigh Michaels
THE BARTERED BRIDE	Anne Weale
THE BOSS, THE BABY AND THE BRIDE	
	Day Leclaire
AN ARRANGED MARRIAGE	Susan Fox
TEMPORARY ENGAGEMENT	Jessica Hart
MARRIAGE ON HIS TERMS	Val Daniels
THE SEVEN-YEAR ITCH	Ruth Jean Dale

On sale from 9th October 1998

H1 9809

Available at most branches of WH Smith, Tesco, Asda, Martins, Borders and all good paperback bookshops

Rona Jaffe

Five Women

Once a week, five women meet over dinner and
drinks at the Yellowbird, their favourite
Manhattan bar. To the shared table they bring
their troubled pasts; their hidden secrets.
And through their friendship, each will find
a courageous new beginning.

Five Women is an *"insightful look at female
relationships."*

—Publishers Weekly

1-55166-424-0
**AVAILABLE IN PAPERBACK
FROM AUGUST, 1998**

DEBBIE MACOMBER

Married in Montana

Needing a safe place for her sons to grow up, Molly
Cogan decided it was time to return home.
Home to Sweetgrass Montana.
Home to her grandfather's ranch.

*"Debbie Macomber's name on a book is a guarantee
of delightful, warm-hearted romance."*
—Jayne Ann Krentz

1-55166-400-3
AVAILABLE IN PAPERBACK
FROM AUGUST, 1998

JAYNE ANN KRENTZ

A Woman's Touch

He was her boss—and her lover!
Life had turned complicated for Rebecca Wade when she
met Kyle Stockbridge. He *almost* had her believing he
loved her, until she realised she was in possession
of something he wanted.

"...one of the hottest writers in romance today."

—USA Today

MIRA®

1-55166-315-5
AVAILABLE IN PAPERBACK
FROM AUGUST, 1998

CHRISTIANE HEGGAN

SUSPICION

Kate Logan's gut instincts told her that neither of her clients was guilty of murder, and homicide detective Mitch Calhoon wanted to help her prove it. What neither suspected was how dangerous the truth would be.

"Christiane Heggan delivers a tale that will leave you breathless."

—Literary Times

MIRA

1-55166-305-8
AVAILABLE IN PAPERBACK
FROM SEPTEMBER, 1998

EMILIE RICHARDS

THE WAY BACK HOME

As a teenager, Anna Fitzgerald fled an impossible
situation, only to discover that life on the streets was
worse. But she had survived. Now, as a woman,
she lived with the constant threat that the secrets of
her past would eventually destroy her new life.

1-55166-399-6
**AVAILABLE IN PAPERBACK
FROM SEPTEMBER, 1998**

JASMINE CRESSWELL

THE DAUGHTER

Maggie Slade's been on the run for seven years now.
Seven years of living without a life or a future because
she's a woman with a past. And then she meets Sean
McLeod. Maggie has two choices. She can either run,
or learn to trust again and prove her innocence.

"Romantic suspense at its finest."

—Affaire de Coeur

1-55166-425-9
AVAILABLE IN PAPERBACK
FROM SEPTEMBER, 1998

Jennifer
BLAKE

KANE

Down in Louisiana, family comes first.
That's the rule the Benedicts live by.
So when a beautiful redhead starts paying a little
too much attention to Kane Benedict's grandfather,
Kane decides to find out what her *real* motives are.

*"Blake's style is as steamy as a still July night...as overwhelming
hot as Cajun spice."*

—Chicago Times

1-55166-429-1
**AVAILABLE IN PAPERBACK
FROM OCTOBER, 1998**

MARGOT
DALTON

second thoughts

To Detective Jackie Kaminsky it seemed like a routine
burglary, until she took a second look at the
evidence... The intruder knew his way around
Maribel Lewis's home—yet took nothing.
He *seems* to know Maribel's deepest secret—
and wants payment in blood.

A spellbinding new Kaminsky mystery.

1-55166-421-6
**AVAILABLE IN PAPERBACK
FROM OCTOBER, 1998**

SHANNON OCORK

SECRETS OF THE
TITANIC

**The voyage of the century
—where secrets, love and destiny collide.**

They were the richest of the rich, Rhode Island's
elite, their glittering jewels and polished manners
hiding tarnished secrets on a voyage that would
change their lives forever.

They had it all and everything to lose.

"Miss OCork is a natural writer and storyteller."
—New York Times Book Review

MIRA 1-55166-401-1
Available from October 1998 in paperback